'I, Me, Mine?'

'I, Me, Mine?':

An Initial Consideration of (Popular Music Record) Collecting Aesthetics, Identities and Practices

By

Veronica Skrimsjö

Cambridge
Scholars
Publishing

'I, Me, Mine?':
An Initial Consideration of (Popular Music Record) Collecting
Aesthetics, Identities and Practices

By Veronica Skrimsjö

This book first published 2016

Cambridge Scholars Publishing

Lady Stephenson Library, Newcastle upon Tyne, NE6 2PA, UK

British Library Cataloguing in Publication Data
A catalogue record for this book is available from the British Library

ISBN (10): 1-4438-8912-1
ISBN (13): 978-1-4438-8912-4

FOR SARA, 1980–2010

"And the songbirds keep singing like they know the score"
—Fleetwood Mac (1977)

CONTENTS

ACKNOWLEDGEMENTS

Many have contributed in so many ways to the success of this book:

Dr Giles Hooper, Prof Stephen Pratt, Dr Laura Hamer and Dr Ian Inglis were invaluable at different stages spanning from the very start till the very end (if such a thing exists). My parents, Ulrika and Stefan, for continued support and storage of all my "collections". My friends who have had their music pried into and still drink coffee with me. All the people who spoke to me in regards to this work, in particular Les, Dave, Sid and "George". And of course Cambridge Scholars Publishing, Sam Baker and Victoria Carruthers.

Dr Mike Brocken—who has been an incredible mentor for so many years now. I am grateful for all the scholarly, intellectual and philosophical debates and advice. I am grateful for all the coffees and all the lifts, and my second LP of *Rumours*.

Brent Thomas—who makes my heart sing and made the stars wanted again, and continually deals with peculiar new collections.

INTRODUCTION

This work aims to consider and present various aspects of record collecting and record-collecting practices, predominantly in the UK. As will be made evident, a number of troubling assumptions and stereotypes have been found to exist regarding record collectors, which have largely stemmed from perhaps outdated critical theories. Throughout this work, a number of approaches will be employed in an attempt to provide a more realistic—and optimistic—account of what record collecting entails and who the collector is. Various methods will be used, and each chapter aspires to provide another piece of the puzzle, as it were.

This work is largely theoretical, although several case studies are involved in the presentation of this theoretical underpinning. However, there are, broadly speaking, three theoretical positions around which this work revolves, and these help us to reconsider not only the record collector, but also the artefact. The first of these is discussed in Chapter One, where John Shepherd's concept of the matrix is discussed. This book takes that a little further, to consider the record as a *kinetic matrix*, in that it holds a vast amount of important information which, when being positioned as an aligned focus, can be extremely revealing and productive in our understanding of how mass-produced products can be representations of the individual. The second important theoretical proposition concerns discourse analysis, and this is principally involved in the understanding of the collector as an interpreter of information. The work, therefore, will proceed by examining how collectors are viewed as ostensibly male outsiders, perhaps even Orientalist "others", and how such definitions lead to the marginalisation of collectors—particularly those involved in popular music—as a potentially deviant collective. Further, this discourse analysis will at all times revolve around the object and, citing the work of Evan Eisenberg, will consider just how unbounded the possibilities are for cultural re-interpretation and re-examination through the medium of recorded sound. Further, from a historical perspective, the very use of the word "record" will be considered before, during and after the advent of recorded sound as a way of suggesting that the very presence of recordings was effectively a paradigm shift of enormous consequences. Recorded sound held unknown possibilities from which later technological developments emerged during the twentieth century via changing formats, technology, and the role of the individual, and as such cannot simply be considered as a mass produced and mass-consumed artefact.

The third underpinning of this book involves the employment of textual analyses. In the first instance, the historical work of the Frankfurt School will be introduced and discussed; Theodor Adorno and Walter Benjamin will then be challenged via a contextual appreciation of their place in time, rather than simply an understanding of their time-bound narrative. Further to this, the *Vertigo Records* record label will also be contextually considered as a significant representational text within the activity of record collecting. At this point, the text will also consider sleeve art as providing a matrix from which the collector can create meaning. Further textual analysis involves ethnographic consideration of a dealer-cum-collector, a collector with a debilitating personal illness, a female collector (myself), and the methods involved in organising and representing collecting electronically in the twenty-first century. Each approach therefore interweaves and connects to the other and, it might be argued, sits within what might be described as a post-modern form of analysis. This in itself is based on theory, yet at the same time does appear to reflect more accurately the unexpected, the misunderstood, and the non-aligned facets of popular music involvement and participation. This writer states this from a position of understanding that even in the twenty-first century, popular music studies is, in effect, a post-modern discipline, and rather than accepting the conventional rhetorical tropes surrounding the persistence of a discourse that continues to conflate a high and low art position, popular music studies is validated by suggesting that issues concerning the popular require close consideration from the perspective of the individual, rather than merely mass production and mass consumption. It is from such theoretical standpoints that this book intends to suggest that the inherent creativity of record collecting has thus far been under-researched, and in fact lies in the hands of a co-creative universe of individual understanding and signification.

Whilst this text is, as discussed above, a predominantly theoretical work, ethnographic methods have also been used. This was mainly in the form of interviews, although observation of the audience in Chapter Six was also important. These interviews were regarded as a vital component by the author as they provided a real—albeit subjective—account of record collecting, from the "horse's mouth", if you will. As ethnography deals with people directly and, as such, involves ethics, it is worth offering the reader further clarification on the interviews and interview subjects in this work. As part of the research for this work, several informal discussions and/or interviews were held by the author with a wide range of collectors (generally) and record collectors (specifically). These have all helped to inform and reinforce the thesis present here, but four interview subjects were included by name—Les, Dave, Sid and "George"—and given primary focus. These four were asked to give their informed consent to be included (all of whom are of sound mind and legal age) in this work, to which they agreed,[1] as they provided the author with useful information regarding record collecting. One may, however, note the absence of a named female interviewee. The author approached and spoke to several female record collectors, but found that—whilst happy to talk about their practices—they were not willing to be included in the book, or did not consider themselves to be record collectors.[2] Most of the collectors this writer spoke to were people encountered in record shops/fairs or in everyday situations. Les, Dave and Sid, however, were all introduced by "George", whom I have known for a number of years prior to undertaking this research.

The interviews themselves were, as indicated, conducted under informal conditions in an attempt to try to recreate an everyday conversation. The author felt those circumstances would yield to most "realistic" responses. Whilst each interview had a purpose, i.e. to gain further insight into record-collecting practices and identities, the author tried not to prompt responses, but to allow the interviewee to speak freely and then respond with comments and questions based on what the interviewee said. Furthermore, it is perhaps worth noting that every effort was made on the writer's part not to inflict personal opinions related to collected objects and/or musical taste(s) as there was an awareness that record collectors frequently encounter (negative) judgements and there was a desire to understand the collectors' (intimate) relationship with their collections without prejudice.

It is also worth bearing in mind how the term "musicologist" is used in this work. Whilst it is understood that there are many scholars and academics that refer to themselves as musicologists, in this work it simply refers to those scholars who give primacy to the score *at the expense* of any other aspects when trying to understand or critically evaluate any kind of music or musical event.

---

[1] "George" is a *nom-de-plume*.

[2] As will be noted in subsequent chapters, it is very important in this work that the label of "record collector" is not imposed on someone who resists it despite displaying the "characteristics" of a record collector.

Chapters—an Overview

The first chapter details the premise and motivations behind this work. However, it also considers how both record collecting, as well as collecting in general, are viewed and written about. The chapter raises the issue of regarding record collecting as a form of musical consumption and how recorded sound can be viewed as a paradigm shift. Furthermore, it is indicated that *as a paradigm shift* recorded sound (and thus records) has been largely misrepresented. This is because the consumption of records has been defined through its production.[3] As will be argued, this is a flawed thesis, if only because the consumption of record collectors themselves has been interpreted through ideology that failed to understand popular culture and its usages (see Chapter Three) and the *individual* is forgotten.

Chapter Two further considers the different methodology used in this work, as discussed above, and then continues with an in-depth review of relevant literature. As academic literature on record collecting is limited, non-academic material is also included alongside relevant material relating to recorded sound and technology, music consumption, and literature relating to collecting generally. This provides a starting point, but also emphasises that this work is only one step in rectifying the lack of (academic) consideration given to the field of record collecting. As such, Chapter Two aims to provide the reader with a basis and an understanding of the climate and narrative that has surrounded the collector and record collector historically.

Chapter Three provides a discussion on a number of key issues within popular music studies, including the notion of "cool" and authenticity, as well as genre. These issues are central to the record collector's understanding of the artefact—or indeed, artifice—that is the record. The chapter then proceeds to consider the theories formulated by the Frankfurt School, particularly those of Theodor Adorno and Walter Benjamin, as this author will come to argue they have been fundamental in creating the demeaning stereotype of the record collector we now have, despite never considering the record collector as such. Finally, a response will be provided to the Frankfurt School's theories, by the end of which it will be clear to the reader that record collecting (and popular culture consumption) cannot be interpreted through such models as, crucially, there is no "one" objective reality.

---

[3] Generally, as mass production for mass consumption.

Chapter Four is perhaps the first chapter that overtly deals with record collecting as such. Les, one of the four central interviewees, is introduced as a case study, and his personal story is considered, including the profound impact record collecting has had on his life following serious illness and how his identity has been shaped and grown, and has evolved in relation to his treasured Lani Hall recordings. The notion of communality, particularly through electronic media, is introduced, and it is highlighted that record collecting is not an activity that requires you to lock yourself away from human relationships. So why, then, do we often believe the opposite? In addition to the theories presented to us by the Frankfurt School, this chapter also explores the notion of deviance in relation to the collector, and how this has been mediated to the general public; mediation is further considered in this chapter in relation to the *Record Collector* magazine. Additionally, the chapter provides a discussion on capital culture and its relevance, which will be of importance to the reader when approaching the following chapter (Five), on *Vertigo Records,* which will initially consider the cultural and historical climate in which *Vertigo Records* was conceived (in 1969) by considering the counter-culture and the musical developments—particularly relating to genre, album art and technology—at the time. The chapter will continue to consider Philips, the founding company of *Vertigo*; the advent of the subsidiary; and a selection of the records released on *Vertigo* from 1969–73. This will lead on to a discussion on why some regard *Vertigo* LPs as highly collectible.

In Chapter Six portrayals of the record collector (in fiction and documentary) will be analysed, followed by a discussion of how and why the record collector is often placed in a position of "otherness" relative to the deviance discussed in Chapter Four. Chapter Six will further indicate that record collectors are not a subculture, but need to be regarded as *individuals*. The majority of the chapter is, however, reserved for an initial discussion on the fictional film *High Fidelity,* followed by the documentary *Sound It Out,* where observational ethnography was employed at a local screening.

Chapter Seven consists of an extended interview with the aforementioned "George" who, in his role as both collector and dealer, was able to provide an interesting analysis of record collecting from the perspective of an "insider". The interview has been arranged in a relative chronology,[4] and is presented as a "whole", and only interrupted when academic literature appears to provide evidence of "George's" argument.

---

[4] See Chapter Seven for further details.

Finally, in Chapter Eight, this work considers how and whether record-collecting practices, communities and identities may have changed in our current digital, information technology age. The writer will consider trading/auction sites like eBay, and how they have come to influence taste and buying practices, but also websites that are centred around a community through various (record collecting) forums and how both these aspects—trading and communality—may come together in a website such as Audiophile USA. While it will become evident that certain aspects have evolved with the development of digital technology, many central aspects remain the same, perhaps only strengthening the impact record collecting has in the collector's life.

It is perhaps also worth highlighting again that, throughout this work, the writer believes in the autonomy of the individual and that the individual's consumption cannot be defined by mass production.

CHAPTER ONE

'I, ME, MINE?':
AN INITIAL CONSIDERATION
OF (POPULAR MUSIC RECORD) COLLECTING
AESTHETICS, IDENTITIES AND PRACTICES

"Why pin and press these specimens when others, alive and just as
lovely, will surely flutter by?"
—Evan Eisenberg (2005),
*The Recording Angel: Music, Records and Culture
from Aristotle to Zappa*

The aim of this work is to highlight record collecting as a form of music consumption, to demonstrate that it is an activity that can show us different, non-passive aspects of interaction with music as a catalyst, and to illustrate that record collecting can both shape identity as well as display aesthetic value in its own right. Previous research by the author[1] has shown that record collectors are largely misrepresented or misunderstood. Such stereotypes (for this is what they are) frequently suggest an eccentric male involved in a solitary activity, a view this book aims to challenge, and this will be achieved by exploring different collecting experiences through the examination of the collectors themselves (who might also be dealers), textual analyses of record collecting media, and an understanding of what it means to collect within the realms of mass-industrialised society. This research will also consider those methods and approaches, which have historically appeared to diminish the roles of such products in our daily lives.

Such modes of enquiry will be held together by a thesis in which the collection, rather than simply the collector, will be discussed as a *matrix*.

---

[1] Currently unpublished work.

This idea stems from the work of John Shepherd,[2] who has discussed how matrixes in popular music can be understood as fundamental to our perceptions of focus, and thus meaning. For example, Shepherd discusses how Elvis Presley can be regarded as a matrix that brought into focus issues related to culture and society in the United States that were previously unfocused. One might argue that this concept should also be used in relation to the record, for throughout the twentieth century the record has created and contributed to one of the most important paradigm shifts in society. Related to this matrix approach, this writer will also be utilizing five points raised by writer and record specialist Evan Eisenberg.[3] His points discuss how and why recordings are, in their own right, aesthetic artefacts, which also arbitrate meaning in some very complex ways not only for the collector, but also for the general public. It is via this combined thesis of kinetic matrixes (seemingly an oxymoron, however, directly connected concepts for this writer) that this work will proceed, drawing attention, perhaps in a post-modern way, to the authenticity and value of the artefact and artifice. It is important for this work to show that many people, perhaps more than one would expect, are engaged in some form of record collecting, and that each collector has their own motivations and strategies, indeed world views, all of which deserve further and deeper investigations. Such enquiries provide not only evidence for rethinking the collector, but also additional confirmation of the strength and diversity contained within popular music *fandom*.

At the outset, it should be emphasised that this work is not intended to be either a history of record collecting or an encyclopaedia of records—such a work would be a vast undertaking, given the range and diversity of recorded sound. It is, instead, intended to be a theoretical work based upon a number of approaches to the consumption of popular culture. For decades, a kind of cultural scholarship tended to dominate the way in which people's interaction with popular culture was theorised. There was, via the direct comments and then later influences of the Frankfurt School, a focus upon popular music consumption as a form of socially maladjusted behaviour culminating, perhaps, in fanaticism. Additionally, collecting in general, while considered to be evidently active, at least in a kind of solitary way, has similarly been considered to be a symptom of maladjustment—an obsessive, isolated pastime which draws human beings

---

[2] John Shepherd, "Definition as Mystification: A Consideration of Label as a Hindrance to Understanding Significance in Music" in *Popular Music Perspectives 2*, ed. David Horn (Gothenburg: IASPM, 1985), 84–98.
[3] Evan Eisenberg, *The Recording Angel: Music, Records And Culture From Aristotle To Zappa* (New Haven: Yale University Press, 2005).

away from the realities of the world and into a netherworld of mania rather than passion, of fixation rather than fascination. Two quotes illustrate this well. First, John Storey characterises what "mass culture" meant for Frankfurtian-influenced theorists: "[...] hopelessly commercial culture. It is mass produced for mass consumption. Its audience is a mass of non-discriminating consumers. The culture itself is formulaic, manipulative [...] and is consumed with brain-numbed and brain-numbing passivity".[4] Secondly, St Etienne's Bob Stanley (himself both a musician and collector), suggests, with regard to football programme fairs: "The musky smell of a programme fair—so much damp plastic, the heating always a notch too high in an airless room—would make most serious people run for the hills. In the very male world of serious football programme collecting, aesthetics don't count for much".[5]

Clearly, opinions are formed both within and outwith popular-culture collecting, similarly obsessed by images of social deviancy. Joli Jenson argues that notions of "the fanatic" and "mass society" still occupied the minds of many cultural critics right up until the 1980s. Jenson suggests that "The fan is consistently characterized [...] as a potential fanatic. This means that fandom is seen as excessive, bordering on deranged behaviour".[6] It is argued in this present work that this continues to be so, but with the emphasis perhaps falling less on the act of popular culture itself, or its fan bases, which have over the years become more understood, and more on the collector-cum-fan as the holder of the fantasist, pathological tags. While there have now been a host of titles dedicated to the understanding of fandom and its associated value systems (see, for example the works of Lewis,[7] Hills,[8] Cavicchi,[9] Ehrenreich,[10] and

---

[4] John Storey, "What is Popular Culture?" in *Cultural Theory and Popular Culture: An Introduction*, ed. John Storey (Harlow: Pearson Education, 2001), 8.

[5] Bob Stanley and Paul Kelly, *Match Day: Post-war to Premiership Football Programmes* (London: Murray & Sorrell FUEL, 2008), 15.

[6] Joli Jenson, "Fandom as Pathology: The Consequences of Characterization" in *The Adoring Audience: Fan Culture and Popular Media*, ed. Lisa Lewis (London: Routledge, 1992), 9.

[7] Lisa Lewis, ed., *The Adoring Audience: Fan Culture and Popular Media* (London: Routledge, 1992).

[8] Matt Hills, *Fan Cultures* (London: Routledge, 2002).

[9] Daniel Cavicchi, *Tramps Like Us: Music and Meaning Among Springsteen Fans* (New York: Oxford University Press, 1998).

[10] Barbara Ehrenreich, Elisabeth Hess and Gloria Jacobs, "Beatlemania: Girls Just Want to Have Fun" in *The Adoring Audience: Fan Culture and Popular Media*, ed. Lisa Lewis (London: Routledge, 1992), 84–106.

Jensen,[11] etc.), there still remains the hoary question of "the collector". While there has been a continuity in the studies of fandom that has effectively "released" the fan from the grip of the Frankfurtian "gloom", this appears to be far less the case as regards the collector who is stereotyped, as in Stanley's comments above: predominantly men who are conducting an esoteric sacrament which is almost unknown, and possibly incomprehensible, to the general public. According to Stanley, they are seemingly collecting things that might crop up in car boot sales, exchanging items with other collectors as forms of Gnostic ritualism. Such is the condescension afforded to most collectors.

Yet, at least according to historian D.J. Taylor, "Any social historian worth his salt who wanted to discover what English life was like in, say, the period 1966–79 [...] could do worse than assemble a couple of hundred football programmes".[12] Within each programme can be found various adverts for local pub cultures long-since vanished, brands of cigarettes no longer advertised, literary languages redolent of specific eras via their gender stereotypes, and so on. They are in fact social documents that actually *demand* to be collected and archived, if only to bear witness to the way popular culture was/is regarded and recorded. One might equally consider (say) the sleeves of LPs of a similar era to discover how, for example, *CBS Records* might have considered their "alternative" record-buying public, or how certain styles of music came to be categorised within what *CBS* called their "Rock Machine" series of samplers, viz:

> The Rock Machine is a machine with soul. The Rock Machine isn't a grind-you-up. It's a wind-you-up. The sound is driving. The sound is searching. The sound is music. It's your bag. So it's ours. It's the Super Stars. And the Poets. It's the innovators and the Underground. It's the Loners and the Lovers. And it's more. Much more…[13]

This marvellously stereotypical hipster language of the late 1960s adorns a sampler LP in which the songs of Big Brother and the Holding Company, Taj Mahal, Leonard Cohen and the Zombies *et al.* are showcased for less than £1 (in fact, 14/6d in pre-decimal UK currency).

---

[11] Joli Jenson, "Fandom as Pathology: The Consequences of Characterization" in *The Adoring Audience: Fan Culture and Popular Media*, ed. Lisa Lewis (London: Routledge, 1992), 9–29.
[12] D. J. Taylor cited in Bob Stanley and Paul Kelly, *Match Day: Post-war to Premiership Football Programmes* (London: Murray & Sorrell FUEL, 2008), 15.
[13] *The Rock Machine Turns You On*, LP (1968) CBS PR 22.

The sleeve is an historical artefact in its own right, and one should surely be thankful that somebody, somewhere, has considered such so-called ephemera worthy of collection—such is its cultural value. Perhaps irrespective of the sounds actually on the record, the signs on the sleeve carry not simply denotative meanings in the explicit messages of its letters, but also connotative expressions of other, perhaps more subtle meanings of its musical genres. Identification comes not simply through the explicit, denotative communication, but through almost literally "spelling out" (as above) the connotations implicit in its musical forms. Not only the recording, but its packaging and marketing help us to not only discover and consider the sociology of music consumption, but also how one should theorise consumption in a modern world. Perhaps like the football programme, these artefacts deserve our fullest attention.

The Record

Before recorded sound, the idea of a record consisted of several important meanings. A record could be the way that, for example, court proceedings have taken place—one might refer to the stenographer in court to be the holder of the keys to some kind of legal truth, making a note of information that could actually end someone's life, or on the other hand release someone from suspicion. One might also say that a record in the nineteenth century is directly related to the expansion of literacy and printing. Popular literature in the nineteenth century gives us a glimpse of what different classes of people came to be influenced by, together with a fascinating picture of the advent of leisure pursuits. As with the above-mentioned twentieth-century football programme or record sleeve, some of this earlier literature was probably not written as a "record", as such, for in the popular sphere such writings were probably regarded as ephemeral. But because of the appearance, content, and then popularity of the reading matter, and because of people's increased literacy, what has been left is a different kind of document to those records from court proceedings. These are documents that similarly provide denotative and connotative meanings. The same documents can, of course, provide both, and they might even be mutually contradictory. For example, one of the very first football programmes from the nineteenth century was a charity match played at the Kennington Oval in 1886. It was a simple card that sold for 2d, and its main purpose, denotatively, was the identification of the players by virtue of the positions they took up on the field of play. However, connotatively the document provides a very different reading from the merely indicative. The match was between "Gentlemen" and "Players"—a representative affair. One can clearly see that this match was indicative of the nineteenth century distinction between Gentlemen amateurs and professional Players, and that the cricket example of staging games between such demographic representatives was part of the authenticities surrounding the class system of the age—a period, one might suggest, of phoney certainties masking real uncertainties. Furthermore, as collecting specialist John Litster points out:

> The fluidity of player movement around amateur clubs is indicated by the lack of team names against the "gentlemen", for whom the famous twins A.M. and P.M. Walters filled the full-back positions. The "Players" came from no further south than West Bromwich. Most represented were Preston North End, and J. Costly of Blackburn Olympic took his place in the forward line.[14]

This is, perhaps, connoting a curiosity in "northern professionals" amongst the London-based elite, and therefore, like a Wilkie Collins "popular" novel, or a Gamages Department Store catalogue, remains of great importance to the historian of popular culture.

In musical terms, a record of music prior to the advent of recorded sound largely depended upon the strata of society at whom the music was aimed. Rather than being simply a tool for the preservation of music, the notated printed form became a representation of what music was supposed to be, and for which instruments. Under such circumstances, where the music score was something to be "afforded" by those fortunate enough to have a musical instrument on which to play it appropriately, music came to be a stylised indicator of not only sound, but also of the differences between class and economics, and as a result of a ruling elite and those who aspired to be part of that elite, good and bad taste. One needs only to look at the parlour music of the late-nineteenth century to see how demarcations via sheet music were made between what one (aspiring) class of society considered either good or bad.

Parlour music was a genre of popular music, which, as the name suggests, was effectively domestic and intended to be performed in the parlours of middle-class homes by singers and pianists. For our purposes it is of interest because it was disseminated and avariciously purchased as sheet music. Its heyday came in the mid-to-late nineteenth century, and was the result of a steady increase in the number of households with enough spending power to purchase musical instruments and take musical

---

[14] John Litster, *Famous Football Programmes: A History and Guide* (Stroud: NPI Media Group, 2007), 7.

instruction. Parlour music is also connotative of issues to do with gender—the woman at home, increased leisure time—and therefore the cultural motivation to engage in recreational music-making. It is indicative, too, of the importance of domestic servants, thereby allowing more time for both the man and the woman in the home to practice playing and singing, and also of the growth of music societies amongst the middle classes, which evolved around domestic concert parties. In addition to the vast sales of individual pieces of sheet music, parlour songs were also collected into anthologies and sold in this format. The most notable collection in the United States, for example, was *Heart Songs*,[15] first published in 1909 by the Chapple Publishing Company of Boston, and repeatedly revised and republished for several decades. Interestingly, and despite its apparent elements of elitist constructions, parlour music is a very good example of how middlebrow tastes came to be despised by those adhering to European classical music. It is especially notable that by the late-nineteenth century classical tastes came to self-consciously distance themselves from the popular via parlour music.

Parlour music's popularity waned in the twentieth century as the phonograph record, and then radio, replaced sheet music as the most common method of dissemination of popular music. So the recorded state of music within what might be described as a bourgeois semi-classical environment (at least to begin with) came to indicate musical hierarchies and battlegrounds. While parlour songs certainly show elements of hierarchical and aspirational social climbing via music, from the elevated perspective of "art" music, they also came to be seen as inferior works and merely "popular". By considering the various written forms such as *Heart Songs* we can quite clearly see (via the explicit symbolism of the cover) and then hear (via the importance of chord-based melodies, rather than harmonic variations) how parlour music came to be looked down upon and considered the substance of the conventional and ordinary.

Other musical forms, which might also be described as popular, are more often than not neglected in terms of any record. But it is true that throughout the eighteenth and nineteenth centuries, what come to be described as broadsides and ballads were printed by the growing print media surrounding music. Broadside ballads (also known as a "road sheet", a "stall", a "vulgar" or a "come all ye" ballad) were a product of the development of cheap print, initially in the sixteenth century. They were generally printed on one side of a sheet of poor quality paper. In their

---

[15] See Charles Hamm, *Yesterdays: Popular Song in America* (New York: Norton, 1979).

heyday of the first half of the seventeenth century, they were printed in black lettering or gothic type, and included multiple, eye-catching illustrations, a popular tune title, as well as an alluring poem. By the eighteenth century, they were printed in white lettering or roman type, and often without much decoration (as well as the tune title). These later sheets could include many individual songs, which would be cut apart and sold individually as "slipsongs". Alternatively, they might be folded to make small, cheap books, or "chapbooks", which also drew on ballad stories and hymns—indeed several religious chapbooks were made available for lower class congregations. These printed records were produced in huge numbers, with over 400,000 being sold in England annually by the 1660s. Tessa Watt[16] estimates the number of copies sold may have even been in the millions.

Many were sold by travelling "chapmen" in city streets or at fairs. The subject matter varied from what has been defined as the traditional ballad,[17] although many traditional ballads were printed as broadsides. Among the topics were love, religion, drinking-songs, legends, and early journalism (such as, for example "The Murder of Maria Marten"), which included disasters, political events and signs, wonders and prodigies. But, then as now, such popular forms were frequently regarded as "here today and gone tomorrow". The evidence for such printed forms of popular music, which might have existed around a song based upon an important event of the day, thus remains scant. Broadsides are seen to have emerged from the beginnings of mass-print culture, and can still therefore be regarded as lacking in authenticity, hence their plight to be subsumed in semi-rarity.

So if the idea of a "record", as far as broader society is concerned, is something to do with recording events, such events, should they happen within different echelons of society, can be disregarded, hence lost to us completely or used perhaps as in the case of classical music, as primary evidence of the popular's lack of musical and/or social substance. The very word "popular", in fact, mutates through several different definitions during the nineteenth century—ranging from those who write about it as being "of the people" to those who suggest that it is a referent of "low and base". None or partial survivals suggest to us that such primary sources are of great significance, but that history is something of a political battleground. John Tosh states that:

---

[16] Tessa Watt, *Cheap Print and Popular Piety, 1550–1640* (Cambridge: University Press, 1991).

[17] *ibid.*

The sanction of the past is sought by those committed to upholding authority [but that] near-universal literacy raises the stakes. In the days when only a minority could read and write, popular memory took shape more spontaneously and relatively free from interference; but [...] mainstream establishment interpretations of our history penetrate everywhere.[18]

This is supported by Thomas Docherty, who concurs by suggesting that:

> The victors in history thus proceed in triumphal procession, bearing with them the spoils of their victory, including those documents which record, legitimise and corroborate the necessity of their victory. Such documents the victors call "culture". The historical materialist, unlike the historicist, is profoundly aware of what is being trampled underfoot in this process: the historical materialist remembers what the historicist ignores.[19]

Such, one might argue, is the relationship of pragmatic popular music histories to the histories of hierarchical art music forms. There is an enormous amount of good emancipatory thinking that can be used for, and drawn from, investigations into the popular. As such, several musicologists now suggests that the way musicology has developed into the twentieth century has been at the expense of popular music, in part given the modes of survival through the record being regarded as ultimately authentic. The score *as* record is therefore awarded primacy at the expense of the so-called pretensions of the popular. One might suggest that artistically, the use of conventional elements of music in what is regarded as ordinary music for the masses still evokes from musicologists associations from these past examples of "records". So the relational character of music as a discourse from this period in time—and its relationship with the score as a record—is precisely what permits the musicological generalisation of issues to do with good and bad taste.

The increasing formalisation of musical language brought about a set of relational logics that embraced the narrowly-defined, and helped bring about a discourse that is only relational but is perhaps ironically recognised as universal. The act of thinking and writing about music therefore stems from a period in time when recording music for specific taste cultures came to be defined by the relationship, as much as the music.

---

[18] John Tosh, *The Pursuit of History: Aims, Methods and New Directions in the Study of Modern History* (London: Longman, 1984), 9.

[19] Thomas Docherty, "Postmodernism: An Introduction", in *Postmodernism: A Reader*, ed. Thomas Docherty (London: Harvester Wheatsheaf, 1993), 11.

In Richard Middleton's view, [20] the study of classical musicology being related so closely to a written score as a record can lead to an emphasis of those parts of music which can only be written down. Middleton suggested there were at least three areas where formal musicology had failed to take account of its own hierarchical terms of reference, especially when inappropriately applied to the popular: the value-laden uses made of terminology; the problems with unsuitable methodology (particularly the use of notation); and the outmoded ideology that supports the uses of musicology in the reproduction of tastes and hierarchies linked to powerful social groups. He suggested that such hidebound methods could not convincingly deal with the popular because of a rootedness in concepts concerned with value. The act of making and listening to popular music (with all of the enunciative strategies that implies) cannot, he suggested, be merely reducible to a "knowledge" of a musical "language", especially when that "language" was at least partly non-applicable (how does one, for instance notate the growl of an overdriven guitar? And, perhaps more is the point, why should one wish to?).

Studies of everyday life and its associations with popular music activities (singing, reading, writing, talking, walking, etc.) suggest that *relationships* determine their terms (not the reverse): each individual is a locus for incoherent, contradictory and pluralistic communications. Perhaps while certain musicologists concern themselves with a kind of singular "methodology-as-truth" approach, they are convincing themselves that they "know" the past via their own pre-chosen methods, and that such methods can indeed appropriate music. The temporal linearity implicit in score-based analysis of popular music should always be cut by an element of the lateral. In this way affiliations, which do not presuppose the overconfidence of a proleptic pronouncement (i.e. that this is the way to do it, and it should always be this way), are relentlessly proposed. Popular music is evidently a spatial horizon, across which affiliations and disaffiliations may occur; therefore a *range* of criteria for choosing how one studies popular music must be approximated. By doing so, we can clearly see that all meanings given to music are kinetic though time and space.

So, the traditions according to which popular culture attempts to define itself are not singular, but eclectic. The result is that, historically, the popular is gloriously "directionless" and amorphous. Via popular music studies, itinerant meanings can be scrutinised for their inherent contextual

---

[20] See Richard Middleton in Longhurst, Brian, "Texts and Meaning" in *Popular Music & Society* (Oxford: Polity, 2007), 150–179.

authenticities and values. Popular music studies uses interdisciplinarity in an attempt to understand the complexities of the sound picture, helping us in the process to question "givens" in society. Indeed, popular music studies helps us to turn issues primarily concerned with musical, political, aesthetic, ethical and cultural worth into discourses. We appropriate, rearticulate and give new meanings to the generative structures of music. These exist within a syntagmatic framework of connotations that refract, not reflect, and continue to ask questions about politicised values and authentications. By the time recorded sound emerged fully into the twentieth century such problematic understandings of what sound is, and how certain sounds are prioritised over others, came so much to the fore that, as the twentieth century moved on, sound recording, its very existence, was gradually seen as something more than just recording sound. The radical (let us say) "relationalist" status (i.e. its relationship primarily to itself) of recorded sound widens the relational logics so much that it opens up a pathway towards a new conceptualization of sound. It suggests new relations and introduces ambiguity.

So by the twentieth century, far from being simply a tool for the preservation of music, the record as it comes to be understood within the emerging music industry, is a catalyst. A catalyst is an interesting expression emerging from chemical equations; it is something that when added to something else speeds up a chemical reaction. One might argue, therefore, that when the record is added to late nineteenth-century society, it too creates an important reaction within society, speeds up change and is therefore no longer seen as something that is merely recording information. This gives rise to an unbreachable abyss between the previously considered "reality" of music and new ideas or concepts (what one might describe as "possibilities"), thus weakening the absolutist pretensions of the classical canon. It should be stressed that this "weakening" does not happen overnight, and in actual fact the classical canon is fully embraced (at least as technology allows) by the advent of recorded sound. However, little-by-little, the inherent vulnerability of musicological concepts, being formed only by and through hierarchical ideas that come to appear somewhat anti-diluvian, especially given the growing relationship of recorded sound with the plurality of our existence as technology advances, redefines them and their so-called status in an unpredictable way. This might be described as the emergence of a co-creative universe, as least as far as aesthetics are concerned.

One of the most significant aspects of the advent of recorded sound is discussed by Mark Katz,[21] and this is to do with the invisibility of the performer to listeners. The process of recording changes forever the relationship between the performer or musician and the listener, because an important channel of communication is removed—the visual. Yet this absence of the visual, he states, is not merely a negative concerning the difference between authentic and inauthentic sound. Katz quotes a 1912 article in the *Musical Courier*, which praises recording for stripping away all unnecessary aspects of the musical experience: "In listening to the talking machine the hearer must of necessity concentrate upon the tonal performance and does not have his attention diverted to extraneous matters, such as scenery, costumes [and] acting [...] that keep him from directing his faculties to the music itself".[22] Actually, Frankfurt School cultural theorist (and anti-popular intellectual) Theodor Adorno appeared to agree with such an idea. He argued that opera, which one might argue is one of the most visual of all musical genres, was in fact best heard on record. In his 1969 article "Opera and the Long-Playing Record", he suggested that staging detracted from the musical experience, whereas "shorn of phoney hoopla, the LP simultaneously frees itself from the capriciousness of fake opera festivals".[23]

Of course, it was not only western classical performers who were affected by the absence of an audience, for it did not take long for the record to achieve a status far beyond its initial meaning. Recorded sound was one of those important technological developments of the late-nineteenth century that were not used for their original purposes. This industrial process cannot therefore be reduced to the sole constituents of either its invention or production—an error of colossal magnitude made by formalist Marxist thought. To Marx, this was the age in which "everything solid melts into air".[24] This was an age of breath-taking developments, of the expansion of material wealth, of the ever-increasing mastery of humankind over its natural environment. The means of production were already "social", both in their character and the private character of ownership. Soon, according to Marx, this private ownership would be the

---

[21] Mark Katz, *Capturing Sound: How Technology has Changed Music* (Berkeley: University of California Press, 2004).

[22] *ibid.*, 21.

[23] Theodor Adorno, "Opera and the Long-Playing Record" in *Essays on Music*, ed. Richard Leppert (Berkeley: University of California Press, 1969), 284.

[24] Karl Marx, *The Manifesto of the Communist Party* (1848), accessed 29 May 2013, http://www.marxists.org/archive/marx/works/1848/communist-manifesto/ch01.htm#060.

last "solidity" to fall. Yet the predetermined outcomes that Marx suggested would occur via such developmental processes have not, by and large, occurred, and increasingly less orthodox historical moments—at least according to the Marxist rubric—have rendered relationships in the modern age far from straightforward. For example, as soon as Edison's cylinder failed as a dictaphone, the intertextuality of human imagination and the co-creative potential of the individual re-contextualised this mass-produced artefact into something completely previously unintended. Historian John Tosh suggests that:

> The truth is that today the Marxist theory of history lies under something of a cloud. The reason is not simply to be found in a keener appreciation of the limits of its application in time and space. The wider intellectual climate has also changed to its disadvantage. Whatever their doctrinal disagreements, Marxists share an optimism about the progressive change in the world, and the ability of an overarching theory to understand and facilitate such change. But during the 1970s and 1980s the tide began to flow strongly the other way [...] the grand theories which legitimate these ideologies lost their appeal.[25]

Many post-modernists have therefore emphasised such intertextuality (the way several discontinuous texts combine together to create a new meaning) as both a strategy and a contemporary reality. This has led to recorded sound being discussed in terms of two precepts; radical eclecticism and suggestive narrative: recorded sound was essentially double-coded and could never be part of a singular understanding of our imaginative universe, as might be suggested by Marxism, even though it could be argued that Marx's attitude towards the bourgeoisie was at times full of admiration for its civilising energies.[26]

This remarkable feat is a good example of the way in which industrial production is often misunderstood and considered to have only negative effects on society, stunting mankind's normal development, for rather than being an invention that was completely dependent upon its modes of production, recorded sound elicited responses from receivers in a completely unintended manner. It therefore might be argued that the social upheavals proper to an age of industrialisation necessitated even more complex articulatory practices than Marx could have ever considered, and as a result, operated in increasingly less orthodox historical ways than

---

[25] John Tosh, *The Pursuit of History: Aims, Methods and New Directions in the Study of Modern History* (London: Longman, 1984), 178.
[26] For example, see introduction to Eugene Kamanka, ed., *The Portable Karl Marx* (London: Viking Penguin, 1983).

could have been predicted. Thus the question posed by such uneven industrial-cum-social development as recorded sound is, "precisely what is supposed to be normal development?"

One might therefore argue that rather than being part of an industrial production, with methodology as an ideology which strips the receiver of their autonomy, recorded sound, by being used against the grain of meaning in the first instance, has always been a relatively democratising form. Adorno and his ideas concerning atomised listening failed to grasp the concept that the unit of sound one listens to privileges the listener, not the music. While Adorno might describe listening to recordings as disconnected moments, one might ask the question, "Disconnected from whom, and from what?" One might even wonder exactly what Adorno means by "disconnected". Certainly, if one was considering the initial idea of a score as a record of a live performance, or of a movement of music, one might suggest that recorded sound does indeed separate the listeners from those intentions; however, if one were to consider reception strategies on behalf of the listener, such apparent *dis*connections are actually *conn*ections. Not to the rest of the music, but to the listeners' ways of life. It could therefore be argued that the recording increases access at a time when hierarchies, having already been formed in western classical music, were consolidating.

Recording technologies, therefore, helped to encourage new ways of listening to music, rather than simply facilitating the act of listening to a record of a score (and being manipulated, in the process). The systematic discovery of discursive areas and floating signifiers brought about by recorded sound, when such areas did not effectively exist prior to recorded sound, was a cumulative enrichment of society and added a different logic to our existence which could not be explained away via Marxist doctrine. It is common in popular music circles to incorporate the listener very early in our analysis of popular music, but this was not always the case. For, given the rise of mass-industrialisation, the growth of broadcast technology, and the development of mass-communication systems throughout the twentieth century, critics have often been inclined to suggest that listening is not a creative act but merely a mode of consumption. However, if one takes the record as a single artefact, rather than one of a million, and if one places that record into specific environments related to particular human interactions, understandings, and aesthetics, the recording itself, indeed the artefact itself, can quite clearly be considered as a matrix, and that this matrix creates, relatively autonomously, a platform within which one can reach for—and indeed at times discover—a sense of identity.

Such significance attached to a single artefact of mass production is remarkable, and cannot simply be reduced to the means of its own production. It needs to be understood in terms of reception, of new ways of listening to music, of distinctive ways in which conspicuous consumption is organised, of performances being unutterably altered, and even of entirely new genres of music coming into existence. The record and its existence within the realism of invention, innovation, and diffusion cannot therefore be considered only through the diktats of either technology or advanced capitalism or the Marxist tradition alone, but rather in extremely complex ways that were entirely contingent upon the actions of the users. It is from such a perspective that this work will proceed, and while acknowledging the arguments of the Frankfurt School and their considerations of mass production as a means of drip-feeding ideology to what they often viewed as the "masses", it will be argued that the record as a kinetic matrix reveals far more about how relational technologies can be both contingent and directly involved in the lives of the individual.

Collecting

Before libraries and encyclopaedias, collections were seen as a source of knowledge.[27] However, as knowledge of the world became more readily available collections took on a more personal role.[28] We also began to collect objects claimed to possess a more fleeting or ephemeral nature, objects of popular culture such as records, football programmes, or cigarette cards. These collections of popular culture can also disclose factual information about the objects themselves in their organisation (what might be described as an indexical indicator), but can be used to tell personal stories about the artefact, the collector and collecting (we might describe this as iconic). Semiotic and structural analysis presents us with many important denotations and connotations under which one can study the collector; however, one of the most important is the division between indexical and iconic signs. For an indexical sign to work it has to carry meaning which relates in an order to other meanings. To paraphrase Philip Tagg,[29] a smoke alarm is a good example of such an indexical sign, for smoke means fire, fire means danger, danger mean get away, and so on.

---

[27] Philipp Blom, *To Have and to Hold: An Intimate History of Collectors and Collecting* (Woodstock: The Overlook Press, 2002).

[28] John Bloom, *A House of Cards: Baseball Card Collecting and Popular Culture* (Minneapolis: University of Minnesota Press, 1997).

[29] Philip Tagg, *Ten Little Tunes* (Liverpool: IPM, 1992).

On the other hand, iconic signs are more personal, and are connected to connotations in a perhaps differing way. Icons are reminders of how one imagines the world and how one would like the world to be. Such indexes and icons feature very strongly for record collectors and their collections, and will be discussed periodically throughout this book; however, this writer would, in the first instance wish to explain her own record collection via such indexical and iconographic tropes.

For centuries, people have invested both time and resources into all kinds of collections, once highly regarded for their educational use and the information they could provide.[30] However, gathering items from around the world before commercial air travel was an expensive and time-consuming endeavour. Collections were thus a great symbol of status and an activity reserved for the wealthy—and regarded as a high cultural practice.[31] Modern-day collecting has moved on from this, and can take on many different forms. People have been known to collect numerous items ranging from baseball cards, Barbie dolls and plastic bags to more "traditional" items such as stamps, books and butterflies. Collecting can, however, be both a conscious and unconscious pursuit,[32] but the people we tend to refer to as "collectors" are generally aware of their actions and pursue their collecting as a hobby.[33] There are as many motives for collecting as there are possible items to collect, though several themes appear to relate back to some sort of nostalgia or innocence.[34] For example, collecting childhood items like toys illustrates this perfectly. In an interesting study, Bloom[35] looks at the practice of adults collecting out of date baseball cards. Excluding the odd exception, these cards are not worth very much in monetary terms, but they still have significant meaning for the collector who can go to great lengths to find the card he or she needs. The interest in these cards, as Bloom explains, can stem from childhood memories and a desire to return to a time when life appeared to

---

[30] Philipp Blom, *To Have and to Hold: An Intimate History of Collectors and Collecting* (Woodstock: The Overlook Press, 2002).
[31] *ibid.*
[32] Randy O. Frost, "Treatment of Hoarding", *Expert Review of Neurotherapeutics* 10, no. 2 (2010): 251–261; Randy O. Frost, "From Dante to DSM-V: A Short History of Hoarding", accessed 27 October 2010, http://www.ocfoundation.org/hoarding/dante_to_dsm-v.aspx.
[33] Walter A. Brown and Zsuzsa Meszaros, "Hoarding", *Psychiatric Times* 24, no. 13 (2007): 50–52.
[34] John Bloom, *A House of Cards: Baseball Card Collecting and Popular Culture* (Minneapolis: University of Minnesota Press, 1997).
[35] *ibid.*

be simpler. For Bloom, the materiality of the cards thus reinforces a sort of "daydream", if you will, of the collector's more naïve years—they offer a direct link back to the past, transporting the collector there in an instant.

Bloom thus identifies the collected object as serving a purpose to link the collector with the past through a tangible object,[36] in essence making history itself appear more tangible. However, the use of the word "daydream" remains problematic—at least for this writer. For, via such a descriptor, collecting continues to be regarded as an escape from the world, not a link to it. It is probably true that collectors as an entity at least appear to have a very pronounced need or desire to connect with a bygone time, be it personal or otherwise. However, all collecting is part of a very complex web of concepts, as we will come to discover through this work, and whilst nostalgia is a very important motivation behind collecting, it is only one possible reason why people choose to collect.

So, too, are economic factors. Many collectors are also stereotyped as being involved in collecting for purely economic reasons. Yet this is clearly incorrect. Take, for example, Bob Stanley's interest in football programmes, which are based on an interest in the graphic design of 1970s programmes—still to this very day of little financial value:

At the turn of the seventies, programme design reached a modernist high-water mark. High contrast, dramatic image adorned covers, frequently two colours—nothing, as Berthold Lubetkin said "jazzy and hideous". Club crests were banished in favour of serious looking men in simple round collar shirts (kits too embraced a new minimalism). [On the other hand] A Hendon Supporters FC programme from 1979 has the production values of an Angry Brigade communiqué; that won't happen again in a hurry.[37]

Premise

As indicated above, before this research had begun a number of troublesome portrayals of (record) collectors and seemingly misconstrued perceptions about the practices involved had already come to the attention of this author, and these are also discussed at some length by Shuker.[38]

---

[36] Stuart Semmel, "Reading the Tangible Past: British Tourism, Collecting, and Memory after Waterloo", *Representations* 69, Special Issue: Grounds for Remembering (2000): 9–37.

[37] Bob Stanley and Paul Kelly, *Match Day: Post-war to Premiership Football Programmes* (London: Murray & Sorrell FUEL, 2008), 21–22.

[38] Roy Shuker, *Wax Trash and Vinyl Treasures: Record Collecting as a Social Practice* (Farnham: Ashgate, 2010).

Having a personal attachment to record collecting, there was a desire to present a more accurate and encompassing picture of collectors generally, and record collectors specifically. There was also a sense of a distinct lack of attention given to the importance of record collecting to the collector's own formation of identity, and that this needed to be rectified. This basis then served as the initial motivations behind the forthcoming work.

Before this, however, it would be beneficial for the reader to have a general understanding of collecting and what it entails. Firstly, there has been a tendency to regard collecting as a "passive" hobby—almost as if it were a mere accumulation of objects rather than an active search for and engagement with them. Adorno,[39] for instance, speaks of the radio ham that, he feels, assembles objects (radio parts) in a predetermined fashion and "brings nothing home which would not be delivered to his house".[40] The radio ham is thus regarded as passive and not creative because his hobby involves the *assembly* of mass-produced parts. Whilst his reflections on the radio ham provides the reader with a different perspective of a collector, even though such a word is not used in the text, Adorno does not, however, consider what the radio ham gets from such items of exchange. But as explored by Robert Pirsig, this activity could for instance be used as a form of meditation with the task allowing the mind to relax and focus:

> The making of a painting or the fixing of a motorcycle isn't separate from the rest of your existence. If you're a sloppy thinker the six days of the week you aren't working on your machine, what trap avoidances, what gimmicks, can make you all of a sudden sharp on the seventh? It all goes together.
> But if you're a sloppy thinker six days a week and you really *try* to be sharp on the seventh, then maybe the next six days aren't going to be quite as sloppy as the preceding six.[41]

Such important worlds are now acknowledged as of vital significance for the health of the mind of the individual. For Adorno, however, there appeared to be effectively two realities: one of immediate artistic appearance, and another of underlying socio-economic explanation. In a way, Adorno represents a sort of anger where things do not appear to

---

[39] Theodor Adorno, "On the Fetish-Character of Listening and the Regression of Listening" in *Essays on Music*, ed. Richard Leppert (Berkeley: University of California Press, 1938).

[40] *ibid.*, 309.

[41] Robert Pirsig, *Zen and the Art of Motorcycle Maintenance* (London: Vintage/Random House, 1974), 325.

match, or fit, his visions of reality, where things as well as people seems to be in conflict. However, the world as revealed by the mind is also a reality, regardless of how it may appear, and those in Adorno's dimension simply have to do more than just ignore it. Belk *et al.*, on the other hand, provide a more objective account, insisting in their study including around 190 collectors that all collecting is an active, not "passive" pursuit, and is part of the mind's sense of the real:

> We take collecting to be the selective, active, and longitudinal acquisition, possession, and disposition of an inter-related set of differentiated objects (material things, ideas, beings, or experiences) that contribute to and derive extraordinary meaning from the entity (the collection) that this set is perceived to constitute. This definition coheres with that of Belk (1982) and Belk, Wallendorf, Sherry, Holbrook, and Roberts (1988). It is also generally consistent with prior definitions.[42]

Furthermore, the above authors understand that some people— collectors, even—have an aversion and resistance to the very classification of "collector". Within society in general, there appears to be a certain stigma attached to the "collector" label. It appears that even some individuals with extensive record collections still resist the term "collector", as they feel it has a negative connotation indicating that a person is simply stockpiling records.[43] One collector and dealer ("George"), interviewed at some length by this writer, was ambivalent about himself as a collector, and although he saw other collectors as real and authentic, tended to give most of them a wide berth because he did not feel altogether comfortable with their presence. Another record enthusiast and audiophile, who responded to the web-based question posed by another web-user on the Audiophile.net forum as to whether being a (record) collector was considered to be a good thing, stated "absolutely *not*… not by me atleast [*sic*]….. in my view, just buying and holding onto vinyls should be considered a *crime*".[44]

This interesting stigma is also often connected to concepts surrounding hoarders. Via this static form of collecting, known as compulsive hoarding (and also pathological collecting), a pattern of behaviour is characterized

---

[42] Russel Belk *et al.* (1991), "Collecting in a Consumer Culture", in *Highways and Buyways: Naturalistic Research from the Consumer Behaviour Odyssey*, ed. Russel W. Belk (Association for Consumer Research, 1991), 3.

[43] www.theaudiophile.net, accessed 5 December 2011; See also Debord's remarks in Philip Auslander, "Looking at Records", *The Drama Review* 45, no. 1 (2001): 77–83.

[44] "sumeet" (2011), www.theaudiophile.net, emphasis in the original.

by the excessive acquisition of (and inability and/or unwillingness to discard) large quantities of items that cover the home and cause significant distress. This can be seen as being clinically significant enough to impair human normality and can prevent the typical uses of space so as to limit activities such as cooking, cleaning, moving through the house, and sleeping. But it would have to be stated that this is not collecting as such, for collectors use, archive, re-visit and supplement their collections. One might suggest that several series of studies are required to separate the collector from the hoarder, at least in the minds of the public at large, because for some there seems to be very little cultural distance between the two—which seems to be more a condition of society's uncertainty concerning what they are dealing with, rather than a problem, as such, for the collector.

It is therefore not uncommon for collectors to be mistakenly referred to as "hoarders" in casual conversations that might imply psychiatric and/or clinical conditions of compulsive hoarding. Such comments are often made in a spirited manner, on occasion even by collectors themselves, but the term nevertheless still holds negative social and clinical associations.[45]

Collecting at Large

As briefly discussed above, collections were used as a source of knowledge before libraries and encyclopaedias were readily available.[46] However, as knowledge of the world became more easily accessible, collections began to take on a more personal role.[47] It has already been stated in this work that people began to collect objects that appeared to be of a more fleeting nature such as records, programmes, or baseball cards. Whilst these popular-culture objects still disclose certain factual information (for instance on the manufacturing processes—which is also of great significance in a world of advanced capitalism), one can also extract very personal information relating to the collector from them— these are connotations of identity, of course. One can perhaps place collected objects into long-term (also known elsewhere as "antiques" or

---

[45] Oxforddictionaries.com, accessed 5 December 2011; See also Hanna Buchdahl, "An Unwanted Inheritance", *The Daily Beast*, 26 January 2011, accessed 5 December 2011, http://www.thedailybeast.com/newsweek/2011/01/26/an-unwanted-inheritance.html.
[46] Philipp Blom, *To Have and to Hold: An Intimate History of Collectors and Collecting* (Woodstock: The Overlook Press, 2002).
[47] John Bloom, *A House of Cards: Baseball Card Collecting and Popular Culture* (Minneapolis: University of Minnesota Press, 1997).

"collectibles") or (perceived) short-term ("ephemera", "memorabilia", "souvenir") value. A few of the collected items in each category might be something like:

Long-term	Short-term
Coins	Postcards
Books	Sporting programmes
Stamps	Tickets
Antique furniture	Newspapers
Paintings	Bottle caps
Natural history items (butterflies, birds' eggs, feathers, stuffed animals, botanics etc.)	Trading cards (baseballs, show horses, ice hockey, etc.)

This is not to say that objects in the short-term value column do not have long-term value (and *vice-versa*), but to illustrate how typically "high" cultural objects are often collected in a different manner and are viewed differently from collections/collectors of popular culture objects. As implied, this method is a very simplified way of viewing things, and crossovers do occur (some newspapers can for instance fall into the "long-term" category, especially if they feature a specific important event), but these distinctions can be used here in order to describe different collecting processes, at least according to the social mores of society where connoisseurship is attached to collecting in order to justify its existence: art history might be such an area, whereas the history of (say) comics, is not.

Objects that are not to be found in the long-term value category might have an initial lower financial value and, as we have already suggested, not intended for long-term preservation. As such, the collectors of such objects might be viewed as somewhat odd for acquiring and preserving them. It may be easier to understand why people would collect objects in the long-term category, as these can be regarded as an investment.

Collections such as coins or stamps (or, indeed, football programmes[48]), for instance, can sell for sizeable amounts of money, and rare items tend to be economically highly valued.[49] However, the objects that sell for particularly notable sums are predominantly cultural artefacts that stem from what is regarded as "high" culture (perhaps paintings, in particular), as such traditional notions of which objects are "worth something" has an effect on values—both socially and economically. Thus perceptions of a high/low dichotomy have a strong effect within collecting as well. Therefore, it is not simply the mechanisms of the market place which take upon themselves the roles of judge or opinion-makers concerning values. Instead, the remnants of the domain of authenticity created by the aforesaid art-based hierarchies still retain their authority. It has long been recognised in popular music studies that authenticity and authority are created by such fragments of the past.

The growing earnestness of collecting, together with incursions from academia, have linked to authorise events, opinions, discographies, and memorabilia administered from within a field of not simply musical, but linguistic, systems. The presence and circulation of information from within such networks of users approves certain types of texts, particularly those that establish an artist as a "gift" to the world, and via interlocutors creates a contract by and through these networks. Collectors emerge as social actors in their own right, authenticating in very specific ways, for example, some attempt to give us insights concerning (say) The Beatles as individuals via recourse to memorabilia. Others merge their Beatles fanaticism with collecting specific recordings, such as for example, out-takes. Observing the regulating of these Beatles "fragments" continues to be of great historical significance.

For the popular music historian and ethnographer alike, "fragments" can be seen as a miscellany of activities relating (in this particular case) to The Beatles. Lars Kaijser,[50] however, correctly states that such Beatles fragments can tend to place a greater emphasis on the present, rather than the actual periods of time in which the group existed. For Kaijser, fragments are best viewed as synecdoches or metonyms: in other words they inescapably link to variable, larger, interesting contexts. These might

---

[48] In May 2012.
[49] Kendall L. Walton, "How Marvellous!: Toward a Theory of Aesthetic Value", *The Journal of Aesthetics and Art Criticism* 51, no. 3 (1993): 499–510.
[50] Lars Kaijser, "Authority Among Fragments; Reflections on Representing The Beatles in a Tourist Setting", in *Fifty Years With The Beatles: The Impact of The Beatles on Contemporary Culture*, eds. Jerzy Jarniewicz and Alina Kwiatkowska (Lodz: University Press, 2010).

be to Beatles-memorabilia valuing, or to the context-based rock discourses of authentication; they might be dialogues of significance surrounding the collector and what they actually collect (see later regarding Diane Tye), or representations of Beatles-collecting as a key to historical narratives during the late twentieth century, etc. All such relational logics can be found in practically every Beatles/Lennon collection pre- and post-John Lennon's death. So it is true, that, for collectors, fragments help to engender historical worlds of their own, but they are also publicly functional and contextual sources of reference for themselves and for others. How fragments are synchronically and synecdochally ordered by collectors, and how they contribute to structuring their worlds discloses a great deal about the contextual policies of entering The Beatles folklore equation.

Collectors are, unlike hoarders, part of an almost "archaeological" field of enquiry, for fresh fragments can be brought to the table. For example, as with an archaeological dig, items still crop up: a new photo, a new recollection, an old piece of music, a new book, a record, etc. So, for the writers of Beatles histories, collectors provide significant definitive documents from which questions and answers can be set forth, and from which a historical sense of proportion can be set into place. In effect, collecting The Beatles has become a significant historical pursuit, and although a historical fragment might have emanated from The Beatles, it does not have to (in fact, cannot) stay the same. A certain "fragment configuration" takes place, so that any "new" fragments "fit" within the ruling order of Beatles historiography. This form of homology serves a support network. Therefore, such aesthetic judgements directly imply economic judgements based on this important social and historical network. This acquisition of cultural objects therefore also brings with it something else—namely, cultural capital. The term "cultural capital" originates in the work of Bourdieu and can be used to both create a bond within a social group or to alienate others.[51] It is used to distinguish (particular) knowledge and, as such, the most knowledgeable person within the specific subject possesses the most cultural capital (see further discussion in Chapter Four). Thus within certain circles of record collecting, for example, one might observe that the person who owns the largest number of rare records holds the most cultural capital as a result. It is also worth noting that people who share beliefs on cultural capital can even develop their own uses of language that are specific to their

---

[51] Pierre Bourdieu, "Cultural Reproduction and Social Reproduction", in *Knowledge, Education and Cultural Change: Papers in the Sociology of Education*, ed. Robert Brown (London: Tavistock Publications Ltd., 1973).

group/s.[52] However, despite several studies concerning cultural capital and popular culture,[53] academia currently offers little information to explain or understand the specifics of how and why, let us say, a teenager might start buying records to gain cultural capital in the 1950s or 1960s, and how that teenager, 30 years-or-so later, leads a generation into the academic study of popular music—for such is the case with popular music studies pioneer Simon Frith. Despite record collecting being at the heart of the growth and development of popular music academia, it still does not appear worthy of study, at least to any great extent, which remains odd. This might be because popular music academia initially sprang from the political left. Brocken and Davis state that such ideology:

> [...] kept many UK popular music critics and scholars such as Simon Frith up at night in the 1970s, as they sought to legitimise popular music as an authentic dialogue, while also acknowledging that the Marxist premise of historical materialism regarding the music industry still encapsulated rhetoric power. [...] It is plausible to state that although history is forged in conflict (as Marx alludes), such conflicts demand that history represents the debates concerning such struggles for ownership, rather than simply reflect the ideology of historical materialism (and indeed the realities of the masses), as a given.[54]

Regardless, people of a certain disposition may find it very desirable to attain the cultural capital attached to certain high-cultural objects typically found in this long-term category (the opposite could likewise be argued for short-term objects, for instance as a tool of defiance). In this sense, it could be argued that collecting objects in the long-term category may be a very valuable cultural pursuit for some, showing evidence of "high" cultural knowledge via the cultural capital the collected items bring with them.

Record Collecting: Indexical and/or Iconic Organisation

One presumes that every popular music studies academic will be familiar with the term "authenticity", relating to (for instance) an act's perceived "realness" or "genuine" involvement/pathos (see further discussion in

---

[52] David Riesman, "Listening to Popular Music", in *On Record: Rock, Pop and the Written Word*, eds. Simon Frith and Andrew Goodwin (London: Routledge, 1950), 5–13.

[53] For instance Michael Emmison and John Frow, "Information Technology as Cultural Capital", *Australian Universities' Review* 4, no. 1 (1998): 41–45.

[54] Michael Brocken and Melissa Davis, *The Beatles Bibliography: A New Guide to the Literature* (Manitou Springs: The Beatle Works, 2012), 30.

Chapter Four). The notion is often questioned by academics, but still in regular use amongst music journalists and fans alike. With this in mind, I have to admit that perceived authenticity has played a big role in how my LPs are organised. Thus, in my record collection I have largely bought in to the myths of rock hierarchy (who is "better" than whom?), hagiography (which single creative, male genius created something more splendid than the next?) and authenticity (who *really* meant it?). As a popular music studies academic I would (i) question why there are no female acts in the "top" positions (see below), e.g. why are The Kinks more important or better than Madonna for instance, but also (ii) what makes The Kinks good or important to begin with?[55] As a fan or record collector however, it is important to note that not one of these questions spring to mind. It must also be emphasised that my organisation is incredibly subjective, as is the case for most record collectors.

First and foremost in the organisation are The Beatles' records, which themselves have a particular order I will return to, followed by The Who, The Kinks, Bob Dylan, Crosby, Stills, Nash & Young and their respective solo albums, Pink Floyd, Jimi Hendrix, Electric Light Orchestra, Jethro Tull, The Rolling Stones, Donovan, Van Der Graaf Generator, The Yardbirds and on to artists of whose records I only own one or two. Some may note the absence of Led Zeppelin, but this was simply because I was not able to obtain any Led Zeppelin records until a much later date, at which point they were slotted in relatively randomly as I felt a major re-organisation was due—a project that requires weeks for it to feel "right", and something which I have continually held in suspension until I feel the "right" moment arrives. Furthermore, the only solo albums by group

---

[55] The academic might argue that Ray Davies's lyrics have made him an auteur with songs like *Waterloo Sunset* and *Sunny Afternoon*, both of which contain un-romanticised, realistic and sometimes even cynical lines such as:

Millions of people swarming like flies round Waterloo underground,
But Terry and Julie cross over the river, where they feel safe and sound,
And they don't need no friends, as long as they gaze on Waterloo sunset
They are in paradise.

and

The tax man's taken all my dough,
And left me in my stately home,
Lazing on a sunny afternoon.
And I can't sail my yacht,
He's taken everything I've got.
All I've got's this sunny afternoon.

As an auteur, one could argue that Davies has brought the Kinks a certain kind of authenticity and cultural capital that made them important in this context.

members to earn a place within their group were Crosby, Stills, Nash & Young as they felt more like a collective than a more regular group like The Beatles or The Who. Their solo albums were also the only ones I felt reflected the same qualities as their music as a group. It is, for instance, fairly common to hear complaints from fans how The Beatles' solo efforts were not as good as their output as a group (with a few, notable exceptions), whereas I felt this was not the case for Crosby, Stills, Nash & Young. This solution also served to "bulk" the Crosby, Stills, Nash & Young section (see below), as their entry was otherwise very small, but could not alter in position according to me.

Apart from "owning" and categorising the Yardbirds in a very specific way, I own several LPs by the aforementioned artists and have prioritised multiple albums from the same acts over single albums. This is complex: even though I understood *Never Mind the Bollocks, Here's the Sex Pistols*[56] to be rather authentic, it ended up further back in the order as I only owned that single album by the Sex Pistols. The Yardbirds' 1966 eponymous album (aka "Roger the Mechanic") achieved a high ranking in the order because my dad found out about my system and told me that it was a cult album that had to be there. Even though some might argue that The Rolling Stones are more authentic than the Electric Light Orchestra, the reason why the latter achieved a higher ranking in my order is simply down to the fact that I really like them, whilst I was never overly excited by The Rolling Stones.

In loose terms, therefore, ranking was (and still is) based on the importance or "seminality" of artist and/or album. This importance was judged according to my own aesthetics—largely a mod, counter-cultural, hippie, psychedelic, progressive aesthetic. Hence *Sgt. Pepper's Lonely Hearts Club Band* would be regarded as more important—and more authentic—than *Goodbye Yellow Brick Road*, seeing as both the music *and* record cover appeared to reflect such an aesthetic in the case of the former whilst it was only reflected in the cover of the latter.

Record covers are an interesting component of records as well as record collecting. As Ian Inglis demonstrates, the record sleeve has four functions: protection, advertisement, accompaniment, and as a commodity in its own right. The final two functions are the primary ones in terms of record collecting, as will be discussed later. With regard to *Sgt. Pepper's Lonely Hearts Club Band*, then, I felt the album art was an "integral component of the listening"[57] experience, whereas it did not appear to me

---

[56] For further album details, see Appendix A: Album Information.

[57] Ian Inglis, "'Nothing You Can See that isn't Shown': The Album Covers of The Beatles", *Popular Music* 20, No. 1 (2001): 84.

that *Goodbye Yellow Brick Road* had the same connection between the cover and the musical content. Later, this work will consider in greater depth the issues surrounding album art, including how sleeves can be used to influence aesthetics, and sleeves as "trophies".[58]

LPs by Swedish artists posed a particular difficulty for me. The Swedish "progg" (i.e. not prog) group Nationalteatern, who released their first LP in 1972 were, for instance, very authentic to my mind because their music often had a (lyrical) connection to their hometown of Gothenburg (which, as it happened, was also my place of birth), but on a global scene I felt they would not be competitive as they are relatively unknown outside of Sweden.[59] I solved this by having a separate shelf for all Swedish music. In some respects, the separate Swedish shelf also made me feel as if I was not fully examining authenticity as a fan, so I excused it as being a tribute to my origins. This system allowed me to rank Swedish artists as a separate entity, but posed difficulties if I encountered any acts that would have been competitive internationally. Some record collectors have probably experienced similar problems if they organise records by genre. Genre classification can be very difficult, and cross-over genres/acts are frequent—for example, should Jethro Tull be called progressive rock or perhaps folk-rock? The case can be made for both genres, and the fan's own understanding or preference of genre will most likely dictate the final decision.

Records by the same artist were organised chronologically within this authenticity order, except LPs by The Beatles—they have their own very specific order. The first Beatles record is *Rubber Soul*, and always has to be regardless of any other changes that may occur, because it was the album that re-awoke my interest in music. I grew up in a house where the radio was always on, usually on a commercial station. When I was 14 I became fed up with commercial pop, and swore off all but classical music. For six months there was a radio and music television ban in our house. I would immediately turn off any popular music being played, for instance on the kitchen radio, when I entered the room. The car radio was a particularly difficult medium to control, but eventually a compromise was reached where it could be turned on, at a lower volume, and not continually. Initially, my family were perplexed, but ultimately my wishes

---

[58] *ibid.*, 84.

[59] Arguably their fame in Sweden could be said to be currently limited as well, although releases such as *Nationalsånger—hymner från Vågen och EPAs torg* (2002), where more current Swedish artists re-recorded famous songs by Nationalteatern, indicate that the group also still have a following amongst younger generations.

were respected (living in a farmhouse with copious space probably helped too). This ban lasted until I found my dad's old record player. I was very intrigued by it for some reason which now escapes me, and I decided to put it back together. When I was finished, and proud of my handiwork, I thought it would be a shame not to listen to anything on it and picked up the *Rubber Soul* LP. At this point in my life I had heard *of* The Beatles, but never actually knowingly, at least, heard any of their *music*. It seemed like a reasonable place to start.

I cannot recall exactly what drew me to *Rubber Soul* on this very first occasion, but I can assume that I was intrigued by the record cover (which to this day is still my favourite as well). There was an air of cool around the four individual Beatles, earthy colours that spoke to me, an interesting fisheye lens, and the *Rubber Soul* logo itself in a font that appealed to my aesthetic senses. With *Rubber Soul*, music was back in my life. *Rubber Soul* is followed by *A Hard Day's Night*, because of the naïve quality in the lyrics and the slightly nasal vocals. George Harrison's contributions to the album are also some of my favourite Harrison moments. The third album is *Magical Mystery Tour*,[60] owing to the pictures that came with the album and the circus-like theme, which (again) spoke to my aesthetic at the time. My collection, which I share with my dad, contains both the EP and the LP version of *Magical Mystery Tour*. My dad, by various means, originally acquired the majority of the collection, though I am unsure how some records were obtained. The *Magical Mystery Tour* EP and LP are one such mystery. Many of The Beatles' records I have come to own[61] were acquired by my dad through complicated pathways, thus it is difficult to remember exactly how the ownership ultimately fell to us. Hence it is hard to say what came first—the EP or the LP. The following LPs were ordered according to similar reasons, but I regarded these as less important albums in my musical development so their place was not as fixed as the first three or the following, as will be discussed. I placed a couple of compilation albums, such as *A Collection of Beatles Oldies but Goldies* and *The Beatles at the Hollywood Bowl*, after *Yellow Submarine* (which was the last of the official studio albums, bar the following LP)—and following these, as the very last LP, was always *Let It Be*. *Let It Be* felt like an unlucky record because it was the last one The Beatles recorded together as a group. The LP itself almost signified their eventual split for

---

[60] It is acknowledged that the *Magical Mystery Tour* set was originally issued in the UK as a double-EP. The album in this writer's collection is an import.

[61] All The Beatles' records were given to me as a birthday present one year. I am also the main proprietor of the entire collection, which is why I commonly refer to it simply as mine.

me, and I still remember the horror I felt when one day the album had ended up in front of *Rubber Soul*. I ascribed the incident to "ghosts", and saw it as an omen until some days later my dad told he had been listening to the album.

I am eternally insistent that whilst my habits of collecting and organising these collections may *appear* neurotic to the outsider, there is nothing inherently neurotic in my behaviour as such: an unorganised or "incomplete" collection does not make me believe the sky is falling down, that I will become fatally ill or cause any other anxieties. This is starkly contrasted by Shuker who writes:

> A major characteristic identified with record collecting was a love of music, with attention also paid to questions of *obsessive-compulsive behaviour*; *accumulation, completism* and collection size [...] For the record collectors, this [searching for records] is a process [...] underpinned by a strong element of compulsion. [62]

Or as Norma, a record collector (as defined by Shuker) who resists the record-collector label, argues, "I see collecting as [...] kind of a useless pursuit, less driven by music or musical taste and more driven by the need to exert masculine power/knowledge".[63] Barry Seven, on the other hand, portrays a very different picture when he writes about his favourite record hunting (shopping) experience during Jarvis Cocker's stag-do, and notes how it was a very social, healthy, and what one could even call "normal", activity:

> We were all record hunters, all friends for years [...] Needless to say, it was a very gentlemanly affair, like an old lady cookery class with loads of hints and tips and admiring displays of knowledge and musical generosity. Looking back we found records that shaped our individual futures. [...] The record shop in all its battered piles and categories is, for me at least, a social act.[64]

This feels like a much more realistic description for me, and the vast majority of the record collectors I have had the pleasure to come across, as my record collecting and organising does not evoke feelings of anger,

---

[62] Roy Shuker, *Wax Trash and Vinyl Treasures: Record Collecting as a Social Practice* (Farnham: Ashgate, 2010), 39 & 110.
[63] Norma Coates cited in Roy Shuker, *Wax Trash and Vinyl Treasures: Record Collecting as a Social Practice* (Farnham: Ashgate, 2010), 36.
[64] Barry Seven cited in Emma Petitt, *Old Rare New: The Independent Record Shop* (London: Black Dog Publishing, 2008), 4.

irritability, erraticism, obsession or depression, either. In fact, engaging
with my collections gives me enjoyment and satisfaction, an activity I will
gladly spend a considerable amount of time on, but that I can also step
away from at any given time *if I so choose*. I resent the fact that people
from all manner of backgrounds—journalists, academics, "regular Joes"—
are so keen to label my hobby with different pathological terms—neurotic,
obsessive, compulsive (obsessive-compulsive), addictive, hoarding—
simply *because they do not understand it*.

To put it in different terms, Pamela[65] enjoys interior design, and in her
spare time frequently helps friends and family members to redecorate, pick
out furnishings and "home style" their homes. She often browses interior
decorating shops without a project in mind or for inspiration and ideas.
This can be helpful when a project does emerge, as she can then return to
these shops and quickly pick out the items she needs. Pamela thus spends
a considerable amount of time on her interior design hobby, but is not
labelled obsessive or neurotic in any way. This is because her hobby is
easy to comprehend for most people as they can see a clear function to it,
for (regardless of choice) interior design surrounds us, and people are
often concerned with having a pleasant home. Even browsing in shops
without a project in mind can be explained by the fact that there *probably*
will be one forthcoming. What some fail to see, then, is the connection and
similarities between Pamela's hobby and record collecting as a hobby.

The next section of this work will consider important texts involved in
the research for this book, which will also be beneficial to anyone wishing
to continue their examination of record collecting. While several texts
have been mentioned in this introductory section, the works collected and
discussed in Chapter Two are testimony to the research process and the
various opinions concerning collecting both within and outwith popular
music discourse that have emerged during the recent past, and the
philosophical positions of certain writers who have offered variable
perspectives on popular music record collecting generally and specifically.

---

[65] Which is not her real name.

CHAPTER TWO

(I) METHODS AND APPROACHES,
(II) LITERATURE, AND THE RECORD

> "Does everyday life cheapen art? Isn't Art tougher than that—can't it
> instead, enrich everyday life even when perceived only glancingly [...]
> And where did we get the idea that art never gains from rubbing
> shoulders with life?"
> —Evan Eisenberg (2005),
> *The Recording Angel: Music, Records and Culture*
> *from Aristotle to Zappa*

Popular music as a discipline has come a long way in rectifying the lack of
attention paid to previously overlooked issues and hidden histories in more
recent years, for example Holm-Hudson's (2002) examination of
progressive rock where he notes:

> Today progressive rock is relegated to a footnote in most rock histories and
> considered a symptom of 1970s excess rather than a genre worthy of closer
> examination.[1]

Or Brocken's (2010) look at the hidden popular music of Liverpool in the
1930s–1970s which, for instance, states:

> Despite several recent attempts to re-configure popular music space in the
> city (for example via organisations such as Creative Bias, Novas, River
> Niger Arts, and the Merseyside Music Development Agency) together with
> a little contemporary national and international success for artists such as
> the Zutons, the Coral, and the Dead 60s, most of the *visible* music-making
> in Liverpool has tended to prolong old (perhaps outmoded) popular music
> stereotypes: white males with guitars. The more diverse musical motifs

---

[1] Kevin Holm-Hudson, *Progressive Rock Reconsidered* (London: Routledge,
2002), 2.

that represent Liverpool's vibrant migrant communities continue to be partially hidden and indeterminate, while others have been all but effaced.[2]

There are nevertheless still areas that remain partially disregarded or altogether ignored. It is this author's opinion that record collecting is one such area. There are several aspects of record collecting that deserve closer examination, but for the purpose of this work the areas of focus will be as follows: the processes of record collecting, its network of activities and connoisseurship and theoretical critiques, and historical perspectives on record collecting as well as representations of the collector as an entity. These three areas will cover major issues in relation to record collecting, problematising the subject and suggesting further areas of research.

It has been suggested that while being a cultural practice enjoyed by many over the past decades, record collecting has also been somewhat overlooked in both academia and to a certain extent broader society. The record, on the other hand, has been subject to several examinations by authors such as Chanan,[3] Morton,[4] Millard,[5] and even Adorno,[6] but the fans, collectors and their actual practices have remained largely unexplored and bypassed. Although there are some academic texts available on record collecting, most of the information found is in magazines, journals or fiction. However, even these sources are limited at least in terminology, if not number. There is nothing effectively wrong with this, of course, for one of the most important ways of understanding issues concerning identity and popular culture is to learn as effectively as possible by trying to understand ideas (even complex ones) in our own vernacular. It is always important to access and consider ideas, and the more penetrable they are, the better. This also means that this writer is fully aware of the danger of over-simplifying things or, on the contrary, making things sound too complicated. However, the overall scope of this work will suggest that a wide variety of thoughts and concepts come into play when we consider the theme of identity and popular culture as it

[2] Michael Brocken, *Other Voices: Hidden Histories of Liverpool's Popular Music Scenes 1930s–1970s* (Farnham: Ashgate, 2010), 2–3.
[3] Michael Chanan, *Repeated Takes: A Short History of Recording and its Effects on Music* (London: Verson, 1997).
[4] David L. Morton Jr., *Sound Recording: The Life Story of a Technology* (Baltimore: John Hopkins University Press, 2006).
[5] Andre Millard, *America on Record: A History of Recorded Sound* (Cambridge: University Press, 1995).
[6] Theodor Adorno, "The Curves of the Needle", "The Form of the Phonograph Record" and "Opera and the Long-Playing Record", in *Essays on Music*, ed. Richard Leppert (Berkeley: University of California Press, 1927, 1934, 1969).

surrounds record collecting. It is hoped that, from this perspective, this writer will be able to help deepen critical thought.

Identity and Popular Music

Several years of research into record collecting by this author has already been able to show that, alongside the aforementioned lack of comprehensive texts, there remains a lack of fundamental insights into collectors' lives, their sense of self, and the gradual building of identity as a continual process of perceiving images that somehow might reflect them (or "us", as the case may be),[7] and that furthermore, several very demeaning stereotypes still remain largely unchallenged about the collector, collecting, and their peripheral activities. Such stereotypes are both broad and encompassing, and can be linked to other typecasts to do with collecting and fandom in general.[8] Often, the collector is seen as a rather isolated, almost anti-social, individual who segregates (usually) *him*self from others in favour of spending time with the preferred objects of his desire,[9] which could be something as peculiar—to the non-collector—as old cigarette cards, records or football programmes. As with any stereotype, these images stem from some sort of truth, but one that has become distorted with time. The point that will be made throughout this work is that record collecting is a mirror and, although we are so much more than a mirror can ever reflect, we can never wholly escape from the mirror that is society. Indeed the pleasure we can take from peering into such "mirrors" lies in the obviously flawed ways in which the mirror reflects us. In fact, unlike what the stereotypes suggest, we can frequently take great pleasure in doing this precisely because the reflection is flawed. But one can usually only reach some kind of conclusion if one knows what a true reflection might actually consist of, and this is an interminably difficult judgement to make when one begins to consider what reflects our thoughts, desires and feelings.

Marxist ideologies and Frankfurt School theorists such as Theodor Adorno have consistently contributed to the concept that such reflections are effectively negatively distorted and do not reflect our "true" selves.

---

[7] Research undertaken as part of this text, as well as (unpublished) research relating to the author's MA thesis.

[8] Rob Strachan, "'Where Do I Begin the Story?': Collective Memory, Biographical Authority and the Rock Biography", *Popular Music History* 3, no. 1 (2008): 65–80.

[9] Theodor Adorno, "On the Fetish-Character of Listening and the Regression of Listening", in *Essays on Music*, ed. Richard Leppert (Berkeley: University of California Press, 1938).

There is strong evidence that all forms of popular culture have the ability to do this, and recorded sound, it has been argued,[10] contributes to this distortion. The role that recorded sound has played in shaping our consciousness is undoubtedly very significant. Many people might argue, for example that (say), *Sgt. Pepper's Lonely Hearts Club Band* by The Beatles was simply meant to be a piece of popular music "relief" from our tedious lives. But for many, it left a sense of either triumph or inadequacy. Not only did a great many people feel included by this record (after all "a splendid time is guaranteed for all", according to the liner notes), but a great many also felt *ex*cluded. Despite the irony of the album's title (The Beatles were actually "being" somebody else), many grew up thinking that popular music was "real art" (whatever that might be), rather than the distorted mirror-like reflection it was actually intended to be. Others, perhaps, might have thought they had been listening to a set of standards being set, social values and ideas being prescribed, and unrealistic expectations being set in motion. Issues concerning race, gender, sexuality, normality were all on display within this recording for people to decrypt, and the extent to which they did so, will remain forever worthy of close study and scrutiny.

It is therefore a great mistake to assume, as the Frankfurt School perhaps does, that all the ears listening to that record were merely being "entertained", and that the entertainment was an accurate yet manipulative reflection of their rather sad, uninformed, and manipulated lives. However, as extremely influential twentieth-century theorists, such ideas have informed (and still continue to inform) modern-day scholars as they deal with subjects related to (cultural) mass-production and reception. For instance in *Understanding Rock 'n' Roll: Popular Music in Britain 1955–64*,[11] Dick Bradley discusses how young people are often seen as atomised, alone in a crowd, an "aloneness" that can be drawn back to these enforced prescriptions of identity (by the superstructure), leading to isolation and depression. Collecting could thus be seen as a variant of these lonely people both within, yet apart from, larger groups of people: such an activity would not be viewed as authentic, but rather a deceitful replacement culture. A great many collectors have informed this writer that they often feel that they are not even perceived-of or prescribed-for at all, as if they had almost disappeared from the cultural landscape.

---

[10] Theodor Adorno, "On Popular Music", in *On Record: Rock, Pop and the Written Word*, eds. Simon Frith and Andrew Goodwin (London: Routledge, 1941), 301–314.
[11] Dick Bradley, *Understanding Rock 'n' Roll: Popular Music in Britain 1955-64* (Buckingham: OUP, 1992).

The Frankfurtian model sees the public being picked up and then dropped where the record industry has "decided" to leave us, and our ideas are thus pre-formed and prefabricated. Collecting is therefore *de facto* syndrome-like: never viewed as developing, either intellectually or socially, and coiling in on itself rather like a fossil. It is probably true that record collectors, like many activities within the gamut of possibilities we call "popular music cultures", can be seen as a clique. However, what is also undeniably true is that when one listens to, looks at, or reads a so-called "artistic" creation, a great part of our response is based on whether one does or does not see something of ourselves in it. We often do this by responding to what we can immediately identify with in a work. So perhaps when one talks of this, one should think about certain kinds of identification—what kind of a reflection is it? Part of the Frankfurt School's argument is that once we have identified ourselves in the reflection, we go on to find more equally comforting mirrors that continue to tell us who we are told we are. But, at least as far as record collecting is concerned, some interesting questions arise: how, and with what means, do we measure the accuracy of the reflection? Do we actually see ourselves in the reflection? If so, all or part of it? Might we prefer to see an increasingly distorted mirror? Should we always feel secure about ourselves before seeking pleasure from such distortions? Can they be anti-social—deviant, even?

So, recorded sound's influences throughout the twentieth, and now twenty-first, centuries have been so evocative as to be felt in a wide range of contexts. Via the creative collecting of sound recordings we now have a vital "record" of the twentieth century, something that could never have happened in the same way in previous centuries: we can hear a Hitler rant or a monarch's speech impediment as clearly as an Armstrong scat or a Sex Pistols' sneer. Often, a recording can show us both what we think we are, and what we think we want to be, at one and the same time. We are constantly struggling to define both who and what we are, and we are always finding our identities being challenged by the cultural product, and the ways in which we do or do not identify with what we hear. The world of record collecting is therefore something that provides deep meaning and value to collectors' lives, for it is a terrain over which such struggles are fought out. While there might be what one collector described to this writer as a "personal form of tunnel vision"[12] created by his hobby, this tunnel vision in no way, shape or form goes towards actually defining that collector.

---

[12] Interview with Les, April 2013.

The Record

But what of the record mentioned at the beginning of this chapter? What, indeed, *is* a record or LP, and what might be a recording industry when these days the (sound) artefact is far more difficult to locate? For half a century the artefact—the vinyl record, CD, cassette tape, and so on—was regarded *as* the music industry, such was its power, popularity and the rhetorical space it occupied, but with the emergence of digital technology and downloading practices one is, once again, faced with this important question. Physical recordings (and arguably certain recording technologies) are intrinsically linked to a historical period, the twentieth century, despite being conceived in the nineteenth. As such, an important paradigm shift can be seen to have taken place. Historians regard paradigm shifts as key moments in the past that significantly alter people's views of themselves. A paradigm could be considered a world-view that helps control the way we understand the world in which we live. A paradigm shift therefore occurs when the dominant paradigm is replaced by a new paradigm. As an example, one might suggest that one of the most significant paradigm shifts occurred in science when the paradigm that united all truth into one was replaced by a paradigm that separated the revealed truth of the Bible from scientific truth. Paradigm shifts can be the result of as key individuals such Newton who eventually change people's conceptions of themselves and their identity. One should bear in mind, however, that technology (and in our case recorded sound technology) is also an important paradigm shifter and, without being overly technologically deterministic, can be seen as an absolutely vital paradigm shifter throughout the history of mankind: the aqueduct, the spinning jenny, mechanical reproduction (or factory conveyor belt, if you will), to name but a few, are all vitally significant paradigms.

In musical terms, technology can be seen as an important development in its own right, but also resulting in serious, unforeseen effects. Consider, for instance, the piano as a paradigm shifter within music. Pianos work through hammers striking strings, and replaced plucked, stringed instruments (such as the harpsichord) as a family gathering point. One could argue that the piano is a result of iron and steel technology because this trade provided its frame, without which the instrument would not have been conceivable. The differences between a piano and a harpsichord are also significant: with the piano the player is even able to regulate intensity of sound with *forte* and so on. This then allows composition to change with the composer being able to indicate touch and feel far more precisely. However, in this instance the change in music is not only compositional, if the recording industry and the record is thought of as an artefact. Gradually, people have almost started to believe that records have always been around, and our capability to record *any* effect (consider Mario Ruopollo from *Il Postino* [Michael Radford, 1994] attempting to record the stars). The recording industry, through records, has almost reached an omnipresent status—which is perhaps one of the reasons that so many have become involved in (heated) discussions about the survival of the record industry as we have known it over the past 50–60 years.

It could be argued that, in historical and cultural terms, there are at least two major ways of looking at records and the recording industry. On the one hand, as evident in *The Recording Angel: From Aristotle to Zappa*, Evan Eisenberg[13] joyously celebrates what is almost a mystery—the idea of the phonograph liberating music from the strictures of time and place. Eisenberg denotes the idea that once the phonograph is introduced it allows people the opportunity to hear music within their own time and space rather than within the place that is occupied by the musician and the concert hall. This perspective then takes away some of the control from the musician, the music industry and certain arbiters of taste, and gives it to the listener, or fan instead, through a process of democratisation. Andre Millard[14] similarly explores the way technology is, in the first instance, also cultural. Hence, in the case of music, Edison's cylinder and player was not invented for recorded music, but was initially intended as a dictaphone for office use. Edison considered his device to be non-musical, and thus the transformation into a musical object was not instantaneous. Nevertheless, Edison began the progress by which sound recording became one of the most notable paradigm shifts of the twentieth century, and which eventually allowed music to "invade" people's domestic space.

Thompson[15] presents an interesting perspective of the advent of recorded sound. Her focus is on the marketing of the phonograph from 1877–1925, and looks specifically at "tone tests" that were being performed to promote the phonograph. Thompson notes that by 1917 the consumer was provided with some kind of framework from which they could evaluate the phonograph's fidelity, and this knowledge could be tapped into and used to promote the Edison phonograph—principally

---

[13] Evan Eisenberg, *The Recording Angel: Music, Records And Culture From Aristotle To Zappa* (New Haven: Yale University Press, 2005).

[14] Andre Millard, *America on Record: A History of Recorded Sound* (Cambridge: University Press, 1995).

[15] Emily Thompson, "Machines, Music, and the Quest for Fidelity: Marketing the Edison Phonograph in America 1877–1925", *Musical Quarterly* 79, no. 1 (1995): 131–71.

because Edison did not really know what his re-invented invention was going to sound like. During tone tests audiences would hear a performer sing alongside a phonographic recording of the same piece, and the audience would have to guess if the singer or indeed the phonograph was performing. The tone tests were, as stated, used as marketing and discovery purposes for the Edison company, but their longevity indicates that they were (at least to a certain extent) successful in proving the phonograph's faithfulness to live music. Regarding a tone test featuring Marie Rappold in 1919, the *Pittsburgh Post* commented:

> It did not seem difficult to determine in the dark when the singer sang and when she did not. The writer himself was pretty sure about it until the lights were turned on again and it was discovered that Mme. Rappold was not on the stage at all and that the new Edison alone had been heard.[16]

The tone tests constantly attracted an audience and allowed listeners to engage critically and evaluate their records and phonographs. Their popularity revealed not only a positive attitude towards the phonograph, or at the very least an open-mindedness to this new "wonder of science", it also suggests that the main focus was, in effect, "hyper real", i.e. being more real than a real performance. This of course was the only matrix by which one could at this stage judge the sonic autography of the cylinder: proving that a disc could be just as good as "the real thing", instead of proving the disc in its own right.

The introduction of the *Victrola* by the Victor Company in 1906 in the US, and shortly after in the UK, was another principal development for music in the home. Phonograph players had preceded the *Victrola* by several years, but the *Victrola* was the first phonograph that was designed as furniture. It retailed at an incredibly high price ($200[17]), and yet people invested in it both financially and culturally, with gusto. In the same year, 1906, one sided records issued by the Victor Company's *Red Seal* label (an indication of high quality) cost $7 each—a significant amount of money at the time, which people were still willing to pay. Thus, alongside the development of music in industrial and technological terms, there are links to several cultural processes. Eisenberg informs us that some records

---

[16] Pittsburgh Post (1919) cited in Emily Thompson, "Machines, Music, and the Quest for Fidelity: Marketing the Edison Phonograph in America 1877–1925", *Musical Quarterly* 79, no. 1 (1995): 131–71.

[17] Evan Eisenberg, *The Recording Angel: Music, Records And Culture From Aristotle To Zappa* (New Haven: Yale University Press, 2005).

were even given the same status as leather-bound copies of Charles Dickens's books: elevated, praised and displayed with pride.

Evan Eisenberg[18] lists several areas where the collecting of cultural objects can satisfy one's needs. His tentative list highlights five aspects. Firstly he identifies the need to preserve beauty and pleasure, not trusting them to return to us unless they are captured: "the market-place might teem with poets, but when would there be another Homer?"[19] This, for the reader, indicates an interesting mistrust of the natural world, which is an important reversal because, rather than mistrusting a product of mass production (the record in our case), it is indeed the natural world that appears deceptive—or, perhaps more accurately, "fleeting". The growth and popularity of the phonograph, and all subsequent recording formats, provide evidence that many have adopted this dichotomy of trust.[20] So, according to Eisenberg, whilst making art is important, so (evidently) is its physical preservation.[21] Thus a mistrust of the world for the sake of the artefact is something imperative to consider in this text—a dichotomy that challenges the Frankfurt School model where the artefact is mistrusted and the natural world is not. It is important to remember this because, as will be made evident in Chapter Three, the values that we use to view and judge the artefact are typically derived from Frankfurt School ideology, as are most critiques of popular music, its artefacts and industries, but can be challenged as models merely drawn from specific contexts at specific times in recent human history.

Eisenberg argues that in order to understand the record and its agency, one is required to study it from the perspective that the artefact is indeed trustworthy. Still dealing with the theme of beauty, Eisenberg continues his list by suggesting there is a need within society to comprehend beauty, and "certainly owning a book or record permits one to study the work

---

[18] *ibid.*

[19] *ibid.*, 14.

[20] Bootleg recordings and (official) live DVDs and records (both on LP and CD) are perhaps particularly strong evidence of this—why else would one purchase or record a live performance one attended, anyway?

[21] Interestingly, this notion appears to be with us from an early age as I recently came to discover. A friend of mine was babysitting her four year-old niece and they were using a "magic pen" that when wet can be used to draw on a special board with. When the "ink" from the pen dries, the drawing fades away. My friend had momentarily left the room and on her return found her niece crying because her "Mickey was gone"—her drawing had faded away—and she could only be consoled by the promise that they could draw a new Mickey on paper, where it would be preserved.

repeatedly and *at one's convenience*".[22] He warns, however, that ownership can be mistaken for mastery, but one might argue that this is exactly the case with recorded sound—ownership *can* lead to mastery. Numerous musicians have, after all, learnt their skill from listening to records and trying to recreate what they hear with their instruments. In fact, the very nature of popular music and the lack of notation within the field would perhaps suggest that it is through listening to records that all kinds of musical possibilities, sounds and compositions are passed on.

Thirdly, Eisenberg suggests that, as perhaps David Riesman[23] also showed in the 1950s with jazz consumers, there are not only heroes of production but also heroes of consumption. What is meant by this is that there are people who spend money on what might be described as a "heroic" scale, or with "heroic" discrimination. In some instances, the overcoming of an obstacle in pursuit of a prized piece of consumption can be truly heroic, in fact so much so that the prize itself can end up being secondary. In terms of record collecting the "hunt" for elusive records is often talked of and tales of rare finds (often at bargain prices, as the myth alludes) can be found in both the *Record Collector* (UK) and *Goldmine* (USA) magazines, both of which are dedicated record-collecting magazines. Roy Shuker writes in great depth of this hunt, but whilst being important, maybe even crucial, to *some* record collectors, Shuker mistakenly attributes the hunt as the ultimate charm of record collecting:

> Many collectors appear to value the process of gathering music more than the actual possession of it, with an element of compulsion underpinning the search. [...] This aspect is most evident in the practice of deliberately moving from the creation of one collection to another; the appeal lies in the chase rather than the ownership of the collection itself.[24]

In this short quote, it is evident that Shuker has misunderstood some crucial aspects that make record collecting an important activity to the practitioners and how it can become intrinsically intertwined with the collector's identity. First of all, it is unclear to this writer *why* this so-called hunt, or desire to find elusive records, is necessarily underpinned by

---

[22] Evan Eisenberg, *The Recording Angel: Music, Records And Culture From Aristotle To Zappa* (New Haven: Yale University Press, 2005), 14–15, my own emphasis.

[23] David Riesman, "Listening to Popular Music", in *On Record: Rock, Pop and the Written Word*, eds. Simon Frith and Andrew Goodwin (London: Routledge, 1950), 5–13.

[24] Roy Shuker, *Wax Trash and Vinyl Treasures: Record Collecting as a Social Practice* (Farnham: Ashgate, 2010), 110.

compulsion, as is also suggested by Shuker. This has been a tendency continually when dealing with the subject of record collecting—using terminology that implies pathology—and it is also evident in the work of other writers: "the obsession with hearing and owning *all* available performances by a favorite [*sic*] artist borders on the pathological".[25] What is more, it is apparent in the above quote by Shuker that he has failed to accredit *ownership* with any great value, and as a result one could argue he fundamentally fails to understand why the hunt is so important to record collectors. For if ownership is worthless to the record collector, why would he or she go to such an extent to acquire the record? The thrill of the hunt is undoubtedly of vital importance, but needs to be considered as representing only one part of a vast myriad of reasons why people collect anything. When discussing statements concerning need, i.e. what we "need" in our lives such as food and shelter but also a watch when enquiring about the time or particular cultures' need to "save face", Paul W. Taylor[26] is able to establish that people often feel that they need more than just the basic supplies of food, shelter and clothing not to survive— but to "live". For some, records and collecting them is a key to life. One record collector fondly informed this writer that some of his favourite records were the ones he had used to roll marijuana cigarettes or "spliffs" on in his youth (he cited the Moody Blues' *In Search of the Lost Chord*, the *Island Bumpers* sampler, and Jethro Tull's *Stand Up* as three such examples) perhaps because those records brought with them a very particular kind of memory and mythology. So, for Eisenberg, throughout the twentieth century the record-collecting pursuit can be seen as a key aspect that turns, for example, jazz and blues lovers into true heroes of their genres. One need only consider the work of Bob Hite, the lead singer of Canned Heat, and his almost irrational pursuit of early blues 78s, which in retrospect can be seen as a massively heroic act for his love of blues, despite his own failing health and the fact that he would never complete his collection, something Shuker also highlights to be of great significance when he states that:

> The collecting process is both open and closed. The desire to complete a collection is in tension with the fear of doing so, since once this has been achieved that purpose of the enterprise is gone. [...] Completism [...]

---

[25] Russel W. Belk *et al.*, "Collecting in a Consumer Culture", in *Highways and Buyways: Naturalistic Research from the Consumer Behaviour Odyssey*, ed. Russel W. Belk (Association for Consumer Research: 1991), 191, emphasis in the original.

[26] Paul W. Taylor, "'Need' Statements", *Analysis* 19, no. 5 (1959): 106–111.

continues to be identified as a characteristic of record collectors (being mentioned by a quarter of my respondents). It can be defined as the need to own all of a particular category, usually one artist's output. This can be regardless of musical quality or artistic merit [...] Such an approach admits the possibility of closure, but this can be indefinitely postponed by a constant extension of the boundaries of the collection. This can occur, for example, by collecting the ongoing output of a living artist, in all its formats and national pressings [...] Or closure can be avoided by simply choosing a goal that is essentially unattainable, given the scope of the subject and the fierce competition for rarer items.[27]

Herein also lies a paradox of vast proportions, also not fully considered by Frankfurt School rhetoric, where the true hero of consumption is actually concomitantly a rebel *of* consumption because by taking the artefact to an extreme, he or she can effectively repudiate it. Both in the case of our dope-smoking collector of 1970s underground music, and Bob Hite's archival activities, Eisenberg correctly proposes: "The prodigal son is not just a show-off".[28] Lyotard has even argued that it is becoming increasingly difficult to subscribe to any great meta-narratives that once organised our lives.[29] What he has in his sights are totalising meta-narratives which in their abstraction deny the specificity of the above local, parochial, and profoundly personal histories that nevertheless represent real experience. These targets would include the narrative of emancipation proposed by Karl Marx and his devotees.

Another theoretical position proposed by Eisenberg, one which is vital to this study, is the need to belong. One might also describe this as an element of nostalgia. This nostalgia may be for a time one has lived in or wishes one had lived in, allowing (any) cultural object of that time to be used as a tonic. Each object, however, "naturally" connects the owner to two important personal eras, the one in which the object was created and the one in which it was acquired. Records fit perfectly into this category and, crucially, allow people to talk about *both* eras from their own particular perspective. Such eras therefore become *their* eras, not simply a generalised, mediated epoch, but something deeply personal. Hence the record collector may tell someone about 1967 and why *Sgt. Pepper's Lonely Hearts Club Band* was such an important release, but they can then also move on to tell about the way in which that particular copy ended up

---

[27] Roy Shuker, *Wax Trash and Vinyl Treasures: Record Collecting as a Social Practice* (Farnham: Ashgate, 2010), 47.

[28] Evan Eisenberg, *The Recording Angel: Music, Records And Culture From Aristotle To Zappa* (New Haven: Yale University Press, 2005), 15.

[29] See J-F Lyotard, *The Postmodern Condition* (Paris: Minuit, 1979), xxiv.

in their collection—perhaps they bought it straight away and kept it ever since, or perhaps, as one collector informed this writer, "[...]bought it, sold it, bought it again, sold it and then received it as a gift",[30] with each part sparking a different, yet connected, memory. As such, the artefact allows us communicate with whoever may want to listen, taking us further away from the stereotype of the atomised loner. These are objects that are part of real life for the collector, not necessarily a fetishism concerning a preferred past in opposition to a putative present.

Finally, Eisenberg considers the need to impress. But the need to impress in this instance is not a need to impress through spending power, but rather a need to impress through cultural capital. A sincere love of culture, he states, can be satisfied by owning records as much as listening to them. Record owners are, in fact, often criticised for (supposedly) not listening to records, but simply "stockpiling" them: "for Attali, the way that music is objectified in recordings *deprives* music of its use-value. *Musical recordings become objects to collect and stockpile, not to hear*".[31] But if there is a need to impress oneself rather than merely an "other", how can we criticise someone for owning an artefact? If this were the case, one might criticise someone for not using a particular knife without considering that it came as part of a knife-set that was desirable. That specific knife may not have any use-value to the owner (as other knives in the same set may or may not), but the set might make the owner feel as if they were a true gourmet—and who is someone else to claim that he or she is not in their own kitchen? With regard to vinyl, a recent trend has been emerging in the US[32] that involves people purchasing vinyl as if by the yard and decorating their walls with the spines aligned (facing outward). Interpreted through a Frankfurt School model this may be viewed as shallow or false consciousness, as there may not even be a record player in the house. However, it is not a case of simply showing off, but instead there are links to what Eisenberg describes as the "sweet weight of culture",[33] whereby the physicality of the records and their presence allows the owner to think about culture, cultural artefact(s) and one's place among them and upon the cultural investments made in these products. Perhaps simply being surrounded by these objects allows us somehow to

---

[30] Anonymous collector to this writer, Muse Music, Hebden Bridge, 2013.

[31] Philip Auslander, "Looking at Records", *The Drama Review* 45, no. 1 (2001): 79, my own emphasis.

[32] The US TV programme *Suits* gives us an interesting example of such themed room or office decoration.

[33] Evan Eisenberg, *The Recording Angel: Music, Records And Culture From Aristotle To Zappa* (New Haven: Yale University Press, 2005), 16.

"feel" the culture around us, and if it improves our life experience why does it necessarily have to be shallow?[34]

It has already been suggested that while certain records may have a high financial value, this is often not the motivation behind record collecting. In fact, for many years existing side-by-side with record collecting as an economic investment, is the one in which collectors deliberately collect the artefacts that appear to be of little-or-no value within the record-collecting marketplace. Collecting items such as Hallmark's *Top Of The Pops* albums, Cannon and Big Six EPs from Woolworths of the 1960s, or Reader's Digest boxed sets (the latter of which even UK charity shops now reject) is an important discourse concerning how the record can be considered as "valuable detritus", even within the "world" of record collecting—representing perhaps more accurately a kind of anti-canonic "world that has been lost". Such collecting even became, briefly, part of a kind of scene in the 1990s ("loungecore"[35]) and can be connected with the post-modern theoretical position of "bricolage"[36]—perhaps best defined as the construction (as of a sculpture or a structure of ideas) achieved by using whatever comes to hand, and in opposition to the meta-categorisations of value and authenticities presented to us as a "given" by the meta-narratives within society.

From this perspective it is worth noting at this early stage that popular music studies generally, and record collecting more specifically, might be studied from what is described as a post-modern perspective. Such reconsideration of culture in terms of value came to the perhaps fullest development in the 1980s, especially via the works of Fredric Jameson, Jean-François Lyotard, Jean Baudrillard, and Charles Jencks among many others.[37] Such discourses acknowledge a "presentist" orientation in which twentieth-century ideas concerning modernism, and that movement's

---

[34] In this instance the author has not even taken album art into account, which is another multi-faceted field that can add layers of meaning to the LP.

[35] Michael Brocken, *Bacharach, Maestro!: The Life of a Pop Genius* (New Malden: Chrome Dreams, 2003).

[36] Thomas Docherty, "Postmodernism: An Introduction", in *Postmodernism: A Reader*, ed. Thomas Docherty (London: Harvester Wheatsheaf, 1993), 1–32.

[37] See Frederic Jameson, *Postmodernism, or, the Cultural Logic of Late Capitalism* (Durham: Duke University Press, 1991); Jean-François Lyotard, *The Postmodern Condition: A Report on Knowledge* (Minneapolis: University of Minnesota, 1984); Jean Baudrillard, *The Consumer Society: Myths and Structures* (Thousand Oakes: Sage Publications, 1998); Charles Jencks, *Critical Modernism—Where is Post-Modernism Going?* (Hoboken: John Wiley & Sons, 2007).

relationship to universal harmony, come to be challenged, and historical periodisation comes to be seen as ideological rather than real. Thomas Docherty *et al.*[38] explore such arguments concerning one of the most important intellectual debates of the present day. This work gathers in one volume a comprehensive selection of articles, essays and statements by leading figures both for and against post-modernism, and the material brought together offers a fascinating way into discovering how the era of post-modernity came upon us, almost by accident, and out of the principal twentieth-century ideology of modernism.

The volume contains no articles on record collecting; however, the very approach that Docherty *et al.* take in writing about divergent artistic terrains is of great significance to the popular music scholar who wishes to consider the diversity, functionality, aesthetic quality and insecure autonomy of popular-music collecting. In other words, such post-modern positions can help us consider how any quality of life depends upon the intensity of cultural exchanges and the value of human bonds. Friendships built upon collecting have not yet been discussed to any great extent. However, to suggest that such human relationships can be threatened by the culture industries and leisure moguls is brought under strain by the post-modern concepts that also form areas of authentic communication via cultural production, and gives rise to the possibility that cultural and mutual aid, and friendship, is often formed out of self-education aimed at countering the dominant ideas and culture of society. Such challenges to formalised narratives, emerging from within a post-modern discourse, are of great significance to this book, for while the record collector is often considered to be a pariah, self-obsessed and self-absorbed, such pejorative terms often disguise self-organisation and mutual values, and are an agent against cultural hegemony. Throughout Docherty's text such issues concerning the condition of mankind living within different ontological ideas are explored.

It would have to be said that record-collecting scholarship is not something within the realms of popular music studies that contains a great number of individual texts. Within popular music studies generally, however, any academic who is drawn to popular music will inevitably have to face the prospect of writing about record collecting. Such is the case, for example, with the work of Roy Shuker, who initially created two undergraduate-level textbooks as a way into studying popular music as a discipline removed from the strictures of formal musicology. The first,

---

[38] Thomas Docherty, "Postmodernism: An Introduction", in *Postmodernism: A Reader*, ed. Thomas Docherty (London: Harvester Wheatsheaf, 1993), 1–32.

Understanding Popular Music,[39] presents a relatively comprehensive discussion concerning popular music, but is rather limited by its top-down approach which throughout suggests that most meanings derived from mass production are consumed first, and re-articulated second. Such people, according to Shuker, are effectively changed by their contact with, and experiences of, popular music consumption. The difficulties surrounding a position such as this (at least as far as record collecting is concerned), is the notion of personality change. While certain aspects are changed via such contact, the historical condition of the collector puts that collector into a certain position in the first place. So it might be argued that the person after the event is, in fact, fundamentally the same as the person before: certain aspects of a collector's personality might have lain dormant, but find the contact with the product to be both a catalyst and a matrix. Shuker's second work is a thesaurus for the undergraduate to consider definitions and, as such, records and record collecting are considered, but not overly-discussed.[40] On the whole, this is also a most helpful text, although definitions are difficult to consider in an environment which is forever kinetic and changing. As a consequence, this text now also appears radically out of date. However, Shuker[41] has also more recently written a text dealing specifically with the activity of record collecting, *Wax Trash and Vinyl Treasures* (2010). This latter Shuker text will be discussed at some length later in the book, though it is safe to say at this stage that he now appears to avoid defining principles and rather considers any popular music activity as a co-creative act and, albeit rather reluctantly perhaps, comes to appreciate that it is not the individual who has changed, but the historical situation of that individual. This, then, demands the appearance of certain catalytic moments that become personal paradigms.

Studying Popular Music by Richard Middleton,[42] one of the seminal texts which discusses popular music, considers the recording industry and the characteristics of recording, but does not essentially consider collecting as a primary link into value and meaning. However, while identity remains at the heart of his excellent and forward-thinking study, Middleton perhaps unwittingly suggests that a primary way into understanding popular music is to consider an interdisciplinary approach which includes ethnography and semiology—both important disciplines in order to understand

---

[39] Roy Shuker, *Understanding Popular Music* (London: Routledge, 1994).
[40] Roy Shuker, *Popular Music: The Key Concepts* (London: Routledge, 2002).
[41] Roy Shuker, *Wax Trash and Vinyl Treasures: Record Collecting as a Social Practice* (Farnham: Ashgate, 2010).
[42] Richard Middleton, *Studying Popular Music* (Buckingham: OUP, 1990).

receivers. Middleton therefore considers the use-value of the popular music artefact as an essential feature of understanding popular music cultures.

Via their contributing writers, Bruce Horner and Thomas Swiss[43] also consider issues to do with identities, youth culture and what something means to be popular, but do not dwell directly upon the activity of record collecting. Frith, Straw and Street[44] do, in fact, discuss issues to do with interpretation and the popular music industry, but rarely place their case studies into a record-collecting framework. Brian Longhurst[45] also considers the social production of music and regards the record as a text, and has a great deal to say on fans and their consumption of records. However, with the possible exception of *Motown*, at no time does he cite a specific record label or record collector as being central to his focus concerning popular music and society. Thus we need to look at more specific popular music texts dealing with what it means to be a record collector and what it means to people and their lives.

From a more recent perspective, one of the texts most directly concerned with record collecting comes from not only Roy Shuker, but also a fellow Ashgate stablemate, Michael Brocken.[46] In his work, *Other Voices*, Brocken is at pains to discuss the hidden popular music histories of Liverpool between the 1930s and 1970s. In each of his chapters, which deal with specific genres of musical activity in Liverpool during this period, Brocken makes sure that recorded music and the purchasing and collecting of recorded music are strongly featured. At one stage, Brocken even talks about how record shops in Liverpool are run not only for profit-and-loss accounting, but also with what he describes as "significant creative communities"[47] in mind. He suggests that record shops in Liverpool between these decades were visible, and socially, culturally, musically and economically indicative of what he describes as a culture of collecting. Record stores such as The Musical Box, Edwards', NEMS, etc. helped to support a genuine set of taste cultures, and eradicate distinction between high and low art. He goes even further by suggesting that a history of record retailing in Liverpool, from 1900 onwards, counts the

---

[43] Bruce Horner and Thom Swiss, eds., *Key Terms in Popular Music and Culture* (Hoboken: Blackwell, 1999).

[44] Simon Frith, Will Straw and John Street, *The Cambridge Companion to Pop and Rock* (Cambridge: University Press, 2001).

[45] Brian Longhurst, *Popular Music and Society* (Oxford: Polity, 2007).

[46] Michael Brocken, *Other Voices: Hidden Histories of Liverpool's Popular Music Scenes 1930s–1970s* (Farnham: Ashgate, 2010).

[47] *ibid.*, 204.

listener in, and perhaps even contributes to Liverpool being described by many as a "music city".

Brocken also discusses local labels in Liverpool, for example how one label (*Stag Records*) actively contributed to earning performance-based point-of-sale money for artists, and how through the passage of time has in itself become collectible. This collectability, it seems, is only in small part based on selective rock genres, rather than popular music, for only two groups on *Stag* could be said to have been rock bands as such. Instead, Brocken suggests that its collectability as a label is via its representation of an authentic pop music activity surrounding Liverpool during the 1970s— a partially hidden history which becomes attractive to collectors who, while at first look for the only two rock bands on *Stag Records* (Supercharge and Pinnacle, respectively), then discover the joy of collecting recordings by the likes of Tom O'Connor and the Jacksons (but do not expect to pay too much money for the privilege). Another of the charms of *Stag* for collectors is the fact that the label created an interesting catalogue system that almost requires code-breaking.[48]

Thus we can see that although there are several academic popular music texts that deal with identities and audiences, very few academic works attempt to understand the nature of the collector in any detail. Our enquiry concerning the historiography regarding the collector is therefore required to broaden its scope. This involves a very close reading of one particular British monthly magazine, *Record Collector,* which has been constantly present for the UK record collector since the late 1970s. *Record Collector* functions as a substantial source of information with catalogues, reports on collectable labels and acts, etc., as well as advertisements for record fairs, an important hunting ground for the avid collector. Initially started as re-issues of the 1960s *The Beatles Book* magazine by publisher/copyright owner "Johnny Dean" (aka Sean O'Mahony) in 1976 (*The Beatles Book* originally began publication in 1963), collectors' growing interest in the advertising section inspired Dean to re-brand the magazine into a dedicated collector's publication with *The Beatles Book* becoming a supplement stapled inside the new magazine. This focus on records rapidly intensified over subsequent issues, changing its intended audience from collectors of "pop memorabilia, 'fanphalia', posters, nostalgia, photos, rare records, etc." to "rare records, posters, pop memorabilia etc."[49] within the space of a few issues in 1979. The

---

[48] *Stag* employed two catalogue systems: one—with an SG prefix—was funded by the label itself; the other—HP—required artists to raise pressing and recording costs themselves—HP standing for "hire purchase".

[49] According to the tagline on the cover of the magazine.

magazine nonetheless consistently maintains it is directed towards the "serious collectors".

A later section in this work will more fully consider *Record Collector* as an arbiter of taste and community. But it is sufficient to say at this point, however, that the main strength of *Record Collector* (and its US counterpart *Goldmine*) probably lies in its authoritative position, its use of authentic language and (importantly) its historical accuracy, rather than opinion-led editorial policies that one might usually find in most popular music magazines and "inkies".[50] For instance, throughout the history of this magazine, writers such as Andy Davis, Spencer Leigh, Peter Doggett, Mark Lewisohn, Mark Paytress, *et al.* have endeavoured to emphasise that record collecting cannot be separated from social context. In fact, so accurate were the writers working for it that *Record Collector* itself became a proving ground where each of these writers learnt their trade and subsequently went on to write seminal texts in the field of pop music.[51] Throughout the pages of *Record Collector*, all writers claim that popular music demands both political and artistic relevance, and that popular music and its collecting activities were all vital historical frames of reference. The arrival of *Record Collector* was (and remains) contextually and symbolically crucial, and its writers developed a growing historical accuracy. Each writer was able to hone his skills in order to explain how collecting certain types of music could be authentic historical representations in themselves.

Although the magazine for many years developed a rock, soul and folk stance, which was problematic via its selectivity, it did also come to discuss and represent, in the mid-1990s, those collectors of exotica and loungecore music who had stepped outside of the rock and folk canon. For Doggett, erstwhile long-standing editor of *Record Collector*, mass production had not rendered popular music unprofitable, and the record

---

[50] The expression "inkies" in relation to the British music press relates to newspapers such as the *NME* (*New Musical Express*), *Disc* (later *Disc* and *Music Echo*), *Melody Maker* and (later) *Sounds*. These weekly newspapers were initially thinly disguised trade papers, but they evolved into important mouthpieces for music fans during times of rapid change. Their "inkie" tag came from that fact that they were produced exactly like a weekly newspaper (i.e. "hot off the presses"), and were printed on low quality newsprint, thus making one's hands "inky" as the papers were read. These days, the only survivor is *NME*.

[51] Peter Doggett, *Are you Ready for the Country: Elvis, Dylan, Parsons and the Roots of Country Rock* (New York: Penguin Books, 2001); Mark Lewisohn, *The Beatles, 25 Years in the Life: A Chronology 1962-1987* (London: Sidgwick & Jackson, 1987); Spencer Leigh, *The Cavern: The Most Famous Club in the World* (London: S.A.F. Publishing, 2008).

and its collectability gave us hard evidence of this fact. Doggett constantly asked the reader to look beyond factors of production in order to explain the popularity and collectability of a mass-produced product.

Such a stance was further discussed by the American writers Vale and Juno,[52] who in 1994 began writing about the collectability of what they describe as "incredibly strange music". Their two volumes, which to this very day stand as vital pieces of source material concerning the complexities of collecting vinyl, spotlight out-of-print recordings which do not fit into the hitherto critically scrutinised genres of rock, jazz and folk. The authors highlighted some of the strangest recordings created in America, for example cash-in records, sexually-orientated records, what might be described as "bad taste records", and moog and synthesiser recordings, as well as sound-effect albums. Furthermore, they suggested that while these recordings were not "worth anything" to rock record "completists", they still stood as testimonies of incredibly significant eras of recorded sound. Such volumes question by their very presence the pessimistic universe extolled by the likes of Benjamin and Adorno, as well as the work of Jacques Attali,[53] who discusses how we physically configure ourselves to our collections of recordings and become effectively subordinate to them.

Vale and Juno take the act of purchasing, keeping and collecting records into far more complex realms of activity than suggested by the mid-century Marxist and post-structuralist critics. They do so by suggesting that a perhaps complex series of resonances exist in relationship to the past. While the Marxist expression of homology (i.e. a structural resonance between producer and receiver) had already been re-created by Richard Middleton as a positive, rather than simply a state of false consciousness, Vale and Juno suggest that without memories and associations of all sorts, life is diminished in meaning. If we think that a record merely represents "what it is"—i.e. a denotation—we will never really come to understand how conventions can be displaced and/or tradition re-interpreted. One might suggest that record collecting therefore has elements of the radical, or even post-modern, if the act of "returning" to something can allow inventive reconfigurations of meaning which transcend replication. Such is the act, one might argue, of record collecting.

---

[52] V. Vale and Juno, Andrea, *Incredibly Strange Music* (San Francisco: Re/Search Publications, 1994).
[53] Jaques Attali, *Noise: The Political Economy of Music* (Minneapolis: University of Minnesota Press, 1977).

Interestingly, most of the few detailed examples of existing record-collecting literature explored here tend to focus on creative, perhaps even artistic, aspects of the act of record collecting, rather than the collecting aspects, especially from the collector's point of view. Pettit,[54] for instance, in her work concerning second-hand records (an advancement to some extent of the Vale and Juno argument), even suggests that travelling to and from important, strategic second-hand shops can be considered to be works of art in their own right, and so her journey across the US from shop to shop was transformative: such detritus of the music industry can, for Pettit, present notions of the sublime. Analysis of collecting, then, within this reflection of art (and of consumer practices actually being art) expands into an aesthetic which is surely an important and acceptable way of analysing how the receiver and collector is affected, and how feelings and meanings are received and experienced through the products of mass production.

Pettit's main focus is on second-hand trading, which may be what first springs to mind when considering the trading of LPs, but as her intentions are to explore the world of record *shops*, she also deals with shops selling new products. From the style of writing, to the layout of the book and choice of photographs and tinted pages, and even the lack of Pettit's name on the spine or cover, all contribute to generating an art sensibility. Criticizing our modern-day mobile phone habits (presumably a metaphor for other modern-day habits as well) and citing America's "wealth of vinyl, and vast musical heritage",[55] Pettit and her partner set out on a three-month film project to explore what they described as *independent* music by and through these record stores. Many of the people she encountered discussed how record shops appear to have an almost magical quality. One might argue that this allows us to consider just how production could be understood as a part of a liberating process. Mechanical production might not be art in and of itself (although this might also be arguable), but via its presence an artefact can present new opportunities and thus be part of a liberating praxis of life. One might take this a stage further and suggest that within such a reality, producer and receiver no longer exist. All that remains is the individual who uses recorded sound as an instrument for living one's own life as best as one can. For instance, in response to a question which asked, what was his favourite record shop, renowned popular music journalist Everett True noted:

---

[54] Emma Pettit, *Old Rare New: The Independent Record Shop* (London: Black Dog Publishing, 2008).
[55] *ibid.*, 8.

There's only one (in London)—Rough Trade in Talbot Road. *It's where my dreams gestated*, and where I busked outside (as part of The Legend! And His Swinging Soul Sisters): it was a ritual, a *reason to survive*, that two-hour trip across London through the 1980s.[56]

Some might well argue that this praise is in actual fact reifying the record shops, awarding them the key to the "Pearly Gates" of popular music authenticity. However, while it may be true that record shops can offer a wealth of musical knowledge, we as listeners have to complete the circle; without guidance it can be difficult to find what you are in search of, but without the complementaries of people expressing continuity and discontinuity, diachrony and synchrony, the shop has little meaning or energy (see this writer's later observations regarding the film, *High Fidelity*):

> They're [the staff/shop owners] the real headmasters of the vinyl trade, it's much more fun to shop around a store with the owner giving you tips about certain quality of sound in opposing albums... and you can't get that online.[57]

The staff can thus work as musical teachers or mentors, but they can also function as gatekeepers or cultural intermediaries. In a famous scene from *High Fidelity* a member of staff refuses to sell a customer the album he wants because it is simply not good enough to sell, an attitude we can also detect in Pettit's journey.

Perhaps it is Pettit's approach—one of understanding how networks of vernacular activity come to take shape and can be transformed into artistic events—that can ultimately assist us in understanding how the didacticism of Adorno and Benjamin has been supplanted by the co-creativity of Juno, Vale, and Pettit herself. These two texts clearly engage with the concept that pleasure is available and multifarious. Pleasure is not simply made up of happiness, and is certainly not part of a collective consciousness imposed from above "for the good of all". Instead, it is argued by such writers that pleasure can be accessed via a negation of the autonomy of art. Pleasure can be achieved through the praxis of life: the production and relatively autonomous individual reception of meaning. If art is not unified with the praxis of life, for these writers, it cannot be "art". For them,

---

[56] Everett True cited in Emma Pettit, *Old Rare New: The Independent Record Shop* (London: Black Dog Publishing, 2008), 58, my own emphasis.
[57] Chan Marshall cited in Emma Pettit, *Old Rare New: The Independent Record Shop* (London: Black Dog Publishing, 2008), 30.

commodity aesthetics effectively prove that consumer behaviour is authentic, not something to do with subjection or sublimation, and can therefore be multifarious: collectors frequently select and de-select, they "read against the grain" of any meaning put forward to them rather than absorb, lint-like, all propositions of mass production.

While Pettit was travelling around the US, Graham Jones[58] was conducting a similar journey across the UK, but for different reasons, looking for the remains of independent record shop networks. Pettit was interested in second-hand editions; however Jones was concerned with the drop in retailing of new products. In one way or another he had worked in the music industry for most of his adult life. Writing his account of the fate of the independent record stores in the UK from a distributor's standpoint, Jones examines why many of these businesses have collapsed, and what others have done to survive. A recurring strategy that Jones discovers is diversification into films, musical instruments, clothing and other merchandise, but that high rents had forced some shops to move elsewhere (or close). Most record shop owners featured in the book have anecdotal stories about seemingly peculiar customers, and even though some of these are undeniably rather amusing, the tone in which some customers are spoken about typifies one of the main issues needed tackling regarding perceptions of record collectors—and perhaps led also to the demise of the aforesaid shops!

The language used by Jones ultimately juxtaposes the independent music industry professional as the musical authority, and the customer as someone who needs to be educated. Yet we should not be all too critical, since record shops—and consequently Jones's own line of work as a music distributor—depend on customers, a fact which Jones acknowledges. *Last Shop Standing: Whatever Happened to Record Shops?*[59] is in essence a critique of how major retailers and supermarkets are taking over the music trade from independent retailers, and Jones urges us to acknowledge and protect independent shops as cultural as well as economic enterprises. Record shops, he suggests, can be valuable establishments, not only for their "novelty" value, but because they provide a place of camaraderie, have functioned as "learning institutions" for musicians and fans alike through the years (as we saw in Pettit[60]), and provide a range that simply is not available in supermarkets. ASDA may sometimes be cheaper, but any

---

[58] Graham Jones, *Last Shop Standing: Whatever Happened to Record Shops?* (London: Proper Music Publishing, 2009).
[59] *ibid.*
[60] Emma Pettit, *Old Rare New: The Independent Record Shop* (London: Black Dog Publishing, 2008).

attempt to get a recommendation from the staff if one liked a CD purchased there is challenging: from a collector's point of view, this writer has still to see (August 2015) ASDA stocking vinyl records.

Unfortunately Jones's[61] account does not take into consideration newer phenomena such as continued technological developments, which have sought to find replacements for the guidance provided by record shops and their staff and other patrons. The Internet website Amazon, for instance, recommends items in which one might be interested, based on previous purchases and searches that others with similar browsing habits on the site have bought and/or viewed. Such devices are called "analytic tools", and are now vital to Internet shopping even though the music industry has been very slow to pick up on such tools. It is clear that websites such as Amazon have had a fundamental impact on people's record-buying habits as high street record shops fail to stay afloat. Most recently, for example, HMV, the UK's last surviving entertainment (originally music) retailing chain, went into administration on the 15th January 2013.[62]

So, while Jones looks directly at the decline of record retailing from within both an industry and collectors' matrix, a few academics have picked out other aspects of record collecting for examination. Lee Marshall, for instance, concentrates on the trading of bootleg recordings,[63] and Will Straw is often mentioned by other (popular music) academics when discussing record collecting as a subject. Articles such as Straw's *Sizing up Record Collections: Gender and Connoisseurship in Rock Music Culture*[64] sound promising indeed, but on closer inspection leave much to be desired. Straw's now somewhat dated article focuses more on masculinity through record collecting rather than record collecting *per se*, and the possible masculinities (and femininities) it creates. Throughout large portions of the text it is easy to forget that record collecting is even in the title of the piece, with its heavy focus on masculine identities. Whilst initially addressing the apparent lack of female record collectors and/or attention given to them, this line of enquiry is all of a sudden dropped, and not sufficiently resolved. What in the end we take away is that men often use record collections around which they socialize, and that

---

[61] Graham Jones, *Last Shop Standing: Whatever Happened to Record Shops?* (London: Proper Music Publishing, 2009).

[62] hmv.com, accessed January 2013.

[63] Lee Marshall, "For and against the Record Industry: An Introduction to Bootleg Collectors and Tape Traders", *Popular Music* 22, no. 1 (2003): 57–72.

[64] Will Straw, "Sizing up Record Collections: Gender and Connoisseurship in Rock Music Culture", in *Sexing the Groove: Popular Music and Gender*, ed. Sheila Whiteley (London: Routledge, 1997), 3–16.

this focus on record collections in male musicians' social lives grants their musical careers greater longevity. Whereas Straw never claims it outright, the article certainly implies that female musicians lack depth, shortening their careers because they do not collect records—and if they do, they do not give them as central a role in their social lives as do men. The article invites the question, is record collecting as heavily-gendered a pursuit as is suggested by Straw?

Philip Auslander,[65] however, provides a different examination of record collecting in his essay "Looking at Records". Examining uses of LPs via the works of situationist Guy Debord and post-structuralist Jacques Attali, he firmly establishes that music is only one part of a record. He cites the aforementioned Evan Eisenberg's[66] examples of Clarence, who collects every record with the word "Clarence" on it, and a deaf record collector with an impressive collection. Using himself as a point of reference in an auto-ethnographic way, Auslander also establishes that gazing at the record (*not* the cover) and gaining pleasure from it is literally "reading against the grain" of the LP, a post-modern concept, to be sure:

> The moments at which I am looking at the record instead of listening to it are not just moments at which I am under the contemplative spell of the commodity; they are moments at which I am consuming that commodity in a way that goes against the grain.[67]

Auslander thus *suggests* an interesting aspect of consuming LPs that could benefit from further consideration. All in all, he touches upon a number of ways in which collectors, and indeed anyone buying records— music even—can consume their purchase without therefore necessarily becoming a victim of commodification or regressed listening.[68]

The few texts that actually deal more or less directly with record collecting also include works of fiction (e.g. Nick Hornby's novel *High Fidelity*, and the 2000 film of the same title, and magazines (such as *Record Collector* in the UK and *Goldmine* in the US). Such works offer

---

[65] Philip Auslander, "Looking at Records", *The Drama Review* 45, no. 1 (2001): 77–83.

[66] Evan Eisenberg, *The Recording Angel: Music, Records And Culture From Aristotle To Zappa* (New Haven: Yale University Press, 2005).

[67] Philip Auslander, "Looking at Records", *The Drama Review* 45, no. 1 (2001): 80.

[68] See Theodor Adorno, "On the Fetish-Character in Music and the regression of Listening", in *Essays on Music*, ed. Richard Leppert (Berkeley: University of California Press, 1938).

important insights into the activity of record collecting, but can at times either stereotype the collector (see the discussion on *High Fidelity*, below) or concentrate more on the artefact than the collector (*Record Collector* offers vast information about records' valuations and such, but seldom mentions the collector's activities). In fact, despite its ubiquitousness since arguably the beginning of the recording industry, the human aspect of record collecting is seldom discussed at length. Effectively, ever since the emergence of popular music studies during the latter half of the twentieth century, a near void exists concerning academic writing dealing with the processes involved in record collecting.

While many years ago popular music studies pioneers Charlie Gillett and Simon Frith discussed records and their value at some length (albeit not necessarily academically) in the *Rock File*[69] series of works (1973–76), Frith's embarkation on a significant academic career did not necessarily include an evaluation of the format. In fact, Eisenberg's *The Recording Angel*[70] (first published in 1987, but revised in 2005) was one of the first serious texts to consider and establish some kind of appreciation of an audio culture where the artefact was taken at all seriously, and the collector considered at any length. As suggested previously, this might have had something to do with the initiators of such studies coming from the political left, and thus being concerned that their own Marxist and neo-Marxist ideologies were being challenged by the very mass-produced artefacts that they might have initially claimed lacked authenticity. Theodor Adorno wrote that in popular music, for example, "every detail is substitutable; it serves its function only as a cog in a machine".[71] This dilemma can also be detected in the writings of Simon Frith, Philip Tagg and Bernard Gendron (and indeed the aforementioned Richard Middleton), to name a few. In all cases, these important popular music studies researchers are evidently working out ideas concerning how to transcend the mass culture critics such as Theodor Adorno (see further discussion below); Gendron, for example, notes:

> The 1956 Eldorado was the first Cadillac model to sport the famous tail-fin. To the mid-fifties consumer, all other Cadillac models paled in

---

[69] Charlie Gillett and Simon Frith, *The Beat Goes On: The Rock File Reader* (University of Michigan, 1996); see also Charlie Gillett, ed., *Rock File* (London: Pictorial Presentations with New English Library, 1972).
[70] Evan Eisenberg, *The Recording Angel: Music, Records And Culture From Aristotle To Zappa* (New Haven: Yale University Press, 2005).
[71] Theodor Adorno, "On Popular Music", in *On Record: Rock, Pop and the Written Word*, eds. Simon Frith and Andrew Goodwin (London: Routledge, 1941), 303.

comparison, though their innards were virtually the same. Not surprisingly, the rest of the Cadillac fleet followed suit with wholly revamped tail-fin models in 1957, though mechanically they showed little improvement.[72]

But then continues:

> He [Adorno] saw no significant differences between swing music and the sentimental ballads of the late thirties, no significant development from the "hot" small combo jazz of the twenties to the cooler big band jazz of the thirties. In effect, he believed that nothing ever changes in popular music.[73]

So it becomes evident, via this albeit limited literature review concerning identities and recorded-sound collecting, that the very history of academic popular music studies involves an attempt to legitimise itself and come to terms with value and meaning in contradistinction to the Marxist constructions from within which many popular music studies academics emerged. What appears to be a burning issue throughout most of the popular music studies texts available to students and researchers alike in the twenty-first century is this coming to terms with the inscription of meaning versus the ascription of meaning. For the Marxist, art is supposed to re-present an already existing world and its structures. For the record collector, however, this relation is reversed: the fact or practice of re-presentation itself produces the possibility of a recognisable world. The Marxist paradigm that a product actually proposes a world that is ethically unrecognisable has therefore been found wanting in the face of multifarious realities where real worlds are created by products. Products can remain mass produced but be different, and different worlds can be produced by the same product—all with real pleasurable and emotional outcomes.

The very basis of knowledge, therefore, and how it "means" things, is challenged by a reversal of the Marxist diktat of false consciousness (singular) into one of "real consciousnesses" (plural): in real terms, record collecting could signify a shift from epistemology to ontology. These academic popular music texts do nevertheless provide some insight into the field of record collecting, but still fail to explore other crucial aspects like the collector's internal dialogue and what effect collecting can have on identity. This means that anyone interested in the topic has to cast a wide net, trawl through a lot of material that may or may not be relevant,

---

[72] Bernard Gendron, "Theodor Adorno Meets the Cadillacs", in *Studies in Entertainment*, ed. Tania Modleski (Indiana: University Press, 1986), 21.
[73] *ibid.*, 23.

and at times hope for the best, hence leaving us with little understanding of what record collectors actually *do*, why it matters to them, why they value it so highly, and how it influences other areas of their lives.

The notion of cultural capital has already briefly been mentioned in this work, so let us briefly reconsider what it entails. The term originates from the work of Bourdieu, and can be used to both create a bond within a social group or to alienate others. It is used to distinguish knowledge and, as such, the most knowledgeable person within the specific subject possesses the most cultural capital. Within certain circles of record collecting then, one might observe that the person who owns the largest number of rare records thus holds the most cultural capital. It is also worth noting that people who share beliefs on cultural capital tend to develop their own use of language that is specific to their group.[74] However, despite several studies concerning cultural capital and popular music studies,[75] popular music studies academia currently offers little information to explain or understand the specifics of such engagement, something this text intends to at least partially attempt.

Seizure of Sound

Before moving on to the next section, it is also worth considering several popular music texts that consider the significance of sound, its relationship to technology and its significance in people's lives. Whilst none of these texts strictly deal with the record collector as such, in their own way they all acknowledge the significance of the artefact as something more than merely a mass-produced item of ephemera. For this work, one seminal text is the work of Andre Millard,[76] who examines how the US came to develop a phonograph and gramophone culture at an early stage, and how throughout the twentieth century the reformatting of such products did not simply emerge in order to create items intended to sell in the market place, but were actually industrial responses to how people wanted to hear music.

---

[74] David Riesman, "Listening to Popular Music", in *On Record: Rock, Pop and the Written Word*, eds. Simon Frith and Andrew Goodwin (London: Routledge, 1950), 5–13.

[75] Michael Emmison and John Frow, "Information Technology as Cultural Capital", *Australian Universities' Review* 4/1 (1998): 41–45; Sarah Thornton, "Moral Panic, the Media and British Rave Culture", in *Microphone Fiends: Youth Music and Youth Culture*, eds. Andrew Ross and Tricia Rose (New York: Routledge, 1994): 176–192.

[76] Andre Millard, *America on Record: A History of Recorded Sound* (Cambridge: University Press, 1995).

The development of recorded formats, according to Millard, not only created a massive industry in the US, but also hitherto unforeseen genres of music. Similarly, in his work *Capturing Sound: How Technology has Changed Music*,[77] the aforementioned Mark Katz understands how musical sounds were effectively captured in order to serve very specific purposes, not the least the way that recorded sound itself influences music. He says in his introduction:

> Simply put, phonograph effects are the manifestations of sound recording's influence. Consider a straightforward example. When Igor Stravinsky composed his Serenade for Piano in 1925, he wrote the work so that each of the four movements would fit the roughly three-minute limit of a ten-inch, 78-rpm record side.[78]

In his autobiography, Igor Stravinsky himself goes on to explain that his composition should be determined by the sonic capacity of the record, and Stravinsky was not the only composer who felt this way. In fact, many *avant-garde* composers, like Pierre Henri, Pierre Schaeffer, Boulez and Stockhausen followed a similar compositional practice. Thus, in this one small example, Katz is able to show how the importance of recorded sound makes a profound impact on the musical life of the twentieth century all the way through to the advent of the Internet. In a series of case studies he explains how the primacy of the technology does not dictate the composition of the music, but instead facilitates composition in several interesting and exciting ways. While he does not discuss collecting, he understands affordability—and by extension one might presume that he also understands the nature of owning and affording the artefact.

David Morton[79] also attempts to trace the complex pathways within which recording devices have come to be understood. He takes the reader from invention through the early years of high culture being recorded, into the era of what he describes as American re-recording culture (in other words the invention of the tape machine), through to his concluding remarks concerning digitalisation. Morton's point is that technologies such as sound recordings have not been "in and of" themselves independent, but instead splice into other systems of communication and, by so doing, transform them. This is in agreement with the great Canadian cultural

---

[77] Mark Katz, *Capturing Sound: How Technology has Changed Music* (Berkeley: University of California Press, 2010).
[78] *ibid.*, 3.
[79] David Morton, *Off the Record: The Technology and Culture of Sound Recording in America* (New Jersey: Rutgers University Press, 2000).

writer Marshall McLuhan and his 1964 text *Understanding Media: The Extensions of Man*.[80] In this text, McLuhan discusses what he calls inter-penetration, where new media take over the roles of old media. This has certainly been an interesting concept carried forward by Morton, who illustrates five case studies to support his theories. Firstly the phonograph record, followed by recording in the radio industry, the dictation machine, the telephone answering machine and finally, and perhaps most importantly for this work, home taping. Each of these case studies dispels the popular notion that recording is all about the music and instead they suggest that the artefacts themselves are facilitators of identity as much as they are facilitators of sound[81]—or, as McLuhan himself put it, the medium is the message.[82]

In 1980, in what may now appear to be a dated account in some respects, Peter Gammond and Ray Horricks[83] looked at the recording industry from Edison's invention of the phonograph in 1877 to what was then the highest technology of its day: quadraphonic sound. This non-academic, but interesting text shows from a British perspective how recording effectively "came of age" and, in a variety of case studies, concerned itself with the record industry that only slowly came to understand the industry in which it was involved. While the music industry is often seen as being in complete control of its product, Gammond and Horricks are able to show how throughout the twentieth century the industry was constantly trying to catch up with popular taste: this is an important point that periodically needs re-emphasising. From producing war records in 1915 on their *Regal* imprint, all the way through to working with The Beatles in the 1960s, *EMI*, for instance, were not fully aware of the market place, demographics, genres or promotion. It was thought at times, according to the writers, that the promotional side of popular music was of secondary importance.[84] It was also believed that the

---

[80] Marshall McLuhan, *Understanding Media: The Extensions of Man* (New York: McGraw-Hill, 1964).

[81] *Cf.* Harrison (2006).

[82] Marshall McLuhan, *Understanding Media: The Extensions of Man* (New York: McGraw-Hill, 1964).

[83] Peter Gammond and Ray Horricks, *The Music Goes Round and Round: A Cool Look at the Record Industry* (London: Quartet Books, 1980).

[84] The creative freedom artists were given with record sleeves when album art first became something more than just protection for the record seems to support this argument further. Gilroy (1993), for instance, discusses how certain black acts used the record sleeve to promote the notion of black liberation without interference from the record companies.

various labels within *EMI* could only provide a certain type of product. Gammond and Horricks thus suggest that the vertically integrated model of the record industry, where every part of developing a single is handled "in-house" from conception, artist selection, recording and promotion and so forth, was effectively one of the problems of the business rather than anything to do with product as such; and furthermore, that the hierarchical nature of *EMI*, predominantly based as it was around the success of classical music on record, meant that as a company they effectively did not keep their eye on the ball.

The late Russell Sanjek's work is also of some interest to this research and in particular the *I.S.A.M. Monograph no. 20*,[85] which concerns publishing in the music industry between 1900–1980. Of special interest was an early chapter in which Sanjek discusses the early music-publishing business around 1900. Here, Sanjek is able to show quite clearly how the phonograph in the US was the most important contribution to the economic development of songs and how the American music-publishing industry before the arrival of recorded sound very much reflected the book-publishing industry, which had effectively begun in England. He goes on to talk about the record and radio in the 1920s and 1930s, where one can clearly see how the music industries came to be synchronised, and sheet music sales to be reduced. Sanjek also discusses the ASCAP/BMI dispute of 1939–41 where the two publishing houses disputed ownership, royalties, radio—and anything else they cared to dispute—for the sake of paying royalties to the radio or not. It is particularly under circumstances such as the ASCAP/BMI dispute where record collecting takes on an identifiable shape, for records released under BMI publication tended to be targeted at ethnic minorities in the US, especially African-Americans. Thus certain styles of music were not only related to certain record labels, but also certain publishing companies. Identifiable signifiers came to emerge on record labels themselves, making the disc generically identifiable and perhaps increasing their collectability as a consequence.

In a different way, yet related to the work of Sanjek, is a more recent text from 2005 by Geoffrey O'Brien, entitled *Sonata for Jukebox*.[86] Written in a very idiosyncratic and original way, it concerns the way certain types of musical styles and songs relate to the author so directly that his musical senses become centre stage around which the rest of his

---

[85] Russell Sanjek, "From Print to Plastic: Publishing and Promoting America's Popular Music (1900–1980)", *I.S.A.M. Monograph no. 20* (New York: I.S.A.M., 1983).

[86] Geoffrey O'Brien, *Sonata for Jukebox: An Autobiography of my Ears* (New York: Counterpoint, 2005).

life seems to revolve. This significant text is very evocative and shows us how music infiltrates daily life. In many respects it is an ode to what can be described as a half-hidden world of meaning being created by and through recorded music. The different essays that O'Brien provides constantly rely on listening and records. For example, in his chapter "Central Park West Side A", itself the title of a John Coltrane track, he discusses how Coltrane's music opens up a lost space to him and that the notes, in a way, have nothing to do with the spaces that are opening up to the writer. Thus O'Brien himself invents and reaffirms the mood and events he wishes to confirm by playing the record, making the notes themselves surplus. What emerges is a kind of "sound movie" about the way in which people live their lives in Central Park West. This seems very intimate and, indeed, O'Brien so regards sound, and throughout the chapter he returns to records as a distinct sign of absolute authenticity. Perhaps we might even suggest that the connotations attached to sound throughout this work form a kind of typology of the real.

At one stage, O'Brien notes that talking to a friend usually reverts to conversations about records, which at times can serve as a kiosk to gather around, to share impressions, and to discuss how things sound, therefore how things actually are. He suggests that records act like a pool of water where one might see one's own reflection, although this could also suggest that were one to drop a pebble into this water the ripples from that pebble and its interaction with the water stretch outwards in almost unending refractions of meaning. O'Brien also makes reference to a strange moment of calm as the needle makes contact with the vinyl record on the turntable. One might suggest that the lyrical value of such contact is similar to the pebble hitting the water. All in all, O'Brien indicates that different people listen to the same record but for different reasons, and that the record may be assessed by a wide variety of reasons by the listener(s). Each person hence "weighs" the music, and in turn is "weighed" by it themselves. When writing about atomisation he further suggests that we are surrounded by people enough of the time, and that recorded sound can intervene in a way perhaps that social workers intervene with our daily problems, and create an essential space within which all of us need to divest ourselves of the ritualism involved in interaction—O'Brien himself is in favour of *allowing* people to do so.

In addition, an even more recent writer, Virgil Moorefield,[87] has traced the evolution of recorded sound, and in doing so he suggests that the

---

[87] Virgil Moorefield, *The Producer As Composer: Shaping the Sounds of Popular Music* (Cambridge: MIT Press, 2005).

producer becomes such an important feature of recorded sound that we need to regard that person as an auteur—in other words, someone who is responsible for their own aesthetic contributions. He even suggests that there is a significant illusory issue often neglected by musicologists of both the popular and classical variety. This is a common error that many highly qualified musicologists fail to recognise when discussing recorded sound. The issue is one of the illusion of reality versus the reality of illusion. According to Moorefield, up until the further development of tape recording in the late 1940s most recordings during the twentieth century were created as a reflection of the sound an artist or orchestra might make in a concert hall: as such, the disc existed literally as a "record" of a performance. This of course is an almost natural occurrence as, for a considerable amount of time many people might have purchased a record after at first hearing the artist in a live situation. However with the growth of radio, film and television, the recording studio took on a personality of its own, and the producer became more and more intertwined between technology as a creative practice and creativity as a technical practice, thus as a consequence creating the reality of illusion whereby the recorded sound one hears may be "constructed" sound (see examples below), and despite being an "illusion" is in fact reality.

Moorefield suggests that the idea of recorded sound as a mimetic space therefore virtually ceases to exist by the time producers as *auteurs* come to be recognised. One need only look back to the vari-speed recordings of Les Paul in the late 1940s, the sound effects created by Mitch Miller, the wall of sound created by Phil Spector, the reversed toilet flushes of Joe Meek on "Telstar" and the sound effects of street drills by George Martin on Bernard Cribbins recordings to realise that the contemporary producer was an artist in his own right during the post-World War II era. While the underlying mechanism for sound production is technological, it also encompasses aesthetics and intellect, and Moorefield suggests that the studio becomes a musical instrument in its own right. His consideration of Pink Floyd's *Dark Side of the Moon* album, together with the growth of hip-hop and the rise of both analogue and digital sampling suggests that music perhaps, in the conventional sense, comes to take on a somewhat secondary role. In hip-hop, for example, he argues that the vocal (in other words the rap) makes the hip-hop track unique rather than the backing track itself, which could actually be used in a variety of settings. This is not to say that the music becomes interchangeable, but that it serves a function that is linked to genre aesthetics and the grain of the voice in many different modes.

Finally in this section, a work that does not concentrate on popular music as such, but instead follows the development of all electronic, contemporary music-making: *Audio Culture: Readings in Modern Music,* edited by Christoph Cox and Daniel Warner.[88] The editors essentially provide the reader with an anthology of recorded sound and by doing so consider the histories of experimental music and sound art. They see this as an assemblage, a growth and an accumulation of sounds, methods and approaches that have piled up during the post-World War II era. They also see and demonstrate how people relate their compositional styles, techniques and authenticities through the medium of recorded sound. Essays from the likes of Simon Reynolds, David Toop, John Cage, Brian Eno and Luigi Russolo show how people have effectively been living in a world of noise, and that recording the world around us is intrinsically important to many. For example, with regard to an essay by Brian Eno, the editors point out that Eno, whilst having a successful career in pop music, was also immersed in the British experimental music scene, performing with both Cornelius Cardew and Gavin Bryars.

In 1975, Eno even founded his own record label with a title that immediately attracted the attention of record collectors: *Obscure Records.* This label disseminated experimental music by the likes of Toop, Nyman and Budd and others, and in its first year issued Eno's own experimental work *Discreet Music,* which contained what he described as self-generating music. Interestingly, and for the purpose of this work, all *Obscure* recordings are now considered highly collectable. Cox and Warner mainly concern themselves with contemporary music rather than popular music, but do draw important correlations between current musical practices and older sonic experimentations. The result is therefore perhaps one of the best introductions to the significance of sound art and production and the way in which recorded sound of all varieties comes to dominate our listening practices into the twenty-first century. This writer found the text of considerable interest owing to the way there appears to be a history of recorded sound which is influenced in some respects by classical music composition, but intends to redraw the ways the composer composes via the medium of recording within a music technological space.

---

[88] Christoph Cox and Warner, Daniel, *Audio Culture: Readings in Modern Music* (New York: Continuum, 2004).

Ethnography

Given that this work has significant elements of ethnographic discourse via interviews with collectors and dealers, it was considered of vital importance to consider several ethnography-based texts. Ethnography is a skill within the discipline of social anthropology, and is therefore vital to the study of popular music. It has been stated on many occasions that the study of popular music is essentially about two things: people and sound. Therefore the ways one goes about discussing sound with people should also prove to be rigorous and disciplined, and should consist of a self-reflexivity concerning the values and opinions of others above any *a priori* concepts and approaches of the researcher. By doing so, one at least attempts to allow the evidence to, as it were, "speak for itself".

To this end, the work of anthropologist Ruth Finnegan is of vital and primary importance. Finnegan's text *The Hidden Musicians: Music-Making in an English Town* does not deal with record collecting at all, but instead focuses upon music-making in a medium-sized "new town" in England, Milton Keynes. Her ethnographic approaches into how she unpacks values and authenticities concerning what people deem good, bad, cool and uncool music has, however, been of vital importance to this writer. For example, she discovered that there were many facets of music-making in the town, and all were considered by adherents to be deeply meaningful and authentic. This multi-faceted understanding of value aids the researcher into record collecting by understanding that "participation in [a chosen music] world was as source of the greatest satisfaction, often by taking up just about the whole of their non-working time [but also] playing a large part in their self-definition".[89] Finnegan was meticulous in her discussion on musical worlds. Concerning one such world—folk music—she discovered that there were guidelines, rules, and sets of generic conventions that created parameters for those involved, but that these rules could be described as much as "lore" as anything. She stated that:

> Above all, the "folkness" of the music was assured for the participants by its enactment within a setting locally or nationally defined as "folk", and by a strongly held, if not always articulated, set of ideas about this kind of enterprise in which they were engaged.[90]

---

[89] Ruth Finnegan, *The Hidden Musicians: Music-Making in an English Town* (Cambridge: University Press, 1989), 58.
[90] *ibid.*, 66.

In other words, such worlds were demarcated, perhaps even limited, by a complex of ideas that was part of a more general philosophy concerning the nature of what they were doing. This writer found this very helpful when considering record collecting, both as a whole and via the very specific.

A consideration of the very specific was an important aspect of this writer's research, and one piece of ethnography was extremely helpful in this respect. The work of ethnographer Diane Tye and her study of a Beatles fan was illuminating, to say the least. Here, Tye's conversation with a self-described Beatles freak in Newfoundland illustrated how, rather than the perception of the industry manipulating receivers, one receiver manipulates Beatles music and memorabilia as "an integral part of his self-concept and world view".[91] Here, not only does Tye show how one fan's desire to collect was central to his own sense of self, but how his search for others to share his interests was never-ending. He created networks of similarly interested fans, spoke very proudly of being consulted by them in settling disputes, and displayed how there was a need to form select groups via an appreciation of mass-produced artefacts. Tye also showed how her participant, "Sean", could be used as a micro-study (i.e. not a microcosm) in the analysis of fandom and what is occasionally described as "odd" or "deviant" behaviour: "Sean never joined a fan club, and he comments that few people he knows share his devotion. Nevertheless, he feels an instantaneous bond when he meets another Beatles fan". Tye was also at pains to create an inventory of Sean's memorabilia-cum-record collection. LPs were arranged chronologically, whereas 45s were arranged alphabetically. Cassette tapes were used to tape his albums but it was also indicated that his cassettes contained interviews and rare items (see Chapter Seven, regarding the dealer ethnography and his comments on cassettes). The young fan had few books, however.

Such significant micro-studies require important ethical and discipline-related considerations, and the work of the widely published Martin Hammersley came to be of significance for guidance during the process of disseminating the research conducted for this book. In particular, his journal article "Ethnography: Problems and Prospects" presented an important review of areas of tensions and conflicts within ethnography concerning taxonomy and methods. Hammersley states in his concluding remarks that we need to take great care concerning "the spatial and temporal perimeters of data collection and the nature of socio-cultural

---

[91] Diane Tye, "Ethnography of a Beatles Fan", *Culture and Tradition* 11 (1987): 42.

phenomena, how context should be taken into account, what can and cannot be inferred from particular sorts of data, and indeed issues about the very purpose of ethnographic work. [...] The very character of ethnography has come to be contested".[92]

The work of Sara Cohen was also considered at some length. She is a renowned popular music studies ethnographer of many years' standing, and her work continues to inform popular music studies. Two key pieces of work were found to be of great use in this instance. Her seminal article for the *Popular Music* journal, "Ethnography and Popular Music Studies",[93] and her work "Identity, Place and the 'Liverpool Sound'" in *Music, Ethnicity and Identity: The Musical Construction of Place*,[94] both illustrate the significance of field-work in anything to do with popular music. Cohen is at all times interested in the local, and she suggests that popular music studies, as a discipline, requires far more locally-based research concerning values, meanings, and authenticities. She understands that, faced with our social, historical, and existential presents, one uses the past as an important referent. Such a contradiction propels lovers of popular culture into complex and interesting inventiveness concerning their own senses of identity (especially in the second of the above, regarding what the "Liverpool Sound" actually meant to musicians in the early 1990s). For these young musicians, the past is approached through stylistic connotation, conveying a "past-ness", not necessarily by any glossy image qualities so often associated with popular music, but actually how expressions such as "Liverpool Sound" sit within their own matrixes of authenticity. For this writer, who came across such oppositions to imaginary and stereotypical "idealities" being similarly opposed by record collectors, Cohen's work proved to be most helpful.

The mesmerizing new aesthetic mode of sound recording emerged as an elaborate system within the waning years of the nineteenth century. It was neither deliberate nor accidental, but came about as a variable response to the lived possibility of experiencing some kind of voice from the past in some active, not passive way. Sound recording, therefore cannot be said to have produced either a passive receiver bent on somnambulation, or a strange occultation within the present (of which it appears to have been commonly accused). Instead, one might argue that

---

[92] Martin Hammersley, "Ethnography: Problems and Prospects", *Ethnography and Education* 1, no. 1 (2006): 11.
[93] Sara Cohen, "Ethnography and Popular Music Studies", *Popular Music* 12, no. 2 (1993): 123–138.
[94] Martin Stokes, ed., *Music, Ethnicity and Identity: The Musical Construction of Place* (Oxford: Berg Publishers, 1994).

recorded sound has demonstrated, through these seemingly contradictory states of false consciousness, the enormity of a situation in which it came to connote genuine authenticity. It could be argued that while at times we seem increasingly incapable of fashioning authentic representations of our own current experiences, record collecting actually assists us in co-creating our musical universe.

Having introduced some themes and literature into this book it is now an appropriate moment to move into the next section in which the methods and approaches of the Frankfurt School concerning mass production will be discussed. A consideration of how the era that represents what one perhaps might describe as modernism (with distinct ideological positions) was being supplemented by a new era that reflected real concerns regarding high and low culture will take place. This has come to be described as an era of post-modernity, within which the emergence of recorded popular culture as a valid art form was central.

CHAPTER THREE

GENRE, CONNOTATION AND THE FRANKFURT SCHOOL

"[…] listeners are distracted from the demands of reality by entertainment which does not demand attention"
—Theodor Adorno (1941), *On Popular Music*

Authenticity, Genre

Roy Shuker[1] writes that one of the central discourses involving popular music creation, mediation and reception is authenticity. As one of the key concepts in popular music studies, authenticity is "imbued with considerable symbolic value",[2] and is often at the centre of our everyday discussions concerning which musician, band (or indeed genre of music) happens to be "better" than another. As such, it also serves an "important ideological function"[3] in that it relates not only to an act's (perceived) creativity but also to their role in history. Both points are of great significance to the popular music scholar, although the latter of these is perhaps important here, for the hegemonic discourses surrounding all music historiography are essentially imbued with authenticities to fit, rather than question, familiarities surrounding historical enquiry. Discounting for the moment, therefore, actual musical skill (or "talent", if one subscribes to romantic notions of authenticity), it is this double-edged notion of authenticity that in most cases renders (say) Jimi Hendrix a better musician and guitarist than Tom Fletcher or Danny Jones from McFly, not simply because Hendrix might have been more skilled, but because "authentic" histories of individual virtuosos "fit" the cultural capital of the way such histories are put together, in the first place. Richard Middleton writes:

---

[1] Roy Shuker, *Popular Music: The Key Concepts* (London: Routledge, 2002).
[2] *ibid.*, 20.
[3] *ibid.*, 21.

Within popular music culture, the discourse of authenticity is familiar. Typically, it is taken to mark out the genuine from the counterfeit, the honest from the false, the original from the copy, roots from surface— oppositions which in turn often map on to further distinctions: feeling as against pretence, acoustic as against the electric, subculture against mainstream, people against industry, and so on.[4]

As (popular music studies) academics, then, there are an almost innumerable number of aspects of such representations of authenticity to analyse and consider. We must, for example, continually acknowledge that our own notions of authenticity may even be part of such hegemonic historiographies; how these notions influence and affect our views on particular artists (or indeed art in general) requires self-reflexive investigation. As mentioned in the first chapter of this book, despite attempting to research issues surrounding popular music and authenticity via the activities of other record collectors and their collections, when it comes to this author's own record collection much academic knowledge can be jettisoned because one's own authenticities can be laid bare by and through the collection.

Under such circumstances, then, a different approach to historiographical authenticity perhaps needs to be considered, that being that a kind of spatial element to understanding our authenticity paradigms should at least be estimated. This is not "anti-historical", but rather an area of critique that expands historical narrative from a chronicle to a level of relative realism. This book, for example, considers how the history of "record collecting spaces" has been created both in people's minds and also in their living rooms; how collecting as a form of authentic emancipatory expression has contributed an "other" history, one which challenges the over-arching narrative of historical temporality and replaced it with an understanding of how spaces and places come to be important areas of authenticity, rather than merely those "on the record", as it were. For example, the very act of record collecting challenges time and narratives of time in a most interesting way. It examines how people and space inter-relate: whether via record fairs, recovering from illness, or contributing to a discourse of record authenticity, electronically. And that is, for this writer, a clear indication that what we perceive as "authentic", whether as fans or music consumers, is not only ontologically very deeply rooted and ingrained into our identities, but perhaps also needs to be historicised in a different, less temporal way, being part of what Edward Soja might describe as a

[4] Richard Middleton, *Voicing the Popular: On Subjects of Popular Music* (New York: Routledge, 2006), 200.

"trialectic of sociality—historicality—spatiality".[5] It is by dealing with authenticity within such spheres that this book suggests that popular music record collecting as an authenticity paradigm requires further "thick" research.

Finally, with regard to this book—unless otherwise indicated—this author defines authenticity in accordance with the above comments and the definitions provided by Shuker[6] and Middleton,[7] which is a definition, by and large, adopted by the academic community within popular music studies. In its common sense value within popular music (both academic and non-academic), then, it is also worth noting that authenticity tends to assume that the creators of the text are authentic because they undertake the work themselves, evoking both creativity and originality, and also sincerity, uniqueness and seriousness. Even though the input of others is recognised on the recording, it is usually the musician who is seen to have a pivotal role. This means the musician usually carries the central element of "cool" as they are pivotal to the entire discourse. Whilst authenticity does not necessarily equate to cool, certain genres, such as cool jazz, Britpop and dubstep, have authenticity embedded within them, rendering them describable as cool, and hence holding a certain appeal for some listeners. One might thus suggest that "cool" lends itself to the popular music sub-discipline of genre analysis, identifying who is, and who is not, cool within an equally cool genre.

Genre analysis will inform the researcher that there are myriad interesting ways of understanding types, and is a key component of the textual analysis of all media texts, including recorded sound. Stuart Borthwick and Ron Moy[8] suggest that while there is no absolutely correct or true way of examining popular music genres, some methodical positions are of significance, and others not. Principally, any examination of the relationship between musical texts and their various contexts demands that we consider aesthetic engagement. This is an important fundamental issue to consider when we cast our glance towards recording and record collectors. In the opening paragraph of Chapter One (above), the issues surrounding collectors, the media, and the meanings of collecting in a modern world were discussed as crucial.

---

[5] Edward Soja, *Thirdspace: Journeys to Los Angeles and Other Real-And-Imagined Places* (London: Blackwell, 1996), 171.

[6] Roy Shuker, *Popular Music: The Key Concepts* (London: Routledge, 2002).

[7] Richard Middleton, *Voicing the Popular: On Subjects of Popular Music* (New York: Routledge, 2006).

[8] Stuart Borthwick and Ron Moy, *Popular Music Genres: An Introduction* (Edinburgh: University Press, 2004).

The structure of consciousness determines what can be perceived, and we process this information in accordance with an internal logic, and the external world around us. There is therefore usually a ritual of engagement, with the material world, but this is only part of the criteria for understanding aesthetic engagement, for the rest of the processing takes place internally. There is, thus, an internal logic which is far more difficult to assess. The argument presented by those who see only ritual in aesthetic engagement with popular culture is that this ritual appears to offer, not a practice of thinking, but rather ritualism turned into thought, therefore ritualistic thought. This, according to "Frankfurtian" ideas, offers only a form without content. Theodor Adorno's (and Horkheimer's) fear was that the popular evades the political because it was actually a mode of disengagement. However, it is argued from within popular music studies that popular-based engagements and relationships divulge far more about music and the societies in which the music is situated than any purely ideological or musicological approaches. The problem with what might be described as "art-based" abstractions are also potentially modes of disengagement—especially of the ideological and opinionated self. If true "art" is viewed as the work of an isolated genius then one might argue that it actually evades the socio-cultural that is embraced by the popular.

Genre analysis is therefore intrinsic to such approaches to understand the aesthetic engagement of the popular. It is dialectical, critical and discursive. Dialectical, because it is rooted in the understanding that there is a relationship between text and context, also that it related to issues concerning social relationships; and critical because it employs theoretical positions and is not just based on facts and lists. Genre analysis is discursive because music is a language system where texts are made to mean things, making semiotics and structure very significant, and very much part of the language system that gives rise to the music as well as the meanings. In the world in which recorded sound came to dominate as a form, signs everywhere announced their presence and demanded to be decoded. Such decoding was often done under the aegis of presiding hierarchies, but as the century progressed required re-evaluation, while high art musical hierarchies remained caught up in a philosophy of identity which negated material and historical realities in the interests of retaining recognisable self-images. A new form of musicology has emerged by and through genre analysis that attempts to understand this noisy world in which we now live, rendering such formal philosophies of identity questionable, at the least.

With regard to records, genre analysis is vital because of the intrinsic organising elements, and as such, genre is vitally important to the record collector. Fans and collectors identify themselves with particular genres,[9] and also demonstrate considerable knowledge about both artist and genre, and indeed an entire "sensibility". Eisenberg[10] identifies a certain "cool" via records awarding the listener the impression that artists understand listeners' understanding of the genre. A reciprocal communication of signs and symbols therefore takes place in which no one has the first or the last word. For example, John Lennon was not cool simply because audiences purchased his recordings; he was regarded as cool by his fans because he appeared to regard his audience, as such, via the medium of the recording as the primary artefact. There is an element of philosophical thought concerning cool. For example, if a listener regards an artist as cool, and the artist is viewed as the creator of a recording, we have immersed within this discourse an acknowledgement that the listener's interpretation has been effectively acknowledged by the artist: the listener is therefore an intrinsic element of the record. It might be argued that classical musicology as it developed in the nineteenth century could not possibly understand the semiotics of such cool and authenticity because its signs were created in an era before recorded sound; it did not truly belong to this circular "audio culture", within which, the primacy of the recording is evidently the item of greatest importance. This benefits the listener because they can situate themselves within this audio culture. The listener, for example, tends to understand that even though a centrality of cool surrounds the "artist", that artist is not the only one involved with the creation of the artefact—it is in fact a collaborative effort right from the start.

According to Eisenberg, the listener thus values the medium that captures beauty, not simply the encrypted message within the medium. Therefore, the artefact can enhance "cool" as it relates to the artist—or not, as the case may be. If one considers the significance of jazz labels, artists can be valued in relationship to the label on which they appear. So, for example, if an artist such as John Coltrane is recorded by a recognised independent jazz label, such as (say) *Prestige*, his value and cool might not simply be attributed to the music on the record, but the label for which the music was made, and the significance attached by the collector to that label. Jazz collectors may therefore generically discriminate between one John Coltrane record and another, depending upon the authenticity of the label. It is a common feature within jazz connoisseurship that collectors openly collect some labels, like *Blue Note*, but not others. As indicated previously, Eisenberg explored the subject in *The Recording Angel* and

---

[9] *Cf.* subcultures.
[10] Evan Eisenberg, *The Recording Angel: Music, Records And Culture From Aristotle To Zappa* (New Haven: Yale University Press, 2005).

concluded that certain artists, such as Miles Davis, Frank Sinatra and John Lennon, enjoyed a certain "cool" appeal because they gave the impression of knowing the listener through and through, yet allowing listeners to make up their own minds. Eisenberg argues that this "cool" mode of projection was only one strategy employed by twentieth-century musicians to overcome the lack of an audience when recording. It can also be of benefit to the listener: the artist's actual, physical presence was not necessary. "Cool" can have multiple meanings, and can be used in many different ways in popular music, but most of us understand what is meant by the phrase when used in popular music recorded-sound terms.

In reality, then, record collecting involves a number of different discriminating proposals and complex processes that, simply put, bring satisfaction to the collector via the record. The text is always the site of a tension between the contradictions implicit in the historical conjuncture of the record itself. This inherent diversity offered by recorded sound means we have a number of different people who can safely regard themselves as record collectors—these can involve a continuum of interpretations or a barrage of disconnected images. It is a hobby that can have a huge lifelong impact on people's lives. Understanding record collecting can thus provide us with information on how a wide range of people from different backgrounds and cultures chose to engage with and own recorded music in a way that can be adapted to fit their own needs—not the other way around.

Ownership

The words "own", "cherish", and "collect" suggest various notions of value, authenticity and aesthetics. It is perhaps easy to understand how the word "cherish", being a value-laden word, implies certain values and authenticities. The Oxford English Dictionary defines the word as being to "protect and care for (someone) lovingly [...] hold (something) dear [...] keep (a hope or ambition) in one's mind".[11] However, owning and collecting both have similar implications. Most people find they are surrounded by objects of necessity or items that aid their lives somehow, like towels for drying oneself with, can openers to access food, or a car to get you places. These are items we to a certain extent need in our lives and do not actively choose to bring in. Whilst a longer consideration of "need" is reserved for another examination, there are some observations we can make:

---

[11] oxforddictionaries.com, accessed 31 October 2011.

A second kind of state of affairs referred to by "need" statements is one in which the something-that-is-needed is a necessary means to the attainment of a goal of the person who is said to have the need. A necessary means is a means without which the person cannot attain his goal. The "need" statement contextually implies that such a necessary means is absent or wanting. If we say, "People need food, clothing, and shelter", the purpose of survival at a certain minimum level of comfort and health is presupposed. We might make this point more emphatically by saying that what people need in this sense is always relative to what they want. A nudist does not need clothing, and a person who has decided to commit suicide does not need food or shelter. [...] However, we also speak of the needs of the members of different groups or societies in statements of type (3). Thus we speak of the adolescent's need for security, the racist's need to dominate others, the Tchambuli's need to be skilled in some form of art, the Zuni's need for strict observance of ceremonial rituals, the Oriental's need to save face, and the contemporary American's need to buy a new car every year (as distinct from his need for a new car every year). In all of these cases, the needs are dominant conative [*sic*] dispositions of typical members of the groups or societies.[12]

The items we choose to keep around us are clearly items that hold certain values for us. This can mean photographs of loved ones, mementos—or records. Choosing to keep (i.e. own) records in our living spaces (as one does when claiming ownership of domestic items) instead of something else we could fill the space taken up by those records, indicates that the consumer places enough value on them to allow them space in their lives. In other words, the records take up space, but give enough gratification to justify keeping them. Collecting records in essence extends this argument: the time, effort and space dedicated to records by a collector are, for them, worth it, valuable and symbiotic. If the satisfaction gained did not outweigh the effort put in, the collector would not persist.[13] One collector informed this writer that space for a record collection is also a changing signifier:

> The number of times I have told myself that I need to reduce the collection is without number. And I have done so on several occasions—I'm not a hoarder. But gradually space is re-occupied, and friends come around and say, "What a pity the records aren't there any more", or, else say "Don't they look nice over there?" They have even said, "We're a bit worried about you—there are too many vinyls here." So it changes and mutates as my life moves on. I tend not to play many of them these days—especially

---

[12] Paul W. Taylor, "'Need' Statements", *Analysis* 19, no. 5 (1959): 107 & 109.

[13] See David W. McMillan and David M. Chavis (1986) on personal investment.

singles—but they look nice enough to me, just sitting there. They make the room look lived in, and cool.[14]

There are, it seems, many different ways to relate to records, and not just for the collector.

As a concrete example, consider from a genre-analysis point of view the Prodigy's inner gatefold illustration for their hit album *Music for the Jilted Generation* (1994). The record is not simply a carrier of gratification or information concerning music, but also a valuable—and, indeed symbiotic—creator of symbolic space. The cardboard sleeve that carries the actual sound recording is a direct symbol of cool in its own right, for the artwork displays an expansion of cool, an illustration of a post-hippie character getting ready to cut a rope bridge between a rave and a city, creating a positioning of the artefact, genre, group, artist and listener. It is colourful, "artistic"—i.e. painted (and rather at odds with the outer cover, as a consequence)—and creates oppositions between the genre of music and open spaces, and the urban environment being graphically represented. It suggests a "new way" via dance music, suggesting that the musical formula can be a judgement on conformity. We have, perhaps, a post-modernist versus modernist opposition right across this gatefold sleeve, suggesting that music is always in a state of flux and is not something that can be determined according to a dialectic of musical appearance and reality—for dance music as a genre is not really "musical" in the formal sense.

Semiotician Charles Sanders Pierce[15] states that many signs and symbols can be either iconic or indexical. For a sign to be iconic, one is concerned with authenticity as follows: the artist becomes an icon who understands the message and the listener, allowing the listener to understand the iconography surrounding the artist. The record can thus be iconic, rather like religious imagery in a church, but simultaneously also indexical. Looking at the *Vertigo* "swirl" label, for instance, the swirl on a record is indexical: it signifies *Vertigo Records*, which in turn means "unusual", perhaps meaning "experimental", suggesting "non-chart" (or outside the mainstream), which in turn signifies "33rpm rather than 45rpm", meaning LP, thus "serious", therefore "counter-culture through progressive rock", meaning hippiedom, and so forth. Thus, what one understands as a record collector is semiotic: cool via the icon (artist) and index (context). Indeed the collectability of some recordings has perhaps

---

[14] Dave, interview May 2013.
[15] For Charles Sanders Pierce see Philip Tagg, *Ten Little Tunes* (Liverpool: IPM, 1992).

less to do with the artist as such and more to do with the relationship of the listener to the carrier and the dialectic elements associated with label, artwork, presentation and generic affiliations. To illustrate this in the words of another record collector:

> For me, there were only two labels worth collecting in the late 1960s. Many of my friends would buy anything on *Tamla Motown*, in fact one colleague collected them numerically from *Tamla Motown* 1 to whatever. For me, less of a soul fan, the two labels I used to collect whenever I saw them were *Island* and *Transatlantic*. Both labels were independents, both labels were quite attractive to look at, and both labels were guarantees of quality. So it mattered little to me whose record I was buying, especially as far as singles were concerned—I just bought everything I could find, usually second hand on *Island* and *Transatlantic*.[16]

Understanding cool, then, from a record collector's perspective, is highly contextual and may ultimately relate more to the index rather than the icon, which may be one of the reasons why some record collectors collect the label rather than the artist (such as this writer). If Eisenberg is at all correct (and this writer would suggest he is), the idea of consumption as being anti-consumer contains some validity. A *Vertigo* collector can be anti-consumerist despite the consumption, and authenticity is attached indexically as well as iconically. Since the consumption is often seen as being iconic (the notion of being "duped by Elvis" or someone similar), indexical consumption is frequently ignored. This is because the artist is seen as holding the key to meaning, whereas the packaging is merely seen as another tool with which consumerist society can be exploited—but consumption is also indexical. The product rather than the icon could function as the authentic artefact and the connoter of authenticity. Mistakenly thinking that issues to do with the indexical relationship of the listener are solely to do with the music, can lead the critic into a deep misunderstanding of collecting. More account thus needs to be taken of the index provided by the packaging and how that relates the consumer to his or her own cool as a member of subculture or indeed counter-culture.

The above discussion might suggest that the connotations of record collecting are widely acknowledged, but they also remain largely unexplored. It has been suggested here that even at a basic genre-analysis level, several complexities arise concerning exactly what is being collected. For some, iconic collecting is central, which may be directly linked to the artist: "cool" can therefore exist between listener and

---

[16] Michael Brocken, personal communication, May 2013.

recorded sound in a more or less direct communication. However, one would have to suggest that this in its own right appears rather simplistic. Philip Tagg suggests that in any recorded sound communication there also has to be a level of codal competence brought on by different levels of social contextualisations, familiarities and sonic indicators and synecdoches.[17] Listeners are therefore effectively versed in an important relationship. If they are not so, the connotations do not work, the reference points do not signify, and the listener is therefore codally *in*competent. For many record collectors who involve themselves in a relationship with both the carrier and the artist, the connotations attached to such relationships are of considerable significance in every possible way. Yet to a large extent popular music academia is still all too focused on neo-Frankfurt School ideologies concerning passive reception. A discussion of the Frankfurt School follows, for having already mentioned this school of important twentieth-century theory on several occasions, it is an appropriate moment to introduce and then critique their approaches from a popular music studies perspective.

Adorno, the Frankfurt School and Popular Music

If one were looking at a classical Adornian statement concerning popular music listening, which has been repeated innumerable times, it would have to be the comments from his 1941 essay, "On Popular Music": "Listeners are distracted from the demands of reality by entertainment which does not demand attention either".[18] It is from such an ideological position that many value judgements, disguised as fact, have emerged. It is therefore important at this stage to consider both Adorno and the Frankfurt School in some detail, in order to develop an antithesis to their pessimistic thesis on the popular. Richard Middleton describes Adorno's polemic against popular music as "scathing", but nonetheless goes on to state that it:

> [...] possesses nevertheless, a striking richness and complexities, demanding to be examined from a variety of viewpoints, notably that of musical production (in relation to general production in capitalist societies), that of musical form (discussed by Adorno in terms of "standardisation") and that of musical reception and function (which he

---

[17] Philip Tagg, *Introductory Notes to the Semiotics of Music* (1999), http://tagg.org/xpdfs/semiotug.pdf.
[18] Theodor Adorno, "On Popular Music", in *On Record: Rock, Pop and the Written Word*, eds. Simon Frith and Andrew Goodwin (London: Routledge, 1941), 310.

sees as almost totally instrumentalised, in the service of the ruling social interests […] Adorno has many strengths[19]

But does he?

The Frankfurt School refers to a branch of learning of early-to-mid-twentieth-century social and cultural theory, heavily influenced by Marxist thought, and particularly linked to the School for Social Research at Frankfurt am Main University. Notable scholars associated with the "school" include Theodor Adorno, Max Horkheimer and Walter Benjamin (amongst others). The School (of thought) began to grow and gain a reputation in the 1930s when Horkheimer became director of the School for Social Research, and began recruiting many now notable theorists. When considering the sometimes perceived ominous quality in the works by Frankfurt School theorists, it is important to remember that the School for Social Research—and thus the centre for the Frankfurt School of thought—was situated in Germany (albeit relocated to New York in 1935) during the rise of Nazism—whilst many theorists (Horkheimer, Fromm, Marcuse, Benjamin and Adorno, *et al.*) were themselves mostly of Jewish descent. Moreover, the Marxist ideas at the centre of the Frankfurt School also contain a great deal of disillusion.

In short, Marx believed that capitalism allowed a wealthy minority to oppress the majority of the population—the working class, or proletariat—and that this would inevitably result in a proletarian revolution where socialism would eventually give way to communism. The notion of different social classes and divisions of wealth were central to Marx's theories, as was the mode of production which consisted of people having to enter into contracts regardless of their will: to survive we must consume, to consume we must produce, and to produce we are reliant on others, creating a superstructure. Of the Frankfurt School theorists, Adorno, who we have already mentioned, is a particularly important figure in our context, as many of his texts deal specifically with music. We have already discussed the radio ham, but Adorno is not short of examples of passivity in art consumption and false consciousness. He even goes so far as to say that people are unable to actively consume music and engage with it as, he argues, listening is regressive:

This does not mean the relapse of the individual listener into an earlier phase of his own development, nor a decline in the collective general level, since the millions who are reached musically for the first time by today's mass communications cannot be compared with the audience of the past.

---

[19] Richard Middleton, *Studying Popular Music* (Buckingham: OUP, 1990), 34.

Rather, it is contemporary listening which has regressed, arrested at the infantile stage. Not only do the listening subjects lose, along with freedom of choice and responsibility, the capacity for conscious perception of music, which was from time immemorial confined to a narrow group, but they stubbornly reject the possibility of such perception. [...] their primitivism is not that of the undeveloped, but that of the forcibly retarded.[20]

This regressed listening, alongside fetishising certain aspects or "charms" of the music, is a result of modern society and mass production. We are invited to conjure up an image of a man "who leaves the factory and [merely] 'occupies' himself".[21] For Adorno, intellectual engagement with music has been sacrificed for popular music that will make a person work at a desired pace in a factory, monotonously assembling whichever part he is told, and then repeat this repetitive act as part of what he sees as his "real" life.

The listener is worshipping what he is lead to believe he should be, picking out individual parts, and not consuming the piece as a whole. For instance, a person declaring they loved a song only when they recognised the chorus after a verse would be fetishising. As for a Toscanini concert ticket, the consumer "has literally 'made' the success which he reifies and accepts as an objective criterion, without recognizing himself in it. But he has not 'made' it by liking the concert, but rather by buying the ticket".[22] Furthermore (and to paraphrase), any endeavour to break away from the passivity of this kind of consumption to "activate" themselves, only leads to a form of pseudoactivity. But what makes Adorno's pseudoactivity "pseudo" is questionable. Is it, for instance, "the enthusiasts who write fan letters to radio stations and orchestras and, at well-managed jazz festivals, produce their own enthusiasm as an advertisement for the wares they consume"? Do they apparently "mock and affirm their loss of individuality", transforming themselves into "beetles whirring around in fascination"? And if they call themselves fans of the "jitterbug", is this term "hammered into them by the entrepreneurs to make them think they are on the inside"?[23]

What is not made clear is exactly how and why we lose our individuality via such activities: it appears that simply ascribing a certain

---

[20] Theodor Adorno, "On the Fetish-Character of Listening and the Regression of Listening", in *Essays on Music*, ed. Richard Leppert (Berkley: University of California Press, 1938), 303.

[21] *ibid.*, 309.

[22] *ibid.*, 296.

[23] *ibid.*, 308–309.

label to a group of people equates to a loss of individuality; such statements are evidently ideological. John Storey[24] suggests there are several different ways of defining ideology and presents five readings particularly relevant to popular culture. Firstly, an ideology that refers to a "systematic body of ideas articulated by a particular group of people".[25] In this instance, an identifiable group of people, such as a specific subculture or professional group, shares an ideology that allows them to articulate certain ideas within that framework. This means we could speak of a distinct ideology of the Frankfurt School, which would refer to a collection of political, economic and social ideas. The second definition is also relevant to the Frankfurt School, as it suggests ideology works to mask, conceal or distort. Questions of taste are usually linked to the questions of time, knowledge and ideology. Ideology can be seen as an aristocracy of culture, disparaging knowledge and experience that does not fit the ideological framework, and favouring a certain refinement awarded to high art, as if to prioritise the connoisseur. Storey's third definition of ideology is "ideological forms". This calls attention to how texts "present a particular image of the world",[26] and suggests that good taste, which develops from this aristocracy of thought can be learnt and passed on in time only when certain classes have developed the correct type of consciousness to appreciate it. This model implies that society is in a state of conflict rather than consensus, and would thus also mean that all texts take sides and present a certain image. In essence, all texts offer "competing ideological signification",[27] making them ultimately political. For Adorno, all aesthetic experiences have to reflect this ideological position, so convinced was he that his rhetoric was correct.[28] But, one might argue, such persistent negation can never be creative.

The final definition of ideology that Storey discusses is one developed by the neo-Marxist philosopher Althusser, and was influential during the 1970s. This definition links ideology to all material practices, rather than simply a body of ideas and beliefs. Althusser further argued that certain rituals, like Christmas celebrations and weekends, temporarily release us

---

[24] John Storey, "What is Popular Culture?", in *Cultural Theory and Popular Culture: An Introduction*, ed. John Storey (Harlow: Pearson Education, 2001), 1–12.

[25] *ibid.*, 2.

[26] *ibid.*, 3.

[27] *ibid.*, 3.

[28] Though it should be noted that Adorno could also be a man of (seeming) contradiction: for instance, initially criticising the phonograph record (1927, 1934), then later claiming it was a vehicle for superior understanding of opera (1969).

from the social order only to return us to it somewhat rejuvenated, bound to, and blinded by, its ideology. One might thus be tempted to ask if the process and activity of record collecting also conforms to this cycle of release from, and return to, a social order. Of course, all ideologies inform an understanding of popular culture, but we should ask whether this particular form of Marxist conjecture can actually define popular culture. The Frankfurt School made formal judgements based upon their own political beliefs because their belief systems suggested to them that capitalist culture was contrived. However, such statements were little more than contrivances in themselves.

Ideology is evidently an interesting word. By taking a contextually-apprised theory from a specific moment in twentieth-century history, statements have been de-contextualised, universalised, and turned into pronouncements of prolepsis (i.e. the assumption of a future act or development as if presently existing or accomplished). Defining popular culture via one ideological, authoritative framework could arguably even be dubbed a fallacy not doing justice to differing and discrete concepts. Different ideological frameworks can cause conflicts for many, for instance when the ideology by which we judge mass production (debased, retaining social order, masking reality) and art (enlightened, unveiling, educating) collide, an interesting situation arises. Many ideologically-bound theorists seem perplexed, dismissive even, of all mass-produced art, but perhaps this is inevitable if ideology is actually a system of language or thought in which certain words, ideas, values, and beliefs are put forward as if they were already defined, understood and agreed.

Walter Benjamin, an erstwhile colleague of Adorno, was concerned that there is a loss of "aura" when art is reproduced, rendering the reproduced artwork meaningless whilst at the same time damaging the original artwork. Perhaps one of the most influential essays on mass communication was written by this powerfully intelligent, young Jewish man, who took his own life in the shadow of what he thought was going to be the triumph of Nazi Germany. The essay "The Work of Art in the Age of Mechanical Reproduction"[29] considers the status of art through time and how it carries traces of history, of human passion and struggle. Such traces, he states, are beyond the tangible surface of the work. When this aura is lost via reproduction, the very function of art is reversed. Were Benjamin alive today one wonders what he might make of photocopiers

---

[29] Walter Benjamin, "The Work of Art in the Age of Its Technological Reproducibility: Second Version", in *Walter Benjamin: Selected Writing, Volume 3, 1935–1938*, eds. Howard Eiland and Michael Jennings (Cambridge: The Belknap Press of Harvard University Press, 1935), 101–133.

and scanners. But his point deserves our attention, for if we return to the mirror metaphor suggested in Chapter Two of this present book, it could be argued that most us want the mirror to flatter us with sameness and are prepared to indulge in a mass market in order to find products that do just that. Musically, however, it is no secret that from the Monkees to One Direction, pop culture has been shaped by market research conducted by (usually) men who think they know what we want to hear. If this is the case, one is forced to question the validity of music in modern society, where music (both classical and popular) is predominantly mechanically reproduced. But from a reception point of view, this is where the mirror begins to distort.

For us, the source of Benjamin's aura would surely lie in the artwork's use-value. While there are some very significant reasons for our love of (say) the Monkees, and some of them might be tied to the industry and the time in which they were produced, others seem to transcend historical specifics in very interesting ways, and appear to speak to a larger, more personal and yet general need that we have. In the midst of all of the mechanical reproduction we appear to be able to contemplate, to ruminate, to meditate. Walter Benjamin's great fear was that, driven by industrial reproducibility and profit, the variety and ritual element of art would be limited,[30] but he need not have worried: he saw the world as divided between classical and romantic understandings. But in terms of any ultimate meaning, a dichotomy such as this has very little use, for the world about us does not split up in that way. For some of us, beauty can be found in the circuitry of a mass-produced computer or in the downdraught of a cheaply cast motorcycle carburettor—"art" is everywhere. Throughout his work, Evan Eisenberg[31] heavily criticised Benjamin. Benjamin mostly discusses the visual arts with one spatial dimension, but in the case of music there are two such dimensions: space and time. While Edison's Talking Machine was indeed a way in to mass production for music, it could also reproduce an "event" in time that is not locked to its historical moment and can effectively become "timeless":

> For a moment the analogy wants to keep going. Doesn't an art event, such as a concert, have a ritual value that depends on its uniqueness? Strictly speaking, "event" is not a ritual category at all, precisely because it does imply uniqueness. To have ritual value an event must recur. In other words, it must not be an historical event at all, but an instance of something

---

[30] Walter Benjamin, *Illuminations* (London: Pimlico, 1999).
[31] Evan Eisenberg, *The Recording Angel: Music, Records And Culture From Aristotle To Zappa* (New Haven: Yale University Press, 2005).

timeless [...] each playing of a given record is an instance of something
timeless. The original musical event never occurred; it exists, if it exists
anywhere, outside history. In short, it is a myth, just like myths "re-
enacted" in primitive ritual. Repetition is essential to ritual, and exact
repetition is what it has always striven to attain.[32]

Time, as they say, is of the essence—most certainly when we come to
understand how mass production can reflect our place in time, not simply
the moment of the artefact's inception. That is one key to the opening of
the matrix that is record collecting. It might have been produced to make
us feel comfortable within an advanced capitalist society, but carries more
signifiers than any moment of manufacture could possibly carry. As
Eisenberg suggests, we do not normally crave the *same* dish over and over
again—in record-collecting terms there is no such thing as the same dish.
Bernard Gendron writes:

> I do not buy records like I buy cans of cleanser. If I like my first can of
> Comet I will be willing to buy another can of Comet that is qualitatively
> indistinguishable. But if I like my record of the Cadillacs' "Down the
> Road" I will not go out and buy another copy of it.[33]

Gendron goes on to establish that he will, however, be interested in
similar products to "Down the Road", and that in such instances, levels of
standardisation in the doo-wop genre will be a source of pleasure for the
consumer. And although this does not mean that the doo-wop collector
wants to, or in fact does, own multiple copies of a certain record, this
seems to be possible in specific circumstances—but the same can be
different (see further regarding this writer's use of Fleetwood Mac's
Rumours LP). Furthermore, if we were to undertake a closer examination
of the motivations of the record collector, as called for above, and then
study the interaction between collector and collection, one might find that
it is very active indeed. The relationship between the collector and the
collected items is complicated, but active choices are being made and are
carefully considered. This is evident in Graham Jones's[34] work where,
albeit briefly, he introduces us to "Bird Woman from Bath". Jones reports
that this woman has frequented a particular record shop (Duck, Son &
Pinker) for several years, and the only items she ever buys are items (CDs

---

[32] *ibid.*, 41.

[33] Bernard Gendron, "Theodor Adorno Meets the Cadillacs", in *Studies in
Entertainment*, ed. Tania Modleski (Indiana: University Press, 1986), 28.

[34] Graham Jones, *Last Shop Standing: Whatever Happened to Record Shops?*
(London: Proper Music Publishing, 2009).

and DVDs) with birds on the sleeve: she is less concerned with the genre of music she buys, and more with the bird on the sleeve. While one might consider this simply a "quirk", clearly this woman has considered her options and possessing sleeves with birds on them would appear to be important to her. The time and history of the mechanically-reproduced artefact does not therefore weigh us down as receivers. We do, in fact, create our own multifarious times and locations depending upon our levels and degrees of interactions with the artefact. This therefore means that the recording is not simply a moment in time effectively preserved in aspic (or plastic, in fact), but is a shifting signifier, a moving target—it is, in fact, a text.

Collectors are generally willing to pay large sums of money for records that will most likely either depreciate in value or never be re-sold in any case. But even so, it is still very tenuous to say that because collectors desire a specific record they neglect the bigger societal picture: we are not stupid, and we know that "things" are meant to flatter us. However, as indicated above, records can be collected for other reasons than simply the music they contain. The record may very well be a materialisation of a significant event or time in our lives, not the life of the record. The record can, plainly, be a representation of something very important for the collector that has very little to do with the "*music-as-art*" on it. Consider the birth of a new baby. Many new parents save newspapers from the day of birth, maybe as keepsakes for themselves or to show to the child once it is older. Whichever way, the papers are not saved because of the news they contain, as such, but rather because of the date they were published— as a snapshot of time in our lives, not the life of the newspaper. Certainly the news plays its part, but had the baby been born the next day, these earlier papers would have been disposed of (and hopefully recycled!).

Perhaps the most significant historical question to ask about these highly influential, yet possibly moribund, Frankfurt School critiques of popular culture concerns Storey's discussion on ideology: how does such ideological rhetorical space develop and consolidate to such an extent that it becomes an almost recognisable entity, i.e. the development of an elevated cultural observation post throughout the last half of the twentieth century? The moment we invoke certain words we are usually invoking a whole ideology. For example, when one speaks of (say) "science", one asserts certain propositions as though they were already defined and agreed. For example, the idea that science is a superior kind of knowledge and that its findings are the best, most reliable kinds of knowledge, is an ideological statement. Furthermore we should question, as does Storey, ideology's relationship to popular culture—in order to do this we must look at the kinds of ideology that surround the production and reception of art, which is what we have attempted to do here regarding the Frankfurt School. It becomes evident that one ideology competes with another, and that some are stronger than others. Maybe one reason for this is that ideology enables cultural surveillance and is part of the striving to deal with the fundamental problem of a "fit" between the world outside and our cognitions of the world. These two elements of signification are constantly being confused as "sense" and "reference", and Paul de Man argues that such confusion is precisely what we know as "ideology". De Man states "what we call ideology is precisely the confusion of linguistic with natural reality, of reference with phenomenalism".[35]

Countering Adorno

Instead of simply falling back on these negative, demeaning illustrations of music consumption, and in particular the record collector, let us consider what the creative and active act of popular music consumption via the artefact is. By doing so, we might discover that the music consumer makes conscious, sub-conscious, and active choices, while at the same time interacting with both music and artefact. As it stands, there are only a few close studies that aim to show the consumer or fan actively engaging with their fandom and, perhaps more importantly, creating something out of it. Whilst some ethnographic research such as the work of Ruth Finnegan[36] and Sara Cohen[37] may show active engagement with music alongside a creative expression, these again tend to highlight the activities of musicians. As a result, and possibly unintentionally, we are yet again given the impression that active engagement with music and a creative expression thereof is only possible by making music oneself. In effect, we are also implying that it is the *only* creative and active response to music—this, of course, is another ideological position in need of review.

---

[35] Paul De Man, *The Resistance to Theory* (Manchester: University Press, 1986), 11.
[36] Ruth Finnegan, *The Hidden Musicians: Music Making in an English Town* (Cambridge: University Press, 1989).
[37] Sara Cohen, *Rock Culture in Liverpool: Popular Music in the Making* (Oxford: Clarendon Press, 1991).

Rob Strachan,[38] however, does look at varying ways in which fans actively engage with musical artefacts. He notes how they express their enthusiasm through record production in his study on micro-independent record labels in the UK. These micro-labels are often run on a small financial margin where breaking even is considered a financial success, and the people involved have regular day jobs to support themselves. Strachan thus establishes that personal and aesthetic satisfaction is a major driving force for the owners/executors as there is very little—if any—financial gain involved. The running of a micro-independent record label undoubtedly requires a considerable amount of time and effort from the staff themselves, which usually consists of the owner/s alone having to find a product/artist they feel artistically engaged with and are willing to produce, taking the artist through production and then finding ways of distributing the product (including packaging of the product, such as sleeve design) and finding a space that facilitates all the needs of a micro-label. Hence the personal and aesthetic satisfaction gained must be considerable for these labels to continue to exist at all. Unfortunately Strachan does not pursue this line of enquiry into the purchase and use-value of the product any further. Doing so would have awarded us a better insight into the ways people can actively engage with, and creatively consume, a musical artefact and express their engagement creatively without necessarily turning them into musicians themselves. We do not have a clear picture of what satisfaction either the label owners or the customers felt, or how and where they began to differentiate between the personal and the aesthetic, and the product and the market. Sadly, Strachan merely brings us back to our starting point: the conflicts, debates and ideologies surrounding recorded music.

We have seen that these can be related to the ideologies surrounding art and technology. The power of widely-held ideological beliefs is so strong that at times we all find ourselves succumbing to that power. However, popular music artists know that what they do is not trivial (as suggested by Strachan), and most receivers find some kind of personal reflection in that work. Once we begin to consider that all forms of music—popular or otherwise—are valid methods of perceiving, explaining, and changing our world, we have to take responsibility for its creation and reception very seriously indeed. So, to perhaps consider Adorno specifically in relation to record collecting it is appropriate to seriously examine one of Adorno's important statements as a case study—

---

[38] Rob Strachan, "Micro Independent Record Labels in the UK: Discourse, DIY Cultural Production and the Music Industry", *European Journal of Cultural Studies* 10, no. 2 (2007): 245–265.

in this case, the one used as this chapter's sub-heading: "listeners are distracted from the demands of reality by entertainment which does not demand attention", in an attempt to seriously critique his ideology as a form of historically-bound rhetoric.

Adorno's Statement

Adorno's statement has five key words, each of which invites discussion: demands, reality, entertainment, attention, and distraction. "Reality" is presented to us as if it were a given, free from ideological selection or interpretation. Adorno implies that there is a uniform reality that all of us can grasp. "Demands" implies that once an agreed reality has been perceived, moral and practical imperatives necessarily flow from it: we must act in our own interests to cope with, or even to transform, reality. As we have already discussed, "entertainment" is here conceived of as something passive that reconciles us to an unexamined reality. The lack of demand for "attention" (concentration, thought) is such as to leave our critical and rational faculties in abeyance, so distracting us from the task of understanding reality and implementing its demands.

Adorno's comments are typically dressed up in Frankfurt School language, and this is a statement of a classical Marxist position on consciousness. According to this view, there is one reality for everyone, but there is also only one key to unlock it: the "true" (or "objective") consciousness that comes from applying historical materialism, scientific socialism, critical theory, or whatever name is given to the method. Lacking this method, a person's consciousness is either undeveloped (Marxists have often used the term "concrete", as distinct from the more laudable "abstract", in this sense[39]) or "false". For a Marxist, traditionally, the worst kind of "falsity" is to perceive reality as a given that is either unalterable, or which becomes altered independently of human intervention. What is regarded as a "true" consciousness is one which categorises reality in the appropriate way (via class, party, nation, economic interest *etc.*), and correctly identifies the agent of its beneficial transformation (class, party, nation *etc.*). Ultimately, of course, this ideological concept is, like Marxism itself, circular (or perhaps "non-falsifiable"). Reality, critical (or revolutionary) consciousness, critical (or

---

[39] Theodor Adorno, "On Popular Music", in *On Record: Rock, Pop and the Written Word*, eds. Simon Frith and Andrew Goodwin (London: Routledge, 1941), 301–314.

revolutionary) action and transformed reality form a clear loop into which no other factor is allowed to intrude.

Adorno's quoted statement is closely related to one of the great unsolved problems of Marxist-socialist ethics and practice. The socialist is both the doctor attempting to cure the ailing patient, and the heir waiting for his demise. The reformist wants any improvement on the *status quo* that brings immediate amelioration; the revolutionist want the situation to deteriorate so that his prognosis of the "crisis" of capitalism is duly confirmed and the dissatisfaction with reality stimulates mass action towards revolutionary change. Adorno's attack on entertainment and relaxation is a restatement, in the private sphere, of the assault on reformism and Social Democracy in the political sphere. The statement is also a reflection of an attitude, especially strong in the German Marxist tradition (heirs to Luther as well as Marx, we must remind ourselves), that education is a duty, and the suspension of education (in the shape of passive relaxation) a dereliction of this duty.

Popular music is therefore an easy target, and unforgivable in the apparently artificial sphere of popular music (in lyrics as well as music) is the monopoly of the "already known": the expression of romantic love devoid of any specific individualising features, the hackneyed I-IV-V-I harmonic progressions, the pseudo-individualisation of "different" pieces of music. Even within the Western art-music tradition, Adorno was unforgiving of all music that did not "stretch" the listener; his critiques of *avant-garde* forms could be as vehement as those applied to popular music. A trace of paranoia creeps into his critique of "undemanding" music. The "repressive tolerance" of the state, in Adorno's world-view, actually plans and plots the lulling of the masses into passivity by facilitating the production and consumption of undemanding music (and other cultural products). It does not actually prescribe "critical" art (Bach, Beethoven, Schoenberg, etc.): that is the "tolerant" side of its nature. It is "repressive" in so far as it does not promote "high" over "low" art, thereby allowing the forces of capitalism, in a free market, to produce the same outcome as formal repression would have done.

So with tragic irony in the light of his victimisation by German fascism, Adorno's views are coloured by their time, place and political tradition. They belong to the heroic, utopian age (between the World Wars) of socialism, where the "planned" society (with top-down control) was seen as necessary and beneficial. But they also carry with them the heavy baggage of German moralism and idealism, together with the urge towards self-improvement inherent in the Protestant ethic. The new lease of life that Adorno (and Marcuse) gained in the years after World War II arose from their clever adaptation of pre-war theories to take account of (relative) democracy, the welfare state and consumerism. One might suggest that, at heart, the worst element in Adorno's philosophy is its aristocratic-cum-intellectual disdain for the ordinary and the repeated. Its dogmatic authoritarianism, its monolithic insistence on *one* right way, its unconscious ethnocentricity, represent the most unpleasant side of the German intellectual tradition. Adorno provides, finally, an object-lesson in how *not* to bring academic thought to bear on culture. He has too little sense of uncertainty or ambivalence, and too little respect for fact, in their inconvenient diversity. His system, with its stock of keywords, such as the ones identified in the quotation, acts as a self-imposed vehicle for an intellectual "repression" of its own. Adorno is yet another of those once-famous thinkers who erected either a marvellously robust edifice or a quagmire (take your pick). A complex love-hate attitude towards the twentieth century saturates all such rhetoric.

As we have seen, Adorno's words are closely related to the interpretations of Walter Benjamin. For this writer, the combined images of these anti-popular diatribes are of tragedy, of twisted dialectics of inextricable contradictions: absolute change in the human condition can only manifest itself in the specificity of individuals and their personal encounters with the world, yet this can only happen under conditions of mass appreciation of change, and indeed revolution. Perhaps, above all, the drama of the popular can be seen to have been played out against a backdrop of Marxist and neo-Marxist thought such as we have seen. One might argue that the success of the popular derives from the tragedy of human inability to assimilate cultural products without a paranoid insecurity concerning material over-abundance. Such observations and concerns, while of genuine concern, have neglected to place enough emphasis on the unbounded resourcefulness of the human spirit in dealing with new forms of creativity. Once set in motion, recorded sound in particular developed its own logic and momentum as it spawned new multiple realities confronting individuals from both the outside world, and the inside one of our imagination.

The richness of recorded sound and popular culture is a result of the cultural abundance of individual human beings, not our cultural poverty. Even if some values had been turned into commodities, they would not have been rendered irrelevant. Adorno was wrong—even if the mechanisms of the popular-music market place took upon themselves the roles of judge and opinion-makers, they could never fully count themselves as the verifiers of values, for values remain in our minds, and in our own individual complex of relationships with artefacts. The individual pathway relating to the way our quality of existence can best be served preselects those items that will be of most use to us; they are not selected "for" us and we de-select as we select. We make such selections in such a way as to synchronize who we are and who we are becoming. It matters less whether the objects are made for us or made for a concept suggesting there are a billion people "like us". It is what we *do* with the objects in our lives that ultimately matters the most.

All in all, the non-physical nature of music means it is very prone to being the subject of rhetorical discussion regarding art and technology. Without the technological means, music remains non-tangible, and we can only experience it in concert or when attempting to perform it ourselves. But as we have seen, the possibility of reproduction also forces us to re-evaluate and question aspects of art. We have looked at two very influential debates on the topic, and will proceed by looking at two areas that become highly interesting in the light of this, and similar, debates. First, we shall look at music's tangibility in the form of the vinyl record. Vinyl is, indeed, an often fetishised sound carrier for a number of disparate reasons, but such fetishisation does not demean its potential for inventive change. The richness of object-based cultures is unlimited. Their frantic searches discussed elsewhere are not appropriations intended to replace lost meanings, but they are in fact enough to create new ones. We will now investigate some aspects of the record collector in society. This will perhaps give us at least a partial understanding of how and why record collectors are viewed as important archivists on the one hand, and dysfunctional loners on the other.

CHAPTER FOUR

CO-CREATORS OF MEANING (I):
RECORD COLLECTING AND MEDIATORS

"[…] the obsession with hearing and owning *all* available performances by a favorite [*sic*] artist borders on the pathological"
—Belk *et al.*, (1991), *Collecting in a Consumer Culture*

In the previous chapters we were looking at what is probably an old philosophical issue, the question of free will in human action as it is connected to the act of record collecting. It has been suggested that the cultures, languages and ideologies we are born into partly determine much of our own thought. As a consequence, questions have been asked about values and authenticities via popular artefacts and the apparent "low art" of sound recording intended for mass consumption. The market economy and commodity reproduction have also been considered, and it has been suggested, in spite of all of the negative associations attached to the latter, that our own individual subjectivities are perhaps relatively less affected by these factors than we might suppose, and that it can be suggested that the constructions of our identities are essentially a private process: an act, if you like, of "relative free will".

In framing our discussions via a metaphor of "reflection", I have suggested that this is a key to our understanding of reception processes associated with record collecting. But what has also emerged during the process of this research is that a philosophical question has additionally been brought to bear. What, for example, might be the relationship of our thoughts to what is actually out there? This is a question concerning the dualism of existence and thought raised in the previous chapter. When we look at ourselves, we are in the act of identifying ourselves. But when we see, we usually recognise things that we have "chosen" in the process of identifying the kind of image with which we feel at ease. The question, as it relates both to issues of identity and social mores, at least as far as record collecting is concerned, is twofold: how do we know whether our version of ourselves is close to the connotations of authenticity we have stored in our mind? And how approximate is this reflection to the way other people see us? In order to proceed with such an important discussion, the theories of the previous chapter concerning the record collector being a member of a "mass" need to be broken down into a consideration of one as an individual.

Further to this, it will be suggested that record collecting needs to be considered via our social interactions. The collector needs to be discussed in ways that also foreground the rules by which society appears to judge and value itself. We all appear to know power when we see it, and we know that money often equates to power, but to paraphrase and re-gender Marx, men (and women) do make their own history,[1] but they do not do it just as they please. There is undoubtedly an element of truth to this comment, but it is not such a forceful statement that it cannot be critiqued and/or modified. It would be true to say that social forces are also dialectic forces, therefore mass-market products such as records are intended not only to please us but, it could be argued, to retain a societal *status quo*. But if we study the individual collector it becomes clear that even multi-national companies do not have it all their own way. They must enter into a dialogue with us, and this dialogue is not always successful from a reception perspective where the receiver can read against the grain of meaning. Philosophical investigation tends to suggest that everything we do is in some sense already done. One might suggest that Marx proposes that our language is determined, that our thoughts are determined by language, that there are symbolic orders in society, and that we have no meaning outside our cultural contexts; this context is often further determined by the work-place.[2]

However, in order to fully understand how collecting popular culture can work to the meaningful advantage of the collector, perhaps one is required to adopt an oppositional point of view. It is important to raise the question of opposition, for sooner or later any co-creative act will be determined by where one stands in relation to the culture in which one finds oneself. Our personal interests will always decree the potential for framing what we do in artistic opposition to the dominant culture, especially if that culture decrees us to be somewhat deviant. This allows scope for personal opposition. One is reminded of the statement made by Liverpool Sound City chairman in 2012 that "even protest is a product". Perhaps even product can be protest?

---

[1] See, for example Marx's Dialectic Materialism from Das Kapital cited in Eugene Kamanka, ed., *The Portable Karl Marx* (London: Viking Penguin, 1983).

[2] Eugene Kamanka, ed., *The Portable Karl Marx* (London: Viking Penguin, 1983).

Case Study: Les

Record collecting as a hobby or practice is an activity the collector can chose to keep private or separated from other people in his or her physical vicinity. In *Sonata for Jukebox*,[3] the aforementioned Geoffrey O'Brien has suggested that a world exists within which recorded sound plays out some very specific roles. However, the specificity of these roles can also be shared and the degree to which the record collector shares his or her world differs considerably from collector to collector. Some record collectors may choose to share their record collecting practices only with fellow collectors in record shops or fairs or, more recently, in an online community. Others may choose to share their collection only within a certain mind-set created by themselves, and for themselves. For some, over a period of time, both might be possible and productive. For instance Les, one collector drawn to the attention of this writer, keenly attested that records were required at specific times of the day not simply (or even) to merely listen to, but to remind him of a particular mental space that he occupied when wishing to "be himself". Les had struggled in recent years after a rather debilitating stroke and had become somewhat house-bound after having given up his job. Strokes, being a serious medical condition, do have a tendency to change people: whilst some can "give up", others chose a different path and can instead re-discover things that had previously been let go. Les used to like to walk, but could no longer do so without some pain. However, he also liked to recall a period of time when he was an active walker and the styles of music that reminded him of these times had now become extremely important. People are faced with their own mortality when they have a stroke, and so all aspects of life become extremely important: new meanings are taken on as memory, mood, and associations are reflected.

Les is from Liverpool, and has always been a record collector—at least since he started to earn money in the late 1960s. His interests have always been broad but he has tended, by and large, to purchase American music. His father was a Hank Williams fan, and this initially was a great influence upon him, particularly the "Luke the Drifter"[4] songs recorded by Williams. Les was also interested in British rock 'n' roll for a while—particularly the

---

[3] Geoffrey O'Brien, *Sonata for Jukebox: An Autobiography of my Ears* (New York: Counterpoint, 2005).
[4] Early in his career, Williams developed the habit of singing preaching-type songs under the name of Luke the Drifter, a *nom de plume* for an idealized character who went across the country preaching the gospel, and doing good deeds, while Hank Williams, the drunkard, cheated on women, and was cheated on by them in return.

work of Johnny Kidd and the Pirates, but this tends to be an exception, for he confesses to being a self-proclaimed "American-ophile", and he continues to be interested in a variety of US genres from different historical periods. He informed this writer:

> Is it odd? I don't know—I'd suggest "not really" really but the thing is, I like to listen to music not from the era I am in. This often means I play a game of catch-up—for example, I currently listen to a lot of late 1990s blues rock like early Joe Bonamassa, but I didn't listen to it at the time. In the 1970s I listened to Johnny Kidd—that kind of thing. So I suppose I'm a bit of a recidivist, although I do come to appreciate music over a longer period of time than its time-span seems to allow. In a funny kind of way I see this as being in opposition. You know, "you tell me to listen to this now, but I'll make up my own mind about it, thank you very much"—that kind of thing. I've just got into Destiny's Child, for example.[5]

However the last time he had directly involved himself in actually collecting rather than listening and purchasing (he makes an important distinction, here) was during the mid-1990s when the "loungecore"[6] revival was at its peak. He does not even collect music of great rarity, but at that time confined himself to a genre of music which was considered by rock collectors and connoisseurs alike to be "uncool", and his particular favourite was a singer by the name of Lani Hall, the former singer with Sergio Mendes and Brasil '66.[7] So the meanings record collecting has,

---

[5] Interview with Les, May 2013.

[6] Loungecore: this was a retrospective "genre" name for Easy Listening music, mostly stemming from the mid-to-late 1960s and early-to-mid 1970s. It is often associated with orchestral- and/or Latin-sounding music with a "groove" that can be danced to. However, it also has film music associations, and carries "uncool" tropes that in the more post-modern environments of the 1990s became "cool". Some influences stem from the ambient house genre, which was effectively dance music for sitting down. Sergio Mendes and Brasil '66, Burt Bacharach, Alan Haven, and assorted types of library music all became popular during this time. One example of loungecore success was the Mike Flowers Pops' version of Oasis' "Wonderwall" in 1995 and 1996 respectively.

[7] Interview with Les, April 2013: Sergio Mendes formed the band Brasil '66 when he replaced his two Brazilian vocalists with the Americans Lani Hall and Janis Hansen (who replaced Bibi Vogel) in 1966. They recorded the single *Mas Que Nada* for Herb Alpert's *A&M* label, which became an incredibly successful hit. The group's line-up remained the same until 1968, after which a number of changes in personnel took place. The group, however, continued to record and release material on a regular basis, which resulted in great fame for Mendes. Hall eventually left the group in the early 1970s to pursue a solo career.

together with its associations with physicality and personal esteem and identity are highly complex, and deal as much with areas within the realms of human psychology as much as they do with industrial notions of mass production and manipulation. So Les's, personal story, "from the off" as it were, reminds us that even though we might be caught up in web of social and cultural practices that enforce great power, at a fundamental level all power generates resistance. In a sense, the generation from which Les emerged was at least a relative culture of resistance (see later regarding *Vertigo Records*). Even in his 60th year Les feels via his listening practices an urge to resist, reinvent, overthrow, or at the very least question the structures of power:

> Yes indeed; it's not that I am hard left or hard right—I see all of that stuff for what it is—voices of authority from donkey's years ago that can't keep up with the pace of change. For me there have been a few important features of the twentieth century that have utterly liberated us from the "old ways", and yet none of them are treated seriously enough, because the old ways and the voices of authority still dominate: TV was groundbreaking—I learnt almost everything I know from the telly in the '60s, recorded sound also changed everything, sound on film changed everything, and sometimes I think above all, photography changed everything. I was looking at an old picture of my old mum the other day—there she was, about eight years of age waving to me from the late 1920s, 30 years before I was born, and with her were other kids I didn't know, and they were waving at me too! Am I a fool to think that this stuff is immortal? I think not.[8]

One might argue that all post-World War II youth cultures show how difficult it has been for competing business concerns to hold a dialogue. Businesses might appeal to you as a unique individual, a rebel, a romantic. But via this appeal they really want you to be ordinary enough to purchase the same materials that millions of others purchase. But such flattery does not always work, for oppositional dialogues emerge from the consumer, concerning identity.

Communality

More recently, online record-collecting communities, most notably online forums, have flourished with networks of communication, information and kinship, creating a virtual community either separated from, or in some cases integrated with, one's non-virtual world. It is evident that the nature

---

[8] Interview with Les, April 2013.

of record collecting allows for both the inclusion and exclusion of differing rituals associated with collecting (and indeed non-collecting) mind-sets. In fact, one of the most interesting questions to ask is, perhaps, whether and how record collectors actively chose to include or exclude others from their activities. The above-cited collector suggested that at first his connection to the work of Lani Hall was "a very private affair" which he did not want to share with others, did not wish to discuss, and did not want to think of himself as being part of a community. However, via the discovery of Lani Hall's website, he did inadvertently find that he was connected to other fans of the artist, and had effectively become part of a community "almost by accident".[9]

Once this had occurred, he informed this writer that he was actually "relieved" to be part of a fan-base, and felt that he was less isolated than he had previously thought. It is interesting to consider this issue of isolation when on the one hand Les felt that his daily rituals were imbued with a relationship to the recordings of Lani Hall (he at no time suggested that his relationship was "with" the singer), and concomitantly the broadening of his interests in company, as it were, with others from around the world. It might be argued that society does still not accept the fact that what appear to be perfect strangers, who do not physically meet, can be supportive of a deeply personal daily ritual. As far as record collecting is concerned, one possible answer to this might be because of the judgemental attitudes record collectors often experience; it is not therefore deemed possible or tangible that people can be both intensely private and genuinely collective via the act of collecting mass produced wares, and presumably "kidding themselves" via subscribing to an online community, although one might argue that this is what one example of co-creation involves. There are ceremonies of the solitary in which, as human beings, we are probably all involved. People are inclined to observe such rituals, and if a record has a special place in one's life one does not cheapen it by playing it at random. If you care deeply about a singer you do not ask that singer to accompany you in every act of the day. The singer provides you with significant ceremonies, which are often singular, and at times solitary, and this appeared to be the case regarding Les. However, as human beings we are also communal, and if we can commune with others who also agree that one should not cheapen the artist by playing recordings at random, then the physical act of communing with others can also be seen as part of that ritual.

---

[9] Interview with Les, April 2013.

Les informed the writer that while turning the radio off as it played The Beatles might be excusable, turning it off for Sergio Mendes was not. He actually related this story to Lani Hall herself, via her website,[10] and the singer personally responded to him, thanking him for giving her an insight into how her voice was appreciated. This had been done through part of a communal blog that was fed into YouTube, and so other fans responded in a similar manner. For Les, then, private passions and rituals also involved—at least eventually, and with some persuasion—an involvement not with cyberspace *per se* but with real people *through* cyberspace in which the music provided him with the opportunity to tell him something about the union of opposites: i.e. the public and private spheres, the solitary and the communal, the nostalgic and the contemporary, or the genre-based oppositions involved in loungecore music; in a way, the musically deceased (i.e. "the sixties") and the living appreciation and fandom created via the mechanical and the aesthetic. Through his so-called solitary isolation as a record collector, Les was able to reconsider his role in this co-creative universe where nobody has the first or last word, least of all himself or Lani Hall:

> I was really chuffed, to be honest; it made me feel really a lot better to get a reply from her—and so quickly. She had been very unwell herself, unable to move out of her bedroom, by all accounts, for quite a long time, so I felt a sense of empathy with her. And then the community of people on-line really came to grow on me. Not at first—I thought they were all a bit "sad". But that was my old so-called political ideas getting to the fore. Why should they be "sad"? They were like me—they cared for the music, were concerned about Lani—and then I found they were asking after me, too. Well, that was really great, because it made me reconsider just about everything, really—who I was, what I was doing—all through the power of a few old LPs and a computer—it was magic, really and I'm sure it all helped in my recovery, I'm convinced it did.[11]

Meanings, values, authenticities are thus a complex series of issues, and once again record collecting needs to be considered as a matrix[12]—in this case, as a deeply personal matrix that helps to arbitrate the reality of the individual. As previously suggested, any kind of matrix brings into focus what was previously unfocused, and in this example, an at times supposedly solitary case, it becomes evident that if we search for meaning

---

[10] https://lanihall.herbalpertpresents.com/.
[11] Interview with Les, May 2013.
[12] If one, for once, wishes to break free from, and question, the stereotype of the record collector that has long been allowed to burden the practice.

in record collecting, we are almost immediately provided with a series of complex "matrixes". Record collecting provides the opportunity to enjoy what might be described as the art of cultural and social diagnoses at perhaps its most pure. Les as a record collector offers a combination of theoretical stringency and practical common sense, which turns into a matrix of praxis via co-creativity. Les cannot write or read a word of music, nor has he ever created a piece of music in his life, and yet the co-creative potential of praxis has given him the opportunity, via his collecting, to understand not simply the pleasures of the artefact or text, but the relevance of his own existence. The matrix, therefore, of several well-played, well-thumbed (i.e. far from pristine) Lani Hall recordings has given him the opportunity for rehabilitation and communication, and a redefinition that other forms of aesthetic practices may not have facilitated at the right time or in the right place:

> I felt really destabilised and debilitated by the stroke—you know, I wasn't an old man when it happened! And it took ages to get myself right mentally. But when I started playing all of that stuff on my player, and then I made a catalogue and archived it a bit (still haven't finished, mind you!), and came across records I'd forgotten I'd bought from car boot sales in the '90s. Things started to make sense for lots of different reasons. It made me happy for a start—so that was good, it reminded me of good walks and good friends, it came to get me up onto the web and buy a few Mendes albums from eBay that I didn't have—that was fun—bidding and waiting to see if I was successful! I started using my left hand a little to help clean the albums so that was also physically therapeutic. There were all sorts of ways that the collection really helped me focus properly on myself—it was a revelation.[13]

Despite the above information, academics researching (general) collecting hint at scepticism towards the *record* collector: "the obsession with hearing and owning *all* available performances by a favorite [*sic*] artist borders on the pathological".[14] This comment may in itself appear innocent enough, but on further examination it is evident that Belk *et al.* do not understand what the practices of record collecting entail—as with the example of Les, above. In this example, the authors have failed to realise that each individual reception can be a unique experience, even

---

[13] Interview with Les, May 2013.
[14] Russel W. Belk *et al.*, "Collecting in a Consumer Culture", in *Highways and Buyways: Naturalistic Research from the Consumer Behaviour Odyssey*, ed. Russel W. Belk (Association for Consumer Research, 1991), 178–215, emphasis in the original.

when a collector might have several editions of the same performance or piece. For instance, this writer recently (April 2013) acquired[15] another vinyl copy of Fleetwood Mac's *Rumours* LP. Despite already owning vinyl and CD copies, and also having access to the album via both Spotify and YouTube, there was still a distinct need to get a hold of another vinyl copy (in good condition, and preferably with the lyrics sheet). The CD copy had in fact been bought in an attempt to avoid buying another vinyl copy of the album, but it failed to fill the "void". This is because the new vinyl copy signified something distinctly different from the first vinyl copy.

The album had first come to bear significance at a deeply personal level after malicious rumours had reportedly circulated amongst colleagues where I had a part-time job during my studies. This personal incident related to what was reportedly part of the conception behind the *Rumours* album, where the artists were, unbeknownst to each other, effectively "having a go" at one another. There was an initial catharsis of listening to the album repeatedly, following which its meaning began to change for me. Around the same time, coincidentally, it was also re-released on 180g vinyl to celebrate its 35th anniversary, which also created a new interest in the album for the general public. In any case, the album came to change me, and I therefore needed a new copy that reflected this and related to the new me. Another copy of the 1977 *Rumours* LP was ordered through eBay, and its arrival symbolised a renewal of me as well. This is not a case of music listography, whereby one's life can be set out by playlists, rather it is a case of catharsis and catalysts. Whilst my two vinyl copies may appear to someone without any investment in either the *Rumours* LP or vinyl records generally to be the same artefact—after all, the music is the same, both are from 1977 and the product is essentially the same "as such"—the two records are very different to me, and carry with them very different meanings, thus *they are not the same*. As Eisenberg might suggest, this is where "the student of Walter Benjamin will be on edge. Mechanical reproduction, he will object, destroys the ritual value of the work of art, its 'aura'. How can a cheap copy of art, like a poster or a record, figure in a ritual?"[16] This failure to understand the pleasure of the collector, one might argue, stems from society's bracketing and misunderstanding of what it regards as a level of social deviance.

---

[15] It was graciously purchased for me as I bemoaned the fact I did not trust eBay, which in itself provides an interesting facet to my collecting—perhaps, unlike Les, I did not share a confidence in this particular vendor.

[16] Evan Eisenberg, *The Recording Angel: Music, Records And Culture From Aristotle To Zappa* (New Haven: Yale University Press, 2005), 40.

The Relativity of Deviance

Record collecting is not necessarily or overtly described as deviant behaviour, but many people do tend to believe that deviance is an objective reality, and that this objective reality needs only to be identified in order that we may understand it. Others insist that deviance can be defined in a subjective way, which relies very heavily on the interpretation of society by the person described as deviant. Thirdly, others view deviance and conformity as labels placed upon people by those with the power to do so. These three viewpoints, it could be argued, illustrate the relativity of deviance.[17] How it can be applied almost at random, rather like both a prescription and a proscription to those who fit, is therefore of relevance to the researcher interested in record collecting. From a broad sociological perspective, no act is intrinsically deviant. Instead, deviance is socially defined through social judgements relative to particular norms and values. Issues to do with collecting, and even the mediation of collecting, are therefore often viewed through these broad collective judgements, which are then taken for granted.

The so-called collectivity of such judgements is taken "as read" because it is part of a syndrome of societal collectivity. In other words, because lots of people say it, it must be true. Many societal norms do not take account of mental anxieties. It might be argued that cultures which develop deviancy as oppositional tropes systematically refuse to alleviate such anxieties of experience; paradoxically, deviancy is used as an example of the "other" not to be ventured into. As a result, notions of who or what deviancy is appear clear cut. But social life is rarely divided into neat dichotomies (deviancy/conformity in this instance). While it might be comforting to think that the "good guys" know best, and the deviants are either locked away or lock themselves away (or mingle with people of a similar ilk), such issues are not so easily defined.

It is therefore important to both consider and understand that deviancy does not simply refer to something necessarily "out of the ordinary". People do out of the ordinary things all the time, whether that be collecting records or winning the Nobel Prize. Their behaviours may be statistically rare, but people nevertheless do lots of things that are statistically rare. In this case, deviancy is an ideological statement created by society's need to legislate. Yet logically we can see that such ideas cannot really deal with human activity, for these are really a web of meanings that can never be

---

[17] William E. Thompson and Joseph V. Hickey, *Society in Focus* (New York: HarperCollins, 1994).

held still, meanings that are constantly evolving and transforming. The word deviant therefore actually refers to a nothingness around which societal judgemental values revolve. Lawson and Appignanesi suggest that if one deconstructs such ideologies we approach the methods of post-modern deconstructionists such as Jacques Derrida:

> The outcome of Derrida's critique is the denial of singular meaning. Meaning is radically unstable in that it is a function of the play of other meanings. Not only does language not refer to reality, but there is no presence for language to refer to. Derrida argues that it is the assumption of presence that has dominated philosophy and thought. In denying presence Derrida is denying that there is a present, both in spatial and in a temporal sense. The corollary of there being no single meaning is that there is no single reality. There is no present.[18]

Yet in order to see how other people define deviance and odd behaviour, four essential elements need to be added to our understanding of how others view recorded sound collecting as a matrix of "otherness". These four elements are norms, acts, actors and audience. If we consider record collectors within such a definition, we can come to understand them far more and how they are considered to be in some people's view out of the norm. Such norms are the guidelines that govern our thoughts, beliefs and behaviour, and can be both prescriptive in attempting to tell people what to do, or proscriptive, indicating what one should not do.[19] It could be suggested that there are at least three types of norms. The first of these is described by sociologists as folkways,[20] which are informal norms that reflect cultural traditions and guide our everyday interactions. Secondly, mores are also informal, but salient, norms that are closely linked to value-judgements about the rightness or wrongness of things. Mores usually have moral connotations and are often codified into the third styles of norms—namely, laws. Laws are often used to create a distinction between deviance and crime. So when acts are defined as being deviant—even casually in relation to the record collector (in other words "he or she's a bit odd or weird")—they do not automatically mean that a person who might be described as the actor will be considered a criminal, but they are considered to be a deviant if they do not subscribe to all of the above norms.

---

[18] Hilary Lawson and Lisa Appignanesi, *Dismantling Truth: Reality in the Postmodern World* (London: Weidenfeld & Nicholson, 1989), xxv.

[19] William E. Thompson and Joseph V. Hickey, *Society in Focus* (New York: HarperCollins 1994).

[20] *ibid.*

In addition to the idea of actors playing a part and acting in a certain way, there is also the importance of the audience, as previously mentioned. In our case, the audience is very significant. The reaction of an audience in relationship, or as a form of society, is a very significant area in terms of record collecting. In small societies it is often easier to find a consensus of what constitutes deviance. In large societies, however, it is more problematic, as the population is larger and, as such, one might argue, contains more "samples". Thus, other groups with other values can appropriate what large social societies regard as deviance. It is this basic appropriation trope that needs to be considered when we think about the co-creative meaning(s) surrounding the record collector. For members of the social group and their regard for norms, which includes folkways, mores and laws, a reaction to deviancy based upon homogenous concepts may be created.

This leaves space for other people in that society with different sets of values to consider such values and authenticities from a completely different perspective. During the twentieth century many norms have been created in society from two important perspectives. On the one hand is advanced capitalism, whereby the folkways, mores and laws exist within the system, yet have a preceding moral judgement which predates capitalism and has its roots in religion nevertheless remaining independent from religion. It is perhaps from this position that the work of Evan Eisenberg[21] is best understood when he discusses the possibility of record collecting being essentially "anti-capitalist"—for what one apparently sees is a form of aesthetic beauty being stored by the collector in full knowledge of its production methods, notwithstanding its inherent beauty.

On the other hand, as we have seen, judgements and values drawn from the Marxist tradition suggest that any potential for co-creativity resides within, and is a reflection of, a community. Furthermore, even a record as a product can be seen as a form of social control, inasmuch as the record actually follows the tradition of capitalism that merely enforces sanctions and imposes false values. Both positions have contributed in their own way to value-judgements concerning popular music, tradition, the artefact as authentic, and thus the collecting of that artefact. Each norm in its own way therefore governs ideas and proceeds to define people as either within or outwith the systems from which the norms have emerged. This understanding of what might in many cases be described as a benign deviance is absolutely vital when we come to understand the mediator and

---

[21] Evan Eisenberg, *The Recording Angel: Music, Records And Culture From Aristotle To Zappa* (New Haven: Yale University Press, 2005).

collectors of sound recordings. Within both of the existing cultures of the twentieth century, capitalism and Marxism, the act of collecting on the one hand what is merely a product, and on the other hand a political artefact designed to illicit a state of false consciousness, can be seen through such lenses to be deviance.

In the case of this book, of course, variables need to be included in order to understand such issues sociologically, and a further four issues need to be taken into account which are highly relevant to the case of record collecting: time, place, situation and culture. As regards time, the post-war era is a very important foundational premise from which society understands the importance of the record, notwithstanding the earlier history discussed in this work. The post-war era creates the historical fact that today's conformists can become tomorrow's deviants. One could argue that the history of record collecting is a history of not only the recording of sound, but a documenting of social deviance throughout the remaining decades of the twentieth century. Some might argue that jazz, folk, rock, punk and dance, to but name a few, are all areas of apparent social deviance, and yet one can quite clearly see that the recordings involved in such important genres are now important historical primary source materials of social change. Similarly, place is very significant. For example, although the concert hall is, and remains, central to many people's listening practices, the significance of the domestic environment and the hardware associated with that environment (e.g. a turntable, boom box, CD player, docking station, etc.), together with the software on which sound is recorded, tell a fascinating story about the rise of liveable, comfortable and amenable space. The so-called deviance of record collecting arguably informs one as much about the rise of suburbia as it does about the deviance of popular music genres.

Historical and cultural situationing are also important to consider. The way that listening tastes have emerged as a consequence of recorded sound can be described as revolutionary (remember, for instance, Edison's original intentions for the phonograph and Les's comments within this chapter), and yet society appears to have absorbed such revolution into its social norms as easily as it has moved on into the twenty-first century. For example, one can now look at the Mod subculture as a folkway and take an interest in the Mod's record collection as a signifier of time, place, situation and culture, whereas in 1964 most Mods were regarded as folk devils around which there were, according to Stanley Cohen, moral panics.[22] Record collecting, therefore, is not a deviant activity if studied from the above three areas. However, perhaps no other variable is more influential in defining so-called deviance than the cultural context in which this so-called deviancy is defined. This is not to say that one needs to strictly examine the social context of the so-called deviant, although it is important, but rather the context of those doing the defining. Whilst it may appear obvious, it is often neglected, but becomes incredibly apparent when the people who are being defined, and the people who are doing the defining, come into contact. Those who understand the significance of ethnography will always inform us that working in the "field" is perhaps of the greatest significance of all, and yet despite the significance of this social anthropology, most critics of popular culture do not conduct field work. It is hardly surprising, then, that so much attention is focused on what one might describe as an "Adornian" way, on the apparently odd or deviant.

The answers to understanding attitudes towards the collector can in many cases be found in either the modes of enquiry or the lack of any such enquiry at all. Interestingly, Pierre Bourdieu uses the world "field" in a different way,[23] yet one that also informs us of the significance of popular culture from the bottom up rather than via deviance. According to Bourdieu, a field generates meaning, and one can quite clearly see that as far as the cultural capital of record collecting is concerned (which will be discussed shortly), collecting exists within an interesting "field of play" where different manoeuvres, networks, similarities and differences can be discovered and unpacked. If this is indeed the case one is provided with an early indication that record collecting, whilst sharing *some* similarities, is also fundamentally different from other types of collecting, meaning it cannot be studied in an identical manner, and the same principals applied to other types of collecting cannot simply be applied directly to record collecting. One stamp collector based in Chester informed this writer:

> I don't think stamp collecting has anything to do with record collecting. Obviously we all collect something, but my feelings about record collecting are linked to a dislike of the counter-culture from which a lot of it comes. It seems to me that record collecting is a product of the counter-culture, and that's something that I've never had anything to do with. I worked at the Post Office for 40 years and was proud to do so, so my

---

[22] Stanley Cohen, *Folk Devils and Moral Panics: The Creation of the Mods and Rockers* (London: MacGibbon and Kee, 1980).
[23] *Cf.* Pierre Bourdieu, *The Field of Cultural Production* (Cambridge: Polity, 1993).

stamp collecting is not only a hobby, but part of my life and part of a system that I greatly admired while I was working. Record collecting to me seems opposed to that, and it's dubious in the extreme.[24]

In contrast to the above, and on the same day, former proprietor of "The Vinyl Grooveyard" in Chester, Dave House informed this writer:

Record collecting has got nothing to do with stamp collecting. When I first started collecting as a kid I must say that I was a bit obsessed with Chris Farlowe. But when I came to finally own all of his singles and I'd actually met him as a consequence, it felt like all my work was done. In fact Farlowe himself acknowledged me as probably the only person he knew in the world with more Chris Farlowe records than Chris Farlowe. In fact, he came out with that old hoary expression that went something like, "he knows more about me than me." Over the years, however, the record collecting and dealing has basically become a communal activity where we talk, swap stories, occasionally records, and drink too much—that's probably why the shop failed in the long run. Stamp collecting always seems to me to be an isolated experience—some guy looking through the lens of a magnifying glass at a postmark and stamp... what fun![25]

Les, my own case study, tended to concur with the above:

I've never really collected anything in my life, apart from records—and even then I don't really consider myself a "collector", although I do like the idea that I might be considered a social deviant—that's good, in my book—it makes me feel that I am not contributing to the industry's or society's definitions of me. I think I might have kept my toy cars for a while, but they were all battered in any case and ended up in the junk shop, and I started taking more of an interest in real cars by the time I was a teenager. I bought, but didn't keep, American comics, never kept a British comic in my youth because I thought they were rubbish—all Desperate Dan and World War Two. I'm not interested in football, so programmes don't come into it. So I suppose am different from other collectors—and funnily enough, even though I love my records, if they all disappeared tomorrow I might shed a tear but not much more... but I like the idea I am a social deviant! I remember a rock band called the Social Deviants, weren't they something to do with Mick Farren? I bet they are quite collectible![26]

It is no less difficult to disentangle the reasons why certain aspects of society react to a form of change than it is to understand why a particular

---

[24] Kevin, former Post Office worker and stamp collector, May 2013.
[25] Interview with Dave House, ex *The Vinyl Junkyard*, Chester Market, May 2013.
[26] Interview with Les, April 2013.

mode of behaviour or attitude emerged in the first place, prevailed for a time, and then became categorised. Society's relationship to record collecting continues to be highly complex and is one which is both driven and analysed by and from a variety of different rhetorical dialectics concerning power and/or the lack of it. The crucial question to ask, therefore, is not simply the trans-functional one of why popular music record collecting has been viewed in some respects as an "aberrant" and an abhorrent activity, but rather how such a common feature of human activity comes to be regarded through time as at the very least marginal, and at times the activities of the obsessive—compared to metal detecting and train spotting—which in their own ways are equally valid forms of behaviour, but also suffer stigmatisation.

Attitudes towards record collecting are both curious and long-standing. Historically, popular music recorded sound has helped to build modern society, its visage has often been at least partially hidden by rhetoric that denies its authenticity through several interweaving strands of socio-political thought concerning the manipulative tendencies of the record industry, mass culture and ideological rhetoric. This is not simply a matter of political bias, however, but can also be attributed to the use of stereotypical modes of presentation which virtually deny the possibility of the music consumer being awarded a broader, and perhaps an even more serious, visage within the underlying social content and context of what was being reported. Thus one must ask, what do most people base their understanding of the record collector on—their own experiences, or someone else's relaying of "information" about record collectors?

Mediation

As Newbold et al.[27] point out, if the average person were to conduct an experiment on themselves to establish how often, when and how they came in contact with media throughout the day by simply making a note of each occasion, they would probably be surprised at the end of the day to find just how many occasions have been noted down. Media has, in one way or another, infiltrated most facets of our lives and become ubiquitous. In some instances people even carry running news updates with them throughout their day on their smartphone, which automatically alerts them to breaking news. New technologies have allowed media to take on new forms, in turn perhaps making it more difficult to clearly define what

---

[27] Chris Newbold, Oliver Boydt-Barrett, and Hilde van den Bulck, eds., *The Media Book* (London: Arnold, 2002).

media in today's society fully entails or fulfils. It is nevertheless important to acknowledge the importance of media in our lives as it plays such a huge part in it. Thus understanding media, how it is created, and by whom, also allows us to gain a better understanding of how we are influenced by it.

One important aspect regarding media, often mentioned or discussed in popular music studies, is the so-called gatekeepers or, more recently, cultural intermediaries, which will be the preferred term in this instance as scholars, such as the aforementioned Brocken[28] and Barnard,[29] have recently begun to favour it as a much more suitable name for the role/activity. These cultural intermediaries (often the "who?") have a very important role, as they are the ones relaying information to the audience and consumer. Cultural intermediaries, journalists in their most obvious form, have the opportunity to push their opinions and feelings upon the consumer. Their choice of words and imagery can become very influential, and they can sometimes even take on the role as auteurs. In such instances, the cultural intermediary is rarely questioned and allowed to "reign free". Some might wonder why this is a problem at all—we often allow ourselves to believe that journalists are objective. For one, it matters because the cultural intermediaries can control not only how they present certain things or people, but can also choose to completely exclude issues or, in our case, music acts or products they do not deem worthy. Thus the consumer only experiences what they are allowed to expose themselves to—a very Adornian sentiment; "He becomes the discoverer of just those industrial products which are interested in being discovered by him. He brings nothing home which would not be delivered to his house".[30]

Journalists, whilst perhaps being the cultural intermediaries we most often come across, are not, however, the only cultural intermediaries. Producers, editors, managers, even CEOs, can function as cultural intermediaries—even the academic. Additionally, cultural intermediaries can have positive functions and effects. By sifting through cultural output and making a selection for the consumer, the consumers do not need to do all the painstaking work themselves. The fact remains that there is a continuous and never-ending production of, for instance, music. For the consumer to sort through all the music available to them would be a

---

[28] Michael Brocken, *Other Voices: Hidden Histories of Liverpool's Popular Music Scenes 1930s–1970s* (Farnham: Ashgate, 2010).
[29] Stephen Barnard, *On the Radio: Music Radio in Britain* (Berkshire: OUP, 1989).
[30] Theodor Adorno, "On the Fetish-Character of Listening and the Regression of Listening", in *Essays on Music*, ed. Richard Leppert (Berkley: University of California Press, 1938), 309.

daunting task. By finding a cultural intermediary that has a similar taste to our own we can allow them to do an initial cull for us. This relationship thus saves the consumer time, and allows the preferred music to reach a receptive audience before the consumer tires of endlessly searching. Media is, however, as already stated, becoming an all the more ubiquitous feature in our daily lives, and whilst most of us would probably accept printed media as media, it may be more difficult for some to regard films—or indeed the internet in some cases—as such. However, the purpose of media is to convey ideas, ideologies and perspectives that influence people on events or texts and—as will be discussed in subsequent chapters—films and documentaries can play a very significant role in this process.

Thus, in today's society, many things are brought to us through the mediation of others. The image of the record collector is no different, and is most often brought to us through the mediation of journalists, directors, screenwriters or novelists, sometimes even academics (however rarely). In the case of record collectors in particular, the author has found this is because people generally do not often reflect on—sometimes do not even know of—the record collectors around them, and as such do not realise they have concrete, relatable examples. Whatever the case may be we can, based on this, make the assumptions that (i) society in general knows little of the process(es) of record collecting, yet (ii) it is still a prevalent enough activity for people to have an opinion on, and thus (iii) we can conclude that these opinions are being shaped or broadcast from somewhere—*what* or *who* is responsible for promoting, creating and/or influencing these opinions? As indicated previously, the author has typically found that, when prompted, people initially have a negative view of record collectors, but on further consideration and discussion of the processes of record collecting discover that they may even know a record collector. In most cases the initial negative attitude is very quickly replaced by a much more positive and open attitude. This change, then, allows the researcher to question what contributed to the initial negative attitude in the first place. Again—what and who has come to shape their opinion of the record collector, and for what purpose? More generally speaking, one might also want to consider how record collectors fare against other collectors in society by examining if and how people hold the same attitudes to collectors consistently, and why the attitudes may differ between different groups of collectors—that is to say, are stamp collectors, record collectors and train spotters all viewed in same light, or are there discrepancies one can point to?

Whilst there are many answers to the question of "who?" generally, in terms of media this particular work will focus on either printed media, through magazines, journals and books, or film and documentaries. Media can, however, encompass many more formats such as, but not limited to, advertising, online newspapers, blogs or radio, an important point to keep in mind. It must also be acknowledged that media alone is not solely responsible for creating an image of, in this case, the record collector, but due to limitations this work as a whole will only tackle the media and academia's role in constructing an image, and the reader is invited to pursue consideration other aspects independently. This work has discussed the shortcomings of record collecting/collectors from a Frankfurtian, Marxist-inspired perception, as well as considering the collector as a social deviant. How these ideas have in turn come to influence the media is also of great significance. One might suggest that the marginal status of the record collector is part of a broader sphere concerning music-related subculture and counter-cultures. Such expressions have a long history, and the theory of marginality is another way of considering how the record collector has effectively been placed at the periphery of society, despite many existing firmly within the rubrics of society. It is no accident that the punk counter-culture of the 1970s turned adult respectability upside down, and that this source of cultural variation was heavily centred upon a particular recorded sound format, the 45rpm single. Furthermore, as punk developed into post-punk, cassette culture became extremely important as formats were further subverted in contradistinction to their initial purposes. What people should do, according to society's norms and values (what some people might describe as "real culture"), was therefore repeatedly turned on its head over a period of roughly five years by value conflicts and recorded sound formats. These cultural variations were also picked up by the mass media.

The media itself should be considered as an interesting way in to understanding the social contexts within which society reports upon itself. The mass media, especially in the UK, one might argue, has developed its stance largely surrounding the aforementioned folkways, mores and laws, and so one cannot really effectively discover a great deal of meaning surrounding record collecting from the mass media. But one can instead actually understand to some degree the social contexts within which the mass media create statements *about* record collecting. Interestingly, our culture will always change as it is exposed to new ideas. These changes may take considerable time, although in many respects one might argue that the media is not necessarily the first place one should look in order to understand, or at least estimate, how cultural values are assessed for their level of conformity or otherwise. In fact, one of the most important points to consider from this writer's perspective, as a lot of this work is concerned with secondary source material, is what one might describe as labelling. Labelling theory concerns the way that labels are assigned to certain people and certain acts.[31] From this perspective, attention is shifted from the actor and the act to the audience and to the process of social reaction that defines or labels people. The media is very significant in this respect. If one looks, for example, at the 1980s, an important growth decade for magazines and journals concerned with popular culture, titles such as *The Wire, The Face, FHM,* and so on that were produced during this time, one can quite clearly see that when applying a theoretical approach to labelling from media about and within popular culture, the record collector is seen in a pejorative light. A short exposition concerning *The Face* and its inauguration during the 1980s might be an illuminating case in point.

The Face was a monthly British lifestyle magazine covering items such as music, fashion and culture, and started in May 1980 by Nick Logan, who had previously been involved with the creation of the teen pop magazine *Smash Hits*, and had been an editor at the *New Musical Express* (*NME*) in the 1970s before the launch of *The Face*. The magazine was influential in showcasing a number of style trends of youth, but on occasion also ran into controversy when, for instance questioning the sexual orientation of Jason Donovan (which resulted in a libel case that Donovan won). During the 1990s, editor Richard Benson aspired to reflect current trends in music, art and fashion, and work was commissioned from photographers such as Stéphane Sednaoui, Elaine Constantine, Craig McDean and David LaChapelle. *The Face* was sold to the publishing company EMAP in 1999, and continued in print until May 2004, by which point sales had declined dramatically and advertising revenues been reduced as a result. Perhaps the main problem with *The Face* was that it tended to over-concentrate upon the latest trend at the expense of some of the fundamental reasons why people involve themselves in popular culture in the first place. A lack of understanding about such issues will often lead to the decline of a seemingly popular journal. One might discuss this as a failure to understand cultural capital.

Cultural Capital and Dr. Z

The term "cultural capital" has already been briefly discussed, but refers to social assets that promote social mobility beyond economic means. The

---

[31] See Howard S. Becker, *Outsiders: Studies in the Sociology of Deviance* (New York: The Free Press, 1963).

concept of cultural capital was first established by Pierre Bourdieu[32] and includes, amongst other things, education, speech (specifically *how* one speaks) and style choices. Bourdieu recognised three different types of capital: economic, social and cultural. Economic capital simply refers to economic resources, whilst social capital relies on resources based on networks or group memberships. Social capital could be membership in a fraternity/sorority or order or secret society such as Skull and Bones at Yale University (US) or the Bullingdon Club at Oxford University (UK).[33] Cultural capital, then, can be obtained through social capital, and is the knowledge, skills and/or advantages a person may have that result in a higher or increased status. This can relate to the child inheriting cultural capital from the parents who pass on certain attitudes or values within society, or the *Vertigo Records* record collector who owns a copy of Dr. Z's *Three Parts to My Soul (Spiritus, Manes et Umbra)*[34] within a group of record collectors (particularly if they, too, collect *Vertigo* releases).

Bourdieu furthermore distinguished between three types of capital within cultural capital itself, namely embodied, objectified and institutionalised (cultural) capital.[35] Institutionalised capital refers to knowledge (or "capital") that is recognised by an institution, typically an academic degree or qualification. Institutionalised capital is primarily recognised in the work place, or when applying for jobs, but as it allows one to enter the labour market with better opportunities (i.e. a high status) it thus translates into cultural capital. Objectified and embodied cultural capital, however, are much more relevant with regard to record collecting specifically—although this is not to say that institutionalised cultural

---

[32] Pierre Bourdieu, "Cultural Reproduction and Social Reproduction", in *Knowledge, Education and Cultural Change: Papers in the Sociology of Education*, ed. Robert Brown (London: Tavistock Publications Ltd., 1973).

[33] Oxford University does not presently recognise the Bullingdon Club as an official club or society, mainly due to behaviour issues, although it did formerly do so.

[34] *Vertigo Records* will be discussed at length in the following chapter, but it is perhaps useful to establish that this particular release is reportedly one of the most rare *Vertigo Records* there is—perhaps only rivalled by Ben's eponymous 1971 album (catalogue number: 6360 052), rumoured to have only sold roughly 100 copies on its release. As such, any collector who owns a copy of the original *Ben* LP, or *Three Parts to My Soul*, is surely one of a select few, and has spent a significant amount of time AND money to obtain the copy (the album is currently valued at an estimated £250–£500, according to some online sources, although arguably demand would certainly dictate the price for such a rare item as *Ben*).

[35] Pierre Bourdieu, "Forms of Capital", in *Handbook for Theory and Research for the Sociology of Education*, ed. J.G. Richardson (New York: Greenwood, 1986), 241–258.

capital cannot play a part either. Embodied cultural capital refers to the cultural capital one has consciously acquired and passively inherited through socialisation of culture and values, as cultural capital is not something instantaneously gained. Embodied capital is the knowledge one has acquired as a result of being immersed in the culture.

Thus a non-record collector may not appreciate the value of an original release of *Three Parts to My Soul (Spiritus, Manes et Umbra),* as they do not possess the cultural capital to understand its value to a record collector—to a non-collector it may just be any other record amongst countless others. Embodied cultural capital also includes the knowledge of being able to speak about the record in a way that indicates knowledge, as an "insider".[36] A *Vertigo* aficionado may, for instance, be able to tell you about the technical production of the album, what kind of vinyl was used during pressing, or distinguish between an authentic catalogue number and a re-issue or fraud. Again, a non-collector presented with the same album might only be able to establish that it is a vinyl record (depending on their generation even this could be a difficult task)—the artwork of the album[37] may even make it difficult to identify the artist and album name.

Objectified cultural capital is perhaps the most important type of cultural capital in this context, but closely related to embodied capital as will be demonstrated, and consists of physical objects that are owned like scientific equipment, books—or records. Whilst these objects can be sold for economic profit, they can also be used to display the cultural capital of the owner. Thus, if one can present the physical object of *Three Parts to My Soul (Spiritus, Manes et Umbra),* one can clearly demonstrate the possession of the relevant cultural capital to (i) acknowledge the album's significance as a rarity, (ii) acquire it, and to a certain extent (iii) display it as evidence of such. In doing so, one is as a result also "consuming" the physical object by understanding its cultural meaning. In order to do so, one must possess the relevant embodied cultural capital making embodied and objectified cultural capital intrinsically linked.

The concept of cultural capital is widely used within a number of academic (and non-academic) fields, although some have also criticised Bourdieu's concept for lacking conceptual clarity,[38] and being overly

---

[36] This is sometimes referred to as linguistic (cultural) capital.

[37] An image search using an internet search engine is recommended by this author for all of the album sleeves mentioned in this text, so that the reader can fully appreciate the context and analysis.

[38] See for instance Alice Sullivan, "Bourdieu and Education: How Useful is Bourdieu's Theory for Researchers?", *Netherlands Journal of Social Sciences* 38, no. 2 (2002): 144–166.

deterministic (as it is closely related to his notion of habitus[39] as well). Originally a sociological term, it is frequently used in relation to the education system, but its relevance to popular music studies—and by extension, given the interdisciplinary nature of popular music studies, popular cultural theory—is undeniable as shown with the example of Dr. Z's album. Sarah Thornton, a prominent popular music studies writer of the 1990s, has even discussed such important forms of cultural understanding as subcultural capital.[40] Thornton asks us to consider languages of culture and language of subculture in relationship to authenticity and value. Such issues are surely part of the record collector's arsenal of meaning.

Record Collector: A Magazine of Obdurate Durability

Record Collector, unlike its failed style press competitor *The Face*, appears to fully understand the logics of cultural capital. As previously mentioned, *Record Collector* started in 1976 as re-issues of *The Beatles Book*, but soon transformed into the *Record Collector* magazine after the supplement outgrew *The Beatles Book*'s popularity. Initially only a section for fans to trade Beatles' records, by 1979 a wide variety of records not exclusive to The Beatles were being advertised in the supplement inside *The Beatles Book*, and *Record Collector* was finally launched as a standalone publication in 1980. *Record Collector* quickly became a lengthy publication, containing over 100 pages, which it still does today, and earlier issues of the magazine predominantly focused on collectable music and artists from the 1950s–70s. Throughout its existence one of the strengths of the publication has been that it never places value-judgements on any particular genre or artist, but simply presents it to the reader as a

---

[39] The concepts of fields and habitus have been a continual feature in the work of Bourdieu. A field, based on a structure of social relationships, is the site of struggle for positions within the field, and is created by the conflicts that arise when the individual involved in the field try to establish what is of value in regard to capital within said field. This means that the cultural capital within that field can be either legitimate or not, depending upon the outcome or development of the struggle, but it is never both at the same time and is consequently dependent on the people within the field—and arbitrary. Habitus, then, refers to lifestyle, values, dispositions and the expectations of particular groups that are the result of life experiences and activities. In short, it can be described as the context of an individual.

[40] Sarah Thornton, "Moral Panic, the Media and British Rave Culture", in *Microphone Fiends: Youth Music and Youth Culture*, eds. Andrew Ross and Tricia Rose (New York: Routledge, 1994), 176–192.

potential area of interest. Whilst some genres, such as progressive rock, have typically been excluded from popular music or rock journalism, or at least treated with great suspicion, *Record Collector* appears to have refrained from such stances and instead concentrates on providing a publication for popular music fans and collectors. Given the wide variety of record collectors and their preferences, this approach ensures that no collector is alienated. However, the features and/or artist profiles in the magazine, which contain some factual details about the act—in some cases some kind of interview and a discography—also ensure that non-collectors, or "just" fans, are not excluded either. The discographies allow the reader to gain cultural capital by engrossing oneself in the necessary embodied cultural capital discussed above. Notably, *Record Collector* (and its US counterpart *Goldmine*[41]) has been instrumental in establishing a valuation system of records to enable traders and collectors to buy discerningly. The system employed by *Record Collector* is generally regarded as the norm to follow and is widely accepted, as becomes apparent when browsing titles on eBay, where many traders rate their records according to this system. The listings, or advertisements, at the back of the magazine have always been a prominent feature of *Record Collector*, although with the increased popularity of sites such as eBay there has been a decline in volume.

Initially, *Record Collector* was one of very few magazines that had a retrospective, or nostalgic, perspective on music—in all likelihood, as a result of the record collector's nostalgic outlook—with magazines such as the aforementioned *The Face* deliberately emphasising the now. From the mid 1980s onwards there has, however, been an increase in magazines with a similar perspective, perhaps with an older demographic in mind, with the launch of magazines such as Q[42] and *MOJO* (launched in 1986 and 1993 respectively). It has yet to be established if these titles will be as long-lasting as *Record Collector*, though—after all, *The Face* lasted 24 years before ceasing publication.

Record Collector has recently embraced the new electronic media and recognised its significance to record collectors by acknowledging online trading and including an eBay feature, but has kept its record fair feature, question and answer pages, review sections (including fanzine reviews) and a focus on anything and everything that might interest the collector. By doing so, *Record Collector* has maintained its popularity and become

---

[41] An investigation of *Goldmine*, whilst perhaps relevant in this context, is reserved for a later date as the main focus throughout this text is on the UK.

[42] Although a recent examination of the covers of Q seem to indicate a move towards more contemporary music.

an important publication for many record collectors. Generally, the visibility of the magazine also helps "normalise" the activity of record collecting and spark interest in the music reissue market.

The notion of "mainstream" media has been referred to a few times in this chapter. The author uses this concept here to differentiate from "specialised" media such as *Record Collector*. Whilst *Record Collector* has a defined objective as indicated in its title, one can assume the journalists at the magazine have specialised knowledge relating to record collecting and/or are record collectors themselves (this fact is often also highlighted). As such, the contributors to *Record Collector* can therefore be assumed to possess important cultural capital relating to record collecting. Contrast this with an "inkie" such as the *New Musical Express*, (*NME*), which details upcoming bands, news stories relating to relevant (typically indie) acts and reviews of new material relating to relevant acts. Throughout the pages of *NME* there is nothing to indicate that the writers possess any kind of specialist knowledge relating to record collecting. The stylistics, formatting, writing and choices of pictures do however indicate an interest—knowledge even—in a specific "indie" aesthetic. In other words, if the consumer is trying to find a new act that fits into this kind of indie genre, looking through the *NME* may be a good starting point. If the consumer, on the other hand, wants information on the value of a particular vinyl LP from, say, the 1970s, *NME* would be of little use whilst *Record Collector* would be a much better option.

Furthermore, someone wishing to read a music magazine just for the pleasure of reading it may find themselves drawn to magazines like *NME* or *Q* rather than *Record Collector*, because *Record Collector* is more precisely geared towards a very particular type of music fan—the record collector. While both *Q* and *NME* can claim a specific demographic, it could be argued that the borders of those demographics are more flexible than the one for *Record Collector*. If one does not have any interest at all in record collecting, it might be argued that there is little to gain from the publication, even though it does also include more general articles about acts. It might therefore be seen as a magazine for "purists" or "specialists". Such descriptors can tend to lead the more general music lover to consider it to be a magazine for "anoraks"—hence the stereotypes start to form.

In defence of the collector, *Record Collector* magazine is a voice crying in the wilderness, and an especially interesting case study for a number of reasons. Firstly, and the initial reason for its inclusion in this work, it is a magazine that is dedicated to the process of record collecting. Also, as previously suggested, the magazine started as part of *The Beatles Book* when it was reissued in the 1970s and therefore retained an element of journalistic authority right from the start. Thirdly, its popularity is based on collecting and is therefore evidence for the researcher of the enormous powers of cultural capital. When one considers how important informal education is to the majority of society, one can quite clearly see that *Record Collector* (rather than say *The Face*) was able to tap in to what is essentially a form of cultural capital. Ironically society labels this form as subcultural capital, owing to the aforementioned deviant tropes.

Indeed, *Record Collector* could be seen to have prospered, perhaps because the forms of cultural capital employed by its writers did not engage in value-judgements concerning good or bad music, but instead acknowledged that for the record collector there is no good or bad, merely titles of interest and titles not of interest. It is hardly surprising that some of the UK's most important popular music writers emerged from the ranks of *Record Collector*—writers like Peter Doggett, Spencer Leigh, Bill Harry and Andy Davis have all gone on to write substantive texts on popular music. Doggett, in particular, has written perhaps some of the most significant popular music works of recent years (e.g. *You Never Give Me Your Money*[43]). The discourse provided in *Record Collector* provides an interesting example, particularly in comparison to other mainstream media, of the power of cultural capital. Such differences in the media are readily detected by those embracing the cultural capital, and record collectors such as Les and Dave appear to fully embrace and comprehend the forms of capital presented by its own specific media representations. It can therefore be suggested that the fates of individual record collectors and record collecting media forms are inextricably linked, despite a sociological model based upon social mores indicating deviance. More signifiers and semiotic tropes need to be examined in order to remove the record collector from the position of a benign, yet problematic, social deviant, and into a position that might present him or her as a representation of how variegated society can be. The objects of desire are the next item on the agenda. If *Record Collector* is able to successfully direct many thousands of collectors towards particular desirable subject matters, then perhaps a closer examination of one of these collectible categories might be revealing.

---

[43] Peter Doggett, *You Never Give Me Your Money: The Battle for the Soul of The Beatles* (Croydon: Vintage, 2010).

CHAPTER FIVE

CONTEXTUALISING THE ALBUM: THE LATE 1960S AND *VERTIGO RECORDS*

**"Vertigo is the least pretentiously and most happily married
of the 'progressive' labels to emerge 'neath the wings
of the large record companies."
—*International Times* (1969)**

Collecting Records—an Overview

What people regard as collectable in a recorded sound sense varies greatly. But there are two constant subjects of dispute among collectors: condition and price—and the latter is often determined by the former. The value to a collector of recordings changes with the passage of time and concomitant changes in collecting trends, although a general rule of thumb can be applied. Older formats such as cylinders, one-sided 78rpm discs and acoustic recordings tend to be collected only by those who have a particular historical and genre-based investment in these older eras, and as such are seldom overly expensive. Collections from this early twentieth-century era can therefore often be made up from assorted visits to antique shops without spending a great deal of money. Certainly, very few record dealers actually handle 78s—not simply because they are fragile, but because there continues to be a general lack of interest in pre-rock 'n' roll recordings from collectors. Some of the hardware from this early era is, however, extremely costly. Whereas flat disc players can be purchased at reasonable cost, cylinder players—even the functional "Gem" models— are frequently auctioned.

In fact, notwithstanding a few important exceptions such as 1920s African-American recordings (e.g. labels such as *Back Swan, Paramount, Okeh*) and 1930s blues recordings—especially those produced during the Great Depression, which can be extremely rare (such as, for example,

Robert Johnson's recordings for *Vocalion*[1])—inter-war 78rpm records are still relatively inexpensive for the collector. Following WWII, formats began to change in the early 1950s, and by the time record collecting in the UK really started to embrace more popular forms (other than jazz, that is) in the mid-1970s, original R&B, folk, rockabilly, doo-wop and rock 'n' roll recordings were becoming scarce. As production levels rose throughout the 1950s and 1960s, reaching a peak of sales in the late 1970s, collectors came to search more for genres, artists, and labels which were special to them. Many of these sounds were of US origin. But recordings that pre-dated the rock era required a certain cachet to be collectible, and so US labels such as *Chess, Veejay, King*, etc. were amongst those sought after, alongside the jazz lover's need for labels such as *Dial, Prestige* and *Blue Note*; in the UK, however, US originals have never been the collector's first choice and UK tie-ins with American labels permitted some, but not all, of these recordings to be re-issued on UK subsidiaries such as *Vogue, London, Stateside, Sue*, and *Pye International*—and these *were* duly regarded as collectible.

This interest in British labels continued throughout the 1980s up to the present day, and although most collectors in the early days of 1970s collecting were predominantly interested in 45rpm discs, LPs and EPs also came to be of interest. Unlike in the US, where independent labels catered for local markets, there have never been many British independent labels, and so collectors tended to focus on those that did exist, making them effectively "collectible" in the process—especially if the releases were poor sellers and production runs were low. Depending upon the genre, a collector might be interested in labels such as *Topic* and *Transatlantic* (folk and folk/rock), *Esquire* and *Tempo* (jazz), *Blue Horizon* (blues), *Top Rank* (pop and imports), *Oriole* (Motown), etc. and such labels, immersed as they were in the rock, soul and folk cultural capital canons, were represented in discographies and prices drawn up accordingly (frequently by the aforementioned *Record Collector* magazine).

During the 1980s the over-production of all recordings, together with the advent of CDs, tended to impact upon the pricing of pre-1980s records, making many such artefacts (perhaps with the exception of pop, disco or some soul and reggae 45s) more desirable because of their musical authenticities and shorter production runs. Some recordings from the 1980s are collectible—especially those representing British indie bands and labels, but these are generally not expensive, so a collector of (say) the

---

[1] Paul Oliver, *Songsters and Saints: Vocal Traditions on Race Record* (Cambridge: University Press, 1984), 180.

Smiths can build up a reasonable collection without too much expense. It is worth reminding the reader that all collectability depends upon condition, and that many 45rpm recordings, being regarded as little more than ephemera when released, are—should they have survived—usually in very poor condition. This does not preclude them from being collectible, but would lessen their economic value. Sub-sets of record collecting would include such items as deejay copies, misprinted recordings, demonstration and promotional discs, etc., all of which are usually of interest to the completist.

Beatles records are usually cited as being collectible, although one can build up a reasonable Beatles collection for very little money, for literally millions of recordings were pressed and sold. Beatles rarities, therefore, tend to revolve around similar classifications as those employed by book collectors, who look for first editions, misprints, etc. Interestingly, Beatles mono LPs fetch more than stereo copies because fewer were sold, and stereo was "the coming thing", while their fan club flexi-discs are usually very highly priced because they were almost disposable and have not lasted, and odd formats such as those singles released in India on 78rpm formats, are extremely rare and valuable. Within some, but not all, such categorisations falls the *Vertigo* label. It is of interest, genre-wise, to rock fans, has a cachet linked to the counter-culture because of the era in which its records were released, and is collectible because, apart from a handful of major exceptions, did not sell particularly well, used art-based sleeves that appealed to a specific demographic, and despite being a subsidiary of the Philips electronics giant, gave off the "aura" of an independent label.

One can therefore identify certain musical and industrial categories that particular collectors are drawn to. This could be collecting certain acts, genres or, as will be examined here, labels. This chapter will therefore provide a case study of a record label that is generally regarded as being very collectable—*Vertigo Records*. By doing so it is hoped that an examination of the reasons why *Vertigo* is collectable, by looking at various aspects of their output such as the music, album art and commercial success—or lack thereof—will give the reader an impression of how recorded sound artefacts can have an enduring appeal despite (or, in fact, *because* of) their lack of initial success. But before this, the cultural environment that allowed *Vertigo Records* to be created will be considered. It is important to understand the shift in musical aesthetics that had been in progress in the years prior to 1969, the year of *Vertigo*'s creation. New genres such as psychedelia and progressive rock were emerging, aided by new technological developments and studio innovation. Ideologies were also changing within music, with a stronger emphasis on an art sensibility, which was being reflected in both music production and content, and even in the artwork featured on the albums.

Albums, or LPs as they were commonly called, became the dominant music media instead of 45rpm singles—in fact, 1969 was the year that album sales came to outstrip singles in the UK in terms of volume (although this was seldom the case with *Vertigo*, who enjoyed only limited singles success, after what had been a promising start[2]). A significant factor in these aesthetic developments came nonetheless from the counter-culture, which had been developing since the turn of the century through bohemianism and folk music, jazz, and beat, or beatnik, culture. Conducting a case study of *Vertigo Records*, while being both valid and worthwhile in itself, does however also raise certain historical issues, primarily the issues of source material. Aside from *Record Collector* articles, the literature available on *Vertigo* is mainly fan- and archive-based, compiled from unedited web articles written by unnamed, albeit enthusiastic, authors. This anonymity compels one to question the historicity of the content. There does not appear to be, as yet, a text concerning this label—which is something of a pity.

Counter-Culture

One would not wish to overstate the significance attached to particular musical "movements", for those involved are seldom aware of the contemporary cultural status of their activities, while others who consider themselves to be outside a coterie are often considered by others to be willingly within. Nevertheless the cultural resonances of popular (in our case, particularly rock) music in the late 1960s and early 1970s, in both the US and the UK, were substantial. Such reverberations present the popular music historian with useful illustrations of particular aspects of identity formed through popular music, in relation to the significance and mapping of the self. They help us to consider how a re-articulated "self" compares with the rites and rituals of the aforementioned social mores in Chapter Four, and how different genres of music and musical products are placed at the heart of such articulations.

Popular music in a variety of styles was undoubtedly an important contributor to such enquiries in both the US and the UK during the late

---

[2] *Vertigo* enjoyed two hit singles in 1970: Juicy Lucy's "Who Do You Love" (V1) and Black Sabbath's "Paranoid" (V2), but were unable to capitalise on this because their roster consisted of bands not normally chart-orientated. Fairfield Parlour's "Bordeaux Rosé" (6059 003) that same year performed well in Europe, but was not a "hit" record, as such, in the UK.

sixties. For example, there are myriad examples of popular musicians—
such as Neil Young, Joni Mitchell and Sinead O'Connor, to name a few—
contributing to a consideration of the cost of urban expansionism and
environmental destruction in material and cultural terms, concerned that
the natural world was being pushed to its limits by post-war economic
growth. Popular music not only drew attention to the US's immersion in
an unwinnable Vietnam conflict, but also rebelled against modern
concepts of resource and championed urban and rural communities.
Several groups linked to the British counter-culture, such as the Pink
Fairies and Quintessence, lived in London communes during the late
1960s. Others, such as the Edgar Broughton Band, were known to raise
funds for local counter-culture causes such as Caroline Coon's "Release"
organisation, an agency established to provide legal advice and arrange
legal representation for young people charged with the possession of
drugs. A new kind of community was attempted, with networks of
communications and a lack of competitiveness, all of which seemed to be
centred on the notion of collective outsidership in some form. A rock
aesthetic, which perhaps might loosely describe a challenging of concrete
musical and social certainties, undoubtedly underpinned these contrasting
works and projects.

    In addition to a variety of political and compositional stimulations,
such discourses were also drawn from a multiplicity of complex critical
fonts: from the imaginative "other America" work of Kerouac, Burroughs,
and Ginsberg, to the critical media analysis of Marshall McLuhan; from
Timothy Leary's *Politics of Ecstasy* to Rachel Carson's *Silent Spring*; and
even seventeen-year-old novelist S.E. Hinton's *The Outsiders* (later filmed
by Coppola), where the alienations of teenage suburbia in Middle America
were put in the spotlight. In the UK, the work of Jeff Nuttall's *Bomb
Culture* was widely disseminated alongside these US texts and
underground newspapers such as *OZ* and *International Times*. A broad
(but perhaps minority) church of social critiques came from such artists
and writers, expressing a gamut of diverse influences creating what might
be described as an alternative "world view", rather than a counter-culture,
as such. Braunstein and Doyle correctly state that "the term counter-
culture falsely reifies what should never properly be construed as a social
movement. It was an inherently unstable collection of attitudes, tendencies,
postures, gestures, 'lifestyles', ideals, visions, hedonistic pleasures,
moralisms, negations, and affirmations".[3] In such a mood as existed in this

---

[3] Peter Braunstein and Michael W. Doyle, *Imagine Nation: The American
Counterculture of the 1960s and '70s* (New York: Routledge, 2002), 11.

post-World War II era (affluent yet uncaring, "multicultural" yet pluralistic, politically powerful yet paranoid), it took a lot of courage to present the values of one's choice as binding—but by at least the turn of the 1960s many young people had indeed done just that.

By 1967, this "world view" had developed into a quasi-utopian pattern of belief systems, containing many paradoxes. For example, the aforesaid communalism contributed towards an attempted reclamation of cultural history via group cohesiveness rather than the systems created by twentieth-century advanced capitalism. But this communalism was also formed within an era of bourgeois (white) prosperity which promoted expectations of post-scarcity and abundance for all. Furthermore, it was also considered by some that the distinction between childhood and adulthood would be effaced, endowing youth with almost heroic heterogeneous attributes along the way. Brocken states:

> This point is perhaps of greatest enduring significance for the popular music historian, for with it developed less a heroic-ism and more an increased youth-based alienated sensibility. We can recognise such scepticisms as something that was also later embraced by punk, post-punk and the emerging pop punk of the mid-late 1990s—despite punk's P.R., then and now, concerning its existence out-with the rock canon, it was (as suggested by Laing) at all times within the musical, social and cultural confines placed upon it by rock's meta-narrative as a so-called counter-cultural representation.[4]

By 1967, the aforementioned ideologies had started to be challenged, and ideas started shifting in rather radical ways owing to counter-cultural influences that had been growing for many years beforehand.[5] These counter-cultural narratives placed a much greater value on what was perceived by certain individuals as the "true" and genuine honesty of the child, which was believed to be untarnished, as well as freedom from authority, or indeed anyone being "in charge". The idea of a community based on outsidership came to emerge from, but develop in direct opposition to, theories discussed by Frankfurt School scholars such as Adorno. In such "Frankfurtian" terms, the notion of being an outsider might itself signify a lack of community and communications and, instead, be an indication of atomisation and alienation.

---

[4] Michael Brocken, "Green Day: Rock Discourse and Dwindling Authenticities", *Brazilian Journal of Song Studies* 2 (2012), http://www.rbec.ect.ufrn.br.
[5] Arthur Marwick, *The Sixties: Cultural Revolution in Britain, France, Italy, and the United States, 1958–1974* (Oxford: University Press, 1998).

Now one generally refers to these ideas that began to form in this way around the late 1960s as part of a hippie culture, but they spread far beyond the somewhat simplistic notions of "hippie" and came to influence many different parts of modern society, such as the development of the Green Party, social acceptance of vegetarianism and open debates concerning renewable energy sources. It can be seen that a variety of counter-cultural ideas, which were concerned with things such as Mother Earth, freedom of the individual, self-regulation and sustenance, were central to the understanding of hippie ideology. Today, the hippie and counter-culture is frequently associated with a very distinct sense of dress and music, often drawing on psychedelic and progressive rock influences. While the choice to follow a rock-related narrative is unconventional in its own right, the way in which rock has responded to certain events has not been very different from many traditional patterns of behaviour (one need only consider Live Aid in 1985). Evidence exists of a *lack* of formalised ideology in the political sense, and more to do with a series of theoretical (albeit rather naive) models which attempted to directly deal with issues that present themselves in everyday life; hence, perhaps, its enduring relevance and appeal. With a more mainstream presence these values also bled into other areas of society where one might not typically expect to have found them. As such, one could start identifying counter-cultural ideas in certain business practices. By the late 1970s, IT businesses were particularly heavily influenced by these new approaches, with workshops offering freedom from an authoritarian manager and IT being seen as a continuation of the hippie "one world" pronouncement.

The counter-culture's influences can still therefore be detected throughout society, especially when one considers general views on small businesses, food, and the ecology. The current engagement with the planet and its climate is, one might argue, a direct result of counter-cultural policies. The specific emphasis on "family" in advertisements for family-run businesses is yet another influence of the counter-culture where organic, "natural" and inclusive businesses were not only favoured, but also believed to be the right way of conducting business. However, whilst climate concern and space for smaller businesses is a positive development, there were also downsides. Andrew Calcutt,[6] for instance, believes the counter-culture was responsible for many negative consequences. He feels that it has resulted in a lack of responsibility, which in turn has led to the infantalisation of the adult and its offspring.

---

[6] Andrew Calcutt, *Arrested Development: Pop Culture and the Erosion of Adulthood* (London: Cassell, 1998).

Calcutt's points are harsh but well-made: he describes a society where no one is essentially prepared to grow up, which also leads to a "super authoritarian" government that creates laws on everything from wearing bicycle helmets to parenting practices, so that we cannot accept personal responsibility. There are many pluses and minuses to Calcutt's argument but, when applied to business, it could be argued that a counter-cultural approach will inevitably result in a different work model because of its fundamentally different views on leadership. Some business might thrive under these conditions, whereas others might not, but the connection between the counter-culture and the business of rock music makes the music industry particularly susceptible to both positive and negative side-effects. As a creative industry, having creativity encouraged through flexible structures and unconventional thinking might be of great benefit to the music industry, but at the same time musicians, and other creative personnel, reneging on their responsibilities to themselves and their colleagues has been a recurring narrative with creativity ultimately being stifled because of loose and destructive behaviour; the examples are numerous and span many generations ranging from Charlie Parker to Amy Winehouse and beyond. Whilst these theories, with some modification, can certainly be applied to different aspects and businesses in society, a case study of the record label *Vertigo* illustrates how a company run on such lines may look. The fate of *Vertigo Records*, which ceased to exist in its original form by the mid-1970s owing to bad management, and then again when *Polygram* was reorganised in 1983, is by no means the only possible outcome of this business model, but undeniably a distinct possibility. Concomitantly, during the late 1960s, popular music had developed towards a more experimental, *avant-garde*, aesthetic. Successful experimental releases such as The Beatles' *Sgt. Pepper's Lonely Hearts Club Band* and Pink Floyd's *Piper at the Gates of Dawn* opened the doors for a continued experimentation with music within a large business recording environment—this had seldom ever been the case in the entire history of recorded sound. Musical aesthetics were thus changing, and there were a number of developments that allowed for these changes to take place.

Musical Developments

The change in musical aesthetics brought about by albums such as the two mentioned above, and others, resulted in the development of new genres as well. Progressive rock was one of these new genres, and whilst some criticise it for being "a music [genre] that failed both as rock music but also as classical music",[7] it was also a genre that pushed the boundaries of rock music. Psychedelia, which had been widely popular in the late 1960s, began to develop into both progressive and heavy rock, and whilst far from everything released was successful, there was still a large enough market to sustain the genres. Bands such as Yes, Black Sabbath, Jethro Tull, Led Zeppelin, King Crimson and, perhaps most notably, Pink Floyd, are testament to the popularity both progressive and heavy rock once had, and are evidence of the genre's market appeal.

Progressive rock had its "golden years", suggested by Macan as being 1969–73,[8] and was hugely popular during this time. As a genre, progressive rock drew upon influences from many different areas, sometimes making its stylistic characteristics difficult to identify. Indeed, some have defined the genre of progressive rock not through its music content as such, but through a "progressive rock ideology".[9] Classical music influences, particularly from the works of Bartók and Dvořák, and lengthy compositions are, however, generally considered to be trademarks of the progressive rock genre. It has been argued that such elements were combined with complex and intricate lyrics[10] to provide us with a genre that is, for better or worse, more concerned with the mind and the intellectual aspects of music rather than those of the body through dancing.

One might presume that such aforementioned aesthetic shifts contributed to the development of new ideas about the authenticity of popular music. But this is not necessarily the case, for while the counter-culture did present alternatives to lived realities, such musical ideas stemmed in the main from nineteenth-century aesthetics concerning high and low art. This was a pity, for almost without exception both heavy and progressive artists tended to shun the popular aspects of their craft and thus alienate the very people who were drawn to them, and gave them purpose in the first place, thus leaving, by the mid-1970s a generation of young people rather disillusioned by what they considered to be

---

[7] Chris Atton, "'Living in the Past'?: Value Discourses in Progressive Rock Fanzines", *Popular Music* 20, No. 1 (2001): 29.

[8] Edward Macan, *Rocking the Classics: English Progressive Rock and the Counterculture* (Oxford: University Press, 1997).

[9] Paul Stump, *The Music's All that Matters: A History of Progressive Rock* (London: Quartet Books, 1997).

[10] Jennifer Rycenga, "Tales of Change within the Sound: Form, Lyrics and Philosophy in the Music of Yes", in *Progressive Rock Reconsidered*, ed. Kevin Holm-Hudson (New York: Routledge, 2002); Deena Weinstein, "Progressive Rock as Text: The Lyrics of Roger Waters", in *Progressive Rock Reconsidered*, ed. Kevin Holm-Hudson (New York: Routledge, 2002).

pretentious and "dinosaur" music. Nevertheless, their impact was significant, and alongside technology was one of the significant developments of the era.

In the latter case, in 1967 the Moog Synthesizer was demonstrated at the Monterey International Pop Festival. Dr Robert Moog had spent most of the sixties developing his synthesiser, but by 1967 parts had become cheaper and Moog had made several further improvements.[11] Despite a number of other demonstrations from 1963 onwards, it was not until this 1967 display that the Moog started gaining widespread recognition, mostly from rock musicians and film and music studios. The Moog was significant in the development of popular music as it was the first practical analogue synthesizer, as such becoming the first widely-used analogue synthesizer, and it allowed musicians to first of all create a spectrum of new sounds and further experiment with them.

Studio equipment such as microphones and recording technology was also being developed, as well as the roles of the musicians themselves, and their producers were also beginning to take on slightly different roles. Musicians developed more craftsmanship, distinct from the showmanship/ performer roles they previously had.[12] An examination of The Beatles in the mid-1960s can provide us with a very famous example of this. After their chaotic 1965 North American tour, where they encountered hysterical fans and had difficulties with sound quality and volume, the group took the decision to stop touring in favour of developing their studio sound. By 1966 they released *Revolver*, featuring tracks like "Tomorrow Never Knows", "I'm Only Sleeping", and "She Said She Said", that show a significant development in musical style compared to their earlier LPs. The group started experimenting with tape loops by playing them back at different speeds or backwards, facilitated by new technological developments, creating a sound, as evident in "Tomorrow Never Knows", impossible to re-create live on-stage—or ever again, at all:

> [...] the group continued the following day by overdubbing tape-loops made by McCartney at home on his Brennell recorders. The tape-loop a length of taped sound, edited to itself to create a perpetually cycling signal—is a staple of sound-effects studios and the noise/art idiom known as musique concrete. Pop music, though, had heard nothing like this

---

[11] Paul Stump, *The Music's All that Matters: A History of Progressive Rock* (London: Quartet Books, 1997).
[12] Richard Peterson, "Why 1955? Explaining the Advent of Rock Music", *Popular Music* 9, no. 1 (1990): 97–115.

before, and the loops created for TOMORROW NEVER KNOWS were especially extraordinary.

There were five in all, each running on an auxiliary deck feed on to the multitrack through the Studio 2 desk and mixed live: (1) a "seagull"/"Red Indian" effect (actually McCartney laughing) made, like most of the other loops, by superimposition and acceleration (0:07); (2) an orchestral chord of B flat major (0:19); (3) a Mellotron played on its flute setting (0:22); (4) another Mellotron oscillating in 6/8 from B flat to C on its string setting (0:38); and (5) a rising scalar phrase on a sitar, recorded with heavy saturation and acceleration (0:56).[13]

While MacDonald goes on to discuss the effects of LSD upon the group's compositional norms, it is more relevant for us to consider in this case how "Tomorrow Never Knows" dealt with the realities of collaborative and contingent composition despite previous examples where recordings reflected an actual composition, and its process. In this case, the recording and the looping was the composition, which further lends itself to Virgil Moorefield's[14] concept of recording establishing itself as the primary artefact via "the reality of illusion". Basically, one might argue, that as we hear it, "Tomorrow Never Knows" never actually happened. The group continued on in this spirit, and in 1967 they finally released *Sgt. Pepper's Lonely Hearts Club Band*, a seminal LP in terms of both musical experimentation and aesthetic development in harmony with the significance of the producer as a co-composer.

So alongside aesthetic, industrial, and technological changes, occupational roles were shifting and, one might argue, audiences were becoming more receptive as a consequence:

At the age of 16 in 1970, I had prepared myself to listen to practically anything, but especially on record. This is why Edwards' record shop became so important to me because they seemed to have everything. I remember one day going in of an afternoon, which was quite unusual because they used to open up around about 4pm, and I came away with a Van Der Graaf Generator album and an electronic music compilation, which was on *Vox Records* and had recordings by Carlos on it. On my way out I also picked up a White Plains single—pure pop really. I went home and thoroughly enjoyed listening to all three purchases, which 43 years later I still have.[15]

---

[13] Ian MacDonald, *Revolution in the Head: The Beatles Records and the Sixties* (London: Vintage, 2009), 190–191.
[14] Virgil Moorefield, *The Producer As Composer: Shaping the Sounds of Popular Music* (Cambridge: MIT Press, 2005).
[15] Interview with Les, April 2013.

Musical content was nevertheless not the only area in which these counter-cultural associations became evident. Style choices, album artwork and public statements all reflected this as well.

However tempting it may be to believe that all fashions of the 1960s and 1970s were inspired by either hippie culture or acid trips, this is not necessarily the case. Looking at the period 1967–1973 (which, some might argue, was progressive rock's last "golden year", and the year *Vertigo* changed their logo from the swirl to the spaceship), it could be argued that we witness the emergence of several important cultural strands. In particular, a fragmentation in British society and culture amongst young people took place, which lead to the formation of specific subcultures employing specific ways of dressing and presentation in order to either distance themselves from mainstream society and/or "hippiedom" while also showing an allegiance to a particular sub-cultural choice. In fact, one need only listen to Mott the Hoople's version of David Bowie's "All the Young Dudes", and watch its accompanying promotional video, to realise how recorded sound was helping to codify new youth movements. Bowie's line, "And my brother's back home with his Beatles and his Stones,/ We never got it off on that revolution stuff,/ What a drag, too many snags", connotes a paradigm shift in the history of popular culture, and thus by extension lifestyle choices and preferences, that is often hidden by rhetoric concerning progressive rock and hippie lifestyles.

Record Sleeves

Looking through album covers from the 1960s to the 1970s one can discern another shift in aesthetics. Whilst album art is, unfortunately, another somewhat neglected area within popular music academia, Ian Inglis[16] provides an eloquent illustration of these aesthetic shifts in his examination of the record covers of The Beatles. He establishes how they were initially a simple "personality photograph" that grew into complex pieces of art (and eventually returned to the personality photograph with *Let It Be*). Inglis argues that The Beatles were at the forefront of a development within album art. Paul Gilroy also notes that album art can be of great significance to certain groups of people for very specific reasons:

> People use these images and the music that they enclose for a variety of reasons. For the black user of these images and products, multivalent processes of "consumption" may express the need to belong, the desire to

---

[16] Ian Inglis, "'Nothing You Can See that isn't Shown': The Album Covers of The Beatles", *Popular Music* 20, No. 1 (2001): 83–97.

make the beauty of blackness intelligible and somehow fix that beauty and
the pleasures it creates so that they achieve, if not in performance, then at
least a longevity that retrieves them from the world of pop ephemera and
racial dispossession.[17]

Gilroy is able to conclude that the album cover was allowed to take on
this important role since its design was not as closely regulated by the
music industry. Record covers had initially consisted simply of a paper
sleeve designed to protect the fragile (shellac) 78rpm record inside. As
record sleeve design advanced into cardboard covers with an inner paper
sleeve over a 33⅓rpm plastic (i.e. vinyl) record, so the importance of the
sleeve duly expanded. The record cover became a tool for advertisement—
for the product inside and other available titles in some cases. Such
developments awarded musicians the opportunity to express certain ideas.
As Gilroy explains, this meant that black musicians, in his example, could
express ideas of "blackness" and being a black person in a largely
Caucasian-centred society. One such example can be drawn from two
contrasting Stevie Wonder sleeves—one designed by *Motown*, *Signed,
Sealed & Delivered*, which placed Wonder in a cardboard box, the other
designed by (the blind) Wonder himself, *Talking Book*, which shows him
meditating in African clothes. Earlier *Motown* albums did not even have
pictures of their black artists on the cover for fear of a drop in US sales. So
album covers are "covered" in significance because they:

> [...] have been developed as an agitational or educational tool which can,
> for example, encourage people to register to vote, to grow their hair a
> certain way, to wear a particular garment or to employ a familiar item of
> clothing in an unfamiliar and "sub-culturally" distinctive way.[18]

In other words, album covers can be used as a tool to influence not
only the music's target audience, but also people who simply buy records
for their covers,[19] making them a very powerful tool indeed when
employed in the right manner.

---

[17] Paul Gilroy, *Small Acts: Thoughts on the Politics of Black Cultures* (London:
Serpent's Tail, 1993), 256.
[18] *ibid.*, 245.
[19] See Philip Auslander, "Looking at Records" *The Drama Review* 45, No. 1
(2001): 77–83; Ian Inglis, "'Nothing You Can See That Isn't Shown': The Album
Covers of The Beatles", *Popular Music* 20, No. 1 (2001): 83–97.

From 1966 album art became more experimental.[20] For instance, whilst regarded as a more psychedelic group, and thus presumably with more experimental album covers than more mainstream popular music groups, the Byrds *Mr. Tambourine Man* (1965) that featured a comparatively straightforward cover. The group is photographed through a fish-eye lens (much like *Rubber Soul*, albeit six months before The Beatles) with the picture being cropped into a circular shape, surrounded by black, and album detail across the top of the cover. By 1968 they released *Sweetheart of the Rodeo*, an album that saw a new musical direction for the group into a much more defined country music genre. The LP is noted for its innovative integration of country and rock music, which had not previously been widely experimented with. The cover features a number of illustrations by Jo Mora from 1933: in the centre there is a blonde woman on a dark background dressed in rodeo/cowboy attire surrounded by, and holding onto, a heart made up of yellow flowers. This centrepiece of the album was originally a smaller detail in Mora's illustration. The borders of the album cover are adorned by smaller framed illustrations in a similar rodeo theme, and the title of the album is inserted between the woman and the heart of flowers. *Sweetheart of the Rodeo* pushed different boundaries in popular music by emphasising a country music style and discourse visually, cleverly using an old illustration which conjures an image of "old-timey" heritage and authenticity, and as such exemplifies how musicians were starting to break moulds they might have previously found themselves encased within.

Thus the counter-culture movement during the mid-to-late 1960s and early 1970s came to influence all kinds of lived experiences, and furthermore helped to change popular music practice, business, and sound and marketing in several fascinating ways. A variety of different people from various socio-economic, political and racial backgrounds were affected in accessible ways that have endured to the present day. Such plans for life are not without their problems (as is highlighted by Andrew Calcutt), although one might suggest that these contexts for recorded sound and its technologies, the record as an artefact, and the development of a "culture" that surrounds these artefacts, have never left us. In fact, it might be argued that such pieces of so-called popular culture detritus mean more to us today than many other seemingly more important symbols of culture. But what did these convergences mean for the *Philips* label?

---

[20] For example, see *Revolver* by The Beatles, the eponymous Doors album, *The Who Sell Out*, etc.

Philips

Created in 1891 by Gerard and Frederik Philips as an electro-technical company, Philips initially gained fame through their manufacture of light bulbs. As a company, they continued to diversify into a variety of different sectors and had already been both manufacturing radios as well as producing radio programmes since the 1920s. Indeed, in the Netherlands Philips played an important part in national radio programming, being one of the earliest players in the field. However, as television broadcasting was beginning to expand after World War II, it was believed that this new medium would result in the death of radio,[21] so in 1949, perhaps as a result of this belief, Philips ventured into the sales of television sets. *Philips Records*, as it came to be known in the UK, started in continental Europe in 1950. Recordings were made with popular artists of various nationalities and also with classical artists from Germany, France and Holland. Philips also distributed recordings made by the US *Columbia Records* in continental Europe. After the separation of English *Columbia* and American *Columbia* at the end of 1954, Philips started to distribute original *Columbia* recordings on the *Philips* label in the United Kingdom: "Philips were interested in a sector of the British record market place, but were determined to use this niche specifically for US product. So they looked at Miller's successful output and directly made a deal with *Colombia*".[22] For example, Mitch Miller-produced US artists such as Frankie Laine and Rosemary Clooney scored several hits in the British singles charts. They also signed Frankie Vaughan and the Kaye Sisters to represent their British market, and further developed a popular music roster via acts such as Marty Wilde, Roy Castle, and Anne Shelton, although these artistes were less popular than they might have been, and *Philips* were forced to re-think their marketing.

However, more success came via their agreement with US *Columbia*, and in the late 1950s they released the first Johnny Mathis products in the UK on their *Fontana* subsidiary. By the mid-1960s this label had proved to be a great success: The Spencer Davis Group, Dave Dee, Dozy, Beaky, Mick & Tich, Wayne Fontana and The Mindbenders, The New Vaudeville Band, Nana Mouskouri, and others, were all signed and performed well in the charts during the 1960s. For one year (1961) *Fontana* was the UK licensee for *Motown Records* (these records are much sought after by collectors); they also distributed *CBS* and *Epic* products until 1962, and

---

[21] Richard Peterson, "Why 1955? Explaining the Advent of Rock Music", *Popular Music* 9, no. 1 (2990): 97–115.

[22] Michael Brocken, personal communication, April 2013.

Vanguard until 1967. The *Philips* label signed Dusty Springfield and the Walker Brothers in the 1960s and enjoyed great success with these artists. When they came to restructure their music operations, *Philips* dropped its *Fontana* label, and this is when *Vertigo Records* first appeared. *Fontana* actually played a crucial part in the formation of *Vertigo* by previously securing distribution deals with smaller, independent labels such as *Island Records*. Founded by Chris Blackwell in 1962, *Island* initially catered for the growing immigrant population in the UK, but had shifted focus by 1967, scoring successes with bands such as Traffic. *Philips*, who had their own pressing plant, also pressed *Island* products.[23]

By 1969, *Island* was also home to acts such as Free, Fairport Convention, Jethro Tull and John Martyn, and the label was able to establish itself strongly in the record industry and become a reputable and influential player, while also appealing to the UK counter-culture because they were seen as being free from any corporate trappings. Their packaging was impressive: sleeves were lavish affairs, mostly gatefold with artistic design concepts. Their success left the major labels in something of a dilemma. From a record-collecting point of view, *Island* was regarded as a sign of absolute authenticity, and they are one of the first labels outside of soul music to be collected via their catalogue numbers. Interestingly, however, because of the aforementioned counter-cultural emphases, it was their albums that were primarily collected, not always their singles. This was quite different from soul music collectors, who tended to prioritise 45s (singles) rather than 33s (LPs). This is not to say that *Island* did not involve themselves in soul and R&B recordings, for they also acted as a licensee for *Sue Records* in America, and it was via this licence that famous producer/deejay Guy Stevens first came to prominence. Also, because *Island* had been established in the first instance to promote Jamaican R&B, it enjoyed a black cachet. But it was via its alternative, heavy, psychedelic output that it came to be regarded as a collectible and authentic British independent label. For example, Les informed this writer:

> I'd buy anything on *Island* when I had the money because I just knew
> without hearing that it would be interesting. I was a big Traffic fan at the
> time, and they'd moved over to *Island*, and as they moved over, their
> music improved. Stevie Winwood had started with the Spencer Davis
> Group, and that was really good, and they were on *Fontana* and when I

---

[23] Donald Clarke, ed., "Polygram", in *The Penguin Encyclopaedia of Popular Music* (Harmondsworth: Penguin, 1990), 923–925; "George", personal communication, November 2012.

found out that the *Fontana* artists were mostly contracted to *Island* I became even more excited. I also remember buying *Stand Up* by Jethro Tull and being absolutely blown away by it, so much so that when I was paid the following week I went to Whitechapel in Liverpool searching for anything else on that pink *Island* label. I came back with Fairport Convention's *Unhalfbricking*—and that was even better![24]

The "majors" such as *EMI* and *Philips* could see that for some record purchasers a counter-cultural genre separation was taking place, and labels needed to reflect this. For example, as far as *Philips* were concerned, artists such as Black Sabbath, Jimmy Campbell and the Spencer Davis Group shared their label with middle-of-the road singers such as Nana Mouskouri, and it was felt that this was not necessarily affording their rock artists a credible reputation.

While *Philips'* plant was pressing LPs for *Island*, the musical material and quantities of LPs being pressed were starting to catch their interest. Furthermore, *Philips* now also had newly-created subsidiaries *Harvest* (*EMI*) and *Deram* (*Decca*) to compete with. This set the wheels in motion for the creation of a similar subsidiary and so, in the autumn of 1969, Philips finally set up *Vertigo Records*. Agents Gerry Bron and Tony Reeves, together with A&R man Olav Wyper, are often cited as key initiators, although the mythology surrounding the creation of labels such as *Vertigo* often makes it difficult to distinguish the precise details. Bron and Reeves did, however, share production duties on *Vertigo's* early releases while Wyper was also a general manager of *Philips Records* in the UK at the time, and is credited with the signing of Black Sabbath. According to Mark Powell:

> A&R head Olav Wyper found the solution by creating a new identity for existing esoteric acts within the Philips group of companies. The creation of Vertigo Records was announced in the autumn and immediately staff were engaged to seek out new talent that would give EMI, Decca and even Island records a run for their money. Vertigo quickly established a recognisable identity with the design of its distinctive 'swirl' logo by Roger Dean that graced the entire label of the A side of each album. [Like *Island*] Album sleeves were almost all gatefold in design and were mostly the work of photographer and designer Marcus Keef.[25]

---

[24] Interview with Les, April 2013.
[25] Mark Powell, *Time Machine: A Vertigo Retrospective*, CD notes (London: Mercury Records 9827982, 2005), 6.

Philips Records later developed into *Phonogram Records*, and after a merger with *Polydor* in 1980 became *PolyGram Records*. Gerry Bron was to leave the Philips organisation, taking his artists under the *Bronze* moniker into Chris Blackwood's *Island* stable, where he joined fellow publishers and managers Chris Wright and Terry Ellis of *Chrysalis*. *PolyGram* was eventually sold to Seagram, a Canadian distillery, in 1999 and was merged into the *Universal Music Group*.

Vertigo Records

EMI and *Decca* had already set up their *Harvest*, *Deram* and *Deram Nova* subsidiary labels respectively between 1966 and 1970, created to promote and sell these new, emerging musical genres—and it was in this cultural environment that *Vertigo Records* came to be created. The counter-cultural schemas present at the time had been disapproving of the major record labels ("the man"), and as a consequence, and to appear more like an independent record label, sub-labels were set up and run fairly autonomously from their major parent labels by people who were regarded as being "in the know". These subsidiaries thus possessed greater cultural capital than their parent labels did in this particular field. Furthermore, by being solely dedicated to these new music genres, the subsidiary labels also benefited from a greater creative freedom in the sense that they only had to cater for the new, emerging audiences of these genres, and did not have to have the same consideration for the mainstream market as their parent labels. Subsidiaries such as *Harvest* and *Deram* attracted a number of very influential and commercially viable acts at the time such as Pink Floyd (*Harvest*) and the Moody Blues (*Deram*), and it was hoped that *Vertigo* would do the same.

Vertigo, however, joined the game at a later stage than its competitors and its success, as we shall see, was relatively short-lived. In 1970 the label:

> [...] scored chart success with its first two album releases, *Valentyne Suite* by Colosseum and Juicy Lucy's self titled debut. The label quickly expanded its roster of acts in its first six months of operation to include Black Sabbath, Rod Stewart, Uriah Heep, Gentle Giant, Manfred Mann's Chapter Three, Affinity, Gracious!, Nucleus, Cressida and many more. 1970 was a particularly good year for the label when albums by Rod Stewart and Black Sabbath became major sellers, allowing Vertigo the

luxury of signing acts such as May Blitz, Dr. Z, Tudor Lodge, Ramases and others that failed to perform commercially.[26]

In 1973, *Vertigo* changed their logo from the eye-catching "swirl" to the spaceship logo designed by Roger Dean. While *Vertigo* continued to live on with this spaceship logo until 1980, the label was considered to be largely in decline from this point onwards, at least from a musical innovation point of view. It is also noteworthy that both Bron and Wyper, who had been influential in both the creation and the (initial) success of *Vertigo*, chose to move on and create their own labels in the early 1970s (*Bronze* and *Logo* respectively), with Bron taking many early, notable *Vertigo* acts with him such as Juicy Lucy and Manfred Mann, and Wyper initially moving to *RCA Victor* to establish another less successful "heavy" label, *Neon*. Michael Brocken interviewed Patrick Campbell-Lyons in 2006 on BBC Radio Merseyside. Campbell-Lyons had taken his group Nirvana from *Island* to *Vertigo* and as part of the deal became a producer and A&R man. He told Brocken:

> Leaving *Island* was very sad because we really fell out with Chris Blackwell, something I have always regretted, but he was acting very differently to us once other artists started to do really well. I wrote a song called "Christopher Lucifer", and it was about him! The deal with *Philips* was that I would make records, I suppose, and perhaps do a little A&R. It was fun, but utter chaos. I was on a wage, so that wasn't too bad, but the bands didn't get paid properly, and there was a mixture of a kind of freelance attitude mixed with this hippie idea around, you know, "Oh, we don't work for 'the man' so we can't pay," etc. I produced a lot of those early albums, and some were really good, others not so good, but there we are—a confusing time in my life, I would say, but not without some happy memories. It was never going to last in that state, however. *Philips* were horrified at some of the expenses, alone![27]

The LPs released on *Vertigo* between 1969 and 1973 are now very rare and very desirable for the niche collector. As one *Vertigo* enthusiast put it, *Vertigo* "swirl" LPs are like the "*Blue Note* of record collections".[28] This chapter will detail *Vertigo's* musical output between 1969 and 1973, and consider exactly what it is that makes the *Vertigo* "swirl" LPs so collectable.

---

[26] *ibid.*, 6–7.
[27] Patrick Campbell-Lyons (2006) talking to Michael Brocken on Spencer Leigh's *On The Beat*, BBC Radio Merseyside.
[28] www.vertigoswirl.com.

Vertigo: The Music and the Sleeves;
Selections from 1969–1973

Vertigo's musical output between 1969 and 1973 was diverse, and crossed many different genres. If one were to summarise it in as few words as possible, simply describing it as not commercial pop would probably serve as the best solution. Some of the acts signed to *Vertigo* include the already mentioned Juicy Lucy and Manfred Mann Chapter Three—who respectively released the second and third LPs with a *Vertigo* catalogue number— Colosseum, Rod Stewart, Black Sabbath, Uriah Heep, May Blitz, Gentle Giant, Graham Bond, Magna Carta, Jade Warrior, Nirvana, and Ian Matthews, amongst many others. These acts alone span a very wide range of genres and represent a number of different aesthetic and musical choices.

For instance, both Black Sabbath and Uriah Heep are correctly regarded as hard-rock acts, and the artwork on their respective debut releases on *Vertigo*: *Very 'Eavy... Very 'Umble* (Uriah Heep, 1970), and *Black Sabbath* (Black Sabbath, 1970), semiotically communicate such values and choices. *Very 'Eavy... Very 'Umble* features a human face with closed eyes and mouth open, as if gasping for air. A thick layer of cobwebs and dust cover the face, making it seem as if it has been left untouched and hidden for some time—very Gothic, one might suggest, and expressing similar gothic imagery to Black Sabbath's eponymous issue. *Black Sabbath* consists of a somewhat grainy photograph of a woman dressed in black, standing in some sort of woodland or overgrown garden (or graveyard?) next to a tree with a white cottage-looking house in the background. The wilderness, the woman's dress and the grainy character of the photograph all contribute to the LP cover's eerie feel. The scene, in fact, is highly reminiscent—for the British public at least—of Hammer Horror movies, a cheap form of horror that by the late 1960s was increasingly dwelling upon macabre subjects. This debut album also created a dark sound, different from other bands at the time, and has been described by fans as "the first ever 'Gothic rock' record", although it is more commonly considered to be the first heavy metal album,[29] being swamped by power chords (fifths). All in all, both covers convey a certain unsettling feel, which it could be argued works in symbiosis with the musical content on both LPs.

---

[29] Paul Stump, Paul, *The Music's All that Matters: A History of Progressive Rock* (London: Quartet Books, 1997).

Ian Matthews, on the other hand, is generally regarded as more of a folk musician. His 1970 LP *If You Saw Thro' My Eyes*, uses a backlit photograph of Matthews looking out through a window. The dark silhouette, the pensive pose and the simplicity of the photograph gives a sense of personal intensity (a "nice guy"?), but also distance, and is in stark contrast to the Uriah Heep and Black Sabbath covers. Matthews also places a larger emphasis on acoustic instruments, notably acoustic guitar, and does not layer his instruments as heavily as the other two acts. Compared to Black Sabbath in particular, Matthews' vocals appear much more natural and folkie, giving the illusion he has simply sat down and recorded the album without the use of a great deal of technology. In tracks such as Uriah Heep's "Come Away Melinda"—a cover of the Tim Rose song (albeit first recorded by Harry Belafonte)—one can detect certain noteworthy similarities to Matthews' music, such as choice of instrumentation and lyrical contents, although there is still a distinct difference in the overall music genre presented on these LPs.

The Jimmy Campbell album *Half Baked* (1970) is wrapped in a full colour gatefold sleeve, with a photograph of two clowns sitting by a tree: one is female and unmistakeably pregnant, while the other (male) sits by her side, perhaps innocently attempting to comfort her. The disarming countryside suggests a level of beauty but also insecurity, loss and innocent transgression. The clowns look foolish, duped perhaps by their immature love for each other: left in a wilderness somewhere, they are clueless. The music is certainly reflected in this sleeve, for Campbell's songs are gently paranoid, almost the subject of a man who is experiencing mental difficulties. Two of the songs, "Forever Grateful" and "Dulcie, It's December", are truly disturbing as they both express disconcerting feelings through a musical style of innocence and a troublesome grain of voice. Jimmy Campbell, who was from Liverpool, also spoke with Michael Brocken about his time at *Philips*, although Brocken did not broadcast the interview, for Campbell passed away shortly afterwards.[30] His memories were patchy, for he recalled being signed to *Philips*, but not the progressive *Vertigo*. Campbell actually cut three solo albums for *Philips*, with this single effort being on the *Vertigo* subsidiary. He did not recall receiving any royalties from the recordings, but remembered "Dulcie, It's December" being recorded by another singer, the Rhodesian Nicky Speero. One memory Jimmy did have concerned the sleeve, and he recalled to Brocken how he was actually asked to discuss the content of the cover, which he thought was "unusual".

---

[30] Michael Brocken, personal communication, April 2013.

Manfred Mann's Chapter Three (1969) has a relaxing forest green cover with the band's name, likewise album title, written across the top in flowing, white handwriting. Underneath it is a three-tiered white border with two faces drawn inside in the same style as Picasso's drawings using only one line, and some of John Lennon's drawings (notably, a famous self-portrait). For this writer there is a beautiful simplicity to the artwork, courtesy of Jack Levy, but also a sense of sophistication and maturity, perhaps reflecting the jazz/rock fusion on the disc. On its release the album was criticised for being pretentious, yet one cannot help but feel that Manfred Mann was unfortunately hidebound by his work with his previous pop ensemble. The track "Travelling Lady" on the record is almost a version of the cover "in sound". *!* by Gracious! (1970) is another illustrated cover, but one that takes the notion of simplicity further into minimalism by only featuring a grey scaling ("ombre") exclamation mark on a white background with the band's name written in the top right-hand corner. By 1970 this was an interesting marketing device that was also used by *Island Records*. In fact, throughout 1970 several adverts appeared in *Melody Maker* with just an exclamation mark in an advertising box. *Island*, on the other hand, placed "if" in a similar shaped box, to advertise the jazz/rock group of the same name. *Seasons* (Magna Carta, 1970) is far more traditional—as might have been expected, because the band were a mixture of light progressive rock and folk music. The sleeve features a photograph of different leaves and flowers on a beige background in different stages of development, very much reflecting the title of the album. The writing is very intricate, reminiscent of writing from medieval times, with the capital letter "s" in "seasons" being particularly intricate and adorned. The cover was designed by Linda Nicol (née Glover), who is reported by some to have designed *Vertigo*'s swirl logo (Roger Dean is also cited[31]). Finally in this brief overview of the album art on the *Vertigo* label, one cannot ignore the elaborate artwork on Dr Strangely Strange's *Heavy Petting* (1970), which has an incredibly complex gatefold sleeve by Roger Dean. Dr Strangely Strange, an Irish psychedelic folk-rock group, is one of the few to have moved effectively "the other way", having crossed the floor from *Island Records* to *Vertigo Records* in the early 1970s. They followed Patrick Campbell-Lyons of Nirvana.

   Vertigo continued in the same rather "scattergun" vein throughout its "swirl years", with a willingness to release LPs containing experimental music (e.g. Bob Downes), heavy rock (May Blitz)—although both Black Sabbath and Uriah Heep had bailed out by 1972—a kind of progressive

---

[31] Barry Winton, "Vertigo: Into the Void", *Record Collector* 314, September 2005.

pop (Campbell, Nirvana, Aphrodite's Child), folk-rock (Magna Carta) and various other genres. Perhaps the most successful were the first three Black Sabbath albums, Magna Carta's blend of folk, Elizabethan music and rock, Gentle Giant's brand of progressive rock, Aphrodite's Child (at least in Europe), and The Sensational Alex Harvey Band and Status Quo, who between them provided the label with a number of hit singles. One could argue that this variation in genre lessens *Vertigo*'s authenticity because some other labels did indeed choose to remain within, or at least retain their connection to, a specific genre. However, others may feel that it is specifically *Vertigo*'s varied output that makes it an interesting, worthwhile and collectable label. Basically the label's motto, at least according to Patrick Campbell-Lyons was "that old adage: if enough shit hits the fan some of it's bound to stick—a mixture of hippie over-optimism and major label incompetence".[32] Perhaps the last word should be provided by a collector and record enthusiast, Bill Hinds. Bill was a collector and then a dealer at Oldham Market for several years, but succumbed to selling his entire vinyl collection in what he describes as "one act of madness several years ago". However while he has fond memories of *Vertigo*, they are not all to do with its supposed inherent authenticities:

> I thought Vertigo to be a bit of a joke, to be honest, at least at the time. You can always smell it when a label doesn't really "get it". Like in the old days when a Tamla-based night club would hold a "heavy night" to get us Troggs in, you know? It would always be a bit shit because the people involved don't know their arses from their elbows... they don't really "get it". That was Vertigo, for me. The more I learnt the more I realised it was a house of cards in any case. Take away Gerry Bron and the people who managed Black Sabbath and what have you got? A few artists who were signed to Philips in any case—like Manfred Mann, Magna Carta and Jimmy Campbell, a few brought in by Nirvana for nothing, probably and that's about it. It's a bit of a misnomer in the annals of proggy rock— especially when "Paper Plane" pays the bills. Actually they are memorable for having one of my favourite "hate" groups of all time—Magna Carta. That's how I felt about Vertigo. I mean Ramases?—that's what makes them collectable, it's like, take away all the good stuff that people really want, and what do you have left? "Uh oh, I suppose I'd better start on Vertigo." I did actually buy that three-CD boxed set, and I must admit there is some good stuff on it—especially Clear Blue Sky.[33]

---

[32] Patrick Campbell Lyons (2006) to Michael Brocken, BBC Radio Merseyside (off-air).
[33] Bill Hinds, email correspondence, May 2013.

There are obviously any number of different factors that all contribute to making *Vertigo* a collectable label, thus a more detailed account is necessary to fully understand what makes *Vertigo* stand out for collectors amongst other labels of the late 1960s to early 1970s.

Collectability

The previous sections of this chapter discussed collecting in general, the origins of *Vertigo*'s counter-cultural authenticities, examples of their catalogue and their potential appeal to the collector. It would be impossible to detail every single reason why someone collects *Vertigo* LPs, but one can identify some general categories. To begin with, the appearance of the LP may be one factor. *Vertigo*'s first logo, the geometric swirl, is very eye-catching and interesting. It was usually printed in a number of different colours on the album covers, usually matching any other writing. On Colosseum's *Valentyne Suite*, the logo was printed in a light pink colour, like the other lettering on the cover. Juicy Lucy's eponymous record featured a yellow logo, again matching other writing, and the *Black Sabbath* album a purple/maroon logo.

The attention-grabbing characteristic of the swirl logo was something *Vertigo* also exploited in their advertisements, where the consumer was encouraged to cut out the logo, put it on the turntable, switch it on and watch the logo spin around.[34] As far as this author has been able to establish, this was, according to Michael Brocken, a successful marketing technique, with consumers following this invitation. It is not, one supposes, inconceivable that some collectors would buy LPs based on their appreciation of the logo. Despite seeming like a small detail to some, and to non-collectors specifically, perhaps, what appears to be a minor detail can mean everything to a record collector.

The album art featured on *Vertigo* recordings is another aspect to consider. Many of the earliest album covers were designed by Marcus Keef, but Roger Dean was also known for his work with *Vertigo*, and reportedly designed their "swirl"[35] and spaceship logos. The album art boasted by *Vertigo* can, at the very least, be described as interesting, even impressive. Covers include everything from straightforward photography to surrealism, and intricate illustrations to complicated pop-out covers.

---

[34] These advertisements are available online via image searches; www.vertigoswirl.com might also be particularly helpful in providing visuals.
[35] There are conflicting reports as to the actual designer, some citing Dean and others Linda Nicol, with no conclusive evidence at hand—no note was made at the time crediting the designer, and memories are hazy in this regard.

The notion of completing a set is by no means unique to the record collector, and is, in fact, a common wish for many different collectors. Sets are desirable because they can add financial value to the collection, but they also give the collector a goal to work towards. Sets can be set up in any way one desires, but usually one can find "natural" sets occurring within a certain collecting practice. This is made evident by Bloom in his study of collectors of American baseball cards:

> It would be a profound understatement to say no two collectors engaged with their cards in exactly the same way, yet there were noteworthy commonalities and trends in collecting behaviour. One of the most important was the phenomenon of collecting sets. Most collectors used the term set to refer to all of the cards produced by a company during a particular year.[36]

But the way baseball cards emerged as both valuable sources of identity and seemingly historical veracity meant cards by the same company in a certain year thus formed a natural set—as if history had a beginning, a middle, and an end. As *a priori* documents they suggest that reality was a continuous synthesis of elements from a fixed hierarchy of concepts concerning the greatness of the "Great Society". Baseball cards therefore stand as a recognition of society rather than an alternative to it. The *Vertigo* catalogue, on the other hand, presents us with a selection of materials for which there is no place in the historical realities of a failed record label. Instead, we are given the opportunity to engage with stylistic choices and aesthetics, in some cases from an ironic standpoint. So that the aesthetics, the relationships with our own senses of at times failed creativity, inspire us to archive this material for an alternative posterity. What could be more liberating? If we are able to consider that concepts in our heads can relate to what we see, in a creative way for our own existences, then we are truly liberated. Record collecting can provide us with such a key. This does not hinder collectors from creating their own sets, their own criteria, their own senses of reality; as Bloom says, "Collectors also sometimes created their own sets, defining a particular category and attempting to complete it [...] such as 'odd-ball' cards, rookie cards, and teams".[37] Bloom states the obvious: we can relate external realities to our own signifying experiences in any which way we chose, so why not "own" it?

---

[36] John Bloom, *A House of Cards: Baseball Card Collecting and Popular Culture* (Minneapolis: University of Minnesota Press, 1997), 47.
[37] *ibid.*, 47.

We know, in any case, that LPs were definitely *not* manufactured in the same way as baseball cards, indicating natural sets will not be formed in the same way as with baseball cards. In such a sense, record collectors may have more of an opportunity to create their own sets to work towards. The completion of these sets can range from being very achievable to categorically impossible. This becomes apparent when we consider the following three collectors. The first one wants to own all official UK LPs by The Beatles. This set could be completed with reasonable ease as there are only a few LPs in question, and they are relatively common. The second collector wants to own every official album ever released by The Beatles worldwide, as well as their solo efforts. Whilst it is not inconceivable that this set could be completed, it would also take a considerable amount of time, effort and funds and resources. The third collector, however, wants to own every single song within every genre ever released. This set would undoubtedly be impossible to complete for a number of reasons such as sheer volume, knowledge and funding. The task, or set, is simply too big for any one person to be able to complete it. And, additionally, some music that has been released is sadly lost owing to various factors like preservation difficulties.

Collecting by Numbers

In addition to the reasons discussed above, *Vertigo* released their LPs with their own, unique *Vertigo* catalogue numbers (VO1–7, and 6360 001 onwards). *Vertigo* used the same sequence of numbers in a consistent manner, with only very few exceptions, for instance when a record was suddenly withdrawn or the release withheld as was the case with 6360 044 by Dave Kelly (which was released on Mercury instead), thus changing the sequence to 6360 043 followed by 6360 045 instead.[38] The general consistency of *Vertigo*'s catalogue numbers is another attractive quality of *Vertigo's* LPs, as a sequence can be followed. As mentioned above, the natural boundaries established by a (radical) change in the *Vertigo* logo in 1973 means one could see this as a natural set. It is easy to explain the premise of one's set, and there are numerous collectors who are attempting to complete that very set. One could nonetheless also argue that it is a "created" set, as *Vertigo* continued to operate after 1973.

The fact that someone may collect records according to their catalogue numbers might again seem somewhat peculiar to the non-collector, but it

---

[38] See Appendix B: *Vertigo* "Swirl" Discography 1969–1973 for a full overview of the *Vertigo* "swirl" catalogue numbers.

is something that this writer has found keeps recurring amongst collectors. For instance, in Chapter Two there was a brief discussion on *Stag Records* and their unique system of catalogue numbering that almost needed code-breaking. In Chapter Seven, below, "George" furthermore mentions the desirability of collecting *London America* records from their first release to the very last. This is even reflected in fiction, it seems, as it would appear that Dick, from the film *High Fidelity* (see Chapter Six) might be inclined to collect records by their catalogue numbers as he displays intimate knowledge about them. Collecting records in this way, whilst being related to creating a set, also allows the collector to create a record of any entire label's output, creating an archive—the importance of which has been stated throughout this book. Catalogue numbers would further display a continuous sequence and, once completed, one might find that this "complete sequence" grants the collector pleasure by impressing themselves (or others!) as discussed in Eisenberg's[39] list of five points in Chapter Two.

Completing a *"Vertigo* swirl" set, then, whilst being *theoretically* possible, is almost practically *im*possible, however —it is in some respects the record collector's equivalent of the search for the Holy Grail. This is not because of the "missing" catalogue numbers in the sequence,[40] but instead as a result of *Vertigo*'s open attitude to new signings and lack of investment in marketing untried musical genres. This meant that the label was not short of commercial failures, and as a result some *Vertigo* LPs are incredibly rare having only sold a limited number of copies before being deleted. It is believed that some LPs exist in as little as 100 copies: Mark Powell, for instance, frankly states that "Dr. Z's Three Parts to My Soul allegedly [sold] less than 100 copies upon release".[41] Consequently, a collector who wishes to possess a full set would have to invest a significant amount of time and resources in obtaining all LPs. This, though, is something that makes the LPs all the more desirable for some.

As a practice, record collecting encompasses many different activities. Some may feel that the organisation of the LPs is the most important aspect, whereas others may value the playing of the record. Searching for a specific LP may take a considerable amount of time, yet for some the

---

[39] Eisenberg, Evan, *The Recording Angel: Music, Records And Culture From Aristotle To Zappa* (New Haven: Yale University Press, 2005).

[40] Because, as the reader may note in Appendix B: *Vertigo* "Swirl" Discography 1969–1973, in some cases the "missing" catalogue numbers can be obtained by purchasing foreign (notably South American) releases instead of British.

[41] Mark Powell, *Time Machine: A Vertigo Retrospective*, CD notes (London: Mercury Records 9827982, 2005), 7.

process of "hunting" for the record is what gives the activity its value. Finding a rare LP will never be unappreciated, but for a person who has invested resources in trying to find a particular LP the rewards will be greater because of the higher investment. Firstly, a record collector who has successfully sought out a certain record shows evidence of certain knowledge. The collector needed to know specifically where to find the disc and having the knowledge of where this LP may be found also shows evidence of cultural capital. Importantly for us, then, the value of the chase, or as Shuker might suggest, the "hunt",[42] and the significance of the artefact, are both two parts of a vital element which creates authenticity surrounding the artefact at least as much, if not more than, the artist. The collector recognises that while a significant amount of time and money can be taken up by the economic investment, a cultural investment involving thought, concepts, and mental space awards the collector a cultural investment that cannot be valued. Indeed, while both these economic and cultural resources are put to considerable effect via the search and acquisition of say, Dr. Z (and that search in all probability would be fruitless), the mirror the search presents to us is perhaps one of the most accurate reflections that we can be provided with, for any collector will see that their distorted image actually represents both tangible and theoretical rewards via the chase.

Therefore, in many respects, the narrative one should attach to the completion of a collection of *Vertigo* records is to do with the process of arriving. Although when we speak of arriving it sounds as if our work is done, in fact the record collector knows that this is never true. Record collecting in general (and the *Vertigo* label in particular) suggests a very important philosophical premise: as human beings we never fully complete what we are or, appear to be, as long as we are still breathing. The record collection, in fact, suggests tangible evidence of the fact that we keep evolving: "I have grown to dislike many records in my collection. My taste has changed and I have been building this sucker [the record collection] since I was a kid".[43] It also suggests that we need to keep checking our reflection as we evolve—the collection is our reflection. The great force behind popular culture generally is its ability to provide us with some kind of a mirror at any given time in our lives. Popular culture reflects the many guises we adopt in the evolution of our various identities. But, as we have suggested, record collecting as a mirror is not simply reflecting us. It is also influencing us, changing us, perhaps even

---

[42] Roy Shuker, *Wax Trash and Vinyl Treasures: Record Collecting as a Social Practice* (Farnham: Ashgate, 2010).
[43] "Recordlove" (2009), www.recordcollectorsguild.org.

coercing us, persuading us to re-think who we are and what we are, and also what we might yet become.

CHAPTER SIX

CODIFICATION:
FILMIC PORTRAYALS OF THE RECORD
COLLECTOR AS "OTHER"

"Laws of nature are human *inventions*, like ghosts. Laws of logic,
of mathematics are also human inventions, like ghosts. The whole
blessed thing is a human invention, including the idea that it *isn't*
a human invention. The world has no existence whatsoever outside
the human imagination"
—Robert Pirsig (1972), *Zen and the Art of Motorcycle Maintenance*

Introduction

Record collectors unquestionably follow their natural feelings and are not
trying to copy anyone: record collecting is not mimesis. However, when
they are looked at as a group by the media (in our case, by filmmakers),
we get the illusion of a "mass" of people, in some cases an anti-
technological mass, that has possibly developed from the counter-culture
of the 1960s ("hippiedom") and 1970s ("punk"). Such readings suggest
that record collectors are "subcultural", and that they loom from the past
exclaiming "stop the technology, go back to the way it was, bring back
vinyl", or other "Luddite" expressions. These images are at least partially
held in place by a gossamer web of logic which suggests that without
social mores, factories and technologies, etc., there are no jobs, and
therefore no standards of living under which one can execute one's
"culture", and that such activities therefore require the over-arching
culture to finance their habits and are by definition "subcultural"—but this
proposition is incorrect.

Via our pre-amble to the discussion of the collectible *Vertigo* record
label in the previous chapter, it could be seen that clichés and typecasts
such as "hippie" were invented to deal with the anti-technologists, the
"anti-system people" of the late 1960s. We should constantly remind
ourselves that such expressions are, indeed, clichés of the highest order,
and that such words do not convert individuals into masses with the simple

coining of that cliché. For example, neither Les Parry nor Bill Hinds are "mass" anti-technology people (both are actually computer programmers by trade) who were drawn to the counter-cultural debates of that era, and then equally drawn to the perhaps Zen-like signifiers of modern computer technologies. In fact, it might be argued that it was against being a "mass" person that many seem to have been revolting—if indeed they *were* revolting, which is also highly questionable! Some record collectors might indeed be on a flight from technology, whereas others might not.

In fact it has already been suggested in this book that this writer feels that technology has actually aided and abetted the record collector in more ways than one could possibly imagine. Yet the counter-cultural critique, from which the pastime partially emerged in the 1970s, has contributed to the cliché of the "record collector", which then supplemented the pre-existing cliché of "the collector" discussed in Chapter One. In some respects, the otherness of the record collector tends to stem from this latter-day pathway, rather than the one from which technology introduced new possibilities for listening, despite the record openly challenging musical, thus social, hierarchies by its very presence in the first fifty years of the century.

One might turn towards subcultural theorists for assistance at this stage, such as those at Birmingham University's Centre for Contemporary Studies in the 1970s, who were among the first to recognise different ways of understanding deviancy in relationship to popular culture. However, in some respects, such subcultural theory merely compounds the "otherness" of the record collector, and does not really help us. It is important to acknowledge the work of Hall and Jefferson,[1] Stanley Cohen[2] and Dick Hebdige,[3] who all suggested in their own ways that subcultural groups take products that are available to them and then transform meanings through a type of "bricolage": this is a process of improvisation where conspicuous consumption is re-framed to transform meanings. All of this appears to be very useful to those studying record collectors, for in some cases this is precisely what they do. Therefore subcultural studies at least offer insights into how people consume popular music cultures.

However, in the first instance, the placing of individuals into subcultural groupings is something of an urban myth. For all the fascination held by historians and sociologists alike for "movements" of

---

[1] Stuart Hall and Tony Jefferson, *Resistance through Ritual: Youth Subcultures in Post-War Britain* (London: Hutchinson, 1977).
[2] Stanley Cohen, *Folk Devils and Moral Panics* (London: MacGibbon and Kee, 1972).
[3] Dick Hebdige, *Subculture: The Meaning of Style* (London: Methuen, 1979).

people, those identified as being part of such groupings do not always recognise such descriptions of themselves. This leaves subcultural theory potentially a little at a loss as to what, and whom, it is supposed to be discussing. Sid Jones of Muse Music informed this writer: "According to most people I'm a hippie, but I never was and never will be: I'm a businessman who happens to do his job properly and is interested in what he sells—that's about it".[4]

So, although subcultural theory can be considered a useful avenue into consideration of record collectors, especially in suggesting that taste and choice are not arbitrary or haphazard, it is productive only up to a point in our analyses. It can, as Tim Wall suggests, develop "our thinking about specific subcultures [should they exist in the first place], but they do tend to marginalise women's roles and ignore the way popular music consumption takes place outside of specified subcultures".[5] It could be argued, in fact, that subcultural theory is *doubly un*helpful for specifically identifying and analysing the vast majority of record collectors as individuals, for if they cannot be defined via their anti-establishment existence, nor fit into society's concepts of social mores, folkways and rules, nor be defined as "subcultural" by society's thinkers, then their outsidership is compounded exponentially by these lacks of "fit" or "homologies", turning them, effectively into an "other".

The "Oriental Other"

The concept of the "other" and "otherness" was first conceived by the cultural critic Edward Said in his book *Orientalism*,[6] where he discusses how the Middle East is typically perceived by the West as an "other". Said argues that Orientalism is the source of inaccurate cultural representations of the Middle East, which is derived from a romanticised view of the region. So far as record collecting is concerned it is perhaps only a slight overstatement to suggest that the record collector is essentially seen as some kind of "other". This is not to suggest that they are seen as a political threat of any description, but rather, according to the matrix of social mores discussed in Chapter Three, that they are seen as relative outsiders. Said further argued that many seemingly academic examinations failed because rather than functioning as an intellectual enquiry striving for

---

[4] Sid Jones to author, May 2013.
[5] Tim Wall, *Studying Popular Music Culture* (London: Arnold, 2003), 172.
[6] Edward Said, *Orientalism* (New York: Vintage Books Edition, 1978).

objectivity (or relative objectivity), they were instead political, self-affirmations.[7]

While Islam and the Arab are constantly identified as a troublesome other, there is little room for a full understanding and exchange of views. Such tropes of European cultural superiority are embedded within Western society to such an extent that they go unnoticed. Even Marxism, it might be argued, as a European-derived form of philosophy, takes little-or-no account of the East and its traditions. The attempt to write a comparative history from within such boundaries has proved to be problematic because it merely reveals common patterns of historical writing. This tends to suggest that the West's historiography is something approaching a litany, an aggrandisement of itself. Said's conclusions are that a great deal of Western writing about the East depicts it as an irrational, weak, and feminised other, a condition which contrasts with the rational, strong, and masculine West; this, it is argued, is a binary relation derived from the need to create a difference of cultural inequality. Such issues concerning essences are interesting when moving closer to home because people are seen as behaving in certain ways since they "just" do this or "just" do that in a similar way in which the oriental other is discussed.

For example Brocken and Davis state:

> When we consider a written text we realise, evidently, that somebody actually wrote it, perhaps re-wrote it, that it was sourced, published, and even re-published to serve changing contextual demands. This realisation then invites the researcher to look further, not simply at the texts *per se* but also at the mores indicative in the texts. Texts are representations offered to the public as a result of relationships between certain kinds of rationality and imagination. They contain tentative suggestions mixed with pragmatic confirmations. There are processual tactics in a text that mark stages of both the writer's practical investigations and strategic ideological representations.[8]

Popular Music Writing as Orientalism

In popular music terms, for example, it became increasingly clear that a kind of "evolutionary narrative" of Beatles writing had re-combined, and at times unwittingly commented upon, earlier instances of its own literary genre and sub-genres, rather than develop new ideas and new frames of

---

[7] *ibid.*
[8] Michael Brocken and Melissa Davis, *The Beatles Bibliography: A New Guide to the Literature* (Manitou Springs: The Beatle Works, 2012), 5–6.

reference. For example, divisions brought about by publishing economies of scale, a rock journalism "elite" (conversely, an artisan-like inventiveness), local and fan-based publishing networks, etc. are all apparent. Growing demographics, canons of national iconography, and the publishing requirements of multinational agencies have also placed Beatles writings into interesting historical subsets. It has been suggested by Brocken and Davis that these texts are therefore part of:

> [...] an almost "archeological" field of enquiry, for fresh fragments can be brought to the table. For example, as with an archeological dig, items still crop up: a new photo, a new recollection, an old piece of music, a new book, etc. So, for the writers of Beatles histories there is almost a mythological definitive document from which questions and answers can be set forth and from which an author's sense of proportion and feelings for this given authority, and for presentation within that authority, can be determined. In effect, writing about The Beatles has become a "Biblical" and enclosed pursuit and although a historical fragment might have emanated from The Beatles, it does not have to (in fact, cannot) stay the same. A certain "fragment configuration" takes place so that any "new" fragments "fit" within the ruling order of Beatles historiography. This literary homology serves, not only the aforementioned support network, but at times blinds the writer to any potential flexible creativity.[9]

The argument put forward is, then, that there exists an entire body of literary constraints, a set of conventions—even within popular music writing—and how each writer paraphrases Beatles images and imaginings and how authenticity is connoted is of significance, for it represents orthodoxy and traditionalism. One might argue that such limitations are what guides Western man towards a consideration of an agreed set of rules and a binary "other" to set these rules against. If texts of any description do not fall within this litany-style historiography, they can be regarded as outsider and "other". So it could be argued that there are many parochial forms of designated "otherness" within Western society that use forms of orientalism. The "otherness" associated with the collector is undoubtedly derived from a kind of orientalism, but it is also strongly influenced by what might be described by sociologists as the modernisation theory.[10]

Modernisation theory recognises global development as progressive, where science and technology guide societies from traditional to complex,

---

[9] *ibid.*, 9.
[10] Thomas Docherty, "Postmodernism: An Introduction", in *Postmodernism: A Reader*, ed. Thomas Docherty (London: Harvester Wheatsheaf, 1993), 1–32.

from regressive to progressive.[11] One can suggest that, linked with Said's model of the oriental other, forms of behaviour that do not necessarily contribute to the development of science and technology as a *guide*, can be seen as "other". These conspicuous discussions about traditional otherness, which do not contribute to a modernised, theoretical world-model, allow us to consider portrayals of record collectors as both individuals and members of an "other" social grouping. Via this mixture of Said's "other" and modernisation theory, we can attempt to see how portrayals work when cast within a modern technological form of media which is intended to portray itself as an arbiter of taste and culture for the modern world about us.

One might consider such a hybrid theoretical form from five specific standpoints. Firstly, modernisation itself is considered to be a confirmation of a Europeanisation concerning the way we live, and that such standards are culturally and politically advanced. Indeed, they are so advanced that they provide a model from which we can live. In some respects, the oriental other of the record collector is seen as an antithesis to this model, a retrogressive, isolated and "orientalised" individual who does not contribute to the progressive development of society. Secondly, modernisation is considered to be irreversible, and according to Said's model, the East needs to "catch up", whether they like it or not. In this model, there is little room for folklore. There is little room for individualisation—and there is no room for nostalgia. Therefore, some of the attributes which make record collecting worthwhile to the collector are not only considered as some kind of exotic other, but are actually reduced to redundancy, surplus to the requirements of the modern age. For example, dealer and collector Dave informed this writer that:

> I wanted to take a stall again in Chester Market, the market is really struggling, and over the last 12 months there has been enormous interest in what has been described as "retro". There are already two retro shops in Chester, but when I tried to convince Chester Council to open a vinyl stall as they once did, I was faced with the problem of being described a "knob head" who won't grow up—in other words they couldn't see the future potential of some kind of retrogressive music stall. If I was asking them to give me permission to sell old-fashioned sausages they might have given me the nod [of approval], but as it was I came across the old ideas of me being a bit odd despite having had a stall there for over 20 years and never being behind in my rent.[12]

---

[11] *ibid.*
[12] Interview with Dave, April 2013.

Dave went on to suggest that it was as if he was considered by Chester Council to be a kind of "one man, Third World country, hindering the progress of Chester Market".[13]

This links with a third point concerning modernisation, that when certain traditional ideas come into contact with futurism they resist the potential for modernisation far too much. Futurism could be defined as an ideology related to the way things might become if human society moved in the "correct" direction, although futurism in this case represents a loose collective of ideas concerning the way we should live. One might, for instance, cite architectural discussion concerning how we should live as "futurism", e.g. Le Corbusier in 1930s France. One might also suggest that the future as presented to us lies in our hands—so it is self-deterministic. Modernisation, it could therefore be argued, is a homogenising process which further isolates Said's oriental "other". This eventually, it has been argued, creates within society people who carry the potential only to resemble one another. The fourth point concerning modernisation and the record collector as other is that its neglect of otherness suggests that there is a long-term benefit from such homogenisation and that by addressing issues to do with the present and the future, the quality of people's lives improves. However this has yet to be proven; one might suggest that this rule is actually of little consequence to the individual, especially given the imprint that politics has left on society during the twentieth and twenty-first centuries. What some people consider to be a lack of reality, or a flight from the present, requires historicisation in a different way, for one might ask why a wish to free oneself from narrow forms of beliefs should be considered to be retrograde, if this flight takes one into the past and the private. If one considers such acts to be sublime, then these must surely be strong emotions which carry pleasure and pain—they are not simply forms of escaping the present and the future.

Finally, the modernisation theory suggests that modernisation is both a phased and a lengthy process in which generations effectively convert from their otherness into a progressively informed person. Given this fact, it is quite easy to see how myth and legends of otherness emerge within society concerning a kind of inherent orientalism. The legend of a record collector will ultimately support modernisation, not the orientalist, and therefore portrayal of the legend ultimately offers, for most people, a level of repulsion from the other so much so that the legend offers a way out of the dilemma of otherness. It is under such terms that it is worth considering the few portrayals of record collecting that have been assigned

---

[13] Interview with Dave, April 2013.

to the visual media. For by looking at such examples we can see that the myth of otherness, if presented as part of a modernisation theory, can suggest that while society allows for such eccentric behaviours, it also offers through its portrayal a way out of it.

The Record Collector as Urban Myth

Visual portrayals of record collectors tend to offer within the modernisation discourse issues to do with word of mouth and legend. It is common to watch what can be mistaken as ethnography, but is actually a series of quotidian examples offering specific supposed validations of the legend of the record collector. One sees collectors invited to offer specific "validations". One sees quotes in the media[14] regarding how collectors perceive themselves, and one sees edits of quotes that can make interviewees look ridiculous, yet harmless. A substantial number of references to record collecting can be found to validate this quotidian sourcing of the oriental other. For example, one usually receives information about the collector's past. One often gets a narrative of the growth of the legend, from a brief initial contact with a record to a full immersion in the "habit". One also often gets a repeated person-to-person narrative which can incorporate media sources and networks.

So, all such representations and portrayals of otherness within the society which is claiming the modernisation are worthy of study if only from the perspective of understanding the theoretical framework within which such portrayals are undertaken. For instance, it might seem unlikely that legends would continue to be created in such an age of widespread and rapid modernisation. Our pioneer ancestors relied heavily on oral traditions and legend in order to pass on important information, and surely one might think we no longer need "folk" reports of what is happening and all of their tendencies to distort facts. However, when one considers the orientalism of the other merged with the modernisation and futurism of society, legends serve multi-purposes: on a basic level they can remind us of the many fascinating and weird things that we do as human beings, and the lack of verification of such stories in no way diminishes the appeal that they have for us. Therefore, while documentation and evidence is vitally important for recognising variables, societal documentation does not seem to be an issue. For documentation will, perhaps, disprove the legend of

---

[14] Ranging from documentaries such as *Sound It Out* to printed media (including newspapers, particularly during events such as Record Store Day, and magazines such as *NME*).

myth. So the legends we tell, and the way that we tell them in the twenty-first century, reflect many of the aforementioned social mores of our time. In short, legends are most decidedly part of our time, just as much as they were within older forms of society.

Urban legends are of great significance. The vast quantity of interchange between human beings tends to include values and associations that we take for granted, and that are punctuated by repeatable stereotypes. Urban legends are not therefore simply what one person might pass to another, but include communication-led portrayals and stereotypes. Indeed the portrayal of a legend, myth or stereotype, if communicated by mass-media methods, especially of the visual variety, requires performance and tells us that urban legends are seldom ever aware of their roles as performers, but performers they certainly are. For, to fit within the matrix of otherness and modernisation, one has to effectively adopt a position through the medium of modern communication techniques. It is all the more ironic that, in the very few visual representations of record collectors that we have received over the past decade, the oriental other is present first and foremost, and that the record collectors, perhaps inadvertently, conform to and accord with the stereotypes into which they have been inserted. One might argue that in looking at portrayals of record collectors we need to consider how the subject matter, style and oral performance contributes to the otherness of the record collector.

High Fidelity

High Fidelity is a 2000 American comedy-drama film directed by Stephen Frears, starring John Cusack and Danish actress Iben Hjejle, and based on the 1995 British novel of the same name by record collector (see further discussion below) and soccer fanatic Nick Hornby. The setting has, however, been moved from London to Chicago, and the lead character's name been changed from Rob Fleming to Rob Gordon. The narrative centres on Rob (Cusack), a self-confessed music "geek" (i.e. record collector) with a very poor understanding of the female of the species (or indeed, most human beings). After getting dumped by his current girlfriend, Laura (Hjejle), because of his apparent obsessions as a collector, he decides to look up some of his old partners in an attempt to figure out where he keeps going wrong in his relationships. He spends his days at his record store, Championship Vinyl, where he holds court over the various customers that drift through. Helping Rob in his task of musical elitism are Dick (Todd Louiso) and Barry (Jack Black), the "musical moron twins", as he refers to them. Armed with an encyclopaedic knowledge of all things musical, they are "listographers" who compile "top five" lists for every conceivable occasion; they also openly mock the ignorance of their customers, and occasionally—and reluctantly—sell a few records. Ultimately, at the resolution of the narrative (or "fairy tale ending", if you will), the viewer finds out that Rob has also started his own label, calling it *Top 5 Records*, and in the final scene Rob finishes his advice about making the perfect mix-tape, which had been an over-arching theme throughout the film and another sign of the "geek", it seems, and says that he is now making one for Laura.

One might argue that *High Fidelity* is a solid representation of record collecting, retailing and fanaticism, being initially written by British writer Nick Hornby, himself (he claims, at least) an avid record collector; however, not only does the removal of the subject matter from the UK to the US present us with narrative problems between novel and film of vast proportions (even if one considers only the emphases of certain London-centric slang used by Hornby in the novel, and its translation into modernised "American-speak"), but also with basic portrayal issues concerning mental health, gender, loneliness, community, and the act of making money from the sales of second-hand records. Reviews, however, were very positive. For example, the late Philip French of *The Guardian*, suggested:

> Nick Hornby's novel High Fidelity is set specifically and convincingly in London. But it touches so amusingly, perceptively and honestly on what it's like to be a confused, self-doubting young man immersed in popular culture in any large city in the Western world at the end of the twentieth century that the transposition to Chicago for the movie version involves surprisingly little reworking. [...] Pop music and films are his [Rob's] obsessive interests, his knowledge of them encyclopedic [*sic*] and, since puberty, he has been troubled by girls, whom he fears, desires and tries to understand. [...] High Fidelity is an extraordinarily funny film, full of verbal and visual wit. [...]The picture never scores cheap points off anybody[15]

The film received further positive reviews. The website Metacritic gave the film a score of 79 out of 100 based on a number of reviews by critics, and 8.2 out of 10 based on user scores.[16] Film critic Roger Ebert gave the film four out of five stars, stating, "Watching *High Fidelity*, I had

---

[15] Philip French, "This One's a Hit...", *The Guardian* [online], 23 July 2000, accessed 30 April 2013, http://www.guardian.co.uk/film/2000/jul/23/philipfrench.
[16] www.metacritic.com, accessed 29 May 2013.

the feeling I could walk out of the theater [*sic*] and meet the same people on the street—and want to, which is an even higher compliment".[17]

In his review for *Entertainment Weekly*, however, Owen Gleiberman was more measured, awarding the film a B-rating and stating: "In *High Fidelity*, Rob's *music fixation is a signpost of his arrested adolescence*; he needs to get past records to find true love. If the movie had had a richer romantic spirit, he might have embraced both in one swooning gesture".[18]

If one were to take into consideration the "other"/modernisation theory, one can clearly see that *High Fidelity* presents us with several problems concerning representation. One might argue that the positive reviews are somewhat bizarre, given the nature of the stereotype of the collector. One might indeed expect collectors to roundly condemn the film for rank-stereotyping, but this is not so surprising, for according to Said the "other" is an image developed in people's minds over a long period of time: the mirror-like reflection, idealism, materialism and objectivity are all parts of the inner sanctum of Western social mores and modernism. In some respects, one might argue that all four of these criteria appear to be fulfilled by *High Fidelity*. We see ideas about reflection as framing a mental structure in words. In this case, the screenwriter gives us what we recognise as a full process of life. Furthermore, in terms of realism, *High Fidelity* could be regarded as a model of Marxist thought because it achieves the adequate reflection of human society as is required by social

---

[17] Roger Ebert, "High Fidelity", 31 March 2000, accessed 29 May 2013, http://www.rogerebert.com/reviews/high-fidelity-2000. Interestingly, Ebert also goes on to state: "This is a film about—and also for—not only obsessed clerks in record stores, but the video store clerks who have seen all the movies, and the bookstore employees who have read all the books. Also for bartenders, waitresses, greengrocers in health food stores, kitchen slaves at vegetarian restaurants, the people at GNC who know all the herbs, writers for alternative weeklies, disc jockeys on college stations, salespeople in retro clothing shops, tattoo artists and those they tattoo, poets, artists, musicians, novelists, and the hip, the pierced and the lonely. They may not see themselves, but they will recognize people they know [are we perhaps to believe they would, or *should*, see themselves if they only 'looked'?]. [...] I am meandering. All I want to say is that 'High Fidelity' has no deep significance".

[18] Owen Gleiberman, "High Fidelity", 31 March 2000, accessed 29 May 2013, my own emphasis, http://www.ew.com/ew/article/0,,275803,00.html. Similarly, Stephanie Zacharek for *Salon.com*, further praised Hjejle's performance: "Hjejle's Laura is supremely likable: she's so matter-of-fact and grounded that it's perfectly clear why she'd become exasperated *with a guy like Rob, who perpetually refuses to grow up* [my own emphasis], but you can also see how her patience and calm are exactly the things he needs".

realism. In addition to this, it is a cultural reflection on the potential of
dialectic materialism, i.e. that our actions lead to consequences, and that
human beings need to intervene in their own lives in order to question the
hierarchies of society. One might argue that there is also a seeming
objectivity to it, wherein Cusack's character is able to objectively reflect
our supposed feelings concerning the subjectivity of life. Given these
criteria, the form, the structure and the genre of *High Fidelity* all seem to
be fulfilling the requirements of a piece of Western art.

For example, John Cusack plays a character with an ostensibly
complex inner life brought about by and through his record collecting,
which is portrayed almost like a drug habit. He finds it difficult to identify
with people especially those who, like him, carry this addiction with them.
This is depicted as a social *problem* brought about by an obsessive,
meandering lifestyle in which he has problems personally relating to
members of the opposite sex, his staff, and members of the general public.
Thus it is suggested that this character has an element of social dyslexia.
As with the book, we are taken into Rob's mind and, for much of the time,
he speaks directly to camera, not just in set-pieces, as if he is talking to
himself—another indicator of the socially dysfunctional. The idea that his
collecting actually contributed to defining him (together with his assistants
in the shop who are predictably geeky) in this way, promulgates the urban
myth and associated legend of record collecting. One can quite easily
understand how a young man can become alienated by society, although to
place the record collection at the epicentre of such meaning merely
contributes to Said's aforementioned "oriental other".

As many of us have a habit of doing, Rob seeks to impose order on his
life by drawing up lists. His most extravagant gesture is to rearrange his
vast collection of LPs as a form of autobiography so that he has to think of
the personal associations records offer him. When Laura leaves him, he
rejects her via a list of "top five most memorable split-ups". However,
such listings are not completely inherent to the record collector
(interestingly, many collectors find archiving their collections tedious and
unnecessary, many commenting on record collecting forums that they only
do so for specific purposes, such as home insurance) and they do not fulfil
the requirements of record collecting. Arguably, in fact, one key feature
that distinguishes record collecting for most collectors (at least according
to the aforementioned Dave and several of this writer's interviewees) is an
emphasis on relationships. There is an element of the nuclear about the
record collector, which is ignored to create an image of the other. Yet
throughout the movie, concepts of the nuclear are set *against* concepts of
the collector as other. Oppositions are therefore established, which fulfil

neither the criteria of the nuclear kinship that the film refuses to suggest, nor the isolation through societal dyslexia that it does suggest. We are therefore left with an image that has no relationship to the potential for an extended family through record collecting: a kind of "perfect polygamy" within which record collecting and a loving relationship can co-exist. This is, perhaps, not surprising because such a concept is oriental and other, not Western and Hollywood.

One might therefore argue that such portrayals are reminiscent of a conventional Western filtering process in which the individual, seeking some kind of culturally acceptable new life, gradually narrows the field of eligible mates and ultimately turns his back on what is depicted as an obsession for the sake of making their final "historical" selection. This is an urban myth, for research thus far undertaken by this writer suggests that many record collectors are able to maintain a balance between stimulus and value. Relationships, for them, therefore pass through various stages of symbolic interaction which do not always end up in an "either/or" situation. Indeed, as previously suggested, over recent years there have been trends amongst middle-class professionals to re-incorporate the presence of vinyl into both domestic and work environments, to effectively "humanise" their lives; vinyl can be regarded as "restful", in fact. The very presence of vinyl in a room creates a sense of harmony for those within the room, and it could be argued that the essentialising dichotomy presented by *High Fidelity* could not be further away from the reality of co-habitation and its relationship to recorded sound collecting. *High Fidelity* is therefore undoubtedly an urban legend and, like many of its ilk, it has been collected, complied, edited, and visualised to serve mythological duties. It is important to recognise that the work is broadly representative rather than definitive, and is an example of otherness created by modernisation concerning the record collector.

In 2011 this writer also attended a screening of the documentary *Sound It Out*, by director Jeanie Finlay. Her intentions were to make a documentary about a Teesside-based independent record shop of the same name, but by the very nature of the project she inevitably also documents people frequenting the shop. Certain record collectors and record shop characters thus feature in interviews, and command a strong presence throughout the film, making it another case study as to how record collectors are portrayed in documentaries. But it is by no means all good news, and also ultimately suggests that collecting, and the collector, is a pursuit of the "other" and perhaps like gambling, needs corrective therapies wherefrom the subject can emerge "clean". Before undertaking an examination of the messages and images of *Sound It Out*, it is however important to introduce the parameters of the case study. Ethnographic study in popular music has been widely acknowledged and conducted for many years now, and we have already discussed this in Chapter Two. In this case, observational ethnography was conducted.[19]

Andrew Hannan of the University of Plymouth offers important advice concerning observational methods and approaches. As part of his advice to undergraduate students he suggests that:

> Observational techniques are an important aspect of many action research studies and of case studies whether undertaken by participants or outsiders [and that] in a way all of us are already well practised in the arts of observation—we all need to observe human behaviour in our personal and professional lives, we are all familiar with the need to come to conclusions based on our observation, to generate explanations and understandings and even to come up with predictions.[20]

Hannan also tells us that it is vitally important that we try to build skills and firstly "exploit those aspects of common sense that are of benefit".[21] However, he also proposes that undertaking such research requires us to:

> [...] go beyond the subjective and impressionistic, we need to be aware of and, if possible, eliminate bias, we need to be systematic and open about our procedures so as to open them up for public scrutiny so that others may check the bases on which we reach conclusions.[22]

It was with such instructions in mind, together with the aforementioned work of Sara Cohen and Martin Hammersley, that this researcher undertook observational ethnography of the screening of *Sound It Out.*

Screening

Sound It Out was screened at the Foundation for Art and Creative Technology (FACT) Picture House in Liverpool on November 10th 2011. FACT is regarded as a more "alternative" rather than "mainstream" venue that hosts exhibitions, events, cinema, and has a café and bar available on-

---

[19] One question relating to the portrayal of the collectors was, however, asked by this writer during the Q&A session.

[20] Andrew Hannan, *Observation Techniques* (2006), accessed 15 May 2013, http://www.edu.plymouth.ac.uk/resined/observation/obshome.htm.

[21] *ibid.*

[22] *ibid.*

site. It describes itself as "the UK's leading organisation for the support and exhibition of film, art and new media".[23] FACT has three conventional screens on the top floor, plus a smaller screen on the ground floor known as "The Box", which typically shows independent films, or films that are coming to the end of their run. It is an interesting venue, but one, at least from this writer's perspective that seems to be "colonised" by people of similar interests, rather than the Liverpool public at large. *Sound It Out* was shown in Screen 3, the smallest of the regular screens, to a roughly half-filled room. One can request a screening of a film through the website,[24] which is presumably what had happened, and it was then screened as part of a music-themed day on the premises. The *Sound It Out* ticket stubs could be used to redeem a free pint of beer at the bar after the screening to encourage patrons to stay and listen to the music being played as a part of this music day. The *Sound It Out* audience were, however, also told a glass of wine was available as an alternative to the pint, but the announcement was made for a pint of lager, which is also perhaps indicative of the "aesthetics" of the evening. A number of local bands were due to perform afterwards, although the author was unable to stay for that part of the evening.

On the whole, the screening was poorly advertised. The event was published on the documentary-makers' website and Tom, the record shop owner, and director Jeanie Finlay were interviewed on the BBC Breakfast sofa on the morning of the screening. However, there were no visible posters in the FACT building (or anywhere else across the city) and attempts to purchase tickets for the screening on the FACT website proved so difficult that your correspondent gave up trying. This was partly owing to the difficulty in navigating the FACT website, but there was nevertheless minimal indication that the documentary was even to be screened at all. Following most of the screenings throughout the UK, a question and answer session was also scheduled to take place, and whilst Finlay attended most of these herself, the Liverpool audience was introduced to the producer Sally Hodgson by a member of staff from FACT, followed by a brief introduction to the film itself.

The Documentary

As mentioned, a FACT staff member and Hodgson, the film's producer, introduced the documentary to the audience before the screening. The

---

[23] www.fact.co.uk, accessed 22 November 2011.
[24] www.sounditoutdoc.com.

audience were also told that the director found inspiration for the film when she sold her old record collection to Tom, the shop owner, to fund her wedding (very authentic). The documentary began with images from the shop's locale, which had a "cold" feel to them. The official website describes it as "a distinct, funny and intimate film about men, the North and the irreplaceable role music plays in our lives" but also as "High Fidelity with a Northern Accent". However they state that *Sound It Out* is not a fictional tale, but aims to *"document* a place [...] and the local community that keeps it alive".[25]

Throughout the film we are introduced to a number of characters, predominantly male, including Tom and his employee David, but also customers and collectors, particularly Shane and Chris (presumably their real names—although we are not informed either way). A number of different collectors are shown making some sort of statement indicating how important record collecting has been to them, and how vital music has been in shaping their lives and identities. One dance music enthusiast states his music-making endeavours have kept him on the right side of the law; he used to get in trouble with the police before he began deejaying, while a young heavy metal fan explains how music, and kinship through music, saved his life.

The Collectors, Their Portrayals

The viewer encounters a number of male collectors throughout the film, who collect a variety of different music genres. There are few women, and from the start, this is a vexed question, for female interpretations are, broadly-speaking, not present, and so the narrative is immediately aligned with the oriental other/modernisation continuum. Shane and Chris are, however, the most memorable voices, but for completely different reasons. Shane appears eccentric, a deviation from the norm—a trait he excuses continually in the film. He is a huge Status Quo fan and collector, and does undeniably have some unconventional ideas, such as the desire to have a coffin made out of his melted-down record collection when he passes ("no one will appreciate it as much as me", he states). Even though the director presents him in a relatively neutral way, at certain points in the film he comes across as a comical figure—it almost feels, at times, as if he is being mocked for the amusement of the audience. This mockery is interesting, for the portrayal appears to suggest that Shane is a bridge between the audience and the "netherworld" of the collector, and as such

---

[25] www.sounditoutdoc.com, accessed 22 November 2011, my own emphasis.

is presented with an almost comical "double vision" where he can embrace both "us" and "them"—the public and the private—with a sense of self-effacing irony. One might suggest that such a parody ill-befits the director of a documentary.

In contrast, Chris is portrayed as very "normal", and as such becomes the most accepted collector in the film. He does not escape the stereotype, however, for because of this he is portrayed as boring. But Chris is evidently very shy and is the only collector in the film to be represented as gainfully employed at the time of filming (Shane is the only other collector to be shown to be in any kind of employment, but he is a night-stocker at B&Q, a job he feels he needs to justify to the camera). Chris's shyness, his sense of reluctance to talk about his record collecting, and the fact that he is immediately introduced to the viewer as an auditor, are all quite ordinary traits and may be why he seems a much more "acceptable" record collector than the others who are featured. Chris has a very large collection, and is almost ashamed to admit that he has organised his records alphabetically, and then chronologically within the same artist (as many do). He also asserts that his collecting never stops and could be a life-long journey.

So we have a classic binary opposition for the audience to embrace. Oppositions are perfect narrative functions for they present the insider (emic) and the outsider (etic) text. Audiences will immediately respond to these typecasts, for the insider is usually responded to in a positive way, whereas the etic outsider tends to fulfil his narrative role by being awarded outsider, oriental status. Audiences always confer their close attention to oppositional motives, both because of the traditional prominence of key individuals in media representations and because the motives of the "great" tend to be painted in glowing colours.

The Audience and Reception

The FACT audience were mainly middle-aged, with a few in their twenties. The younger members of the audience appeared to be students or young professionals, and some were apparently reviewing the film: the slightly older people seemed well-educated and in distinguished jobs (including university lecturers). In view of the examination of the audience reception and reactions which follows below, it may also be useful for the reader to keep in mind that because of the poor publicity for the screening, one might assume that the members of the audience either actively sought out the screening (like the author), were interested in the general music day held at FACT, or were regular patrons who learnt of the event by simply being "in the know" (such as FACT members)—in other words, people with a clear interest in the arts generally, and more specifically, music and/or record collecting.

Throughout the film, the audience were audible in their responses to it, but some responses were occasionally very troublesome. To give one example, the heavy metal fan who stated that the music he listened to and the kinship it brought with it had saved his life provoked laughter when he said that without music he would not look the way he did (a very distinct heavy metal-style with long hair and leather jacket, etc.) or be the person he was. A few moments later he also revealed that he had made a number of suicide attempts, but with the help of the music he interacted with, and his friend, who was also featured in the documentary, he had been able to put such feelings behind him—thus literally saving his life. The film swiftly changed scene, and there was a sense of shame among the audience for having mocked.

In fact, there were several instances in the film, especially during interviews with collectors, when they were met by laughter from the audience, and the only collector not to be subject to the audience's amusement was (of course) Chris. In stark contrast, the audience could not take Shane seriously. Shane felt it necessary to constantly make excuses for his collecting and passion ("I like me Quo. People say I'm mad, but I don't smoke, I don't drink, I don't have a woman so… [*ain' it*] What more do you what?"). This behaviour, however simply suggested that he was "odd", an outsider, and "other".

Those audience members who stayed for the question and answer section—a little more than half the original number—insisted several times that Finlay had been respectful in her depiction of Teesside. Others, however, also noted that there was something in her depiction of the collectors that marked them as peculiar:

> At time it feels a bit like director Jeanie Finlay looks down on collecting and the men who do it, because there are almost only men or boys in the entire film. All the interviewees are portrayed as slightly crazy according to me, they are aware of this themselves and often mention it in defence before giving different explanations for things.[26]

During the Q&A session the audience also appeared to have an aversion to, and negative perception of, the featured collectors. They spoke of them with both arrogance and pity, and in a sense diminished the

[26] www.vaxjuntan.wordpress.com, accessed 24 November 2011, my own translation from Swedish.

social difficulties they faced as a result of the environment in which they lived (a socially deprived area). This somewhat resentful attitude towards the collectors is a typical example of Said's other, and the modernisation theory: these collectors are out of touch with modern society, live in a world of their own, and take part in Gnostic-like rituals that do not appear to make sense to the public.

Critique

So, in spite of what might be described as a valiant attempt to document and portray record collectors, there are troublesome aspects to the film. We are confronted with statements indicating that record collecting is an almost entirely *male* pursuit[27] (the film's synopsis even states it is a film about men[28]), both Tom and David make claims that record collecting is something that men do because men like records and collecting, and Finlay asserts in a film asking for further funding that *Sound It Out* is "an observational documentary about men collecting vinyl records".[29] There is, furthermore, an implication that only one per cent of record collectors are female with comments such as "Tom is at the helm of this distinctly (99%) male environment",[30] a sentiment repeated in the film. In fact, the only two women featured in the film—apart from the odd musician—are Tom's sister, who stereotypically nags him about lack of organisation, and a seemingly drunken man's partner with a penchant for Meat Loaf and unconventional eye make-up, who is also met with laughter by the audience.

The film and its related websites give off an air of authority similar to that mentioned in the Said section of this chapter. There is an attitude expressive of an old-style anthropologist looking for strange people with bones through their noses without any reflection on their own methods and approaches, together with that fact that there are certain collectors who would not venture into such shops for various reasons, and so the sample is too narrow. Secondly Finlay, and perhaps even Tom, employed an agenda akin to Western enlightenment Orientalism. When questioned during the question and answer section, producer Hodgson insisted that the characters in the film had been portrayed fairly, and that Finlay had been

---

[27] It should be noted that this author vehemently disagrees with this—perhaps if filmmakers, journalists, academics, etc., do not find female record collectors, then they are simply looking in the wrong places.

[28] See www.sounditoutdoc.com, accessed 22 November 2011.

[29] www.jeaniefinlay.com, accessed 22 November 2011.

[30] *ibid.*

very "careful" in choosing her participants because she was more interested in the more shy and introverted patrons who she could "weave a story out of". This smacks of an arrogance discussed by Said, together with a classic *a priori* posture. The air of authority is further enhanced by the use of apparently neutral language and intertwining of facts ("over the last five years an independent record shop has closed in the UK every three days"[31]), and we are almost led to believe that we are being presented with the absolute truth. Perhaps the greatest critique, however, must lay in Finlay's portrayal of the collectors and how the audience perceives them. Finlay, consciously or not, sets up the collector as "other" throughout the film, a discrepancy from the norm—unfamiliar and different—which inevitably invites the reactions detailed above.

As such, even though there is a need to highlight the subjects that are approached in *Sound It Out*, the way in which the film sets about doing it does not present the subject matter in an open-minded way. The record collectors are stereotyped, their activities trivialised, and one could argue that Tom (and, to a certain degree, David—Tom's shop assistant) is presented as being socially "above" his customers despite maintaining a friendly relationship with them. If one is able to look beyond Finlay's portrayals of the collectors and focus instead on what they are actually saying in their interviews, one does gain certain insight into their worlds and motivations. However, the audience's reaction at FACT indicates that this might be a difficult task for many. Finlay has ended up with a document not only of the *Sound It Out* record shop, but also of the theoretical knowledge-based background of Western society's approaches to the "oriental other". One might have made a very similar and equally disappointing film about a group of young men attending a mosque in Bradford. Interestingly enough, the release of Chris Morris's film *Four Lions*[32] puts the oriental/other/modernisation discourse squarely into the public sphere. It is the reverse of both *High Fidelity* and *Sound It Out* by suggesting that these documents merely follow a tradition of negation rather than discourse. Dealer and collector Dave, who saw the documentary on TV when BBC4 showed it 12 months later, commented as follows:

> It reminded me very much of a poster, which shows Martin Luther King on one side and Charles Manson on the other and said something like: the

---

[31] www.sounditoutdoc.com, accessed 22 November 2011.
[32] *Four Lions* (2010) is a British black-comedy. It was Chris Morris's directorial debut, and written by Morris, Sam Bain, and Jesse Armstrong. The film is a satire on *jihad* and follows a group of home-grown terrorist *jihadis* from Sheffield.

man on the left is more likely to be stopped by the police than the man on the right. The man on the left in the poster is Martin Luther King. *Sound It Out* made the record collector appear like the man on the right, Charles Manson, whereas in actual fact I feel that the record collector is more associated with the man on the left. The man on the right [Manson] is clearly mad, self-obsessed and dangerous to society. The man on the left [King] is regarded as subversive, but actually is able to help society find some kind of moral place for itself. The division between either one thing or something else is always absurd, but seems even more absurd when films like *Sound It Out* are able to portray binary oppositions in such a simplistic way. I couldn't get over it and for days it reminded me of the way Islamic people are demonised for their religious beliefs.[33]

Record Store Day

According to the official Record Store Day website:

> Record Store Day came into being in 2007 when over 700 independent stores in the USA came together to celebrate their unique culture. The UK followed suit and 2013 will see the sixth celebration of the UK's unique independent sector. This is the one day that all of the independently owned record stores come together with artists to celebrate the art of music. Special vinyl and CD releases and various promotional products are made exclusively for the day and hundreds of artists across the globe make special appearances and performances. Festivities include performances, meet & greets with artists, DJ's, in store quizzes and many other events.[34]

However, while the communication itself is a valid attempt to arrest and reverse the closures of independent record stores, and has been greatly assisted by the work of Graham Jones and his *Last Shop Standing*,[35] the aesthetic displayed on the website—a primary form of communication for Record Store Day—indicates a conformity to a particular indie aesthetic, one that not many vinyl record enthusiasts will recognise or identify with.[36] This is perhaps particularly because this specific aesthetic originates from a period of time that is by and large more recent than the original releases of the records in one's record collection.[37] There is an

---

[33] Interview with Dave, May 2013.

[34] www.recordstoreday.co.uk, accessed 07 May 2013.

[35] Graham Jones, *Last Shop Standing: Whatever Happened to Record Shops?* (London: Proper Music Publishing, 2009).

[36] *Cf.* previous discussion concerning *NME* v. *Record Collector*.

[37] Despite the recent resurgence in sales and collecting of newly released LPs, collectors of older releases still represent the majority of record collectors.

undeniable disparity between the records being represented, the collectors who do the collecting, and the modernising narrative of the present.

This was further brought home to this writer via the BBC's run-up to Record Store Day in 2013, where presenter/deejay Danny Baker fronted three TV programmes about how important vinyl has been in people's lives.[38] Perhaps predictably, one programme concerned rock, the other concerned pop, and a third concerned soul. If ever a series of programmes representing the bureaucracy of the organisation that put the programmes into place (i.e. the BBC), it was this triptych of so-called record collecting categorisations. Not only were the programmes delivered in a way to culturally separate black from white, and in fact gay from straight, they unerringly suggested a separation of social interaction: as if, for example, a rock collector would not wish to buy a Stevie Wonder album, or that a pop collector used the genre as a celebration of his/her sexuality. Once more, a level of "otherness" informed the programme makers, this time suggesting that such genre categorisations indicated forms of knowledge that were ultimately "emic" to those involved, but "etic" and strange to the mainstream.

Muse Music, Hebden Bridge

In *Last Shop Standing*, Graham Jones discusses Sid Jones, the proprietor of Muse Music, at some length, and this information does not essentially require repeating here.[39] However, in an interview with Sid by this writer in 2012, he expressed a certain distaste for Record Store Day, which would also benefits from documentation and further analysis from the perspective of "otherness". Sid has been trading in Hebden Bridge, West Yorkshire, for decades, and has witnessed the growth, flat-lining and potential demise of artefact-based recorded-sound retailing. He was also the victim of severe flooding when his entire stock and shop was destroyed by a flash flood during the early summer of 2012. Sid, however, remains very philosophical about his area of expertise, has since re-opened his shop, and realises that he is part of an ever-shrinking niche market-place. He does not trade on the internet, cannot be contacted via email, and does not involve himself in any web-based audiophile culture. While this might look like economic suicide in the twenty-first century, he appears to

---

[38] *Danny Baker's Great Album Showdown: File Under: Rock*; *Danny Baker's Great Album Showdown: File Under:Pop*; and *Danny Baker's Great Album Showdown: File Under: R&B*, most recently aired on BBC4 Jan–Feb 2016.

[39] Graham Jones, *Last Shop Standing: Whatever Happened to Record Shops?* (London: Proper Music Publishing, 2009), 210–211.

understand the basic nature of record collecting: similar to the thesis offered by this work. He considers the record collector and the record retailer to be part of the same company of friends: he knows that people come to him not only to buy things, but to "spend money", which he sees as a completely different thing from simply buying a CD.

> People come to me to come into the shop, talk to me, ask advice and feel part of a community which in some respects is under pressure. Therefore a need for them to buy something is far outweighed by their desire to spend money. Even the most pragmatic of analysts do not often understand the fundamental difference between these two expressions. Put simply, one buys something in a supermarket, but one spends money in order to sustain a business. I know people come here to help sustain this business, that means that despite market downturns and natural disasters this shop will stay open for the benefit of the people who spend money.

Sid went on to discuss Record Store Day, thus:

> I've been asked to involve Muse Music in Record Store Day year after year, but so far I've refused. For me, it just doesn't seem to capture the essence of how popular music and the popular music record seems to capture people's sense of themselves. It's not that I'm against Record Store Day, but it seems too short-termist. No sooner do some colleagues of mine see the records leave their shops, then see them on sale on eBay at an increased price from that which they paid. Apparently, or so I'm told, this seems to make money from the purchases and I've no objections to this whatsoever. But I actually wonder if this does make money for the people, and if it does, it renders the entire Record Store Day to be a waste of time. I run a comic shop next door and it would be like me selling all of my rare comics at a ridiculous price in one fell swoop so that the act of seeking out, finding, coupled with the joy of buying that comic that you needed to complete your set is totally removed from the experience. For me, part of the fun is about the chase.[40]

The reader might recall this writer's concerns not simply about "otherness", but also about long-term and short-term value. Whereas short-term items still appear to be categorised as ephemera by society at large, and the collector of such ephemera is similarly categorised as a representation of mild deviancy, long-term collecting is often classified as a form of connoisseurship. Sid Jones, in his comments above, continues to be concerned about this dichotomy, and while on the surface Record Store Day appears to be addressing issues to do with so-called ephemera and

---

[40] Interview with Sid Jones, proprietor of *Muse Music*, Hebden Bridge, 2012.

popular culture, according to Sid, at least, it is perpetuating the old stereotypes (as presented in Chapter One of this work).

Summary

It is worth perhaps summarising the perception of record collectors via "otherness", "Orientalism" and the modernisation of society. If social interaction is the mutual and reciprocal influence by two or more people on each other's behaviour, then the five basic forms of interaction— exchange, cooperation, completion, conflict and coercion—are not represented by any of the above-mediated portrayals. Most human activity occurs in groups and in private, and not least record collecting, which consists of two or more people interacting with each other in networks, patterns and routes. To deny the co-creative potential of what is, according to Eisenberg, a "ritual", is a denial of the "other". To paraphrase him further, music lives in time and unfolds in time: "It lets the eye and mind set their own pace".[41] So, although music is an object that can be owned by the individual and used according to his or her own convenience, it is also subject to the influence of primary groups of people interacting regularly, emotionally committed to the relationship formed through recorded sound. Sid Jones complained that record collecting was only really viewed as a secondary operation, where people only interact on Record Store Day in a formal and impersonal basis to obtain a specific objective, e.g. that "one-off David Bowie single—which will end-up on eBay two days later, in any case".[42] He was correct: formal organisations attempt to achieve specific goals, create specific rules, and maintain a rational world view. Record collecting does not fit such formalistic, secondary concepts, and is therefore relegated to the symbolic role of "other".

---

[41] Evan Eisenberg, *The Recording Angel: Music, Records And Culture From Aristotle To Zappa* (New Haven: Yale University Press, 2005), 10.

[42] Sid Jones, interview with author, 2012.

CHAPTER SEVEN

CO-CREATORS OF MEANING (II)
AND ARBITERS OF TASTE:
INTERVIEW WITH A RECORD DEALER

**"Vinyl rarities have also left their mark in a more surprising arena—
the regular auctions of rock and pop memorabilia staged in London by
Christie's and Sotheby's. Signed albums, one-off acetates and ultra-
rare collectibles regularly turn up in these sales, often fetching
remarkably high prices."**
—The Editors, *Record Collector Rare Record Price Guide 2002*

It has already been stated in Chapter Two (above) that ethnography is
intrinsically linked to popular music studies. This chapter will discuss how
record collectors and dealers can be one and the same, and how the
primary motivation for such interwoven activity is not solely economic. In
order to do so, this writer used the methods and approaches discussed
principally by Diane Tye,[1] who considered her ethnographic goal to be one
of understanding how Sean, a Beatles fan, while apparently isolated
through living in Newfoundland, could actually build up a network of
associations and friendships through this apparently isolated activity. Tye
spent a considerable amount of time with Sean, and it was this starting
point that helped this writer come to terms with the subject in question.
Tye's methods and approaches in getting to know and enjoy mutual
respect with her subject was considered ideal for this researcher,
considering the profile that popular music played in Sean's life. It was
here, however where the similarities between Tye's and my own
participant ended, for Sean appears, at least according to Tye's study, to be
using his collecting as a way of gaining confidence in the present world,
whereas my participant was far more confident about his place in society
and came from what might be described as a counter-cultural background

---

[1] Diane Tye, "Ethnography of a Beatles Fan", *Culture and Tradition* 11 (1987):
41–57.

which was still of great value. He informed me that "the lunatics had taken over the asylum".[2]

"George" has been known to this writer for over ten years, and a relationship built up around shared interests and trust. "George" is in his late 50s and has been a fan of popular music and record collector for all of his adult life, as well as being a professional musician (guitarist) and broadcaster for something like twenty years. He is married with one adult daughter, and lives in the north-west of England. In "George's" case, there did not seem to be an overt lack of confidence or an insular view of the world. In his case, his messages of communication appeared to come from a position of relative authority, and he also appeared to understand the music industry well, and from an "insider" position. He was also deeply interested in the various histories of popular music, its formats, technologies, and business set-ups equally as much (if not more than) those making the music.

The following transcription covers an extended discussion that occurred during the original research for this work.[3] Several points raised by "George" were discussed on different occasions and in different ways, and have therefore been paraphrased here. I have thus compiled this transcription into a chronological narrative, which was not necessarily the case at the time, but which will perhaps aid the reading process in order to convey how "George" considered himself to be not only a fan and collector, but also an arbiter of taste and a decision-maker concerning the marketability of collecting. Because of this being a compilation I have been careful not to alter any words as they appear to be spoken—hence the pauses and occasional misunderstandings in transcription.

The Extended Interview

We began the process of interviewing with an explanation from "George" concerning how he became involved with record trading.

> Okay [...] Well, it goes back really to when I was a kid and we didn't really have a gramophone player that was up to date or suitable enough to play newer records. My dad had a collection of 78s that I think he'd picked up from second-hand shops really and we had a second-hand gramophone player. So, once The Beatles and all that sort of happened and I started to get interested, we didn't really have the facilities to play records and couldn't afford them. So all throughout the 1960s up till the late '60s I just

---

[2] Interview with "George", March 2013.
[3] Between 2009–2013.

relied on the radio, but by the late '60s, I started buying the music press as well and I was desperate to get involved in buying records, you know they were so expensive really. I remember the first single I purchased: it was from Boots in Liverpool, and it was "Race With the Devil" by The Gun—it was late 1968 8/6d, I only used to get 10/- pocket money per *month* [emphasis in original], so this was a lot of money for me.

And then I stumbled across a second-hand record shop in Liverpool, a second-hand shop called Edwards' who were legendary [...] And Edwards' was just amazing. It was one of those places where you'd go along after school, they wouldn't always open during the day, and you'd go along after school and they'd put boards up outside the shop with lists of singles on it—you know stuff like "The Supremes—You Can't Hurry Love: 2/-", things like that. So anyway, Edwards' was really good because you could buy singles and LPs and EPs for very small amounts of money, so it was affordable for me. In my last year of school I started to build up my collection of records. I also started to buy some new ones as well, but it was at that point... going to Eddie's and all that, that got me interested from a business point of view, because I could see they were making a little bit of money out of it, so that always interested me. And I kept trading with them right up until the time I left the UK to go to America, which was in 1976.

Brocken has also written about this particular shop, and states:

Mr. Edwards' back room was out-of-bounds to all but the most trusted. It was in this inner chamber that items were rather cursorily examined for defects, and priced accordingly. The risk of buying a defective album from Edwards' was relatively high, but this was not the fault of the shop. By the late 60s vinyl faults such as white lining and impurities, not always visible to the naked eye, were an increasing problem for all record collectors. [...] I well-remember observing Mr. Edwards inspecting a copy of the first Bert Jansch album in the backroom. I returned to the shop several times thereafter, only to disappointedly see it in the hands of another collector before I was able to part with my 25 /-.[4]

When "George" returned from America, in 1977, he started getting interested in selling some of his own records. He had built up a sizeable collection by that stage:

And so by '77–78, record fairs had started throughout the country. Now, record fairs were really interesting because they were kind of linked to the

---

[4] Michael Brocken, *Other Voices: Hidden Histories of Liverpool's Popular Music Scenes 1930s–1970s* (Farnham: Ashgate, 2010), 210.

way popular music was starting to look back on itself, being what you might describe as repertory, so in the 1970s, especially once punk had arrived, people started to, um, you know, collect things more and value things in different ways. So even though there might have been people who collected the *Vertigo* label in 1970, it wasn't in the same way as people started to collect the label in '76 or '77. It came to be viewed more as an artefact. I'd noticed this in America as well, but when I came back from the States, the *Record Collector* magazine started—now you're going to do work on that—and that linked together with record fairs so I thought I'd do a record fair. 'Cause I had that much stuff, and it must have been either '77 or '78, can't quite remember to be honest, but I did a record fair here at the Bluecoat Chambers in Liverpool.

I just put a stall up; you'd pay, I don't know £5, £7, whatever it was back then for just a table in the Bluecoat main room and it would be a Saturday afternoon, Saturday morning. Say you'd get there about ten o'clock, uh, they'd let the public in about eleven o'clock and you do it till about three o'clock. But I found that I was able to clear a lot of my unwanted records in that way. So that started to get me interested in doing it again, but in order for me to do it again I had to buy some records then.

"George" placed a "wanted ad" in the *Liverpool Echo*, stating that he was to buy records for cash. The late 1970s were a time of economic depression and he felt that such an advertisement would attract those in need of quick money. He was also running a business at the time, which involved him being mobile throughout the working week:

So, I started to pick records up around the Wirral, Birkenhead, Liverpool, Huyton, Widnes, Chester, I remember going to. And I'd picked up effectively in about six months, some very, very interesting stuff. On one occasion I went to Blacon in Chester after I'd had a phone call from a bloke who had loads of Elvis stuff. I went in the afternoon and it was like finding gold in the middle of the desert. He had loads of Elvis albums—right back to Elvis 1 and 2. I made a deal for them and drove back to my home in Liverpool. I was covered in fleas—although the albums were immaculate! The following week I did a fair in Leeds and when we arrived I put a blanket over the stall so that the other dealers couldn't get a look-in. When the public came in at 11am I pulled back the blanket and there was a queue to the door—the other dealers were livid because had they seen the Elvis stuff they would have bought it before the public had a chance—it was very competitive.

"George" informed this writer that there were several independent record shops on Merseyside by this stage and they were conducting brisk business in all kinds of recorded sound outputs. In Birkenhead there was

Skeleton Records that dealt in new and second-hand copies, principally albums. However they also sold bootlegs, which was a growing trade throughout the 1970s, and came to develop a small independent label of the same name (i.e. *Skeleton*). There was also Probe Records in Liverpool, and Penny Lane Records in Liverpool and Chester, both of which specialised in punk singles and rare West Coast recordings. Similarly in Liverpool there was the long-standing Musical Box shop on Rocky Lane, which Bill Hinds admitted to Michael Brocken:

> [...] has to loom large in my legend as it's the place [...] I bought my first ever 45 [...] but even before that, before we had a record player (!) their window acted as a kind of news board as to what was out/available. [...] A great shop—always worth asking for old deleted stuff right into the 70s.[5]

However, not everyone would fully agree:

> The Golden Disc was the only record shop in Liverpool I remember NOT having a deletion bin! But the Musical Box towered above even the major city stores in my opinion. Nothing was too much trouble. [...] When I walked in with my long hair and trogg-like clothes she [Diane] probably knew I was after something a bit more unusual, but by and large she had it and if not, she'd always order it.[6]

Les also described the Golden Disc as the kind of shop that one went into only under sufferance. He stated that:

> It was one of those shops that if you asked for a single they would say "is it in the charts?" you might reply "yes" and they would say "sorry, we've sold-out". If you said "no" they'd say "we don't stock it".[7]

Probe Records was, it seems, a little different. Brocken recalls:

> All of the Probe employees were regarded as arbiters of "good taste". So much so that one Saturday I went in to buy a country rock album: Poco's *Rose of Cimarron*. Pete Burns, later of Dead or Alive fame was working behind the counter and he was the only one in the shop at the time. I picked up the sleeve and took it to him and he wouldn't let me have the record. He

---

[5] *ibid.*, 206.
[6] *ibid.*, 207.
[7] Interview with Les, May 2013.

said I could pick something else, but he wasn't going to soil his hands with a f*****g Poco record.[8]

It becomes quite clear that record collecting by the 1970s was reaching something of a zenith and a community of traders and collectors was establishing itself. Artist Trevor Jackson commented to Emma Pettit that:

> I owe a huge part of my musical interests to people who have served me, and people I have met whilst shopping. Record shops are more than just a place to buy product, the best are cultural landmarks, social places to converse and debate, a retreat from the mundane, an escape. Music is one of the most powerful and enjoyable forms of communication and deserves to be delivered in an environment that fully panders to every music-lovers desire.[9]

"George" continued to say that he concentrated for the most part at this stage on singles, "because it was the single at this stage that was quite collectable". There were two areas in particular that seemed (to him) to be important for collectors. First of all, soul singles were already collectable and had been a bastion for collectors for some considerable time. People are still interested in the back catalogues of *Stax* and *Atlantic Records* and others perhaps more obscure. Many also collected *Tamla Motown* singles:

> *Motown* was one of those labels that you could almost collect start to finish if you wanted to—and also anything on *London America* was very popular, black and silver label, because you could basically do the same thing, that was one of those subsidiaries of *Decca* and they just released stuff without any marketing to speak of. So you could almost collect from *London America* "number 1" through to *London America* "The End", you know. So that became important. I was also interested in EPs because they're an interesting artefact that people collected, although I didn't. And EPs by a variety of different artists: some were collectable and some weren't, but you know EPs being very much a '60s thing and going with, say, Elvis all the way back to the '50s.

> Around about the same time as this I was also in wholesale, but by about 1980 we'd moved to Chester, we moved December '80, um, I was starting to wonder about which direction I should go in, because I was running two very successful businesses. One, the wholesale business that I took over

---

[8] Michael Brocken, *Other Voices: Hidden Histories of Liverpool's Popular Music Scenes 1930s–1970s* (Farnham: Ashgate, 2010), 213.
[9] Trevor Jackson cited in Emma Pettit, *Old Rare New: The Independent Record Shop* (London: Black Dog Publishing, 2008), 89.

from my dad, and the second business was the record business. I'd also started dealing a little bit in, um, re-issues and occasional bootlegs as well. People would canvass you with the new records at fairs first saying "we're issuing these rockabilly tracks, would you like some?", and I'd go "yeah, give us a box", a box would hold twenty, and you'd be able to sell them for a pound each or something like that. So by 1981 the spare room at our place was full of records, some of which were worth 50 pence and some of which were worth pounds and pounds and pounds and pounds. And what started to develop then was, um, I'd started to kind of get a bit of a name for it as well so we were doing fairs here in Liverpool, we were going down to Burslem, in Stoke, we always went there, we'd go to the YMCA in Birmingham, we'd go to Leeds, the one at Leeds was very, very good. We'd go down as far as Nottingham. So we do these fairs and it turned out to be sometimes twice a month. And I was earning a lot of money from it and at the same time I was picking up records all of the time—so I started to think about packing one job in for the other.

"George" informed me of a particular period of time when a record shop in Prenton, in Birkenhead, closed down and he bought the entire stock that was left. Some of it, he states "wasn't much good, but it didn't matter". He tended to find that even if one was purchasing items that did not appear to be sellable, there might always be somebody around who would collect things for different reasons:

Even with cheap, *Top of the Pops* albums or, you know, that kind of thing I'd find that somebody would always come along and buy things from you. So by the early 1980s it was becoming quite a serious business and my wife and I decided to go to America and try to meet a bootlegger. So we got a flight out to the States and went to Greenwich Village. We were staying there for a week, went to Greenwich Village, and went into a record emporium, I think it was on Bleaker Street, and met this bloke called "Bob". And I said to "Bob", you know, "where do you get all this stuff from?", he said "who wants to know?", and I said "well, I'll buy all of that off you now", and his attitude changed. What I was looking for at the time, and this'll date it quite nicely, it was the early days of the 1980s, and it was just in that period of time when Bruce Springsteen was getting his live reputation together. He'd already had a pretty good reputation, but then once punk came along, um, he was knocked in this country [UK]. People knocked him a little bit. So he kind of had to step back from the British market and he went and toured America a lot. His live performances were renowned, and I wanted to get some live Springsteen albums. Also it was a the time when the Danny Sugarman book had just come out about The Doors and that started the whole revival of interest in Jim Morrison, which lead to the movie. So I was looking for Doors bootlegs as well. Also there was an Elvis Costello live album out there I knew, bootleg, *Live at The El Mocambo* and I'd been asked for that several times, so I did want that, too.

Also there was a really good bootleg, I wish I still had this actually—sold them all—of all of The Beatles' Christmas discs on one album and I bought as many of those as he ["Bob"] had. So I bought tons of stuff off him there-and-then, cash, and the best of all were these live Bruce Springsteen singles that were on multi-coloured vinyl! So it'd be Springsteen live in America somewhere doing covers or some of his own material. We brought all of this stuff back to the UK—walked it back through the customs in Manchester. We never got questioned. So the following weekend, we got back, I think, on the Friday, I was due at Birmingham YMCA on Saturday—and I can honestly tell you that the entire week's visit to the US was paid for by the trade that I did on the Saturday. There were queues out of the Birmingham YMCA just for my stall. *We made a small fortune* [emphasis in original]… that was the day that I purchased a Beatles 78 [rpm] because I'd done so well. George Reddington had a stall there, he was a big dealer in Birmingham, and he had the Beatles 78 on the wall and he wanted 150 quid for it, I said, I'd had a really good day so I said "I'll give you £100 for that, George". And he hadn't had a good day, probably because of me, so he took my £100. So, what eventually happened with "Bob" was I used to send him an international letter of credit usually for about £200, which would be converted into [US] dollars, and he would send me a box of records every month, or so. So that went on for about another two-three years. And I made a lot of money out of that. And it just came through the post, a box of records, nobody ever checked it, looked at it, or anything.

Each time "George" booked a stall at a record fair, he would be armed, not only with his second-hand and new stock, but also with the latest bootlegs. He expanded his scope from Springsteen into Beatles bootlegs, although these latter recordings did not sell that well at the time. Interest in The Doors' book however meant that interest grew exponentially in their recordings. Most of their albums were actually still available on vinyl, however out-takes and live material were always in demand:

That's what it's like with popular music: stuff kept on coming really, that was the stuff that did really, really well in the 1980s because they were just "it" for a couple of years with record collectors. And anything really "Bob" would advise me on, you know, I'd buy. And it would be, I don't know, a box of about 50 [records] at a time and I made loads of money [out] of it. Eventually I sent him an international letter of credit and the records never arrived! I followed it up and I found out that he'd been arrested (laughs). Looking back I think [he] had a direct connection with a New Jersey pressing plant somewhere. I've got a feeling it might have been coming out of Camden. Now Camden was, um, the factory where *RCA* were based and it's common knowledge that people on the night shift would do their own thing, you know. So I think a lot of this stuff might have been coming out of the *RCA* factory in Camden. I have no evidence to suggest it was, however. If I still had some you'd probably be able to check on the vinyl now. I know that the vinyl was very, very shiny and was also quite flexible which was like something called Dynagroove, that *RCA* used to produce, so I've got a feeling it came out of the Camden factory. So that was the dealing... Anyway, it grew to such proportions by the mid-1980s that I had to make a decision whether I was going to go into it, full-time, or stay in the business I was involved in, which was wholesale. And I decided to stay in wholesale. Finding that "Bob" had been arrested was a bit scary, but what started to affect me was that bootleg cassette culture had come in, in a big way.

People were making lots of bootleg cassettes at the time, and I wasn't interested in cassettes. I wasn't then, and I'm not now. I've never been interested in cassettes. And by the mid-1980s takings were dropping because of these bloody cassettes. You'd be sitting next to somebody in a stall and it'd be nothing but bootleg cassettes. They'd bootleg every single thing because they were very, very cheap. So I kind of saw the writing on the wall really, and I think the last gig I did was at Burslem again and I thought "I'm not doing any more of these". I think we might have only taken £100-or-so and I thought "well this isn't worth while really". Even though we were still making a bit of money, we were still buying records and that sort of thing. But it just seemed like a waste of time for 100 quid, you know, once you got your petrol and stall rental out of the way it wasn't really worth it. But I had thousands of records, you know, um, so a friend of mine from Manchester was packing in his job, I think it was at the Co-op at the time and he offered to buy my business. So I sold it to him. I sold it to him lock, stock and barrel. I took a few things out that I wanted to keep and I sold it to him. He set up a stall; I think it was in Oldham Market. I think it was a permanent stall, and he carried on trading right up until the early 1990s I think. I don't know what happened to the stock after that, but I think he might have moved it on, as well.

"George" stated that it was a really important time for him because he could keep up with trends and for him it was made evident that vinyl was never going to "die". He stated that when he first started in the 1970s the market place was about singles. But by the time he was trading in the early 1980s, it was mainly about LPs and bootlegs:

By the time it was drawing to come to an end, though, people had become interested in "proggy" rock again. Because if you can imagine in the late '70s, progressive rock was completely out of fashion, you know, and apart from the Motown and rock 'n' roll/rockabilly things that I used to do from the '50s and '60s, you'd always sell punk singles anyway, you know. New or second-hand there'd always be someone looking for "Anarchy in the UK" or something on *Stiff* or *A Step Forward* or *Chiswick*, those independent labels. But by the mid '80s that had started to change and that's when this issue surrounding, at least as far as I was aware, progressive rock as a collectable entity, started to emerge in a big way. There were always people who'd come along asking you for, you know, *Vertigo* singles. You could always tell them a mile off because they'd still have long hair, you know, flares and all that. But by the time I started to get out they were becoming more and more prominent and it became more of a, it became more of a, kind of a… lads' club… It became a kind of, you know, smelly bloke with a builder's arse behind him, you know, looking at, sifting through records. And they were the guys looking for the gatefold sleeves. They were the ones who were looking for anything on, say, Sensational Alex Harvey Band, you know, stuff on early *Island*, or the Mighty Baby album: things like that. And that's when, if you look at *Record Collector* too, you'll find that the adverts at the back of become very, very specific. They become less to do with soul and rock 'n' roll from the '50s and more to do with "head music" as we describe it as, so stuff that was on *Island*, stuff that was on *Vertigo*, stuff that was on *Harvest*, and hadn't sold.

So that occurred to me, and I was never very interested in that stuff anyway really because psychedelia was my area so that's one of the reasons I let it go. It was all based on my own interests, which were all based on this idea of Edwards' record shop back in the day. Edwards' is really important for me because it first of all allowed me to get into the market through second-hand records; you know, I didn't have any money, hardly any money. You might have even bought it a month ago from Eddie's, so you'd take it back to Eddie's and he'd give you money for it again and then you'd buy something from his window. So it was really, it was like a real Aladdin's Cave and it made vinyl very desirable to me.

And that's why I've always had this, you know, interest in vinyl, because I think it was unobtainable to me at the time, it was always very expensive and till I started working in the 1970s I didn't have any money to speak of, might have a little bit of pocket money. So the idea of trading, buying and selling was with me right from the word go, with records. If you spoke to a lot of the people of a certain age in Liverpool, they'd tell you that Edwards' was very, very important. Eventually they moved from Kensington down to London Road, just here, but the shop didn't really… it was too big and it was during the punk period and they didn't really keep up with trends so I don't think it lasted very long before it closed. It might have lasted till the early '80s—I don't know. But you'd get to know a network of people as well.

I knew a guy called Trevor Hughes and he had a record shop in New Brighton, second-hand. I got to know a fellow from Stoke called Chris Savory and he was a dealer of things in Stoke. I got to know a bloke in Leeds and he was a dealer up in Leeds. So you'd start to deal, as well, with people. If you knew that somebody liked Elvis stuff you'd keep things back for them. If somebody likes *London America* singles you keep them back, if you got them in good nick, because the idea for collectors was always to get stuff in mint condition. I must say it was never an issue for me, because if I wanted a single I'd sometimes get the single just as an artefact anyway if it was cheap, even if it was scratched to hell. Because also, I often like the idea that someone's really played this 100 times. But that didn't square with most record dealers who liked things to be "mint" or "near mint", very good condition. So that meant that I wasn't really in a way a record collector myself in the same way.

I did collect, but I used to distinguish myself between a collector and a dealer and a junkie, a "vinyl junkie", and I never considered myself to be a vinyl junkie because I'd sell them. Vinyl junkies never sell anything, I thought at the time. So I made a very important distinction between being a record collector and dealer, so it was for about probably seven years I was a dealer, and being a vinyl junkie. If I was a vinyl junkie I'd have been buying all of this stuff and just filing it and cataloguing it and all the rest of it. I did catalogue things, but I've never considered myself to be a vinyl junkie.

One of my favourite albums of all time, which you probably have actually is by a British hard rock-cum-progressive rock group called T2, which is "t", "2". And they only had, I think, one album out on *Decca*. I think they had another one out later, but they'd shot their bolt by then. It [the *Decca* LP] was called *It'll All Work Out in Boomland*. And I'd bought that album second hand from Edwards', then I sold it, then I bought it from a dealer, then I sold it, then I bought it from a friend, then I sold it and now I've just bought it again from Sid up in Hebden Bridge and it's a new copy of a reissue. So I, you know, I do kind of like to have things, but I do like to let them go. And for me there's a difference there. I find there's a difference between me and sort of "vinyl junkie-dom", you know. I'm always prepared to let things go.

I then questioned "George" about people's desires to own certain items and not others. Where did the authenticities lie? What formats were authentic and why? And what was the appeal of a bootleg? From my own perspective bootlegs and out-takes have never been priority items and so this interest in an "other" recorded sound history was fascinating. It was stated at the very beginning of this book that recorded sound supplemented, and at times replaced, the "live" in performance, however according to this dealer, such live performances were of great interest to record collectors. Also "George" was at pains to point out this "other" history, consisting of the detritus and leftovers of an industry which, while not considering certain tracks to be of interest to the public, merely left them "in the can" as it were, was yet another contextual strand that linked together the realities of the impact of recorded sound. Bootlegging was for him therefore another example of a record collector's independence of thought and deed, where value judgements were made, and an alternative industry catered for such judgements.

Well, um, there were two things that I found that people wanted. They wanted live stuff at the time so anything that was, um, based around a live performance was very interesting. So in the first instance, the first bootleg I ever bought was in the early 1970s was *The Beatles Live at the Hollywood Bowl*. I think it was the Hollywood Bowl, might have been somewhere else. But when we, when I first started realising there were bootlegs it was very much based around live stuff and then on the other hand out-takes of stuff. So the first bootleg I ever remember was *The Great White Wonder*. That was a Dylan bootleg and that was based around, if I remember correctly, out-takes from Woodstock. So when he was based up in Woodstock for a while he, you know, did a lot of music with the band. Bits and pieces that were done. Songs like "Million Dollar Bash" and, um, that kind of stuff, that were recorded and never released officially. So *The Great White Wonder* had a lot of that stuff on it. There were Hendrix and Beatles bootlegs that were very popular for live performances and Stones bootlegs that were based around live performances as well. The appeal changed gradually as the bootlegs became better. Some of the early ones are really, really poor quality. I mean the Grateful Dead used to get involved with production of bootlegs of their own as well. They sort of helped their Dead Heads find this material too. But I always, it must've been the audiophile in me a little bit, I was never very impressed by live music recordings. In actual fact, if you look through my collection I haven't got very many live albums. I'm not bothered really. If you look at The Who's *Live at Leeds* album, that's dressed like a bootleg. It could be a bootleg, you know. So they were quite interested in them. But I'm not a big fan of live recordings because I always think something's missing from them. I remember, I've still got *The Doors Live*, which is good, you know, and a bootleg of that album was also issued on *Electra* was also popular on the stall funnily enough. So that was the appeal of that. So that's two or three areas really. There's the area of any possible out-takes, so alternative recordings, and there's the live thing—and then in some respects there's the rarity value. So what I did come across quite a few times were bootleg singles and EPs by the late '70s and early 1980s. So you'd get, I did quite a lot of rock 'n' roll and rockabilly records and you get rockabilly societies in the UK bootlegging early to mid '50s rockabilly. So you'd get an EP with four tracks on it. That was popular, that was quite popular. In fact they, those labels often, those bootleggers often turned themselves into legitimate labels because they'd made money on the bootlegs. So eventually they became legit labels, they'd ask for the licence to copy these records as well.

And it was only really later when, you know, when we got to the mid 1980s that this retrospection of, say, let's say *Vertigo* became more prominent. There weren't, as far as I recall, in the late '70s many people looking for, I don't know, a DJ copy of a Uriah Heap single or for a nice copy of the first Yes album on *Atlantic*. I don't really remember that happening at that stage. In fact if they were looking for anything it would be things like an original copy of *Velvet Underground and Nico*, or an original copy of the first Quicksilver Messenger Service LP. So it'd be kind of based around either precursors to Bowie, say the MC5, the Stooges, the Velvets, that kind of thing, or west coast music, so it could be Grateful Dead, some of the Dead spin-offs, Quicksilver, Love, The Doors, Jefferson Airplane. That was the stuff people were looking for then. They weren't, as far as I can remember, really interested in British "proggy" rock. They were like the precursors to prog, so singles by groups like Nirvana, *Island* singles by Spooky Tooth and Art, Mott the Hoople, earlier singles by the likes of Bowie, Davy Jones and the Lower Third, those kind of singles, they were all very, very much in demand at that stage, but I don't think anybody was looking for a Ramases album at that stage. Do you know what I mean? So there was a shift.

There was almost like a cultural shift, as I recognised it between looking for the '50s and '60s goodies, then punk singles and bootleg albums and the rest of it, and then came "oh, I think we'd better revaluate *Vertigo*". That's how I remember it anyway. So the idea of authenticity and value did shift. It shifted quite a lot. I mean, even when I used to deal, even the Beach Boys were very collectable. Beach Boys singles always used to go. The early black *Capitol* label, and purple *Capitol* label, singles. Beach Boys albums didn't shift very much, but you'd often get bootlegs of *Smiley Smile*, you know, and that kind of stuff so the Beach Boys were popular even at that stage. All rock 'n' roll's very popular. Elvis albums, you know, Elvis was always collectible. Any ten-inch rock 'n' roll albums, rather than twelve-inch. Because in the first instance some labels did ten-inch albums rather than twelve-inch ones. I think Elvis' albums were always on twelve-inch, but there was a Johnny Burnett Trio album I remember being on ten-inch and people would almost kill each other for that. But then came that important cultural shift.

As a *Vertigo* fan, myself, I further discussed this with "George" and we moved into the area of rarities and out-takes, once again. "George" was asked what he thought draws the collector to such rarities (rather than bootlegs) in particular:

Some collectors like to have everything they can, by their favourite artists, or even artists who are loosely connected with somebody. So I remember there was a guy who, he was very interesting, he was a big Elvis collector, but he'd buy Jordanairs stuff, he'd buy James Burton albums. Anything that was even loosely connected with being with Elvis, he'd buy. So that's in a way buying kind of out-takes, in a way. Um, Beatles collectors and Lennon collectors, as I remember, were very interested in two aspects of their careers: first of all the out-takes, 'cause there were a lot of Beatles out-takes and there were quite a lot of Beatles songs that didn't make it on to their records. Their quality control slipped as the years went by, but in the first, say, five years this was very good so that meant they had quite a lot of out-takes. As I say, later on, they didn't have as many, as their quality control had slipped and anything would do. But Beatles fans are very interested in that. Also as a dealer I found that *Apple* was in great demand. Anything connected to *Apple*. So, Beatles fans weren't just interested in Beatles' stuff. They were interested in stuff that was on *Apple*. They'd be very interested in it because *Apple* wasn't a successful label really, if you take the Beatles and Badfinger out of the equation, there's probably only Mary Hopkins that had hits. So, there's quite a lot of *Apple* rarities, out-takes, misprints, unissued stuff so that's another element of completism. Not only would you want all the Beatles records, maybe even a pirate cassettes of their out-takes, but you might want a Lon and Derreck Van Eaton single as well. You'd also maybe want something on *Zapple*. You might want something by the Modern Jazz Quartet because they also recorded on *Apple*. You might want a Jackie Lomax single.

So there's that element of completism. But also, I think, there's an acknowledgement that there's value in this stuff. So they would say "well even Jackie Lomax made some good records so it would be good to buy Jackie Lomax stuff". So there's an idea of, I think, records are very much part of your sense of identity, aren't they? Very, very important to your identity. And I would have thought that if completing an *Apple* collection made you very, very happy about yourself, that's got transformative qualities, hasn't it? It's a really, really important thing. It's almost like when people come up to me and say "oh, look at that, she's had a few nips and tucks and, you know, had a hair piece put in or dyes her hair or something". There's nothing wrong with that. If that makes you feel more happy, if that makes you confident about yourself, if you start to feel as if you can, you know, engage with the world a little bit more, well for God's sake go ahead and do it! I'd be the last person to object to that. I think record collecting helps you like that, you know. It's a very important point of connection with people. And I've seen it, you know, standing behind a stall every other Saturday at Burslem Town Hall, or whatever. These people, you know, they're not isolationists, they want to talk about it. There was more tea drunk at some of those record fairs than could fill a kettle hundred times. People wanted to talk about it, they wanted to discuss things, they wanted to meet people, they want to trade, they want to do all sorts of things.

Here, perhaps, is the missing link that people often forget about record collecting: it is not actually there to keep you from the world, as the stereotype often eludes, instead it asks you to converse with the world on your own terms. This leads to a sense of empowerment through human contact, and if one attends a record fair there is a really important point of contact. One might even be of help to other people. "George" suggested that "you might say 'well, hang on a minute, you know, that wasn't good, don't buy that because that's been reissued'", and build up a relationship with a dealer that lasts for a lifetime. One can also speak with a voice of relative authority not only within the matrixes of the world within one is immersed (relating to the scope of collecting), but also within the broader sphere of life. And what one might have done in the process is to create a discourse, a form of cultural capital. If one deals with one's own form of cultural capital, this is bound to be of great significance for one gains such authority, not via systems, but through experience, "on the hoof" which, it could be argued is one of the best ways to learn. This is reversing the idea that one has to go to the right school, say the right things to the right people, go to university, etc. One can form one's own kind of understanding of the world through a self-generating form of cultural capital and, for this writer (and it seems, "George"), this is what record collecting is about:

> [...] it's not about smelly old people, you know, even though there are people like that. I think it's about a real aid to people's communication. And that, that cuts across, that's about collecting really, isn't it, that's not just about record collecting. People who collect all sorts of things are able to communicate their ideas to other people who collect those kinds of things. I find that very stimulating, to be honest. And it could be, I don't know whether it is or not, but it could be one of the reasons why vinyl's made a comeback. Not just because it's something that, um, was better than people gave it credit for, but also because it allows people to communicate. It's really helpful, you know. It allows you to talk, it allows you to converse. So I think you could argue it is important in its own right, but it's also a vehicle upon which people communicate with other people.

Finally I mentioned to "George" that as a record fair dealer, he was not in any fixed location for long and that I found this of interest—almost in a way like the transient "chapmen" mentioned in the first chapter of this book:

> People would regard you as a bit transient, but one of the good things about it was, even though you were a dealer they could see that you were an enthusiast as well. Now, there's an element of that still has some presence in the very few lingering independent shops that are around, like Sid's in Hebden Bridge, where you've been. Sid is regarded as an enthusiast, but he's regarded as a retailer really. What we were regarded as, were *fellow* [emphasis in original] enthusiasts—at least until the cassettes turned up because they were obvious forms of exploitative bootlegging. We were thought of as on a level with the people we were dealing with, which was really good. It was a different type of engagement. Um, they tell you things very often. They'd be looking through singles and, you know "have you got TMG1049". And you'd go "what's that?", they'd go "ah, don't you know...". It's a *Tamla Motown* thing and I'm not a *Motown* fan anyway, really.[10] But then you'd learn *from* [emphasis in original] them. So they'd be looking for specific things.

> Some of them would come armed with little memo books with lists of numbers that they didn't have. And occasionally they'd find things. Very often those kind of guys were looking for almost the Holy Grail sometimes, that none of us dealers had a copy of it because, you know, they were very, very rare records. So the idea of being transient and dealing through stalls meant that it was quite democratic really. And it also meant that they could haggle with you. So if you had an Elvis album up for sale for, I don't know, 30 quid or something, you know, these guys would look at it, you know, and go "how much is the album?", "it's such and such", "let's have a look", "okay"... give it back. At half past two they'd be back, because they knew you'd want some money towards the end of the gig, "I'll give you £20 for it", "okay", because you knew it was going to a good home then. So you would connect, and if they got a good deal from you, they'd be back. Or they'd even say "when are you back next?", you'd go "oh, next month I think we're booked in for", "okay, if you find any more Elvis stuff or this, would you give us a ring, let me know that you're coming and keep it to one side for me and I'll turn up and I'll look at it", "okay".

> So it was like, it was almost like barter except money was involved, you know. Quite democratic really. I mean, some weirdos, but you always get that, don't you? And you didn't get too much bartering. It wasn't like a marketplace. So you'd have an understanding, I think. They'd be looking

---

[10] TMG1049 is the catalogue number for the Four Tops single "Reach out I'll be There".

at you and you'd be looking back at them, all of this stuff meant that there was some kind of an understanding. So it'd be kind of, a lot of it would be unspoken, so it'd be kind of I'd be trying, you'd be trying to buy a record from me and you'd be looking at me and know I'd over-priced it, you know, and I'd knew I'd over-priced it and you'd say "okay, well that's really a really nice record", you'd be telling me you'd really want it, but there was no way you were paying £50 for it, you know. So you'd kind of give me that look and then go and then come back later, you know. That happened a lot. It was different with the bootleg stuff. People would just rush in and buy them. And of course, something I didn't mention earlier, the profits were extraordinarily high. The one I made most money out of was a bootleg triple *Springsteen at Winterland*. It was a triple album, nicely sleeved-up actually, only black and white, nice pressing and I think I paid something like $10 a-piece for it and I got £30 a-piece for it. $10 would mean in those days probably about seven quid. I was selling them for £30… and there was no bartering. People would come in and say "what's that?", "it's a triple album, *Springsteen at Winterland* six months ago", "how much?", "30 quid", "thank you". So there was never any bartering or that sort of thing. So you could argue there was a slightly different trade going on there. And, to get back to the point again, that's what the cassette trade ruined. They came in and just ruined it. They ruined it, and it's a legacy now, isn't it. You can tell that, you know, nobody's interested in those cassettes anymore, I don't think. They're probably in some bin somewhere, in a skip, you know, whereas they still want vinyl. So that was never going to last, but it lasted long enough to do away with a lot of the trade. I've always been half excepting an article on it from *Record Collector*, but they never done it as far as I'm aware: this idea of how cassette bootlegging in the '80s nearly put paid to the record fairs we came to know.

We came to the 1980s and what "George" described as "the over-production" of all music formats over the past thirty years:

There must be still warehouses across the country somewhere full of unsold CDs. We did think the same with vinyl, well that was getting that way by the mid-1980s. But they're the albums that crop up all of the time. You know, you can go to a junkshop and probably find *Bad* Michael, three copies of Michael Jackson, or various copies of, you know, Asia or Europe or, you know, those sort of overproduced rock albums of the 1980s. Loads of Simple Minds albums, loads of Dire Straits albums, loads of old Rush albums, AC/DC ones—that's because of over-production. So whether even those records will ever be collectable is a different matter. Because you don't have to pay any money for them, but you can certainly find them on eBay. They're on eBay, aren't they. You know, if you wanted to build up an AC/DC collection you could probably pretty well get it in a week, I would say.

You'd probably get all of their vinyl cheaply. Just, you know, bid a pound for this, 50 pence for that, maybe four or five pound, maybe more, £10 for their Australian albums, you know, before they came over to the UK. So I wonder whether anything will ever replace vinyl in that collectability form; I wonder if any other format following on from vinyl will ever have the appeal of vinyl precisely because vinyl appears at a particular moment in history. Not because vinyl is better than anything else, it's just that *vinyl reflects a very, very interesting period of time in popular music and cultural history anyway* [my own emphasis]. Just like in the mid to late 1990s when the "loungecore" thing developed isn't it. How some of that stuff started to become collectable, Burt Kaempfert albums, Andy Williams albums, sound-effects albums; and while those albums were "collectable", they weren't worth much, in monetary terms. It's still the *Vertigo* and *Island* and *Harvest* albums that continue to be worth the big bucks, isn't it? So I think it's a very special case, vinyl. Vinyl is a special case—partially because it appears at a very specific time in cultural history.

Summary

One might argue that record collectors are very special people. They have taken it upon themselves to archive the entire history of popular music, while at the same time subscribing to a different set of value judgements about taste and authenticity, and at least partially removing themselves from the ideologies around them. They have created an independence of thought—which, it might also be argued, is what life is all about.

This ethnographic example is perhaps both poignant and informative. While "George" expressed an element of self-confidence, the fact remains that he never stopped looking for ways in which recorded sound could articulate value and meaning in uncharted ways. Whether he was dealing in punk singles, Springsteen bootlegs or even cassettes (!), he never stopped believing in the aura of recorded sound (quite the reverse of the Benjaminian "loss of aura"[11]). There was always something new, and if all of this has fallen within an era of post-modernity, which for some has emerged and has been distinguished by abandoning any search for meaning, record dealers and collectors such as "George" (and others cited

---

[11] Walter Benjamin, "The Work of Art in the Age of Its Technological Reproducibility: Second Version", in *Walter Benjamin: Selected Writing, Volume 3, 1935–1938*, eds. Howard Eiland and Michael Jennings (Cambridge: The Belknap Press of Harvard University Press, 1935), 101–133.

here) have not convinced themselves about the futility of such a search. Instead, they have reconciled themselves to a life under conditions of uncertainty in which one of the competing forms of mass communication can reveal its own value for their own historically-shaped conventions.

This is not to say that record collecting has certainty to it, but it is certainly important to suggest that such collecting and trading has few requirements for a modernist universal grounding, as might be suggested by the Frankfurt School. One might even describe the dealer and the collector as being partially representative of a metaphoric fall of the authorities. We can see now that dealers and collectors are not mutually exclusive. Dealers and collectors make sense together, as manifestations of the same authenticity complex. How different this situation appears to be when compared with the otherness, Orientalist, and deviant visages proffered by what we might describe as obedient social narratives. The point is that the dealer/collector has found better and more efficient ways of producing power on an individual level than the norms and realms of society could offer. One might even argue that conventional authority within such matrixes has become relatively redundant; certainly, the reproduction of authority appears somewhat surplus. If a member of a record shop staff can refuse to sell a record, it seems that whosoever continues to immerse themselves in such cultural goings-on perceives their situations as intrinsic and vital.

CHAPTER EIGHT

IN SEARCH OF THE MATRIX:
RECORD COLLECTING AND NEW MEDIA

"Sweeping across the country with the speed of a transient fashion in
slang or Panama hats, political war cries or popular novels, comes now
the mechanical device to sing for us a song or play for us a piano, in
substitute for human skill, intelligence, and soul"
—John Philip Sousa (1906)

This work has tried to develop a thesis by which the record collector and
the artefact of the record can be considered from a variety of perspectives
that challenge the conventional wisdom concerning collecting in general,
and record collecting in particular. The suggestion has been from the
outset that the history of both collecting and recorded sound have been
stereotyped and have suffered from neglect in relatively equal amounts not
only by society at large but also by popular music academia, both areas
having struggled with ideological decisions that have led to narrow and
unwholesome definitions of not simply the collector but also the very
object of desire—the record. It has been further suggested that in the case
of the latter, such ideologies have been formed out of the hierarchical
manner in which musical records have been considered in the prioritisation
of the score as an indicator of the excellence of society and culture, the
unexpected impact of recorded sound, and the ideological standpoints,
perhaps dressed up as definitions that emanated from the mid twentieth-
century concern with mass movements and mechanical reproduction,
brought about by the apparent success of Marxism as a philosophical tool,
the movements of masses of people for the first time in history, and the
technological wizardry which by 1945 could also destroy the human race.
It has been argued that such pessimism was understandable, yet rather
premature in its designation of all mass-produced forms of entertainment
being limited in scope by the nature of its production.

This work has considered issues to do with deviance from a
sociological perspective in order to locate opinions and urban myths
concerning the record collector, yet suggested that drawing down

collectors to the individual asks us to concern ourselves with the duality of existence from our thoughts to realities, and how tastes and authenticities are very much in the "ear" of the beholder. Individual perception has been explored via a model of a reflective and perhaps even refractive mirror-like view of ourselves where the negativity of distortion suggested by such as Theodor Adorno could be reversed into a positive. Such positivity was certainly found via the ethnographic case studies presented in this work. Among those interviewed, Les suggested that his record collection was at least some kind of matrix of meaning—in other words his collection helped him at a very vulnerable time in his life to focus upon what he felt was very important—in his case, recovery after a stroke. Others, however, such as "George", Dave, Chris and Shane also felt that the collection itself contained important signifiers and connotations, in one case preventing one collector from suicide. We have also considered the concept that the binary division between "collector" and dealer is false if we take into account the important use-value quotient that records have in people's lives, both privately and communally. So much so, in fact, that it is suggested here that this matrix was also a catalyst—spurring people on to important decisions and activities.

Above all, perhaps, this book has attempted to remind the reader that the focus of attention was as much on the collection—the artefact—as on the collector, and as such this has raised very significant issues within the study of popular music, where the focus, at least according to this writer's research, still appears to concentrate upon the collector (human) rather than the collection (artefact): for some, that is arguably a step too far from their initial inspirations coming from the ideologies of the left. This final point, of course, is somewhat radical—i.e. applying meaning to an inanimate object—but it follows a narrative that could be described as both historical and ahistorical. In other words, it suggests that the impact of recorded sound was so much greater than humankind could have predicted that individual perceptions out of juncture with time with the recorded sound artefact were perhaps of such great significance that they became "timeless" and were important embodiments for individuals. Such embodiments were discussed within the realms of cultural capital—a theoretical model that emerged from Marxist thought, but one that has been taken far beyond such limiting discourse into the realms of perception. An examination of a "classic" Adornian statement, it is hoped, helped to offer to the reader how and why this writer feels that such preconceived ideas masquerading as philosophy have been mistakenly considered as profound.

Further, via a short treatise concerning the contexts, rationales and impacts of one particular British record label—*Vertigo*—it has been suggested that the complexities surrounding the label's appearance and disappearance are both contextual and de-contextual. That the fact that the label is regarded as collectible stems from important issues involved in its conception: industry, technology, culture and counter-culture, but also that a collector might find the label alluring for a wide variety of different aesthetic reasons. Such pronouncements were not simply rhetorical, for alongside the presentation of a theory concerning cultural value via a matrix, social concerns over deviance and "otherness", and conceptions of identity via the subjectivisation of the object, the work of Evan Eisenberg was used as a model for understanding the significance, impact and reception of recorded sound. The collector was then placed into a "kinetic matrix" from which he was examined. All of this was given a backdrop of a questioning of consensus via the rubric of ideology, thus leading the writer to consider post-modern theory as a way of understanding popular culture from the so-called, "bottom-up". This was akin to Emmanuel Levinas's concept—expressed here in this final chapter—of a different "other" to that which was discussed within the work of Edward Said. It appears that we simply have to judge; it is probably human nature that we do so. But Levinas proposes that our ground for judging has no base, that ideology has no grounding, and that "the face of the Other [is in our case] the original site of the sensible". Levinas continues:

> The proximity of the Other is the face's meaning, and it means in a way that goes beyond those plastic forms which forever try to cover the face lie a mask of their presence to perception. But the face always shows through these forms. Prior to any particular expression and beneath all particular expressions, which cover over and protect with an immediately adopted face or countenance, there is the nakedness and destitution of the expression as such, that is to say extreme exposure, defencelessness, vulnerability itself [...] In its expression, in its mortality, the face before me summons me, calls me, begs for me, as if the invisible death that must be faced by the Other, pure otherness, separated in some way, from any whole, were my business.[1]

The face, it seems, points the finger directly at us. In the demands of humankind to be social beings we simply must behave correctly and justly towards any "other" we encounter. Levinas suggests, however, as does this work, that we cannot do so according to pre-determined systems and

---

[1] Emmanuel Levinas, *The Levinas Reader*, ed. Sean Hand (London: Blackwell, 1989), 82–83.

ideologies that have been contextually-apprised from similarly pre-determined political theories that were unable to fully consider (in our case) the full impact of recorded sound upon the human imagination. Such systems will only ever reveal the systems themselves to be incomplete and incapable of dealing with the other. The other, according to Levinas, is always other than itself—in other words, it always has more overwhelming capacity than the social structures which appear to define it, for such social structures—in our case mores, myths, folkways and laws—have not been constructed to deal with otherness, but to define and dispatch it.

In fact, it has been suggested via this work that the other is not simply a displaced identity but a distorted mirror in which we may continue to recognise, re-invent and thus reconstitute ourselves as we, not society, see fit. In this respect, the demand made by this work is one of the potential for records and their collectors to be viewed as progressive, not regressive, productive not passive, artistic not pathological: the demand, in fact, is one of alterity, in other words for one to accept changes to something or somebody, or to be changed or become different through such practices as record collecting. There is also, of course, the concomitant demand that we accept a cognition of the event of heterogeneity, for if ever there was an impact, difficult to record by (say) Marxist and post-Marxist thought, it is the "event" of becoming, the event of the diverse nature of humankind, and our ability to co-create "on the hoof". If ever there was a need for such acceptances, it is perhaps now that the twentieth century is behind us and a new century beckons us forward.

In short, therefore, by this sample of record collecting, stereotyping and partial studies of the popular, this work has attempted to suggest that we must discover—produce, even—non-aligned justice in our values of others. It is here that the real burden and trajectory of post-modern enquiries can actually be discovered, for they lead us to the search for understandings not hidebound by formalistic thought produced at specific times and relating only to those specific times. Perhaps the worst thing one can do to collectors is to homogenise them under a cloud of mediocre theory.

Eisenberg Revisited: Collecting Records as a Matrix in the Modern Age

Before considering the specificities of this chapter it is worth revisiting Eisenberg's[2] five points regarding the satisfaction from collecting cultural

---

[2] Evan Eisenberg, *The Recording Angel: Music, Records And Culture From Aristotle To Zappa* (New Haven: Yale University Press, 2005).

objects, discussed at some length in the initial sections of this book. Eisenberg's listing still carries great resonance with regard to record collecting practices, and actually become more applicable when one views the web-based collecting of music. To remind ourselves of the important five positions: firstly, Eisenberg identified a need to preserve beauty and pleasure as sources of satisfaction to the collector. This aspect, perhaps naturally, remains unaltered, for the collector still collects and thus still preserves the perceived beauty. Hence, whilst certain practices may change, the desires one has to collect or the pleasures and enjoyments one accrues from collecting remain relatively unchanged, perhaps they are even enhanced by electronic media.

This, it seems to this writer, is a philosophical issue of great proportions, for the need for beauty appears constant across technologies. If, as is occasionally argued, there is no beauty in electronic media, this might suggest that only rationality remained. But the world, it seems, cannot function without concepts of beauty,[3] irrespective of electronic media formats, and so it can clearly be seen that such formats are "naturally" adapted to serve the search for beauty. Not only does this make sense, but it is also of great significance: if a worldwide media system existed without a search for beauty, life would probably not be worth living. This is in opposition to those who suggest that such forms have effectively "ruined our lives". Actually, like recorded sound before it, the World Wide Web has enhanced our lives beyond measure by our inclusion of it in our search for the sublime. Digital technology allows the collector to search with a greater scope and without the limitations of geography. As one record collector noted, "[I like] eBay because it makes searching so easy and because you can find things in 20 minutes that you've never seen in 20 years of record-store-going".[4]

One small piece of ethnography supports this well. A PhD student who had just commenced her research on "sunshine pop" in 2013 came across The Peppermint Rainbow, a group of whom she had never previously heard. She was at the time compiling a list of all such groups that might, upon investigation, fit into this retrospective genre, and was taken aback to find that there was a group she had overlooked. She went online and her first port of call was YouTube, where she found several tracks, and even a couple of TV performances, that had been uploaded onto the site by fans of the group. Thrilled by this she trawled through the references and

---

[3] One might also wonder if it would *wish* to function without concepts of beauty: *cf.* George Orwell's 1984.

[4] Keir Keightley cited in Roy Shuker, *Wax Trash and Vinyl Treasures: Record Collecting as a Social Practice* (Farnham: Ashgate, 2010), 123.

discovered that they were from Baltimore, USA, and had enjoyed a Hot 100 hit in 1969. The song, "Will You be Staying after Sunday?",[5] had been released on a US *Decca* 45rpm, so her next port of call was eBay, where, lo and behold, the single was available on their auction site. After the bidding had ended one week later, she received the single in the post for the price of a couple of cups of coffee. She told this writer:

> When I heard the song, I wanted it, but as both a collector and a researcher I did feel a real need, not a desire, to have it on the original 45 format and label. American or British, it didn't really matter, but it was nice to find a US copy—and, of course, these are usually cheaper than the British equivalents, less desirable, I think. My search could have taken forever, I suppose, but my natural inclination was to look on eBay, and hey presto! I don't know how anyone can say—if they do—that the web is not an aid. I found the purchase of the single to be not only a personal triumph, but a real aid to my research. And what is more, someone posted it up there in the first place, so there must be a market for this stuff, so I'll look again, when I'm ready.[6]

Eisenberg's second point, the need to comprehend the beauty, also remains, like his first point, largely unchanged. Again, whilst electronic media can alter certain behaviours exerted by record collectors, their cognisance and rationale for collecting does not, by and large, need to change substantively. In fact, the unending panorama of sound and recording creates a vista that could be equated with sound painting:

> As he takes hold of the power to record selectively the sounds that make up his world, Mario is overcome with excitement. Wherever he points the microphone, it seems not only to capture sound but to register his feelings about the world he perceives. Finally, he points the microphone at the night sky. "Starry sky over the island", he says. He has become intoxicated with the magic of this machine, and in the process has forgotten that it can only record sound. To Mario, the machine seems capable of capturing and replaying anything that engages his emotions or leaves a trace on his imagination [and perhaps it is?].[7]

---

[5] The publishers of this recording were Kama Sutra, owned by the renowned pop producer Paul Leka, who was also responsible for hits by The Lemon Pipers, and Steam, amongst others.

[6] Dori Howard, personal communication, May 2013.

[7] Albin J. Zak III, *The Poetics of Rock: Cutting Tracks, Making Records* (London: University of California Press, 2001), 1

It should be noted, however, that greater access to a larger (perhaps unending) variety of sounds, records and other people's record collections, can also swamp a collector with information. One programme collector, who wished to remain anonymous, informed me that he "used eBay all the time to build up my collection but this was just for bargain bundles and the like. I'd rather reserve judgement on quality in the case of the good stuff and go to programme fairs to continue the chase. I think the instant gratification of immediately finding what I was looking for on the web would somehow deflate me".[8]

So the comprehension of a route to find beautiful things to archive remains strong for many. Although we are faced with the possibility of having our desires satiated, we still appear to find the web very useful: the use of such modernity in a social, historical and perhaps even existential, way does similarly appear to satisfy our cognition of what beauty is for us. Perhaps the inherent contradiction of this new/old model is not lost on most, and might even contribute to the, albeit at times brief, search. Approaching the past via stylistic and technological connotation does not stereotype or purvey an imaginary past for, in the case above, it is evidently also an aid to research, as well as a thing of beauty.

While before electronic media it was almost impossible to find and acquire certain records, such as a few of those discussed in the *Vertigo* chapter above, eBay and other and various forums open up the field. In fact, one might discover that someone who did not previously perceive themselves as a record collector ad started collecting, almost by "accident", because he or she became *aware* of what records were available. As regards eBay and the opportunities it allowed for record collectors, another collector offered similar thoughts to the example of the above PhD student, quite plainly: "It is fun to find unusual items and expand one's collection, and sometimes music tastes".[9]

It is, perhaps, in Eisenberg's third point that we begin to see changes in applications when we consider record collecting through electronic media. While electronic media still allows for—and perhaps even encourages— consumption as an act of heroism, such as bidding in the face of economic non-affordability, or doing without an interpreter and/or interlocutor to help you along your journey or search, it does bring with it changes in ways *of* consumption. Firstly, one does not need to leave one's home in order to consume vast quantities of records—and in some cases, the records may even be delivered to your door. This may indeed remind the

---

[8] "C", programme collector, March 2012.
[9] Gary Shuker cited in Roy Shuker, *Wax Trash and Vinyl Treasures: Record Collecting as a Social Practice* (Farnham: Ashgate, 2010), 110.

reader of Adorno's statement that "he brings nothing home which would not be delivered to his house";[10] Adorno might still be mistaken, however, for regardless of his warnings, something *is* brought home. It is Adorno who is reduced to a consideration of the artefact only as a product. In this work, however, we have considered the artefact as much more than this, and have described it as a kinetic matrix. Therefore, the artefact also facilitates "real" quality moments, not simply in its "being", but also in its "arriving" (literally, in this case). Pirsig discusses this kind of transient transcendence as "Quality", something almost indefinable, something one tends to only notice when it ceases to exist, but it is there, and only we know where to look because of its innate subjectivity—therefore, he suggests, theorists tend not to acknowledge its presence at all, or if they do, wish to lance it as if a boil:

> On the intellectual side [...] he now saw that Quality was a cleavage term. What every intellectual analyst looks for. You take your analytic knife, put the point directly on the term Quality and just tap, not hard, gently, and the whole world splits, cleaves, right in two—hip and square, classic and romantic, technological and humanistic—and the split is clean [...] here was Quality; a tiny almost unnoticeable fault line; a line of illogic in our concept of the universe.[11]

If one yet again considers that important Fleetwood Mac album, *Rumours*, discussed previously (and of great significance to this writer), *both* vinyl copies in possession of the writer hold meaning to her, but the latter, more recently-acquired copy[12] also holds a distinctly different meaning from the first, despite being "the same" record. This meaning was created and forged through what Pirsig might describe as a "Quality" moment: the mixture of contemporary context, listening, and sentiment attached to the discourse surrounding the album; such complex paths of meaning could not have been "home delivered" as it were, but were searched for and found through processes of finding that Quality moment. Furthermore, if Shuker[13] was also correct in his analysis that the "hunt"

---

[10] Theodor Adorno, "On the Fetish-Character in Music and the Regression of Listening", in *Essays on Music*, ed. Richard Leppert (Berkley: University of California Press, 1938), 309.

[11] Robert Pirsig, *Zen and the Art of Motorcycle Maintenance* (London: Vintage Random House, 1974), 218.

[12] Which, to whomever it may interest, arrived safely in May 2013, intact and *with* the desired lyric insert.

[13] Roy Shuker, *Wax Trash and Vinyl Treasures: Record Collecting as a Social Practice* (Farnham: Ashgate, 2010).

within record collecting was a significant element of consumption, one of the things that mattered most—"[the hunt is] more important than the end result"—and

> [the hunt is] every bit as absorbing as the collection itself—probably more so, because I've been guilty of chasing a particular item for years, then, having finally got it, putting it away in the collection without even listening to it, and promptly becoming obsessed with the next elusive treasure on my list.[14]

Then one has another example of Pirsig's "Quality" element (which might also be described as cognition of beauty). For if, as has been suggested in this work, the impact of recorded sound was/is "timeless" and not historical in the linear sense (as Eisenberg also suggests), then the time factor may be less to do with common conceptions of time and space and more to do with mental time and space, in which case the literal time it takes to find that Dr. Z album, were it possible, is not really the issue. Instead, the hunt can be compressed, condensed by a technology that re-allocated and redefines time. Just as Levinas suggested that the other can reconstitute itself, perhaps technology asks important questions about time, the construction of time, and our approaches to time. The hunt, therefore, is not dispensed with by electronically acquiring a record, it is reconstituted by the typing-in of a title of an album or artist into a search engine: "I collect as a passion and enjoy the auction aspect of internet buying: hunt, chase and… kill!"[15]

Of course, unless choosing the "Buy it now" option, one can never be quite sure of successfully purchasing anything from eBay, for someone

---

[14] Greg Crossan cited in Roy Shuker, *Wax Trash and Vinyl Treasures: Record Collecting as a Social Practice*, Farnham: Ashgate, 2010), 110. Interestingly, this quote is not further examined by Shuker, where it can originally be found. For this writer, this might suggest a lack of understanding of a fundamental element of record collecting—the importance of owning the record as an *artefact*, not as a musical carrier—one of the main features of this book. It is an all too common error to assume the only value a record has is its sound, and that if it is consumed in a different manner one must be obsessed or stockpiling for some reason. This is a deep-rooted flaw in understanding consumption, where, arguably, consuming any artefact *against the grain* is viewed suspiciously.

[15] Gary Shuker cited in Roy Shuker, *Wax Trash and Vinyl Treasures: Record Collecting as a Social Practice*, (Farnham: Ashgate, 2010), 110.

else might just as easily place a higher bid at any given time.[16] As previously suggested, some collectors do not, however, feel that eBay auctions are a substitute for the reality of the hunt, or chase, and still express a preference for physically browsing and shopping. Shuker notes: "This preference is based on a combination of the immediacy of the act of acquisition, and wanting to have the cultural artefact, the record, literally in hand".[17] It is not only a question of immediate satisfaction, which might draw the critic's mind to stereotypical images of Freud's *id*, but "on a more pragmatic level enables a careful inspection of the condition of the recording",[18] and there are few things that are of such value that one would happily purchase blindly, without inspection. However, record sales on eBay are a little different, for there is always the possibility of community coming into play: while we might not be able to legislate or mediate on what we buy, there is always the fact that record collectors do belong to some kind of community and are there for us to understand the instance, the event and whether we relate it to our sense of Pirsig's "Quality". A number of record-collecting forums visited by the writer in the process of researching this book[19] had, for instance, boards dedicated to eBay where members could discuss anything eBay-related. Many of the posts encountered were warnings to other members about precarious buyers or sellers, indicating a concern that they did not want fellow members to come across the same problems they had—or at least approach with caution.

This leads us to Eisenberg's final two points, ones that perhaps resonate most in regards to record collecting in this electronic age: the need to belong, and the need to impress. As will be made evident later in this chapter, networks of communication and kinship have formed around record collecting via such online forums as the Record Collectors Guild.[20] A closer look at this particular forum will take place in due course, although it is safe to suggest at this stage that one can already observe that by offering a network of communication, forums such as the Record Collectors Guild could be seen as providing a real level of cyber-

---

[16] Some "eBay regulars" even gain quite some pleasure from out-bidding someone in the closing moments of an auction (which of course also pretty much guarantees them the affording bid and, thus, the item), this writer is informed.

[17] Roy Shuker, *Wax Trash and Vinyl Treasures: Record Collecting as a Social Practice* (Farnham: Ashgate, 2010), 113.

[18] *ibid.*, 113.

[19] Particularly www.audiophileusa.com, www.recordcollectorsguild.org, www.theaudiophile.net.

[20] www.recordcollectorsguild.org.

community. This was something to which Les, in Chapter Four, could also testify: through Lani Hall's website he had found a community to which he felt he could belong. Previously, fans of Lani Hall, Colosseum, The Beatles or The Outlaws[21] (or whoever) might have been spread out geographically, with few chances to physically meet or socialise, and thus may never have had the opportunity to learn of each other's existences prior to online communities, as such forums can be seen to provide "roads to people".[22] As Eisenberg establishes, the need to belong is an important one, and something people seek. If belonging to a fan club or online community where one can find networks of support and exchange thoughts with like-minded people enhances or brings pleasure to our lives, it is necessarily relevant.

Eisenberg finally discusses the need to impress, but here it was identified that he did not simply mean the desire to impress others, but to award a level of satisfaction to the self, to bolster one's opinion of one's self by suggesting that correct decisions had been made, and to lift one's spirits as a consequence of coming across a timeless moment that will live in the memory beyond the strictures of high and low art, social mores, and laws. Online forums provide ample opportunity to impress both one's self and others. Often, the online forums provide a resource where one can find information already posted, and crucially also ask questions of other members. Thus being able to answer questions using language that displays mutual cultural capital can bring satisfaction to both the person asking and/or answering the question by impressing themselves (a sort of "this is what I have achieved"), and can also impress others as being a respectable part of a community not restricted by politics, ideology, time, space, or geography, but existing in cyberspace, across geo-political boundaries and without the conventional rubric of representation (a category which of course comes under pressure because of shared interests in aesthetics that are usually regarded as low art by "real" society). Similarly, knowing the right questions to ask, and hence creating a discussion or debate, can satisfy the need to impress, as that too can be a sign of cultural capital. One could also argue that the more permanent nature of the forums through the written word allows for a greater spread as well. In other words, a post that may have impressed the author and other readers during the time of writing may later impress others, as an

---

[21] An early 1960s instrumental group, with associations with Ritchie Blackmore and Joe Meek, amongst others.
[22] David Riesman cited in Evan Eisenberg, *The Recording Angel: Music, Records And Culture From Aristotle To Zappa* (New Haven: Yale University Press, 2005).

online post can continue to affect others indefinitely—it is, like recorded sound itself, "timeless".

As with so many aspects of life, the electronic age has an impact on record collecting. As researchers, we need to formulate understandings concerning how record collecting deals with the absence of mediators, authority, social mores and ideologies (apart, of course, from the self-made authority related to the collectors themselves). In the current electronic age, and with other changes in the practices that may have occurred as a result of new developments and opportunities, the lack of external limitations of social mores is only part of the story; another part, arguably, comes from the growing independence of electronic media. This enables arbiters of collecting taste to cleverly manage their authority and their authenticity, one result of which closes down certain types of cultural capital (education, elitism, class, etc.) and opens up different types of cultural capital in which traditional authorities hardly recognise how to use their previous skills, systems and power. This is a significant addition onto the collecting environment: taste cultures can be both collective and anonymous, and value can only be gauged by on the one hand the speediness of a bid on eBay, or the approval of a given value continuum by an audiophile dealer on the other. In such modes of creative consumption, one is seldom seen as the old aforementioned "lone voice crying in the wilderness", because in the search for (let us say) our rare sunshine pop 45 we are all lone voices, but none of us *are* lone voices: we are all individuals, but we are all part of a community. In these circumstances we would have to concede that just as recorded sound was an innovation introduced as a commodity but became artistic via its unbounded and non-prescribed potential, so we now have consumption introduced as art in a constantly fluxing cyberspace of record collectability.

In what is a mammoth piece of scholarship, Brocken and Davis have discussed how they feel cyberspace is now contributing to Beatles fandom, creative writing (and one might suggest, collecting) in myriad ways:

There are several small archives and communities on the web (some "live", some not), described by contributors as "Beatles Slash" IT media fandom sites; slash fiction is a subset of RPF [Real Person Fiction]; the term "slash" is commonly used to describe stories where two people have an intimate relationship of a homosexual nature. Such fan fiction will usually concern men who also happen to have been significant characters from history. These writings are not necessarily intended to promote the idea that (say, in this case) The Beatles were gay, but suggest to writers a "what if" factor: always an interesting authorial premise. One anonymous writer informed this researcher via email that he "couldn't really explain mine or anyone else's fascination with this type of writing, other than it seems to

me to be very creative, given the fact that most Beatles books just go
through the same old stuff. It has also helped me a great deal as a writer,
that's for sure, because I can also put ideas up there and watch them get
shot down".
[...] Incidentally, there are now Beatles Slash fiction awards and there are
several Beatles Slash video productions hosted by YouTube. Here, slash
producers edit together songs with images of The Beatles (particularly
John and Paul) glancing at each other. There is also a "slash novella":
Plastic Jesus, by Poppy Z. Brite (2000), which postulates a love affair
between (a very thinly disguised) John Lennon and Paul McCartney. To
paraphrase situationist Guy Debord (1988), perhaps the most important
changes in society tend to lie "within the continuity of the spectacle".
However, the spectacle succeeds not simply by raising, as Debord suggests
"a whole generation moulded to its laws", but also when given an
opportunity to creatively subvert from within.[23]

The possibilities are evidently quite endless and if, as Brocken states in
his opening essay to the above work, we are (to paraphrase him) possibly
bearing witness to the growth of a new electronic historiography which
has little or no recourse to either fact or place (or indeed time) and we
have interspersed ironic interpolations of previously supposed objective
propositions or "givens", then the future looks exciting indeed. Here, all
previous directives of myth are re-mythologized for different modes of re-
consumption as "other". It is via the web that fictional works such as
these, and collecting communities such as mentioned above, can allow us
to witness and be part of another authentic fracture of time and space. In
one hundred years' time, perhaps, researchers will be suggesting that the
present day made as enormous an impact on the hierarchies and social
mores of society as recorded sound did at the turn of the nineteenth
century. As Brocken suggests, "Surely the imagination is where our
authenticities are primarily sited".[24]

Audiophile USA

Margaret Wertheim, in her excellent historical charting of cyberspace *The
Pearly Gates of Cyberspace* informs us that:

> Like physical space, [...] "cyber" space is growing at an extraordinary rate,
> increasing its "volume" in an ever-widening "sphere" of expansion. Each

---

[23] Michael Brocken and Melissa Davis, *The Beatles Bibliography: A New Guide to
the Literature* (Manitou Springs: The Beatle Works, 2012), 51–52.
[24] *ibid.*, 17.

day thousands of new nodes or "sites" are added to the Internet and other affiliated networks, and with each new node the total domain of cyberspace grows larger. What increases here is not volume in any strictly geometrical sense—yet it is a kind of volume. In cyberspace each site is connected to dozens, or even thousands, of others through software-defined "hot buttons." These digital connections link sites together in a labyrinthian web that branches out in many "directions" at once.[25]

She continues:

Businesses, too, are staking out a presence in cyberspace. Seemingly every corporation from IBM and Nike on down now sports a Web site packed with corporate PR and product information. Included in an increasing number of sites is also the ability to purchase online. Clothes, books, cosmetics, airline tickets, and computer equipment (to name just a few items) can now be bought over the Net. According to a recent Commerce Department report, ten million people in the United States and Canada had bought something online by the end of 1997. The report estimates that electronic commerce should reach $300 billion by 2002. The virtual mall has arrived.[26]

Wertheim's text is a most valuable source, for it not only records, but also projects. The author correctly identifies that cyberspace is the new place to both socialize and play. To paraphrase, she states that chatrooms, newsgroups, IRC channels, online conferences, forums, and fantasy worlds known as MUDs promise an unending scope for social interactions of all kinds. We have already seen that Brocken and Davis have identified such areas in relation to Beatles historiography, and that record collecting is now at least partially led by eBay, and similar sites. It is becoming clear that in cyberspace we can readily search for friends with similar interests. As online pioneer Howard Rheingold suggested almost twenty years ago, while "you can't simply pick up a phone and ask to be connected with someone who wants to talk about Icelandic art or California wine, or someone with a three-year-old daughter or a forty-year-old Hudson, you can, however, join a computer conference on any of these topics".[27]

---

[25] Margaret Wertheim, *The Pearly Gates of Cyberspace: A History of Space from Dante to the Internet* (New York: W. W. Norton & Company Incorporated, 2000), 221.

[26] *ibid.*, 225.

[27] Howard Rheingold, *The Virtual Community: Homesteading on the Electronic Frontier* (San Francisco: HarperPerennial, 1994), 27.

The intellectual level of discussion in many public forums is highly variable,[28] but serious private online discussion groups abound on many forums, and the academic world, particularly in the United States, has long since used such forums for genuine academic debate and research. So there now exist myriad imaginative ways of creating online communities and making a living via record collecting. One record-collecting site which this writer has enjoyed dealings with over the past ten years is Audiophile USA, an interesting project right from the start, which seems at times to lurch from crisis to financial crisis and then at other times to prosper. They continue to trade—buying and selling all kinds of LPs from all over the world (popular *and* classical forms, in fact) and appear to subscribe to the online dictum discussed by Wertheim that there is indeed a valuable community out there with no geographical boundaries.

It is of significance that one does not examine such sites from within the dualist notions we have spent a considerable time exposing and critiquing. One of the key features of this book is that the separation of life from "doing"—whether that is older notions of art or business, are out-moded and require substantial reconstruction. It would therefore not be wise at this stage to consider Audiophile USA as a business rather than a forum. Cyberspace has so greatly challenged what we consider to be reality that it has broken down conventional logics concerning what both space and time actually is, so it would be incorrect to re-situate old dualistic notions in order to explain such activities as businesses only. We no longer live in a world of such fractionalisation—and in fact we have not done so for more than a century. As Pirsig suggests:

> I think that the referent of a term that can split a world into hip and square, classic and romantic, technological and humanistic, is an entity that can unite a world already split along these lines into one. A real understanding of Quality doesn't just serve the System, or even beat it or even escape it. A real understanding of Quality captures the System, tames it, and puts it to work for one's own personal use, while leaving it completely free to fulfil his inner destiny.[29]

It has become increasingly evident to those who feel that systems are to be avoided, that actually they can be re-employed in a profound way.

---

[28] One need only compare the discussion on forums such as Record Collectors Guild (www.recordcollectorsguild.org), Football365 (forum.football365.com) or Malaria World (www.malariaworld.org).

[29] Robert Pirsig, *Zen and the Art of Motorcycle Maintenance* (London: Vintage/Random House, 1974), 223.

Cyberspace, therefore, is literally an "other" place. Unleashed into the internet, one's location can no longer be fixed purely in a physical sense—which is exciting if one sees cyberspace as the potential face of the "other", for it effectively mirrors a multifarious reality, rather than simply a binary dichotomy (between, say home and work, pleasure and duty, freedom and drudgery, supplier and customer—the Marxist oppositions that have always been ontologically unsound and have now actually "melted into air").

But what does it mean to talk about this digital age in direct relationship to record collecting? It is evident that the Audiophile website is able to attract major search engines, and thus almost guarantee a level of trade throughout the lifetime of a business. It is perhaps of little use bemoaning, as does Graham Jones,[30] the loss of high street record shops, when such outlets lose money, do not carry enough stock, and do not appear to understand how to trade in a non-dualist "dealer and customer" relationship. If that important search, that hunt, can be transferred to the different spaces, different times, who are we to grumble? Facilitators such as Audiophile USA are there to serve us and help us to effectively join a community:

> We've had over 13 years of success in supplying records and CDs to collectors worldwide. We've grown from humble beginnings in 1989 as 'The Record Connoisseur' in England to our current operation near Sacramento, California. We've also personally been avid record collectors for over 25 years. Through the years we've developed a keen sense of the needs of both the connoisseur and the collector who is just starting out on his musical odyssey. We carry a superb collection which is continuously updated and encompasses all genres of music to satisfy even our most demanding customers. Outstanding condition is our standard and expert packaging and fast friendly service is our specialty. As shown in *The Wall Street Journal*, we are THE reliable source for your musical inspiration.[31]

One newsletter from 2011 even informed collectors that Audiophile was struggling with recorded sound authenticities (and bootleggers!). The collectors were the first to be informed that:

> We have cut way back on carrying vinyl reissues and new releases due to the widely varying quality, not only of the pressings, but in many cases, the completely unknown sources and mastering for these reissues. It seems

---

[30] Graham Jones, *Last Shop Standing: Whatever Happened to Record Shops?* (London: Proper Music Publishing, 2009).
[31] www.audiophileusa.com, accessed 31 May 2013.

like everyone and their uncle is jumping on the reissue bandwagon with a resultant mad rush to get product out and a consequent drop in quality. That said, we are still stocking titles that we think are worthy additions to our site. One label of note that takes great pains to release excellent vinyl and packaging is Light In The Attic. Two outstanding recent releases from this label are: Kris Kristofferson's "Please Don't Tell Me How The Story Ends" —A 2LP hand-numbered limited edition of 2,000 pressings featuring all previously unreleased songs from 1968–1972. A personal favorite of mine is the self-titled Lou Bond album originally released on the rare We Produce subsidiary of Stax. I've never been able to locate a quiet copy of this lost masterpiece for my own collection, so it is a great pleasure to hear this re-master by Dave Cooley in a deluxe numbered gatefold with lyrics and extensive insert notes. From Mobile Fidelity we have new releases from Madeleine Peyroux, plus a great reissue of Little Feat's "Dixie Chicken".[32]

While a more recent communiqué reads:

MID MAY UPDATE 2012

Welcome to our short and sweet Mid-May flyer,

I have just returned from yet another buying trip, with over one thousand quality LPs. Click here to see our latest arrivals. ......

For the next month we are having a sale on all 12 inch singles with 20% off any title either sealed or open. Click here for all the new 12 inchers....... And click here for all the used 12 inchers....... We have over 1,000 in stock.

Thanks for visiting, John Turton and crew.[33]

The language is of one communality, it suggests that we are all part of a community and that the division of labour is never certain: we know that John Turton is the proprietor, but we also know he collects; we know he sells, but he also buys; he buys to sell, but also buys to collect; he appears to employ others, therefore sustaining other families, other lifestyles. The interlocking imaginative and social mesh of Audiophile USA means that actions taken by one contributor may affect the lives of hundreds of others. As in the physical world, relationships build up over time, and bonds and trusts are established, with responsibilities evident. The very vitality and

---

[32] www.audiophileusa.com, "June 2010 Flyer", accessed 31 May 2013.
[33] www.audiophileusa.com, "May 2012 Flyer", accessed 31 May 2013.

robustness of Audiophile USA emerges from both an individual and collective will into a social matrix that is by no means any less "real" for being virtual. To quote Wertheim:

> Before we get too upset about this bifurcation of reality, it is well to remember that those of us born after the mid fifties have already been living with a collective parallel world—the one on the other side of the television screen. We who grew up with Bewitched, I Dream of Jeannie, Gilligan's Island, and Get Smart—are we not already participating in a vast "consensual hallucination"? One that, as in Bewitched, is deeply imbued with magical qualities. The collective drama of soap operas and sitcoms— be it the daytime fare of Days of Our Lives and General Hospital, or the nighttime fare of Melrose Place and Seinfeld—are these not "consensual hallucinations" which engage tens of millions of people around the world every day of the week? What is the cartoon town of Springfield in The Simpsons if not a genuine "virtual world"?[34]

The Record Collectors Guild

The Record Collectors Guild[35] has its own fascinating website;[36] it appears to have been put into place with the sole intention of creating a locatable site for enthusiasts who wish to share ideas, advice, stories, and perhaps even write articles concerning their chosen mode of interest. This concurs with the various sets of ideas put forward concerning meaningful fandom and audience tropes by Tim Wall where, to paraphrase: (i) we do not choose music in isolation from each other, and that (ii) the music that we choose to consume is also relevant and meaningful to somebody else. Further, the way in which we consume music amongst fellow like-minded people (whether in our own home or in cyberspace—and in some cases we might ask: "what's the difference?") actually transforms any meaning it might have carried from the composer and mediator into our own meanings: "Acquiring our music as a vinyl LP from a second-hand stall on a market, as a CD from a high-street store, as a 12-inch vinyl single from a specialist dance music shop, or as an MP3 file over the internet, are all meaningful choices".[37]

---

[34] Margaret Wertheim, *The Pearly Gates of Cyberspace: A History of Space from Dante to the Internet* (New York: W. W. Norton & Company Incorporated, 2000), 241.
[35] The site itself refers to its name as "collectors" rather than "collectors'" (note the apostrophe) or "collector's".
[36] www.recordcollectorsguild.org.
[37] Tim Wall, *Studying Popular Music Culture* (London: Arnold, 2003), 171.

In this way, one act of consumption simply has to relate to other
similar acts, or indeed other social practices. Unlike, perhaps, Dick
Hebdige's[38] 1970s image of this, which suggests that the consumer's
fashion and style are paramount (and from which many popular music
scholars still receive inspiration), in our case it might be suggested that the
physical, outward styles of one consumer no longer have to bear a
resemblance to the styles of another—at least in physical terms. *Just*
perhaps, then, the internet might also be partially responsible for
questioning issues to do with our associations with the social veneers that
support notions of self-indulgence via an avant garde. What this writer
means by that is that record collecting in cyberspace posits the proposition
that collecting in and of itself becomes a continuous widening of spaces,
with an ever-increasing amount of "quality-based" topics of interest that
might be shared. Recorded sound has already contributed to a
demystification and then re-mystification of Western cultures, and has
logically led to searches for "alternative" perspectives outside the
hegemonic spaces of the "First World"—which, one might argue, includes
notions of the *avant-garde*—society's so-called artistic, futuristic
reflection of itself. It is within such illumination, therefore, that this
emergence of cyberspace as a viable critical engager and signifier must be
comprehended.

Our collecting, categorising, organising, etc., becomes the central
focus. This, as we have suggested throughout this book, is one of the
significant tropes that should always be remembered—i.e. that the
collection itself consists of meaning, not simply the actions of the
collector, and it could be that it is the transference of such meanings—
how, as was suggested in Chapter One, a collection is actually organised—
that might be shared with new friends as a way of discussing "quality".
These methods and approaches are not only personal, but are also coherent
sets of ideas that can be transferred via cyberspace to others who will
relate distinctive meanings within their own specific contexts. This, oddly
enough, is not really "democratic" in the conventional sense, for thereby
lies a politics of the past. Instead, it appears to be an attempt at some form
of reconciliation, which is what often appears to be missing from our own
present: a resourceful territory from which we can embark upon shared
experiences and investigations.

Thus while the Record Collectors Guild website remains a non-
commercial site in the conventional sense (although it does sell banner

---

[38] Dick Hebdige, "Style as Homology and Signifying Practice", in *On Record:
Rock, Pop and the Written Word*, eds. Simon Frith and Andrew Goodwin (London:
Routledge, 1979), 56–65.

advertising space), it fulfils commercial requirements in the broader sense by providing various keys to consumption within a collecting framework. Therefore it *is* commercial in the global/"own" world sense. We are invited, via our interest in consumption to ratify our habits against others, and then to proceed further into our modes of consumption as quality moments. This is not a narrative that can be easily reabsorbed into the twentieth-century capitalist system, for it does not effectively play by such rules.

Neither is it a cynical rejection of capitalism: a system within which the rest of our lives are played out. Instead, it is a set of culture-specific periodising concepts which release the user from what post-modernists describe as a "meta-narrative" into an "other" world,[39] which has moved away from culture-bound visions of value and authenticity. The co-option of art by society's hierarchies inevitably led to its downfall. The political dimension of the *avant-garde* illustrates how it has failed to deliver on different ways of understanding our various realities. Rather than sever political, social, and aesthetic chains, it has compounded them. Cyberspace collecting might be merely one small way of liberating such repressed energies. The Record Collectors Guild site is therefore similar to, but has different requirements from, John Turton's Audiophile USA site.

For example, even a brief scan of the articles on the site reveals artistic sensibilities emanating from commercial detritus. There is one essay entitled "Article: record covers more than just protection", which contains several interesting propositions concerning one of the important topics raised in this book, i.e. how one's identity can relate to the packaging of a record, as much as the musical contents. There is also an interesting article entitled "Album Cover Art—A Priceless Commodity"; another, "Album Art: A Brief History of the Picture Disc", followed by "How Records are Made", and three historical items entitled (i) "Vinyl Record Collecting, Alive and Well", (ii) "Gramophone Recordings-post-war and Present", and (iii) "V-discs Boosted Troop Morale..." Finally, there are items concerning legal issues such as "Vinyl to CD: The Public's Right of 'Fair Use'", etc. All such works are anonymous and are, one presumes, written with others in mind. They are not articles in the journalistic sense, for they do not subscribe to the aforementioned fashion-ability quotient by which all such popular music journalism is usually destabilised.

---

[39] Thomas Docherty, "Postmodernism: An Introduction", in *Postmodernism: A Reader*, ed. Thomas Docherty (London: Harvester Wheatsheaf, 1993), 1–32.

There are also items concerning good music ripping software and how one might extract such software free of charge, news of new releases, record accessories such as inner sleeves, cartridges, and cleaning devices still on the market or being remanufactured, and music cataloguing software, and so on.

Comments

The great British Marxist historian Eric Hobsbawm argued many years ago that the industrial revolution marked the most fundamental transformation in the history of the world.[40] For instance, he described Britain's rise as the world's first industrial power, its decline from the temporary dominance of the technological pioneer, and the effect such peaks and troughs had on the lives of the British people. It was a masterly survey of the major economic developments of the past 250 years, but he made several crucial errors concerning leisure. His concern over social control and his adherence to Marxist thought meant that he was forever viewing leisure pursuits as "inauthentic". Whether he was considering Marconi's radio, the motor industry or the music hall, he felt that there were limited ways in which one should approach issues to do with leisure. Hobsbawm did concede that during the 1960s recorded sound and popular media could generate authentic responses, but he was still hidebound by the concept that a mass consumption society was led by the false consciousness of its largest mass market:

> The truth was that a mass-consumption society is dominated by its biggest market, which in Britain was that of the working class. As production and styles of life were therefore democratized, not to say proletarianized, much of the workers' former isolation melted away; or rather the pattern of isolationism was reversed. No longer did the workers have to accept goods or enjoyments essentially produced for other people; for an idealized petty-bourgeois 'little am' [...] for a degenerate version of the middle-class matinee-going (as in most of popular music), or by a moralizing teacher (as in the BBC).
> Henceforth, it was their demand which dominated commercially, even in their taste and style which pressed upward into the culture of the non-working classes; triumphantly in the Liverpool-accented tones of an entirely new pop music, indirectly in the vogue for authentic working-class themes and backgrounds which swept not only TV but even that bourgeois stronghold of the theatre.[41]

---

[40] Eric Hobsbawm, *Industry and Empire* (Harmondsworth: Pelican, 1978).
[41] *ibid.*, 283–284.

A plausible account, no doubt, with some irrefutable historical facts contained within; yet this comment is also largely rhetorical, for while Hobsbawm evidently looked beyond fellow Marxist Adorno for an understanding of meaning and value, he could still not bring himself to write about the potential of co-creativity, rather than simply potentially meaningful collective working-class consumer marketplaces. His writing still evokes a reluctance to accept consumerism as an authentic site for discourse, rather than manipulation, apart from when he sees popular music as part of a vanguard of authentic working-class representation breaking through, from the "bottom-up", as it were. No credit for this falls at the feet of the industry: technology is still viewed as a manipulator, nothing is mentioned about the impact of recorded sound as an arbiter, and nothing to speak of concerning the consumer as a cognisant co-creator of taste. One might even suggest that he got it wrong as far as The Beatles were concerned, for it is indeed arguable whether they ever were on any lower social rungs related to working-class consciousness. Yet this is the rhetoric of authenticity that as popular music researchers we are faced with—perhaps what might be described as a search for tradition.

In fact, from a view of the field of popular culture one can quite clearly see that it was the breakthrough of pop that inspired a series of art movements (from Opus, to Fluxus) the members of whom could clearly see that recorded sound and technology was as exciting as it was commercially profitable. Recorded sound bridged the gap between home and stage that no other form could do. The tradition, should we choose to find it, lies in the increasing flexibility of the record (both physically and corporeally) as the century moved on. Now that we have passed the first decade of the new century, and are halfway through the second, it can also be seen that popular culture, communication via electronic media, and the use-values to which we put such developments, are moving us further and further away from the models of history described by Adorno and Hobsbawm. We have a cyberspace no longer subject to the protestations of historians who have cleaved to an ideology that clearly misunderstood early twentieth-century impacts of technology. Such writers, as noble and erudite as they were, should not be used as a model to understand our new co-creative universe. One is reminded of the attempts by the French Revolutionaries to stop the fashions for (and indeed destroy) automata; so, too, the efforts of Marxism to belittle the effects of recorded sound. However, from Jacquet Droz to Thomas Edison to Bill Gates, the homeostasis of the cam (circles, cylinder and wheels) survives to give us new imagined spaces.

A Future Projection

This research-based book has suggested that the historicisation and contextualisation of record collecting, the record collector, and the history of recorded sound, all require re-evaluating and re-considering as major factors in not only the history of the twentieth, and now twenty-first centuries, but also as a way of understanding our personal relationships with artefacts, values and meanings. It has been suggested that the disciplines of history, social studies, economics, and politics need to be re-evaluated in order to release the collectors and their collections from the shackles of imposed value-ridden statements, ideologies, and histories in which the oriental other is placed at a counterpoint to the norms and traditions of society. It has also been suggested that closer investigations of collectors, their collections and their modes of interaction with others—especially via cyberspace—needs to be given greater focus and awarded serious value as historical narratives about the modern world, in their own right.

It has become clear then, at least to this researcher and collector, that the search for the sociology of the music consumer is far from over, and in fact still has a long way to go. Studies have been thus far bogged down by political rhetoric that failed to fully understand recorded sound's impact in the first place, and by seemingly not getting beyond theorising about the dualism between the imaginary and the real, could not come close to understanding the cartography of cognitive "quality" moments. However, it is suggested that a far closer investigation into the personal lives of collectors, without the aforementioned chains of social studies ideologies, might indicate that records and their sleeves, and the ways that they are stored and cherished all appear to point towards important life-giving quality moments that lend themselves to feelings of very special awareness, friendships and compatibilities, together with positive mental and physical health.

Future research on record collecting will simply have to respect such aesthetics of the mind. In fact, it could be argued that a respect for a kind of pedagogical popular culture in which self-learning is at the heart of people's meanings via collecting should be more fully acknowledged. If we are sure that we should endow popular music and the individual subject with new heightened senses of their real and imagined places in a global system, then we simply have to respect this enormously complex representational dialectic and consider radically new forms of understandings to do it justice.

And *that* future research will have to hold a self-evident truth, that the world of multinational capital can at times achieve breakthroughs (as yet unimaginable) in new modes of representing our lived experiences—whether that is/was the intention or not—and that our re-positioning as individuals as a consequence cannot be reduced to the means of production or to rhetoric surrounding the "masses". To paraphrase the great left-thinking cultural studies pioneer Raymond Williams and his wise words from many years ago: he stated that there are no such things as "masses" of people, just ways of thinking about them[42] (how true). Perhaps the final word should go to collector Les, whose similarly wise words have featured throughout this book: having at least partially recovered from a debilitating stroke, Les found the right words to say about his inanimate collection of cardboard, paper, and plastic:

> I can honestly tell you that that bunch of old records, LPs, albums over there's like having a friend constantly in the room. And I don't just mean memories: it helped me to get over my depression, it helped me to meet new people, it helped me to come out of myself. What I would have done without it is anybody's guess. I can't imagine why and how thinkers consider all of this to be unreal, or false, or whatever they say. To me, nothing could be more real, except my feelings of gratitude towards it, which in a way is gratitude towards myself, I suppose, because I collected it in the first place!—oh, and gratitude to Herb Alpert and Jerry Moss for forming *A&M*, and gratitude towards Elton John for writing "Come Down in Time", which is my favourite Lani Hall track, and gratitude towards Lani, of course... I'd better stop there—this could go on all night—gratitude for being alive.[43]

And so say all of us.

---

[42] Raymond Williams, cited in Tim Wall, *Studying Popular Music Culture* (London: Arnold, 2003), 230.

[43] Interview with Les, May 2013.

APPENDIX A

ALBUM INFORMATION

Album	Artist	Year	Catalogue Number
!	Gracious!	1970	6360 002
A Collection of Beatles Oldies but Goldies	The Beatles	1966	PCS 7016
A Hard Day's Night	The Beatles	1964	PCS 3058
Black Sabbath	Black Sabbath	1970	VO 6
Bumpers	Various (Island Sampler)	1969	IDP 1
Dark Side of the Moon	Pink Floyd	1973	SMAS-11163
Discreet Music	Brian Eno	1975	OBS 3
Goodbye Yellow Brick Road	Elton John	1973	DJLPD 1001
Half Baked	Jimmy Campbell	1970	6360 010
Heavy Petting	Dr Strangely Strange	1970	6360 009
If You Saw Thro' My Eyes	Ian Matthews	1971	6360 034
In Search of the Lost Cord	Moody Blues	1968	SML 711
Let It Be	The Beatles	1969	TC-PCS 7096
Magical Mystery Tour (EP)	The Beatles	1968	SMMT-1
Magical Mystery Tour	The Beatles	1968	SMAL-2835 (US)
Manfred Mann's Chapter Three	Manfred Mann Chapter Three	1969	VO 3
Mr. Tambourine Man	The Byrds	1965	SBPG 62571
Music for the Jilted Generation	The Prodigy	1994	XLLP 114

Nevermind the Bollocks, Here's the Sex Pistols	Sex Pistols	1970	TCV 2086
Piper at the Gates of Dawn	Pink Floyd	1967	SCX 6157
Revolver	The Beatles	1966	PCS 7009
Rubber Soul	The Beatles	1965	PCS 3075
Rumours	Fleetwood Mac	1977	K56344
Seasons	Magna Carta	1970	6360 003
Sgt. Pepper's Lonely Hearts Club Band	The Beatles	1967	PCS 7027
Signed, Sealed & Delivered	Stevie Wonder	1970	TS304 (US)
Stand up	Jethro Tull	1969	ILPS 9103
Sweetheart of the Rodeo	The Byrds	1968	S 63353
Talking Book	Stevie Wonder	1972	T 319L (US)
The Beatles at the Hollywood Bowl	The Beatles	1977	EMTV 4
The Yardbirds (a.k.a. "Roger the Mechanic")	The Yardbirds	1966	SCX 6063
Three Parts to my Soul "Spiritus, Manes et Umbra"	Dr. Z	1971	6360 048
Very 'Eavy... Very 'Umble	Uriah Heep	1970	6360 006
Yellow Submarine	The Beatles	1969	PCS 7070

All catalogue numbers are UK based unless indicated.

Single	Artist	Album	Year	Catalogue Number
"Telstar"	The Tornados	*Telstar* (EP)	1962	DFE 8511
"Tomorrow Never Knows"	The Beatles	*Revolver*	1966	PCS 7009
"I'm Only Sleeping"	The Beatles	*Revolver*	1966	PCS 7009
"She Said She Said"	The Beatles	*Revolver*	1966	PCS 7009
"Will You be Staying After Sunday"	The Peppermint Rainbow	*Will You be Staying After Sunday* (45)	1969	32410 (US)

All catalogue numbers are UK based unless indicated.

APPENDIX B

VERTIGO "SWIRL" DISCOGRAPHY 1969-1973

Catalogue Number	Artist	Album	Year	Comments
VO 1	Colosseum	*Valentyne Suite*	1969	
VO 2	Juicy Lucy	*Juicy Lucy*	1969	
VO 3	Manfred Mann Chapter Three	*Manfred Mann Chapter Three*	1969	
VO 4	Rod Stewart	*An Old Raincoat Won't Ever Let You down*	1969	
*VO 5	Ancient Grease	*Women and Children First*		Not released. Released instead on *Mercury* 6338 033 in 1970
VO 6	Black Sabbath	*Black Sabbath*	1970	First press had "A Philips Record Product" on the label. The label and the backcover still mention the "old" number before *Vertigo* was fully conceived: 847 903 VTY
VO 7	Cressida	*Cressida*	1970	
6360 001	Fairfield Parlour	*From Home to Home*	1970	
6360 002	Gracious!	*!*	1970	

6360 003	Magna Carta	*Seasons*	1970
6360 004	Affinity	*Affinity*	1970
6360 005	Bob Downes	*Electric City*	1970
6360 006	Uriah Heep	*Very 'Eavy, Very 'Umble*	1970
6360 007	May Blitz	*May Blitz*	1970
6360 008	Nucleus	*Elastic Rock*	1970
6360 009	Dr Strangely Strange	*Heavy Petting*	1970
6360 010	Jimmy Campbell	*Half Baked*	1970
6360 011	Black Sabbath	*Paranoid*	1970
6360 012	Manfred Mann Chapter Three	*Manfred Man Chapter Three Volume 2*	1970
6360 013	Clear Blue Sky	*Clear Blue Sky*	1970
6360 014	Juicy Lucy	*Lie Back and Enjoy It*	1970
6360 015	Warhorse	*Warhorse*	1970
6360 016	Patto	*Patto*	1970
6360 017	Colosseum	*Daughter of Time*	1970

* indicates "missing" catalogue number

Catalogue Number	Artist	Album	Year	Comments
6360 018	Beggar's Opera	*Act One*	1970	
6360 019	Legend	*Legend*	1970	
6360 020	Gentle Giant	*Gentle Giant*	1970	
6360 021	Graham Bond	*Holy Magick*	1970	
***6360 022**				Not issued
6360 023	Gravy Train	*Gravy Train*	1970	
6360 024	Keith Tippett	*Dedicated to You, but You Weren't Listening*	1971	
6360 025	Cressida	*Asylum*	1971	
6360 026	Still Life	*Still Life*	1971	
6360 027	Nucleus	*We'll Talk about It Later*	1971	
6360 028	Uriah Heep	*Salisbury*	1971	
6360 029	Catapilla	*Catapilla*	1971	
6360 030	Assagai	*Assagai*	1971	
6360 031	Nirvana [UK]	*Local Anaesthetic*	1971	
6360 032	Patto	*Hold Your Fire*	1971	
6360 033	Jade Warrior	*Jade Warrior*	1971	
6360 034	Ian Matthews	*If You Saw Thro' My Eyes*	1971	

*6360 035				Not released in Britain, but in Argentina as Manfred Mann Chapter Three— *Dama Viajera*
*6360 036				Not released in Britain, but in Argentina as Juicy Lucy—*Juicy Lucy*
6360 037	May Blitz	*Second of May*	1971	
6360 038	Daddy Longlegs	*Oakdown Farm*	1971	
6360 039	Ian Carr	*Solar Plexus*	1971	
6360 040	Magna Carta	*Songs from the Wasties Orchard*	1971	
6360 041	Gentle Giant	*Acquiring the Taste*	1971	
6360 042	Graham Bond	*We Put Our Magick on You*	1971	
6360 043	Tudor Lodge	*Tudor Lodge*	1971	

* indicates "missing" catalogue number

Catalogue Number	Artist	Album	Year	Comments
*6360 044	Dave Kelly	*Dave Kelly*		Not released. Released instead on *Mercury* 6301 001 in 1971
6360 045	Various Artist	*Heads Together, First Round*	1971	
6360 046	Ramases	*Space Hymns*	1971	
*6360 047				Not released in Britain, but in Brazil as Black Sabbath— *Black Sabbath* in 1973
6360 048	Dr. Z	*Three Parts to my Soul "Spiritus, Manes et Umbra"*	1971	
6360 049	Freedom	*Through the Years*	1971	
6360 050	Black Sabbath	*Master Of Reality*	1971	Poster included in some copies
6360 051	Gravy Train	*(A Ballad of) A Peaceful Man*	1971	
6360 052	Ben	*Ben*	1971	
6360 053	Mike Absalom	*Mike Absalom*	1971	
6360 054	Beggar's Opera	*Waters of Change*	1971	
6360 055	John Dummer	*Blue*	1972	
6360 056	Ian Matthews	*Tigers Will Survive*	1972	

*6360 057				Not issued
*6360 058	Assagai	*Zimbabwe*		Not released. Released instead on *Philips* 6308 079 in 1971
6360 059	Paul Jones	*Crucifix in a Horse Shoe*	1971	
6360 060	Linda Hoyle	*Pieces Of Me*	1971	
*6360 061				Not released in Britain, but in Peru as Various Artists— *Superheavy Vol. 1*
6360 062	Jade Warrior	*Released*	1971	
6360 063	Legend	*Moonshine*	1971	
6360 064	Hokus Poke	*Earth Harmony*	1972	
*6360 065				It is rumoured that this number was reserved for a re-issue of Nuleus— *Elastic Rock*
6360 066	Warhorse	*Red Sea*	1972	
6360 067	Jackson Heights	*5th Avenue Bus*	1972	

* indicates "missing" catalogue number

Catalogue Number	Artist	Album	Year	Comments
6360 068	Magna Carta	*In Concert*	1972	
6360 069	Gordon	*Gordon*	1972	
6360 070	Gentle Giant	*Three Friends*	1972	
6360 071	Black Sabbath	*Vol 4*	1972	
6360 072	Freedom	*Is More than a Word*	1972	
6360 073	Beggar's Opera	*Pathfinder*	1972	
6360 074	Catapilla	*Changes*	1972	
*6360 075				Number was assigned to Paul Jones's aborted second album
6360 076	Ian Carr	*Belladonna*	1972	
6360 077	Jackson Heights	*Ragamuffin's Fool*	1972	
*6360 078				Not released in Britain, but in Peru as Various Artists—*Superheavy Vol. 2*
6360 079	Jade Warrior	*Last Autumn's Dream*	1972	
6360 080	Gentle Giant	*Octopus*	1972	
6360 081	Alex Harvey	*Framed*	1972	
6360 082	Status Quo	*Piledriver*	1972	
6360 083	John Dummer	*Oobleedooblee Jubilee*	1973	

* indicates "missing" catalogue number

Catalogue Number	Artist	Album	Year	Comments
6657 001	Various Artist	*Vertigo Annual 1970*	1970	
6360 500	Rod Stewart	*Gasoline Alley*	1970	
6830 032	Various Artist	*Vertigo Sampler July 1970*	1970	White label promotional copy
6325 250	Thomas F. Browne	*Wednesday's Child*	1971	
6342 010	Lighthouse	*One Fine Morning*	1971	
6342 011	Lighthouse	*Thoughts of Moving on*	1972	
6830 067	Various Artist	*New Vertigo Popular Material*	1971	White label promotional copy
6333 500/501	Aphrodite's Child	*666*	1972	Double LP
6360 700	Jim Croce	*You Don't Mess around with Jim*	1972	
6360 701	Jim Croce	*Life and Times*	1972	
6499 268/269 (6641 077)	Kraftwerk	*Kraftwerk*	1972	Double LP, reissued with spaceship label
6360 609	Atlantis	*Atlantis*	1973	A German import that retained its original German catalogue number

* indicates "missing" catalogue number
Italicised catalogued numbers indicates numbers out of sequence (this can be due to the album being an import, a compilation album, a double LP etc.)

BIBLIOGRAPHY

Adorno, Theodor, "The Curves of the Needle", in *Essays on Music*, ed. Richard Leppert, Berkeley: University of California Press, 1927
—. "The Form of the Phonograph Record", in *Essays on Music*, ed. Richard Leppert, Berkeley: University of California Press, 1934
—. "On the Fetish-Character of Listening and the Regression of Listening", in *Essays on Music*, ed. Richard Leppert, Berkeley: University of California Press, 1938
—. "On Popular Music", in *On Record: Rock, Pop and the Written Word*, eds. Simon Frith and Andrew Goodwin, 301–314, London: Routledge, 1941
—. "Opera and the Long-Playing Record", in *Essays on Music*, ed. Richard Leppert, Berkeley: University of California Press, 1969
Arnold, John H., *History: A Very Short Introduction*, Oxford: University Press, 2000
Attali, Jaques, *Noise: The Political Economy of Music*, Minneapolis: University of Minnesota Press, 1977
Atton, Chris, "'Living in the Past'?: Value Discourses in Progressive Rock Fanzines", *Popular Music* 20, no. 1 (2001): 29–46
Audiophileusa.com, www.audiophileusa.com, accessed 01 June 2013
Auslander, Philip, "Looking at Records", *The Drama Review* 45, no. 1 (2001): 77–83
Barker, Martin and Julian Petley, *Ill Effects*, London: Routledge, 1997
Barnard, Stephen, *On the Radio: Music Radio in Britain*, Berkshire: OUP, 1989
Baudrillard, Jean, *The Consumer Society: Myths and Structures*, Thousand Oakes: Sage Publications, 1998
Becker, Howard S., *Outsiders: Studies in the Sociology of Deviance*, New York: The Free Press, 1963
Belk, Russel W., Melanie Wallendorf, John F. Sherry, Jr., and Morris B. Holbrook, "Collecting in a Consumer Culture", in *Highways and Buyways: Naturalistic Research from the Consumer Behaviour Odyssey*, ed. Russel W. Belk, 178-215, Association for Consumer Research, 1991
Benjamin, Walter, "The Work of Art in the Age of Its Technological Reproducibility: Second Version", in *Walter Benjamin: Selected*

Writing, Volume 3, 1935-1938, eds. Howard Eiland and Michael Jennings, 101–133, Cambridge: The Belknap Press of Harvard University Press, 1935

—. *Illuminations*, London: Pimlico, 1999

Bennett, Andy, Barry Shank and Jason Toynbee, eds., *The Popular Music Studies Reader*, Abingdon: Routledge, 2006

Borthwick, Stuart and Ron Moy, *Popular Music Genres: An Introduction*, Edinburgh: University Press, 2004

Bourdieu, Pierre, "Cultural Reproduction and Social Reproduction", in *Knowledge, Education and Cultural Change: Papers in the Sociology of Education*, ed. Robert Brown, London: Tavistock Publications Ltd., 1973

—. "Forms of Capital", in *Handbook for Theory and Research for the Sociology of Education*, ed. J. G. Richardson, 241–258, New York: Greenwood, 1986

—. *The Field of Cultural Production*, Cambridge: Polity, 1993

Blom, Philipp, *To Have and to Hold: An Intimate History of Collectors and Collecting*, Woodstock: The Overlook Press, 2002

Bloom, John, *A House of Cards: Baseball Card Collecting and Popular Culture*, Minneapolis: University of Minnesota Press, 1997

Bradley, Dick, *Understanding Rock 'n' Roll: Popular Music in Britain 1955-64*, Buckingham: OUP, 1992

Braunstein, Peter and Michael W. Doyle, *Imagine Nation: The American Counterculture of the 1960s and '70s*, New York: Routledge, 2002

Brocken, Michael, *Other Voices: Hidden Histories of Liverpool's Popular Music Scenes 1930s–1970s*, Farnham: Ashgate, 2010

—. "Green Day: Rock Discourse and Dwindling Authenticities", *Brazilian Journal of Song Studies* Volume Two (2012): http://www.rbec.ect.ufrn.br

Brocken, Michael and Melissa Davis, *The Beatles Bibliography: A New Guide to the Literature*, Manitou Springs: The Beatle Works, 2012

Brown, Walter A. and Zsuzsa Meszaros (2007), "Hoarding", *Psychiatric Times* 24, no. 13 (2007): 50–52

Buchdahl, Hanna, "An Unwanted Inheritance", *The Daily Beast*, 26 January 2011, accessed 5 December 2011, http://www.thedailybeast.com/newsweek/2011/01/26/an-unwanted-inheritance.html

Bunzl, Martin, *Real History: Reflections on Historical Practice*, London: Routledge, 1997

Calcutt, Andrew, *Arrested Development: Pop Culture and the Erosion of Adulthood*, London: Cassell, 1998

Campbell-Lyons, Patrick to Michael Brocken on Spencer Leigh's *On The Beat*, BBC Radio Merseyside, 2006

Cavicchi, Daniel, *Tramps Like Us: Music and Meaning Among Springsteen Fans*, New York: Oxford University Press, 1998

Chanan, Michael, *Repeated Takes: A Short History of Recording and its Effects on Music*, London: Verson, 1997

Clarke, Donald, ed., *The Penguin Encyclopaedia of Popular Music*, Harmondsworth: Penguin, 1990

Cohen, Sara, *Rock Culture in Liverpool: Popular Music in the Making*, Oxford: Clarendon Press, 1991

—. (1993), "Ethnography and Popular Music Studies", *Popular Music* 12, no. 2 (1993): 123–138

Cohen, Stanley, *Folk Devils and Moral Panics: The Creation of the Mods and Rockers*, London: MacGibbon and Kee, 1980

Cox, Christoph and Daniel Warner, *Audio Culture: Readings in Modern Music*, New York: Continuum, 2004

De Man, Paul, *The Resistance to Theory*, Manchester: University Press, 1986

Dean, Johnny, ed., *Record Collector* 1–46, including *Beatles Book* 46, London: Diamond, 1979–1983

Dean, Johnny, ed., "Guide to Collecting Vertigo LPs", *Record Collector* 79, London: Diamond

Debord, Guy, *The Society of the Spectacle*, New York: Zone, 1995

Dimery, Robert, ed., *1001 Albums You Must Hear before You Die*, London: Cassell Illustrated, 2005

Docherty, Thomas, "Postmodernism: An Introduction", in *Postmodernism: A Reader*, ed. Thomas Docherty, 1–32, London: Harvester Wheatsheaf, 1993

Doggett, Peter, ed., "Vertigo: Updated Guide with Star Ratings Parts 1-2", *Record Collector* 123–124, London: Diamond

Doggett, Peter, *Are you Ready for the Country: Elvis, Dylan, Parsons and the Roots of Country Rock*, New York: Penguin Books, 2001

Doggett, Peter, Andy Davis and Jack Kane, eds., *Record Collector Rare Record Price Guide 2002*, London: Parker Mead, 2002

Doggett, Peter, *You Never Give Me Your Money: The Battle for the Soul of the Beatles*, Croydon: Vintage, 2010

Ebert, Roger, "High Fidelity", 31 March 2000, accessed 29 May 2013, http://www.rogerebert.com/reviews/high-fidelity-2000

Ehrenreich, Barbara, Elisabeth Hess and Gloria Jacobs, "Beatlemania: Girls Just Want to Have Fun", in *The Adoring Audience: Fan Culture and Popular Media*, ed. Lisa Lewis, 84-106, London: Methuen, 1992

Eisenberg, Evan, *The Recording Angel: Music, Records And Culture From Aristotle To Zappa*, New Haven: Yale University Press, 2005

Elliott, Anthony, *The Mourning of John Lennon*, Berkeley: University of California Press, 1999

Emmison, Michael and John Frow, "Information Technology as Cultural Capital", *Australian Universities' Review* 4, no. 1 (998): 41–45

Fact.co.uk, www.fact.co.uk, accessed 22 November 2011

Finnegan, Ruth, *The Hidden Musicians: Music-Making in an English Town*, Cambridge: University Press, 1989

Frame, Pete, *Rock Family Trees: The Development in Histiry of Rock Bands from Gene Vincent and the Blue Caps to Ian Dury and the Blockheads*, London: Omnibus, 1980

French, Philip, "This One's a Hit…", *The Guardian* [online], 23 July 2000, accessed 30 April 2013, http://www.guardian.co.uk/film/2000/jul/23/philipfrench

Frith, Simon, *Sound Effects: Youth, Leisure, and the Politics of Rock 'n' Roll*, London: Contable, 1978

—. *The Sociology of Rock*, London: Constable, 1978

—. *Music for Pleasure*, London: Polity, 1988

Frith, Simon and Andrew Goodwin, eds., *On Record: Rock, Pop, and the Written Word*, London: Routledge, 1990

Frith, Simon, Will Straw and John Street, *The Cambridge Companion to Pop and Rock*, Cambridge: University Press, 2001

Frost, Randy O., "Treatment of Hoarding", *Expert Review of Neurotherapeutics* 10, no. 2 (2010): 251–261

—. "From Dante to DSM-V: A Short History of Hoarding", accessed 27 October 2010, http://www.ocfoundation.org/hoarding/dante_to_dsm-v.aspx

Frow, Gerald, *'Oh, Yes it is!' A History of Pantomime*, London: BBC, 1985

Gammond, Peter, *Your Own, Your Very Own! A Music Hall Scapbook*, London: Ian Allan, 1971

Gammond, Peter and Ray Horricks, *The Music Goes Round and Round: A Cool Look at the Record Industry*, London: Quartet Books, 1980

Gendron, Bernard, "Theodor Adorno Meets the Cadillacs", in *Studies in Entertainment*, ed. Tania Modleski, Indiana: Indiana University Press, 1986

Gillett, Charlie, ed., *Rock File*, London: Pictorial Presentations with New English Library, 1972

Gillet, Charlie and Simon Frith, eds., *Rock File 3*, London: Panther, 1975

Gillett, Charlie and Simon Frith, *The Beat Goes On: The Rock File Reader*, University of Michigan, 1996

Gilroy, Paul, *Small Acts: Thoughts on the Politics of Black Cultures*, London: Serpent's Tail, 1993

Gleiberman, Owen, "High Fidelity", 31 March 2000, accessed 29 May 2013, http://www.ew.com/ew/article/0,,275803,00.html

Gordon, Steve, *The Future of the Music Business: How to Succeed with the New Digital Technologies—A Guide for Artists and Entrepreneurs*, New York: Hal Leonard Books, 2008

Gronow, Pekka and Ilpo Saunio, *An International History of the Recording Industry*, London: Cassell, 1998

Grossberg, Laurence, "Is There a Fan in the House? The Affective Sensibility of Fandom", in *The Adoring Audience: Fan Culture and Popular Media*, ed. Lisa Lewis, 50–68, London: Methuen, 1992

Hall, Stuart and Tony Jefferson, *Resistance Through Ritual: Youth Subcultures in Post-War Britain*, London: Hutchinson, 1977

Hansson, Nils, "Ordning på punken", *Dagens Nyheter Kultur*, 23 July 2008

Hamm, Charles, *Yesterdays: Popular Song in America*, New York: Norton, 1979

Hammersley, Martin, "Ethnography: Problems and Prospects", *Ethnography and Education* 1, no. 1 (2006): 3–14

Hand, Sean, *The Levinas Reader*, Oxford: Blackwell, 1989

Hannan, Andrew, *Observation Techniques* (2006), accessed 15 May 2013, http://www.edu.plymouth.ac.uk/resined/observation/obshome.htm

Harrison, Anthony Kwame, "'Cheaper than a CD, Plus We Really Mean It': Bay Area Underground Hip Hop Tapes as Subcultural Artefacts", *Popular Music* 25, no. 2 (2006): 283–301

Hebdige, Dick, "Style as Homology and Signifying Practice", in *On Record: Rock, Pop and the Written Word*, eds. Simon Frith and Andrew Goodwin, 56–65, London: Routledge, 1979

—. *Subculture: The Meaning of Style*, London: Methuen, 1979

Hegel, G. W. F., *Philosophy of Right*, Mineola: Dover Philosophical Classics, 2005

Hills, Matt, *Fan Cultures*, London: Routledge, 20002

Hmv.com, www.hmv.com, accessed 18 January 2013

Hobsbawm, Eric, *Industry and Empire*, Harmondsworth: Pelican, 1978

Holm-Hudson, Kevin, ed., *Progressive Rock Reconsidered*, London: Routledge, 2002

Holt, Fabian, *Genre in Popular Music*, Chicago: University of Chicago Press, 2007

Horn, David, ed., *Popular Music Perspectives 2*, Gothenburg: IASPM, 1985

Horn, David and John Shepherd, eds., *The Continuum Encyclopaedia of Popular Music of the World Volumes VIIII-XIII: Genres*, London: Continuum, 2012

Hornby, Nick, *High Fidelity*, New York: Riverhead Books, 1996

Horner, Bruce and Thom Swiss, *Key Terms in Popular Music and Culture*, Hoboken: Blackwell, 1999

Inglis, Ian, "Men of Ideas? Popular Music, Anti-intellectualism and the Beatles", in *The Beatles, Popular Music and Society: A Thousand Voices*, ed. Ian Inglis, London: Macmillan, 2000

—. "'Nothing You Can See that isn't Shown': The Album Covers of the Beatles", *Popular Music* 20, no. 1 (2001): 83–97

Jameson, Fredric, *Postmodernism, or, the Cultural Logic of Late Capitalism*, Durham: Duke University Press, 1991

Jeaniefinlay.com, www.jeaniefinlay.com, accessed 22 November 2011

Jencks, Charles, *Critical Modernism—Where is Post-Modernism Going?*, Hoboken: John Wiley & Sons, 2007

Jensen, Joli, "Fandom as Pathology: The Consequences of Charactarization", in *The Adoring Audience: Fan Culture and Popular Media*, ed. Lisa Lewis, 9–29, London: Routledge, 1992

Jones, Graham, *Last Shop Standing: Whatever Happened to Record Shops?*, London: Proper Music Publishing, 2009

Kaijser, Lars, "Authority among Fragments; Reflections on Representing the Beatles in a Tourist Setting", in *Fifty Years With The Beatles: The Impact of the Beatles on Contemporary Culture*, eds. Jerzy Jarniewicz and Alina Kwiatkowska, Lodz: University Press, 2010

Kamanka, Eugene, ed., *The Portable Karl Marx*, London: Viking Penguin, 1983

Katz, Mark, *Capturing Sound: How Technology has Changed Music*, Berkeley: University of California Press, 2010

Kusek, David and Gerd Leonhard, *The Future of Music: Manifesto for the Digital Music Revolution*, Boston: Berklee Press, 2005

Laing, Dave, "A Voice without a Face: Popular Music and the Phonograph in the 1890s", *Popular Music* 10, no. 1 (1991): 1–9

Lawson, Hilary and Lisa Appignanesi, *Dismantling Truth: Reality in the Postmodern World*, London: Weidenfeld & Nicholson, 1989

Leigh, Spencer, *The Cavern: The Most Famous Club in the World*, London: S.A.F. Publishing, 2008

Levin, Thomas Y., "For the Record: Adorno on Music in the Age of Its Technological Reproducibility", *The MIT Press* 22 (October 1990): 23–47

Lewis, Lisa, ed., *The Adoring Audience: Fan Culture and Popular Media*, London: Methuen, 1992

Lewisohn, Mark, *The Beatles, 25 Years in the Life: A Chronology 1962–1987*, London: Sidgwick & Jackson, 1987

Litster, John, *Famous Football Programmes: A History and Guide*: Stroud: NPI Media Group, 2007

Longhurst, Brian, *Popular Music and Society*, Oxford: Polity, 2007

Lyotard, Jean-François, *The Postmodern Condition*, Paris: Minuit, 1979

—. *The Postmodern Condition: A Report on Knowledge*, Minneapolis: University of Minnesota, 1984

Macan, Edward, *Rocking the Classics: English Progressive Rock and the Counterculture*, Oxford: Oxford University Press, 1997

MacDonald, Ian, *Revolution in the Head: The Beatles Records and the Sixties*, London: Vintage, 2009

Marshall, Lee, "For and against the Record Industry: An Introduction to Bootleg Collectors and Tape Traders", *Popular Music* 22, no. 1 (2003): 57–72

Marx, Karl, *The Manifesto of the Communist Party* (1848), accessed 29 May 2013, http://www.marxists.org/archive/marx/works/1848/communist-manifesto/ch01.htm#060

Marwick, Arthur, *The Sixties: Cultural Revolution in Britain, France, Italy, and the United States, 1958–1974*, Oxford: University Press, 1998

Mabey, Richard, *The Pop Process*, London: Hutchinson Educational, 1969

McLuhan, Marshall, *Understanding Media: The Extensions of Man*, New York: McGraw-Hill, 1964

McMillan, David W. and David M. Chavis, "Sense of Community: A Definition and Theory", *Journal of Community Psychology* 14 (January 1986): 6–23

Melly, George, *Revolt in Style: The Pop Arts in Britain*, Harmondsworth: Penguin, 1970

Metacritic.com, www.metacritic.com, accessed 29 May 2013

Middelton, Richard, *Studying Popular Music*, Buckingham: OUP, 1990

Millard, Andre, *America on Record: A History of Recorded Sound*, Cambridge: University Press, 1995

Moorefield, Virgil, *The Producer As Composer: Shaping the Sounds of Popular Music*, Cambridge: MIT Press, 2005

Morton, David, *Off the Record: The Technology and Culture of Sound Recording in America*, New Jersey: Rutgers University Press, 2000

Morton, David L. Jr., *Sound Recording: The Life Story of a Technology*, Baltimore: John Hopkins University Press, 2006

Negus, Keith, *Popular Music in Theory: An Introduction*, Cambridge: Polity, 1996

Newbold, Chris, Oliver Boydt-Barrett and Hilde van den Bulck, eds., *The Media Book*, London: Arnold, 2002

O'Brien, Geoffrey, *Sonata for Jukebox: An Autobiography of my Ears*, New York: Counterpoint, 2005

Ochs, Michael, *1000 Record Covers*, Hong Kong: Taschen, 2005

Oliver, Paul, *Songsters and Saints: Vocal Traditions on Race Record*, Cambridge: University Press, 1984

Oxforddictionaries.com, www.oxforddictionaries.com, accessed 5 December 2011

Pearce, Susan, *On Collecting: An Investigation into Collecting in the European Tradition*, London: Routledge, 2005

Peterson, Richard, "Why 1955? Explaining the Advent of Rock Music", *Popular Music* 9, no. 1 (1990): 97–115

Petitt, Emma, *Old Rare New: The Independent Record Shop*, London: Black Dog Publishing, 2008

Pirsig, Robert, *Zen and the Art of Motorcycle Maintenance*, London: Vintage/Random House, 1974

Powell, Mark, *Time Machine: A Vertigo Retrospective*, CD notes, London: Mercury Records 9827982, 2005

Ramqvist, Philip, "Musik på vinyl får allt fler köpare", *Dagens Nyheter Kultur*, 18 July 2008

Recordcollectormag.com, www.recordcollectormag.com, accessed 01 June 2013

Recordcollectorsguild.org, www.recordcollectorsguild.org, accessed 31 May 2013

Recordstoreday.co.uk, www.recordstoreday.co.uk, accessed 07 May 2013

Rheingold, Howard, *The Virtual Community: Homesteading on the Electronic Frontier*, San Francisco: HarperPerennial, 1994

Riesman, David, "Listening to Popular Music", in *On Record: Rock, Pop and the Written Word*, eds. Simon Frith and Andrew Goodwin, 5-31, London: Routledge, 1950

Rogers, Mary F., *Barbie Culture*, London: Sage, 1999

Roject, Chris, *Celebrity*, London: Reaktion, 2001

Ruddock, Andy, *Understanding Audiences: Theory and Method*, London: SAGE, 2001

Rycenga, Jennifer, "Tales of Change within the Sound: Form, Lyrics and Philosophy in the Music of Yes", in *Progressive Rock Reconsidered*, ed. Kevin Holm-Hudson, 143–166, New York: Routledge, 2002

Said, Edward, *Orientalism*, New York: Vintage Books Edition, 1978

Sanjek, Russell, "From Print to Plastic: Publishing and Promoting America's Popular Music (1900–1980)", *I.S.A.M. monograph no. 20*, New York: I.S.A.M., 1983

Semmel, Stuart, "Reading the Tangible Past: British Tourism, Collecting, and Memory after Waterloo", *Representations* 69, Special Issue: Grounds for Remembering (2000): 9–37

Shepherd, John, "Definition as Mystification: A Consideration of Label as a Hindrance to Understanding Significance in Music", in *Popular Music Perspectives* 2, ed. David Horn, 84–98, Gothenburg: IASPM, 1985

Shuker, Roy, *Understanding Popular Music*, London: Routledge, 1994

—. *Popular Music: The Key Concepts*, London: Routledge, 2002

—. "Beyond the 'High Fidelity' Stereotype: Defining the (Contemporary) Record Collector", *Popular Music* 23, no. 3 (2004): 311–330

—. *Wax Trash and Vinyl Treasures: Record Collecting as a Social Practice*, Farnham: Ashgate, 2010

Soja, Edward, *Thirdspace: Journeys to Los Angeles and Other Real-And-Imagined Places*, London: Blackwell, 1996

Sounditoutdoc.com, www.sounditoutdoc.com, accessed 22 November 2011

Stanley, Bob and Paul Kelly, *Match Day: Post-war to Premiership Football Programmes*, London: Murray & Sorrell FUEL, 2008

Stokes, Martin, ed., *Music, Ethnicity and Identity: The Musical Construction of Place*, Oxford: Berg Publishers, 1994

Storey, John, "What is Popular Culture?", in *Cultural Theory and Popular Culture: An Introduction*, ed. John Storey, 1–12, Harlow: Pearson Education, 2001

Strachan, Rob, "Micro Independent Record Labels in the UK: Discourse, DIY Cultural Production and the Music Industry", *European Journal of Cultural Studies* 10, no. 2 (2007): 245–265

—. "'Where Do I Begin the Story?': Collective Memory, Biographical Authority and the Rock Biography", *Popular Music History* 3, no. 1 (2008): 65–80

Straw, Will, "Sizing up Record Collections: Gender and Connoisseurship in Rock Music Culture", in *Sexing the Groove: Popular Music and Gender*, ed. Sheila Whiteley, 3–16, London: Routledge, 1997

—. "Exhausted Commodities: The Material Culture of Music", *Canadian Journal of Communication* 25, no. 1 (2000): http://www.cjc-online.ca/index.php/journal/article/view/1148/1067

Stump, Paul, *The Music's All that Matters: A History of Progressive Rock*, London: Quartet Books, 1997

Sullivan, Alice, "Bourdieu and Education: How Useful is Bourdieu's Theory for Researchers?", *Netherlands Journal of Social Sciences* 38, no. 2 (2002): 144–166

Tagg, Philip, *Fernando the Flute: Analysis of Musical Meaning in an Abba Mega-Hit*, Liverpool: IPM, 1991

—. *Ten Little Tunes*, Liverpool: IPM, 1992

—. *Introductory Notes to the Semiotics of Music* (1999), http://tagg.org/xpdfs/semiotug.pdf

Taylor, Paul W., "'Need' Statements", *Analysis* 19, no. 5 (1959): 106–111

Taylor, Timothy D., *Strange Sounds: Music, Technology and Culture*, New York: Routledge, 2001

TheAudiophile.net, www.theaudiophile.net, accessed 30 May 2013

Thompson, Emily, "Machines, Music, and the Quest for Fidelity: Marketing the Edison Phonograph in America 1877–1925", *Musical Quarterly* 79, no. 1 (1995): 131–171

Thompson, Paul, *The Voice of the Past: Oral History*, Oxford: University Press, 1978

Thompson, William E. and Joseph V. Hickey, *Society in Focus*, New York: HarperCollins, 1994

Thorgerson, Storm and Dean, Roger, *Album Cover Album*, East Sussex: Ilex, 2008

Thornton, Sarah, "Moral Panic, the Media and British Rave Culture", in *Microphone Fiends: Youth Music and Youth Culture*, eds. Andrew Ross and Tricia Rose, 176–192, New York: Routledge, 1994

Tosh, John, *The Pursuit of History: Aims, Methods and New Directions in the Study of Modern History*, London: Longman, 1984

Tye, Diane, "Ethnography of a Beatles Fan", *Culture and Tradition* 11 (1987): 41–57

Vale, V. and Andrea Juno, *Incredibly Strange Music*, San Francisco: Re/Search Publications, 1994

VanMaanen, John, *Tales of the Field: On Writing Ethnography*, Chicago: University Press, 1988

Vaxjuntan.wordpress.com, www.vaxjuntan.wordpress.com, accessed 24 November 2011

Wall, Tim, *Studying Popular Music Culture*, London: Arnold, 2003

Walton, Kendall L., "How Marvellous!: Toward a Theory of Aesthetic Value", *The Journal of Aesthetics and Art Criticism* 51, no. 3 (1993): 499–510

Watt, Tessa, *Cheap Print and Popular Piety, 1550–1640*, Cambridge: University Press, 1991

Weinstein, Deena, "Progressive Rock as Text: The Lyrics of Roger Waters", in *Progressive Rock Reconsidered*, ed. Kevin Holm-Hudson, 91–110, New York: Routledge, 2002

Vermorel, Fred and Judy, *Starlust: The Secret Fantasies of Fans*, London: WH Allen, 1985

Wertheim, Margaret, *The Pearly Gates of Cyberspace: A History of Space from Dante to the Internet*, New York: W. W. Norton & Company Incorporated, 2000

Winton, Barry, "Collecting Vertigo LPs", *Record Collector* 123–124 (November–December 1989)—See Doggett, Peter, ed.

—. "Vertigo: Into the Void", *Record Collector* 314-315 (September–October 2005)

Zak III, Albin J., *The Poetics of Rock: Cutting Tracks, Making Records*, London: University of California Press, 2001

INDEX